Be different.

Speak out of turn.

Enjoy your body.

BE WHOEVER THE HELL YOU WANT TO BE

Be loud.

Ask questions.

WANT MORE

And if anyone says you shouldn't, tell them to buzz off! ;)

Lasairiona McMaster

Wanton & Wicked Ways

Lasairiona McMaster

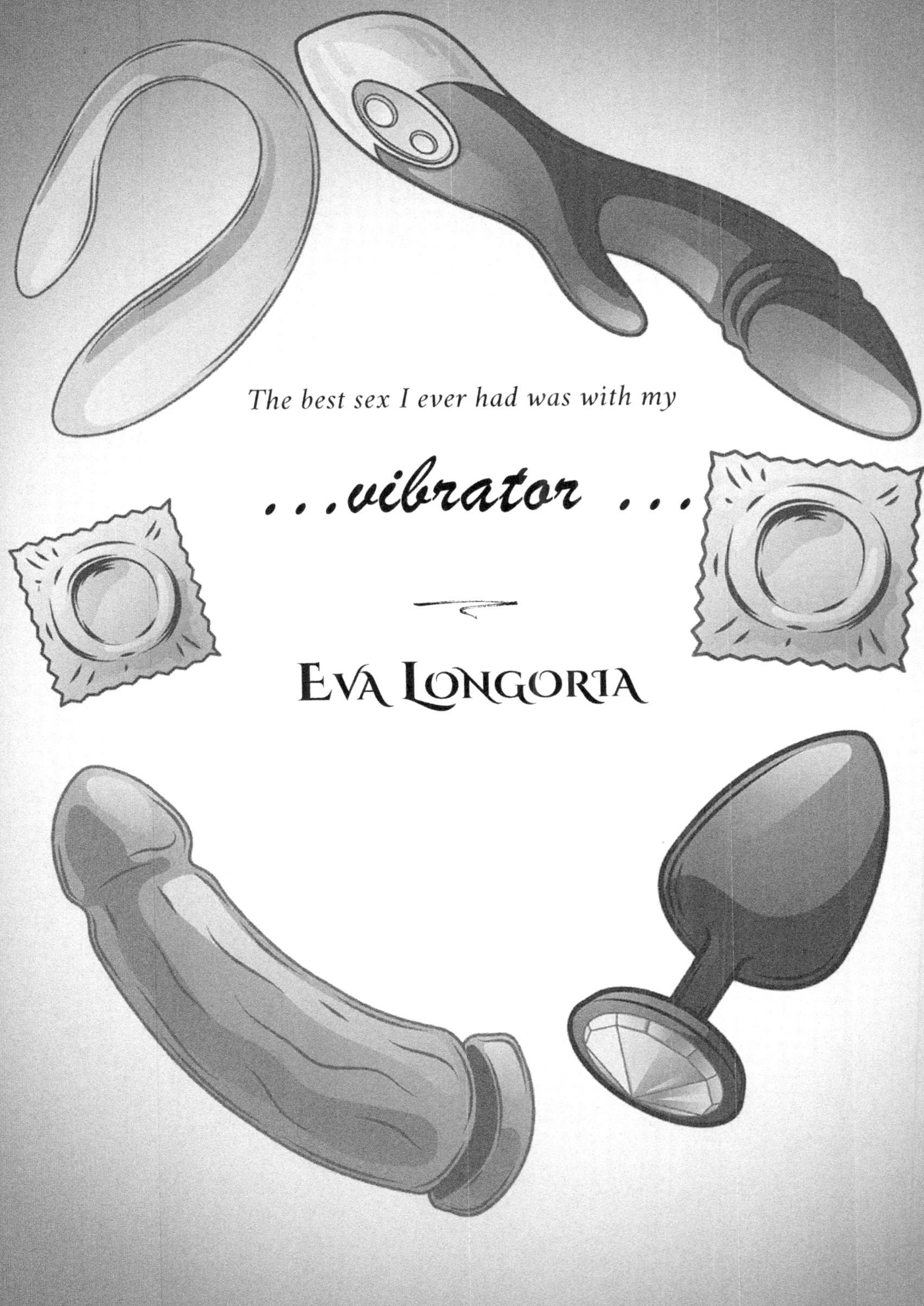
The best sex I ever had was with my
...vibrator ...
Eva Longoria

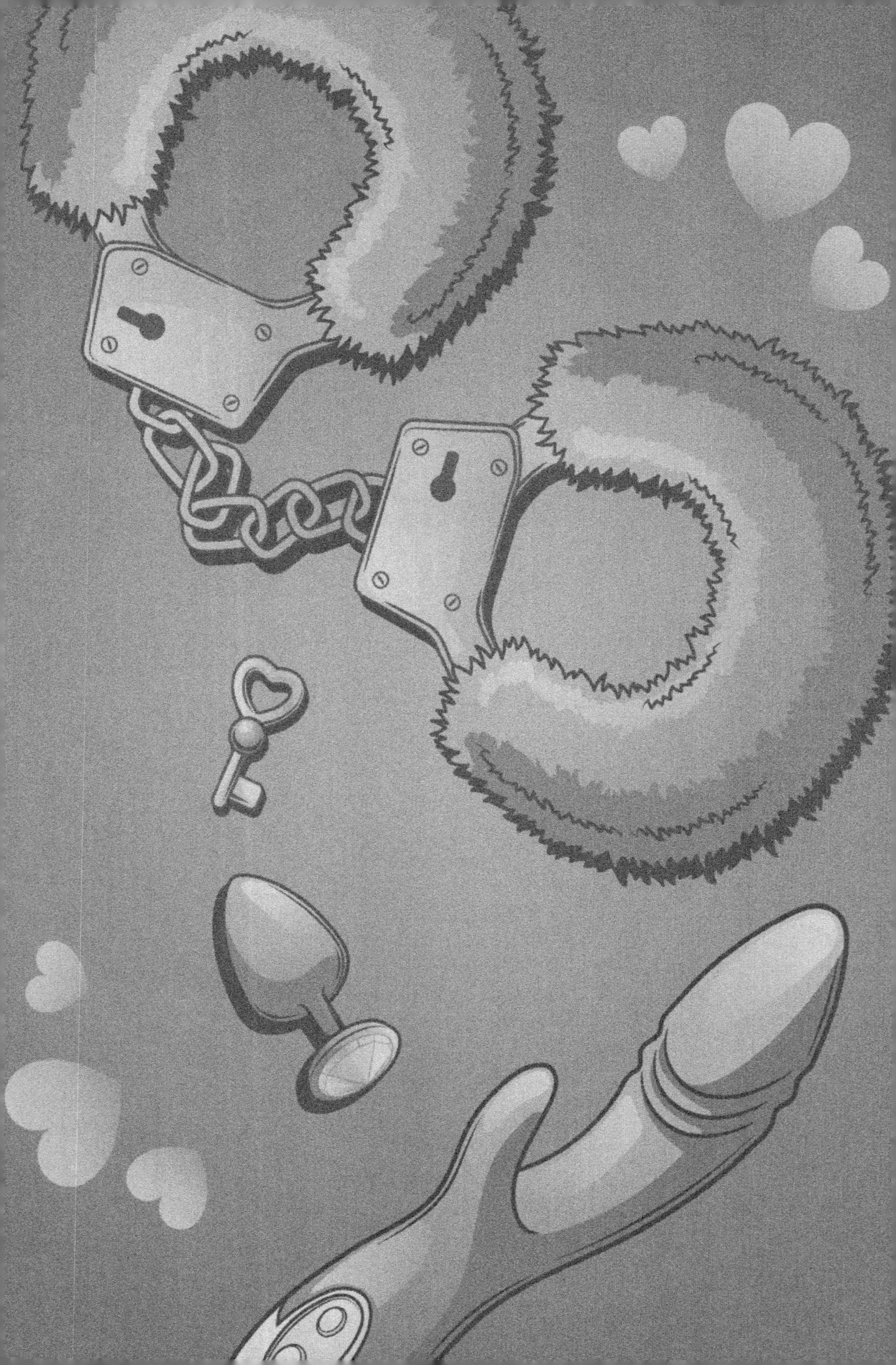

One

"Ma'am, your luggage is moving."

Lisa tilted her head and pursed her lips. "Moving?"

The TSA agent in front of her nodded. A heavily pregnant Lisa, AJ, and Olivia were at their gate in Kuala Lumpur International Airport, ready to board the first of their flights back to Alabama. "Might be my toothbrush. Can you just turn it off?" *Please don't make me move.* The man's broken speech and blank expression suggested he was not fluent in English, and her level of any of the ten dialects of Malay lingered somewhere around 'non-existent'. She was going to have to move.

"Come with me, please."

She groaned and braced her hand against the back of the cold metal seat, ready to push herself to standing.

AJ reached out to stop her. "I'll go."

Lisa nodded, her swollen feet and aching back grateful for the reprieve. Three weeks of exploring everything Malaysia had to offer had taken its toll. Not to mention, she was growing a person in her uterus. A person who had no regard for sleeping hours, the limitations of her ribcage, or the size of her bladder. "Okay." She sighed. "It's probably your damn beard trimmer anyway." AJ rolled his eyes, passed Olivia to Lisa, and followed the TSA agent out of sight.

"If I was a gambling woman, I'd guess daddy left the battery in your twist-and-spin Lion again, Miss Liv. I'll resist the urge to say 'told you so' when he comes back." Lisa turned Olivia so she was sitting sideways on her lap and pulled the diaper bag from two seats away onto the chair next to her. She tugged open the bag, producing a well-worn copy of The Gruffalo, her daughter's favorite book.

"Grubo!"

Lisa chuckled. "You want to read The Gruffalo, baby girl?" Olivia nodded and bounced on Lisa's lap. The movement revealed a damp patch on the thigh of her jeans. "Do you need your bum changed, peanut? Did you pee pee?" Lisa leaned the blonde haired, blue-eyed toddler forward, tucked the book back in the bag and gave the baby's bottom a gentle diaper-test squeeze. She scrunched her nose at the smell permeating their surroundings. "Oh, Livvy. Is *this* why Daddy volunteered to go turn off whatever battery powered object is freaking out Malaysian TSA? Hmm? He didn't want to change a dirty bum?"

"Poop, poop, poop-poop!"

Lisa laughed and slid the strap of the diaper bag onto her shoulder. "Aye, you stink wee woman."

"'tinky." Olivia scrunched her face to match Lisa's.

Lisa shot off a quick text to AJ to tell him they might be in the bathroom when he returned before scooting to the edge of the chair. She silently counted to three before hauling herself to stand, patting the diaper bag to make sure it made the transition to upright with her. She was approaching the stage of pregnancy where if she dropped something, she did a thorough evaluation as to how much she needed whatever it was. Unless it was deemed urgent, she wasn't desperate enough to bend and pick it back up. They'd checked the car seat into the hold, and gate checked the stroller. AJ was carrying the backpack full of emergency provisions for the long haul flight: snacks, spare clothes, the tablet her parents had bought Olivia for Christmas despite Lisa's best protests. It was as close as anyone came to 'traveling light' across the globe, pregnant, and with a small child in tow. Stepping out of the way of the trickle of people leaving the ladies restrooms, Lisa made her way to the changing table and plopped Olivia onto her back.

"Poop-poop. Poop-poop, mama!"

"Oh ... oh no." Both of their hands were covered with poop. "This is bad with a capital 'B' kiddo. Guess not all of us have recovered from that God-awful tummy bug yet." She dropped the bag onto the counter next to the sink and washed their hands. "Here you go." Lisa handed her four bright-colored interconnected rings to distract her from touching anything that might get her hands messy again.

"Hang in there, little one. I just need to grab the wipes and a diaper and I'll get you out of those icky clothes."

"Icky."

"She's adorable." A North American lady with a sleeping toddler in a stroller emerged from a bathroom stall.

"Thank you. She's usually much less … eh … decorated with feces." Warmth rushed to her face as she busied herself with finding the necessary provisions for the poonami which had surged up her darling daughter's back. She laid out a change of clothes, wipes and diaper rash cream next to a poop-bag on the counter, but there were no diapers to be found. "Oh God." Frustrated tears sprung to her eyes as her brain tried to figure a solution. "Shit. Shit. Shit!"

"Somethin' wrong?" The lady had finished washing her hands but was lingering next to the sinks. From the drawl of her accent, Lisa guessed she was from the south. Carolina, perhaps, or Texas.

"Shit!" Olivia echoed.

Lisa groaned and raised her hand for a face-palm, stopping short when the faint smell of baby poop wafted towards her. She gritted her teeth and blinked back the tears. "I'm going to kill him."

"He didn't put diapers in the bag, did he?"

I don't think you're supposed to confess pre-meditated husband murder to a complete stranger. And yet ... the sonofabitch deserves it. Lisa pinched her bottom lip between her teeth, and shook her head, refusing to allow the tears to fall.

"Hey, it's okay. I have extra. I'm an over-packer, and I didn't let my husband near the diaper bag." The stranger pulled open the bag draped over her stroller handles and rummaged through its contents. "Been there, done that. Australia to San Francisco with only two diapers and a teething nine-month-old who was shittin' fire." She pulled out a handful of diapers and thrust them towards Lisa.

"I can't take all these."

"You can and you will, and then you're going to clean aaaaaall that shit up and we're going to find wine."

"Wine?"

"Yeah, wine. I feel like if you don't get wine, you might end up throwing your husband's ass out of a plane at thirty five thousand feet. Eve." The woman reached her hand out, but scrunched up her nose and stopped herself. "Nice to meet you."

"Lisa. Nice to meet you, too. We can shake hands when I'm not covered in a thin layer of someone else's crap. And thanks for these, maybe I'll use them to beat AJ to death with." She tucked all but one of the diapers into the bag and got to work stripping off Olivia's clothes. "This poop-covered monster is Olivia."

"My little one is Noah. Where you flying to? Maybe we could be travel buddies, at least for the first leg."

"Alabama. You?" Lisa cringed as she peeled the pungent, sticky clothes from Olivia's wriggling body. Lisa hadn't opened the poo-bag, and the trash can was too far away to leave Olivia unsupervised, but Eve was sporting a sympathetic smile and holding out a wide-open bag for her to dump the poop-covered clothes into.

"No freakin' way. Us too. Birmingham, you?"

"Huntsville."

"Close enough! Well, it's official. The universe has just delivered my new best friend." Eve tied the bag up, crossed the bathroom to the garbage can and got rid of the offending clothing.

"What a meet cute we have to tell the world. We met in a bathroom over a poop-splosion."

"They'll write songs and sonnets about it. What a thing of beauty."

A short time – and a hell of a lot of soap – later, Lisa, Olivia, Eve, and Noah emerged from the restrooms, smelling much less like poop. AJ leaned against a pillar, arms folded, brows furrowed, and cheeks flushed a dark shade of 'grumpy'. *Oh God. What happened?*

"I'm going to find Robert. I'll see you at the gate, okay?" Eve took off in the direction of their gate while Lisa attempted to decipher the fury radiating from her husband's body.

I'm pretty pissed at you, too, Pim. Don't come at me right now. Unless there's diapers in that backpack of yours ... but ... even then ... But for the kindness of a stranger in the loo and you'd be doomed for death.

"You got something you wanna tell me?" He pushed off from the pillar and straightened himself, arms outstretched to take Olivia.

"Yeah. As a matter of fact, there is. You didn't pack nappies in the nappy bag."

His jaw dropped open and snapped closed. "Well, I guess what I lack in packing skills, you more than made up for in *your* packing."

"What the f—udgesicles does that mean?"

He lowered his face so his mouth was next to her ear. "I thought our marriage was solid enough to talk about when one of us is unhappy." His words were laced with sadness and disappointment.

Her stomach dropped and ice cold terror seized her chest. "You're unhappy?" It came out as a croak, and she grabbed onto the pillar to steady herself. "I—I know the holiday was tough on us, what with all the vomiting and poop, but I thought we were stronger than a lil bug."

"What?" His brows pulled into that deep frown of confusion he wore when trying to solve a jigsaw puzzle. "I'm perfectly happy in our marriage Lisa, I'm not the one who had a freakin' lightsaber-esque vibrator crammed into the side pocket of her suitcase!"

Two

"Wait, what? I didn't pack a vibrator."

"Really? 'Cause Sir Girth-a-lot in the luggage hold begs to differ. Jesus Lis, you could beat someone to death with that thing."

A voice over the PA system told them their flight was boarding and to make their way to the gate. Lisa burst into fits of giggles.

"Lisa, it isn't funny."

They set off towards the gate, dodging bustling passengers as they walked. "That's where you're dead wrong, Mr. Williams, it's hilarious. While the vibrator *is* my vibrator, I did *not* pack it for this trip. It must have been in the bag from my trip to the US from Ireland. I can't believe you thought your pregnant, sleep deprived wife was of sound enough mind to pack a monster vibrator for a trip across the world. Don't you think if the notion for a screaming 'O' were to overrule my instincts to nap all the time, I'd just, I dunno … use my husband's real life attachments instead of something made of sparkly silicone?"

He stopped dead in his tracks, almost crashing into a traveler with her nose buried in her phone. "Well, yeah, I kinda did think that. Yet somehow, here we are." They arrived at their gate and joined the back of the line.

Eve gave her a small wave from the line next to them. "Hey, y'all get to board early 'cause of the little one. Get yourselves over here."

Lisa threw her a grateful smile and shuffled across to the faster moving line.

"Glad to see you haven't yet killed him for Diaper-Gate." Eve spoke in a stage whisper and gave Lisa an exaggerated wink.

"There's still time."

"He sure looks madder than a wet hen about something."

Lisa nodded, swallowing down another giggle and turned to face her still-stewing husband.

"You know I can hear you, right?" AJ's jaw twitched. His eyes darted between Eve and Lisa, and he shook his head.

"I can't believe you thought I was having ... fun ... behind your back." Lisa lowered her voice and directed her words at AJ. His brows were still drawn low.

"The evidence kinda speaks for itself, Lisa. Nothing says 'my wife isn't happy in the bedroom' like finding a freakin' vibrator big enough for the goddamn hulk hidden in her suitcase."

Eve choked on her drink, spraying it out her nostrils and over her shirt. "Well, shit. This just got all kinds of interesting." Her chest heaved and eyes watered. She accepted a Kleenex from her chuckling husband and patted her face dry. "Kinda wishing I'd brought popcorn for this. I'm so glad we're officially besties. It means I can listen to this conversation without having to pretend I'm not."

AJ's brows rose in question. Lisa knew all his looks. This one was his "unsurprised she'd made a friend in the airport, but waiting for an introduction" look. "AJ, this is my new bestie Eve. We met in the toilets over poopy clothes and a bare arse since *someone*, who shall – for now – remain nameless, didn't pack nappies in the nappy bag. Eve, this is my husband AJ, or Pim. He is the aforementioned nameless someone, in case you didn't make the connection."

The two shook hands and Eve introduced her husband, Rob, to the group. "Pim? As in penalty minutes? You play?"

AJ nodded as he shook Rob's hand. "Recreationally these days, house league. I played in college, though."

Eve covered her face with her palm. "We might need to switch up our seats for a while during the flight. Rob *loves* hockey, but doesn't have any hockey friends in Birmingham. From that look of glee sparkling in his eyes, he's gearing up to talk your poor husband's leg off about The Game."

They all took a step forward as the line moved towards the podium. Eve turned her attention to Noah who was waking up from his nap and demanding to be let out of the stroller.

"I'm *not* unhappy in the bedroom, Pim." Lisa circled back to his earlier declaration with a hushed whisper and burning cheeks. He wasn't going to let it go, and she'd learned the easiest way to clear the decks with him was to just have it out. It was bothering her, too, and while she should have waited until they had a little more privacy in their seats on board the plane, she couldn't stop herself from continuing the conversation. "I told you I didn't put the damn thing in the bag, Pim. Why isn't that enough proof to you that I didn't bring it? Do you think I was waking up at 3am and getting my jollies off in the bathroom?"

"Well, I sure as shit didn't pack it."

"Shit!" Oliva chimed in as they approach the counter.

Eve smothered another grin with her hand and handed her family's passports and boarding passes over to the agent at the door. AJ and Lisa let out a collective groan. As they stepped forward to hand their documents to the gate agent, Eve chimed in from a few feet ahead. "They don't understand, girlie. The peen-folk, I mean. I dunno about you, but when I was pregnant with Noah, I could barely reach my vajungle, let alone get all up in my lady garden."

Are we talking about my lady garden right now? The gate agents both attempted to hide their laughter, and a blush warmed Lisa's neck and face. "Thank you," she croaked, taking their paperwork back and walking down the jetway. *If the ground could open up and swallow me that would be great.*

"Tell me I'm wrong." Eve unclipped Noah at the door to the plane and handed him to Rob while she collapsed the stroller and left it to the side out of the way of traffic. "Okay, wait, even if you *can* reach your bajingo, you can't possibly have the freakin' energy, right? I mean you're growing a human, that shit takes it out of you."

"Shit!" Olivia clapped her hands together in glee at the repetition of what seemed to be her new favorite word.

"Bajingo?" AJ shuffled behind Lisa, who waddled behind Eve, down the cramped aisle towards their seats.

"Yeah, you know, bajingo?" Eve spoke louder than any human being should about what she called her vagina, in public no less, but she gave zero shits which enamored Lisa to her all the more. "Penis fly trap … furry taco … vajayjay … see … you … next … Tuesday …?" She spun around to face AJ over Lisa's shoulder and burst out laughing. "Look at your face, all fifty-shades-of-outrage! It means *vagina*, AJ. And I can tell you now, I may have just met your wife in the restroom, but I know she hasn't used that vibrator since you knocked her all-the-way up with the real deal. I'd give her a twenty right now if she could even reach her cooter."

AJ's face had paled and his eyes were wide. "Do women really call it their bajingo?"

Lisa laughed and patted his arm. "No dear, we don't. But let's take a moment to point out that of the list she gave you, *that's* the one that caused you most concern. In you go if you want the window." She stopped at the end of the row and let him scoot across into his seat. Eve and her family were serendipitously seated across the aisle from them perhaps in a bid to keep all the kids clustered together to contain the chaos. Lisa and Eve sat in the aisle seats for ease of chatting.

"I guess they thought keeping all us crazies together was a good idea." Eve reached across the seat and fastened Noah's seatbelt.

"We just met. How could you *possibly* know I'm crazy?"

Eve arched her brow, narrowed her eyes and pursed her lips. "Oh, are we in denial? Mmkaaaay. I'll pretend like you don't have a bedazzled, flashing 'I'm batshit cray' sign hanging around your neck."

"Damn. Thought I switched that off."

A round faced balding man was struggling to put his hand luggage into the overhead compartment in the row in front. He was mumbling something about being an irresponsible mother, but the rest of the seats next to him were empty. He could only be talking about someone in their group.

And of course, Lisa was going to find out who. "Excuse me sir, did you say something?"

"Yeah, I said you're irresponsible. Flying while so heavily pregnant."

She instinctively reached a hand across Olivia's seat and grabbed AJ's arm, giving him a gentle squeeze. *Don't start anything on board a plane on foreign soil, Pim. Let's just get everyone home without a criminal record.* "Not that I owe you an explanation, *sir*, but I was cleared by my doctor to fly."

"And that makes it right?"

Dude, never mind my husband, I'm about to rip your head off your shoulders.

"Perhaps not. But I *can* tell you that last time I was this pregnant on a plane I gave birth right outside the cockpit, so I'd suggest you don't give my blood pressure cause to rise."

The stranger blanched and thumped the overhead call button, demanding to be moved from the hysterical pregnant woman. As he fumed at an unsuspecting air hostess, Eve offered Lisa some Chex Mix across the space between them. "Great move telling him you had Olivia on a plane. I don't think I've ever seen anyone so terrified of a pregnant woman before."

Lisa scooped a handful snack mix and cradled it against her body, offering Olivia a pretzel from the pile. "Oh, I did give birth to Livvy on a plane. I wasn't saying that for dramatic effect."

Eve's jaw dropped open, clamped shut, and she swallowed hard. "I take it back, you're not just crazy, you're a freakin' badass."

AJ leaned over Olivia and nuzzled his head against Lisa's. "You okay?"

She turned her head to his and inhaled, her muscles loosening at the small gesture of intimacy. She nodded. "Kinda wishing I had that murder weapon dildo handy right about now though."

THREE

"I want to see it."

"Shit! You scared the crap out of me, Eve!" Lisa spun to face her new friend in baggage claim in Newark International Airport. Every muscle in her body ached, her chest seared with heartburn, and her eyes stung with tiredness. Any time she'd gotten comfy during the flight, the baby shifted and lodged a limb in her ribcage.

"Were you asleep? Can you sleep standing up with your eyes open? I've heard about mothers who can do such things, but I've never been able to master it. I want to see it." Eve's hair was kempt, her makeup untouched, and there were no dark circles underlining her eyes.

"Okay, I'll bite. See what?"

"Thor's hammer." Eve's stage whispers needed work. She continued at what must have been an expression of 'what the hell are you talking about?' on Lisa's face. "Y'know … your silicone schlong … weapon of ass destruction … big red riding rod …" She snorted with laughter.

"Oh God." AJ's groan alerted Lisa to his presence. He'd pulled their luggage from the moving carousel and placed the cases next to Lisa while she cuddled a napping Olivia against her chest. "She's talking about *it* again, isn't she?"

Eve grinned at him. "I want to see it."

His only response was to curl his lips between his teeth and shake his head. He ignored Lisa's wide-eyed silent plea to be rescued from the woman who wanted her to throw open her luggage and whip out her ten inch red vibrator in front of three hundred people.

"Can't I just send you a picture when I get home?"

"And how would I get an idea of scale then, eh? C'mon, you know you want to. I don't want to wave it around like a flag or anything ... just wanna see why it's such a big deal."

Lisa's face burned with embarrassment as she put Olivia in the stroller and tugged her case into a quiet corner. She plopped it on the ground and crouched down beside it. "I hate you right now, you know that, right?"

"Mmmmhmmm. But not for realsies. You can't hate your bestie, even if I'm a shiny new bestie. Them's the rules. Out with it, Williams. Show me the pocket rocket."

Lisa unzipped the case and lifted the lid, the Malaysian TSA had left it sitting pretty right on top of all her clothes.

Eve gave a low whistle. "Hot damn. That is one fine and dandy disco stick."

"Did you Google a list of things to call a penis before you came up to me? I feel like no one has this many names to hand for a dude's junk."

Eve laughed. "Stop deflecting." She squatted next to Lisa and placed her hand next to the vibrator in the case. "How do you get it all in?"

"In my case?"

"In your *box,* girl."

Lisa laughed. "Oh! I didn't, not at first."

"Wait, didn't I hear you tell him it was the same size as him so he had nothing to worry about?" Eve gasped, clutching a hand to her chest before fanning her face. "Why, AJ, what a big ... semen demon you have ..." She burst into uncontrollable giggles. "Daaaang girl. I feel like sex with him should be an Olympic sport ... that's quite the javelin he's got tucked in those jeans. Didn't it take a while to make him fit?"

Lisa covered her face with her palm. "He's going to kill me."

"Nuh uh. I'm not kidding. I need ... *details*. I can't figure out how that fits in ... well, anywhere. Did you need to do like ... stretches ... before you did the horizontal bop for the first time with ... *that*? Hell, even now. Do you stretch? I feel like stretching first must be a prerequisite. And pooping. Y'know, to make space."

A giggle escaped Lisa as she zipped up her case and pushed to stand. "We did a long distance thing for a while first. It's why I got the toy in the first place. I went shopping with my best friend Chelsea during one of my trips to visit her. I'd never been to a sex shop before and she insisted it was not only a rite of passage, but necessary, so when I met AJ in the flesh, he wouldn't break my vagina."

Eve nodded and her face turned thoughtful. "She sounds like a wise woman. So she took you to buy a fake peen to get you prepped for the real deal. That's a good friend right there. Protecting your lady garden from that. Brings the phrase 'ride or die' to a whole new level. She was clearly making sure you didn't die while riding. I dunno, girl … I feel like there's no prepping for something like that. But that doesn't answer the real question. Why's he so hung up over a toy when he's so well hung?"

Lisa shrugged. She didn't have an answer. She tugged the case back to where the bemused husbands stood watching the women talk loud and proud about vibrators. AJ's gaze burned into her and she shook her head in response. *Not now.*

They walked their bags through customs, left them off at bag drop, and exchanged numbers before the two families parted ways. Lisa hugged her new friend. Her conversation buffer was walking away towards her gate, and Lisa was about to enter a confined space with her inexplicably still-angry husband, who, for some reason, still needed closure on the vibrator thing. Part of her wanted to throw it in the trash and be done with it when they landed in Huntsville. But the more stubborn part of her yelled that he was being irrational and wanted to beat him over the head with the damn thing instead. How the flight went would decide the fate of both AJ and Buzz Nightgear.

FOUR

Eve: Holy shit - it just hit me. NEED TO KNOW and we're besties now so you have to answer.

Lisa: O...kay ...?

Eve: Have you ever done anal with the monster cock? Didn't it hurt like a white-hot, foot-long poker was stuck in your poop chute?

Lisa groaned and dropped her phone on the kitchen counter.

"'Sup?" Jeremy was helping himself to the meagre contents of her fridge.

"Am I at least going to get some of whatever witchcraft you're making from that empty fridge?"

"It's not empty. I grabbed some basics before you guys got home last night. And I even made you some stuff to reheat cause I'm nice like that." He leaned further into the open fridge, and for a moment she feared he'd disappear through a secret panel in the back. Would that be so bad? Her stomach growled in response. Good call. Let's at least eat first.

"And you knew you'd be here today so you saved today Jeremy the hassle of having to make food?"

He raised a casserole dish and cocked his head. "Exactly. Thank you, past Jeremy. Stop distracting me from whatever face you just made, with food. We both know it always works and I wanna know what made your face twist up like that."

Lisa plopped onto the dining room chair and huffed out a sigh. AJ had taken Olivia upstairs for a nap, leaving Lisa to fend for herself against the energizer bunny that was Jeremy. She should be grateful. He'd kept her dog alive while they were gone, sure, but she'd arrived home to extra dogs in her house, and she wasn't quite ready to forgive him for that just yet.

"Is this about the vibrator thing?"

"How the fuck do you know about the vibrator thing?" She folded her arms on top of her bump and glared at him. Her cheeks warmed. It had bothered AJ enough to mention it to his best friend, but she had no real idea why. "What's his damn deal? It's not like we've never used toys before."

"He told me last night. He's always been self-conscious about his size. You know that. Girls are all 'size matters,' but when he brings the size they're like 'fuck no'. He never dated a hell of a lot before you, partly because of the reaction he got when chicks saw his cock."

Lisa arched an eyebrow and gestured at him to continue.

Jeremy turned on the oven and popped the casserole dish in before continuing. "Guys are jealous as shit, but the very, very, very few girls in the world who have seen it, were terrified. He was freakin' out before you guys first had sex. I guess seeing the size of it in all that silicone splendor brought him back there? It's definitely a him thing rather than a you thing. What about I take Livvy tonight for a sleep over? You two can get some solid rest, sleep off your jetlag and reconnect. Y'know ... to his dick I mean."

Lisa held up her hand to silence him. "Thanks, mansplainer. I got what you meant." She drummed a finger against her chin. "You're sure Chels won't mind?"

"Won't mind spending time with our badass goddaughter? For real? Stop trying to make excuses where none exist and just say 'thank you Jeremy that sounds epic.'"

She rolled her eyes. "Fine. Thank you, Jeremy."

He tilted his head and widened his eyes.

"What?"

"You didn't say the whole thing."

"Ugh. You're a monumental douche nozzle sometimes. You know that?"

"As a matter of fact, I do. But I'm your douche nozzle, and there's a no refund policy with me, so you're kinda stuck. Sorry, not sorry."

Her phone chimed and Jeremy handed it across to her from the counter.

Eve: I know you're ignoring me. I demand an answer. Did he deflower your chocolate starfish with his mondo-cock?

"Oh God." Lisa dropped her head onto the dining room table with a dramatic thud.

"Someone who makes you grumble more than I, Sir Douche Nozzle, does? Say it ain't so, Lis. Of all the people in the world who grind your gears, I'm number one, right?"

"Do you need your ego massaged, Jer? Then yes, you are the number one pain in my ass." She grimaced at the wording and waved her phone at him. "I think you'd like Eve. They're gonna come visit soon, she wants a barbecue, and her hubs wants to skate with you guys."

"Okay, none of this sounds bad. What's the groan-fest for?"

Lisa's face grew hot, and she shook her head. Before typing out a reply, she made sure Jeremy wasn't looming over her shoulder trying to read.

Lisa: Should I be concerned? None of my other friends have ever asked what I've stuck up my ass before.

Eve: Amateurs. How can they even call themselves your friends? Tell. Me. ALL.

Lisa: FINE. YES. We have had anal. Took a while to train my ass to take something so … eh … girthy, and he had no idea I was working up to it. I'd never had anal before him and he mentioned it was something he'd like to try some day, so I surprised him by being ready for him when we got together.

Eve: And they say romance is dead. Hey honey, lube up, my Hershey Highway is ready for a-poundin'.

Lisa: Well, I didn't *quite* put it like that.

Eve: Trained your ass first, eh? I knew you were a smart cookie. Did you use that toy to help? If so, he shouldn't be so mad about it, he kinda owes it a debt of thanks.

Lisa: We're done talking about my ass now, right?

Eve: Fuck no. Did you like it?

She lifted her head and was met by Jeremy's piercing stare. "Well?" He smirked. "Did you?"

Nerves fluttered in Lisa's stomach as AJ unboxed the takeout dinner onto plates on the table. She traced her finger around the rim of her wine glass – filled with Martinellis sparkling apple cider in a bid to fool her body into thinking it was something alcoholic. She couldn't wait to get her hands on an ice cold, top shelf margarita when the baby was born.

"You're quiet." He tipped the rice onto the plates and set aside the empty container.

"Just tired, I guess."

His face fell, making her heart swell. Even ready-to-pop pregnant with swollen fingers and toes, having not shaved her legs since who knows when, and resembling a swamp witch most days, he still wanted her.

"Not *too* tired." She sought out his gaze as he served cashew nut chicken onto the rice.

"Did my face do that thing where it didn't hide its disappointment again?"

She nodded, dunking the crab Rangoon into the sweet dipping sauce, taking a bite, and moaning in appreciation. "It did. But it made me feel better about myself, so I'm kinda glad."

"Please don't tell me you need reminded that I want you. I always want you." He slid a palm along her jaw and stroked her cheek with his thumb.

"I know. I just … I'm feeling spectacularly blah and unattractive right now. I had a bath earlier and decided to shave my legs. We both know it's been a while. It took me an hour! I know …" She held up a hand to stop him. "You don't care whether I have hairy legs or not, I just … *I* care."

His deep chuckle warmed her. "You're right, I don't care. I thought you'd fallen asleep in the tub. I went up to check on you, and you were cussing something out, so I left you alone. I could have helped, you know."

"You'd shave my legs for me?"

"Damn freakin' straight I would. Zero hesitation. You're literally growing my child. If you needed your ass wiped, I'd help you with that, too. Just say the word."

"In some moments, I feel like you're a fictional character in a book. Men like you don't exist."

He leaned over the plates of food and planted a kiss on her lips. "I'm every bit as real as you are, Mrs. Williams."

Her phone chimed on the table, but she ignored it, snaking her arms around AJ's neck, and kissing him again. "As much as I'd love to drag you up to bed and have my wicked way with you, your child is demanding food."

"That's okay, wontons first, wicked way later."

"Sweet and sour before spanking?"

He coughed around the mouthful of food he'd taken as he sat down. His eyes watered, and he covered his mouth with his hand.

"You can't die before I get laid, Pim. That's just rude."

He gulped down some milk and laughed. "Spanking, eh? It's been a while."

"I like alliteration."

"And spanking." Desire burned in his grey-blue eyes as he held her stare for a moment. "Eat your food, Lis, before I end up eating something else for dinner entirely."

FIVE

"It's useless!" Lisa grabbed a pillow from the bed next to her and smushed it over her face. "I'm destined not to get laid until after this baby comes out."

AJ plucked the pillow from her face. "What was that? I didn't hear you, what with the face-full of pillow."

"The basic gist was, I need your cock."

"What you *need* is to be patient. Okay, so it doesn't work with me on top, and you were uncomfortable on top, but those aren't the only two sex positions in the world, you know. There's a whole freakin' book written to tell the world how to make it work in many, many other ways."

"Agh!" She threw the pillow at him, and he caught it with ease. "I *know* that, Pim. I don't want to be patient. I'm just frustrated. I want this baby out of me. Right *now*!" When he didn't reply, she lifted herself up onto her elbows and narrowed her eyes. "What?"

"You're beautiful."

"And you need your eyes tested." She reached over onto the nightstand and picked up her phone, pretending to search. "I'm calling the optician, or whatever Americans call the optician."

He plucked the phone from her hand and put it back on the bedside table. "Eye doctor? And I mean it. I know you're frustrated and impatient to have your body back but you're doing really well. The trip was tough, but we bossed it, and you're on the final stretch now." He picked up her foot and kissed the inside of her ankle. Spreading her legs, he kissed the inside of her knee. "I know I can't do much to help you with the watermelon you're carrying, or the heartburn, the back ache, the insomnia, and general discomfort." He trailed his tongue along her thigh and a flutter of need shot straight to her core. "But I can definitely help you relax. You've never been a quitter, Lis. So the first few positions weren't what we needed them to be. So what?" He dragged his finger through her wetness and groaned, dropping his head onto her thigh. "Fuck, you're so wet."

"I told you. Need. Your. Cock."

"If you're not careful, I'm gonna shut your whining mouth up with my damn cock."

She grinned. "Promises, promises, Mr. Williams. Actually, I think that's a great idea." She ran a hand through his hair and tugged him up her body until he kissed her. "I mean it." She pushed his chest. "Stand up beside the bed." He protested but she grabbed at his dick and slid her tight hand down the length. "Don't argue with me." She turned to lie on her side and took him into her mouth. With as big as he was, she couldn't maneuver him too deep, but he never complained that it wasn't enough, or forced her beyond where she was comfortable.

A low growl rumbled deep in his chest as she wrapped both hands around his length and teased at the head with her tongue as she pumped. He reached behind him, the sound of the drawer opening causing her to raise her eyebrows but his fingers weaved their way into her hair. His hand grabbed the back of her head, his hips jerked and he moaned in appreciation as she sucked. Something cold brushed against her leg and she gasped around him.

"Shhhh." He stroked her hair and refocused her on teasing him with the tip of her tongue.

He pushed his hand against her knee, and she opened her legs for him as she sucked. His fingers trailed through her folds and he brushed a gentle thumb over her clit. Her sensitivity had increased since getting pregnant, and she pressed herself into his thumb, groaning at the chuckle he gave in response.

"So hungry, baby."

"Mmhmm."

He slid a finger inside her, then two. "So empty."

She whimpered when he slid his fingers all the way out before sliding them back in.

"We should fix that."

She tilted her head upwards, taking him deeper as she did. He brushed her hair out of her face with his left hand and with his right he slid her toy into her. Her breath caught at the unexpected intrusion and she pulled her brows together in a questioning frown.

"I don't have anything against using toys, Lis." He pushed the large vibrator another inch inside of her. "I guess I just got self-conscious for a sec." He inched the toy all the way in as he continued. "You know how the irrational thoughts can snowball when something kicks off your inner demons." Turning the vibration on, she dropped her hands from the base of his cock, and grabbed onto his hips. He pulled it out and dragged it over her clit before sliding it back in. Her hips tilted towards him and she ground against the toy buzzing in his grip. "What's the matter? Not enough for you?" He pulled it out again.

She rolled her eyes and flopped back onto the bed. "Ugh. You know it's not. It's never enough. Is that what you need to hear? That no matter how big or powerful the toy is, it's never going to compare to my husband's huge and talented cock? Because I'll say it as many times as you need to hear it." She half hiccupped, half shrieked as he rammed the toy into her.

"Turn over." He withdrew it, turned it off, and threw it onto the bed next to her.

"Since when are you so bossy?"

"Since I'm determined to give my wife what she needs and fuck her senseless. All fours."

Her jaw dropped open, but she complied and rolled onto her hands and knees. Aching need replaced her frustration, and a shiver of anticipation erased her impatience. He widened the gap between her legs before easing himself into her on a low moan. She sighed, driving her hips back against his.

He chuckled. "So impatient, Lis."

His fingers curled around her hips and his thrusts grew harder and faster as she rocked back.

"Deeper." She rasped. When she'd been pregnant with Olivia he'd been afraid of hurting the baby, but this time he complied without protest and pounded his every inch deep into her.

She gripped the comforter in clutched hands. The only sound in the room was the slapping of skin and their heavy grunts and breathing as they chased their climax. He slid his hands up her sides and cupped her breasts. She moaned when he squeezed. He teased at her nipples before sliding a hand over her bump and between her legs. He only needed to circle her clit a few times before she came undone, grabbing the headboard of the bed.

"Don't. Stop."

He only said two words in reply, but she could hear the grin in his voice as his palm cracked against her ass cheek and he wrapped a handful of her hair around his fist. "Yes ma'am."

SIX

"Feel better?"

Lisa fought the urge to throw her breakfast at Jeremy's smug face, but that would mean she'd have no burrito, and her growling stomach didn't approve of that plan.

"You're moving a lil slowly today, Lis. Overexert yourself?"

"Jeremy Lewis." Lisa's tone conveyed everything he needed to know. She stopped at the chair next to the dining table and sank onto the hard wood with a groan. "Murder is on my mind."

"It's premeditated if you say it out loud, though."

"And yet I'm okay with that. To answer your question, I am two hundred weeks pregnant. That's why I'm slow moving."

"Ah." Jeremy finished his burrito and pulled another from the plate between them. "So not because of all the bow-chica-wow-wow, sweet, sweet lovin' you guys got up to last night while we had Princess Livvy?" He made a circle with the thumb and forefinger on his left hand and slipped his right index finger in and out of the hole a couple of times, chuckling to himself.

"Ugh. You're such a pig."

AJ reached over Lisa's shoulder and plucked a burrito from the diminishing pile. "I'm gonna help you out here, man and suggest you change the subject. Can't you feel that seething rage rolling off of her today? Read the signs, Jer. Or you're gonna die, and there won't be a damn thing I can do to save you."

Jeremy laughed. "She loves me too much to get rid of me. And your unborn child loves my burritos. I'm safe."

"For now." Lisa unwrapped her second burrito and took a bite, savoring the bacon, egg and cheese explosion on her tongue. A moan escaped her.

"Lis, do you need a moment? You seem to be having a biblical experience right now and I feel dirty watching."

It was AJ's turn to chuckle.

"See? AJ's getting flashbacks to last night and all the noises you made during sexy times." Jeremy's head darted between her and AJ. "Oh God, Pim. Did you fall asleep and leave her unsatisfied? Is that why she's so mad today?"

"I. Want. This. Baby. Out. Of. Me." Lisa thumped the table as Olivia ran into the kitchen, arms outstretched for a cuddle.

"Up!"

Lisa couldn't help but smile. She'd missed the adorable little hurricane while she was away for her sleepover and was only too eager to cuddle.

"No more dirty talk with little ears around, okay?"

"Sure, but could you at least tell me you got some? Are we past vibrator-palooza? AJ's no longer self-conscious about silicone Jurassic Pork?"

A flush crept up AJ's neck, cheeks, and even the tips of his ears went pink.

"Ah ha! Y'all got your buzz on with the ... ah ... grown up toy, didn't you?"

"Toys!" Olivia wriggled down from Lisa's lap and toddled back out of the room.

"Jeremy." Lisa covered her face with her palm. "Your interest in our sex life is unhealthy, you know that, right?"

"Lies. You can't tell me that Eve woman you met in the airport wasn't texting you first thing this morning demanding to know everything."

"As a matter of fact, that's exactly what she did. I told her she was a weirdo too." Lisa's cheeks warmed and there was every chance her ears were as red as AJ's. Even after all this time, Jeremy still had the ability to make them both squirm with his probing questions about their sex life. "They're coming to visit next weekend. I guess we made an impression on them."

"Her husband skates, I told him he could come to practice, maybe set up a pick-up game of ball while we're at it."

"Sounds good to me. Just say when. We're cookin' out, right? Beer, dawgs and s'mores?"

Having taken too big a bite of her breakfast, Lisa nodded. "Mhmm."

"Now who's the pig?" Jeremy waved the end of his third burrito at her. "Didn't you learn your lesson about putting too much in your mouth last night?"

"Hey, hey. You doing okay? You look tired." Chelsea flopped onto the chair across the two-person table and placed her phone face-down next to Lisa's.

"Thanks, Chels. You sure know how to make a girl feel beautiful."

"Any time. You ordered?"

"Order for Lisa." The barista squinted at the words he'd scrawled on the side of the cup as he yelled.

"Sit. I'll get it." Chelsea leapt from her seat and collected Lisa's drink. "Hot chocolate?"

Lisa nodded, popping the plastic top from her drink and setting it on the table. She picked up the cinnamon shaker and dusted the top of the whipped cream with cinnamon before stirring it into the warm chocolate with the wooden stirrer. "What did you order? Venti caramel macchiato?"

Chelsea smiled. "I guess we're both predictable."

"After all these years as friends, we ought to be. Thanks for taking Olivia last week, I needed it."

"I bet you did. Jer mentioned something about AJ and a monster vibrator, I figured he was making shit up but after your texts ... well, don't sweat it. You know we're always happy to take her for a sleepover. It doesn't even need to be a vibe-crisis."

Lisa giggled. "He really got up in his anxiety over the damn vibrator. It was the strangest thing."

"We've all had weird shit set off our inner monsters. I'm just glad he didn't let it fester."

Lisa took a sip of her drink and licked the cream from her top lip. "Yeah, nothing worse than a festering vibrator."

Chelsea laughed and the barista called her name. She grabbed her drink and settled back at the table, facing Lisa. "Things are okay with you guys now though, right? I mean, I know they weren't broken or anything, but from the sounds of it, your trip was … trying, then AJ's … eh … tantrum? Wobble? Whatever it was … and you're basically in your fifth trimester. You've got a lot going on and we don't need another stress induced early arrival." She tipped her cup towards Lisa's belly.

Lisa patted her bump. "Yeah, no. We're fine, and this little one doesn't seem in any rush to join the outside world."

"Pups doing okay?" Chelsea grimaced. Lisa wasn't sure if it was because her coffee was too hot or the fact that Lisa was still pissed that she left one dog in her and Jeremy's charge and came home to additional dogs.

"Yeah, we're in the process of trying to find homes for them. I for sure thought you guys would take one."

"Shhhh." She checked over her shoulders. "No dogs. We can't. I mean, Jer would have taken all three of them, but hell no."

Lisa laughed. "You think saying the word 'dog' will summon Jeremy?"

"Stranger things have happened. When do your guests arrive?"

"Tomorrow. You wanna come over while the guys are out throwing each other into the plexi?"

"Finally!" Chelsea sniffed and popped out her lower lip in a melodramatic pout. "I thought you'd replaced me with this new Eve person."

Lisa gave her friend a playful shove. "Lies. You'll like her though, she's our kinda crazy."

"Ten bucks says she brings you a new sex toy."

Seven

"I brought you something." Eve stepped back from their hug and produced a small, hot pink gift bag. "Best put it somewhere out of little people's reach."

"And Jeremy's reach." Chelsea's knowing smirk made Lisa roll her eyes.

She crossed the kitchen, slid her purse across the counter and pulled a crisp ten dollar bill from her wallet. "Is what's in this bag …" She raised her hand with the bag in. "From an adult store?"

Eve's face dropped. "We've only been besties for like two weeks and I'm already predictable? What the hell?"

Lisa handed the money to Chelsea, who plucked it from her hand with an arched eye brow and a 'thank you' before tucking it into her cleavage. Olivia tugged Noah by the hand and the two scampered off into the play room.

Eve's husband handed AJ a six pack of beer. "I didn't bring you a vibrator, man, but I've got meat in the car."

"Shouldn't leave your meat out there. It'll go funky in that heat." Jeremy stepped forward with an extended hand. "Jeremy Lewis, nice to meet you. Let's go rescue your meat."

"There's gonna be meat jokes all night now, isn't there?"

"You know it, cupcake." Jeremy followed Robert out to the car and Lisa sat at the table. AJ put the beer in the fridge and pulled out the guacamole.

"Let me help." Eve sprang into action, taking the dish from AJ and placing it on the table. "What needs done?"

Lisa pressed a palm into her lower back and made a move to stand.

"Nope, stay there. We've got this. Use your big girl words and tell me what needs done."

"I like her." Chelsea stirred the guac. "Chips are in that cupboard."

Eve's eyebrows shot up her forehead and Chelsea gave a dramatic sigh. "Oh, I see. For her you'll do it, but you don't love me enough yet. Give it time. Fiiiiine, I'll help."

Between the two of them they warmed the homemade queso, and brought out the rest of the appetizers. Jeremy had made man candy and a cheeseball as big as Lisa's head. Eve had brought potato salad, and a strawberry, mozzarella and spinach salad with a balsamic dressing, an apple pie and she'd even brought some non-alcoholic wine for Lisa to enjoy.

The kids watched *Moana* while the guys fired up the grill and got started on cooking.

"How did you and AJ meet?" Eve dragged a chip through the guacamole and popped it in her mouth with a loud crunch.

"Online. Chelsea dragged me into a Gmail chatroom with Jeremy and AJ one day and we got to talking. I fell for him pretty hard and fast. But we're one of those clichéd couples who met on the net. Not a very original meet cute, eh?"

"It's adorable, and you have good friends for bringing you both together."

"I'll drink to that." Lisa raised her wine glass and clinked it against Eve's bottle of beer.

"I feel like Rob's going to want to move here now that we've met y'all. He's been looking for his boy-tribe, he misses hockey. He's from Wisconsin so he's pretty sick of the firey inferno that is Alabama, but I think if he had his tribe he'd shut up whining about it."

"If you make me this salad every day you can move into our garage." Lisa heaped another scoop of spinach salad onto her plate as AJ came back inside.

"Grub's up. Want us to bring it inside? There's a lot of bugs out there and it's kinda sticky."

Lisa groaned. "Yeah, I don't wanna be skeeter-dinner. Bring me my food, waiter man."

The doorbell rang and she furrowed her brow.

"Oh. I eh, I might have suggested the neighbors come over for a burger when I saw them over the fence this morning."

"Shit. AJ, I'm not people-presentable, damnit."

"Uh, you know we're people, right?" Eve stood and walked towards the door.

"You don't count. You're not peopley people." Lisa waved a queso-dipped chip at her new friend.

"Thanks, I think." Eve pulled open the door and Alex and Sandra walked in carrying a bottle of red wine.

AJ and Lisa hadn't talked much to them since moving to the neighborhood, they were the prim and proper couple in the neighborhood. He wore a sweater tied over the shoulders of his polo shirt and there wasn't a hair out of place on Sandra's head. As they walked in and across the kitchen displaying the bottle wine as though it was a gift for the Messiah, Lisa imagined twelve different ways she could murder her husband before the sun came up.

"Oh, I'm sorry. We totally forgot you can't drink."

Lisa strained to pull herself up off the chair.

"Don't get up." Alex rushed forward and squeezed her shoulder.

Noah's squealing giggles pealed around the room as he weaved between the bodies dotted around the kitchen. Jeremy and Rob had come in with plates of food and Jeremy was standing eating from a piled-high plate, eyes dancing with amusement at the gleeful child bounding around the room.

Horror clenched Lisa's stomach and her breath stopped in her chest when Olivia chased behind him, wielding the ginormous red, sparkly vibrator, clutched between both hands. As she ran after the little boy, she yelled, "Buzz, buzz!"

Sandra's eyes widened and Alex's eyebrows shot into his receding hairline. Jeremy smothered his laughter by shoving a hotdog in his mouth and Eve doubled over in hysterics. Chelsea hid her smirk behind her hand and AJ's face looked as hot as Lisa's.

"Well, we just stopped by to drop this off and say thanks for the invite but we can't stay." Sandra handed the bottle to AJ and backed away.

"Buzz! Buzz! Take that!" Olivia and Noah had made another lap of the room and none of the adults took the enormous vibrator from the little girl.

No one moved as the neighbors spun on their heels and bolted out the door, not even pausing to close it behind them. AJ followed their steps and shut the door with a dull thud before tipping his head against the wood. His shoulders sagged, then juddered. His laughter was contagious and before long tears were streaming down Lisa's face as she clutched her aching ribs.

Eve grabbed another bottle of beer from the fridge and sat across the table from Lisa who was still struggling to breathe between bouts of giggles. "Damn, girl. That chick stick sure does have a lot to answer for."

"No shit. Now, which one of you is gonna go wrestle BOB from the clutches of my toddler before I need to order new batteries?"

About The Author

Lasairiona McMaster writes sassy, classy and badassy women and strong, yet vulnerable men. She challenges reader's expectations by openly dealing with mental health issues, often exploring tough-to-handle topics and 'taboos' and books with a whole lotta heart.

She can either be found enjoying a gin and lemonade by the Irish sea, or baking sweet treats in her kitchen while singing at the top of her lungs. When she's 'home' in Texas, and isn't eating fresh-popped popcorn while buying things she has absolutely no need for in Target, she can be found at Chuys eating her body weight in chips and queso and washing it down with a margarita swirl.

https://www.amazon.com/Lasairiona-E-McMaster/e/B07V8DCB8M

Strawberry Lipstick

L. Ann

Sometimes it's nice to have a little extra
...something ...
when you're getting it on.
Alicia Silverstone

Love Song - YungBlud

One

Gabe

"Gabe?" I opened my eyes at Harper's voice and found her standing in the doorway to our bedroom.

How the fuck did I get so lucky?

I thanked the universe every day for letting me keep her, even though I didn't deserve to.

"Are you awake?" she asked quietly. I knew why she was cautious—I didn't sleep much, usually going two or three days without until my body demanded I crash and burn. She didn't want to disturb me if I wasn't ready to wake up.

"Yeah, I'm awake." I yawned, propped my head up on one hand and waved her over to the bed. "Everything okay?"

"It's your birthday soon. I was thinking … It'll be the first one since we got back together. I want to do something to celebrate." She moved further into the room, paused to run her fingers through my hair, then settled beside me.

I turned my head to look at her. "You know I don't celebrate my birthday, Frosty," I reminded her gently.

Birthdays hadn't been my favorite time of the year when I was growing up. They had always come with particularly bad beatings from my da. I knew *now* it was because my birthday reminded him strongly of the woman—my mother—he'd lost too soon and, for whatever reason, he'd blamed me for her death. It had taken me a long time, *and* Harper, to finally realize her death *wasn't* my fault.

"I know," Harper was saying. "But maybe we could start making better memories out of them?"

Did you have something in mind?" I relented, because truthfully, if it made Harper happy then I'd do it for her.

"Well, what would *you* like to do?"

I smiled slowly, leering at her, then laughed when she rolled her eyes at me and punched my shoulder. "Frosty, come on. Did you think my mind would go anywhere else?"

"Having sex isn't unusual."

I leaned in and stole a kiss. "But it's *always* special. And it's *definitely* memorable. We could make a big thing of it like you want to. Hell, you can even make me a birthday cake. In fact, we'll go out for a meal." I grinned, an idea forming in my head. "Yeah, I could get that all I-can-eat buffet under the table at Joyeuse like I wanted. Then back here to play some more."

"You want to have sex on your birthday? That's the ultimate gift?" Her brows pulled together, and I recognised the action—she wasn't convinced.

"No, Frosty, I want to have sex with *you* on my birthday."

"We have sex all the time."

"But we've never had sex on my birthday," I pointed out.

She huffed and rose to her feet. I laughed. I was gonna get sex on my birthday. The day was already turning out to be a good one and it was still a month away. First though, we needed the warm-up act. I picked up my cell and started researching.

Three days later, I'd put the first part of my plan into action *and* managed to keep it a secret from Harper. I was reading the email notifying me of the delivery date when she called my name … my *full* name.

"*Gabriel!*"

Gabriel? Hmmm, now what was that about? There were only ever two reasons she used my full name. If I'd annoyed her somehow or when she was about to come and, right now, neither seemed likely.

I rolled off the bed, where I'd been lounging, dragged on the pair of pants closest to me—an old pair of grey sweats, ammunition just in case she *was* annoyed with me—and padded out of the bedroom, following the sound of her voice. My footsteps slowed when I heard other voices and I stopped to listen. I could make out Harper's soft tones, another woman and a male voice—both I recognized.

Striding through into the main living area, I crept up behind Seth, who was leaning against one of the kitchen counters, and wrapped my arms around his waist from behind, so I could slap a wet kiss onto his cheek.

"Hey, gorgeous," I greeted him, caught Harper's eye roll and winked at her.

"I've been your assistant for years and you *never* greet me like that," Candice complained from the other end of the kitchen.

I squeezed Seth's waist, dropped my arms and turned to face her. "Your husband would squash me like a bug if I put my dirty hands on you." I plucked Seth's coffee out of his hand and took a sip. "What are you two doing here, anyway?"

"I told you he forgot," Seth moved around the room to pour himself a fresh drink.

I frowned, mug halfway to my lips, and glanced between the two of them. "Forgot what?"

"The band has an interview with Generation Music tomorrow. You're *supposed* to be packed and ready to leave for Detroit. I reminded you a *week* ago. You said you had it all in hand," Candice told me.

Fuck. That explained the *Gabriel* thing.

I'd forgotten all about it. With everything that had gone on over the past couple of months—getting back with Harper, the kidnapping, almost dying, and the constant worry about Harper's safety, the interview had gone completely out of my head. It had been arranged months ago and even though Candice reminded me every week, I *still* managed to forget to mention it to Harper. I twisted to face her.

"Come with me," I said, and she immediately shook her head.

I understood why—she still wasn't comfortable with the attention which came from being with me, but I still felt the rejection like a knife to the gut. None of that showed on my face when I nodded. I knew she didn't mean it like that, but it didn't make it sting any less.

"I'll leave Remy here with you, then. We'll only be gone for three days. Don't go anywhere without him."

"Gabe—"

I shook my head. "It's not open for discussion, Harper. Remy stays or you come with me. Those are the only two options on the table."

Our eyes clashed and I waited for her to argue with me. She wasn't going to win this one. There was no fucking way I was leaving her without any security, and the *only* person I trusted with her safety, other than myself, was Remy.

Sweet Child O' Mine – Guns N Roses

Two

Harper

The penthouse was quiet without Gabe. It wasn't that he was particularly noisy, but I *knew* when he was there. His presence filled the apartment, held my attention like no one else could. When he was home, he was either writing, humming, or singing—sometimes all three. I would find him at all hours sitting outside, strumming an acoustic guitar, or scribbling down song lyrics. And when he wasn't doing those things, he was wrapped around me, not always physically, although our sex life was better than *good*. We'd talk, tease, watch movies, and just *be* together. Sometimes we'd sneak out, with Remy keeping a close guard, and go to Molly's—where we'd hide in our favorite booth and share whatever their daily special was.

Without him there, it made me realize just how much he'd filled up my life since we reconnected. And I *missed* him. I laughed at myself—he'd only been gone for a day, leaving with Seth and a promise to call me as soon as he landed in Detroit.

When had I become so reliant on him? I'd spent eight years looking after myself and the moment he came back into my life, I reverted to the girl whose entire existence revolved around him. That wasn't who I was. I *loved* Gabe, but I still had to keep some semblance of independence; otherwise, he'd take over my life completely, without even meaning to. That was just who he was—he'd spent so many years looking after me that, even after a lengthy time apart, the need to protect me remained strong … especially after recent events. Which was why I hadn't put up much of a fight about him leaving Remy with me. It would give him peace of mind, leaving him free to concentrate on band-related business while he was away from home.

And, anyway, I had a birthday to plan.

I'd known when I asked him that he would tell me he didn't celebrate his birthday, and *that* was my biggest reason for wanting to do something. I'd seen firsthand how his father had treated him, and yet Gabe had *always* made my birthdays special. I wanted to do that for him. I wanted to show him that things were different now, that birthdays weren't things to avoid but something to celebrate. But to do that, I needed help ... *specialist* help. And there was only one person I could turn to.

I reached for my cell. Siobhan picked up on the first ring.

"Hey, Harper."

"I need your help." I didn't bother with pleasantries. "Gabe's birthday is coming up and I want to surprise him."

"Now *there's* a problem. What to buy the guy who has everything?"

"No, I know what I want to get him. I just ..." My cheeks heated and I stumbled over my words. "I just need to know where to get it," I blurted in a rush of words.

"Oh, now this sounds interesting." Siobhan's voice was rich with curiosity. "Keep talking."

I'd never been so thankful to have decided to *call* Siobhan instead of going to her apartment as I was after I finished explaining to her what I needed *and* she'd stopped laughing.

"Can you help me or not?" I demanded when she finally fell silent.

"Of course I can. There's a place over in Brentwood that will sell everything you need."

"I'm not going *into* a sex shop, Siobhan!" I screeched. "If anyone saw ..."

Siobhan laughed again. "Stop panicking, Harper. They have a website and will deliver."

"I don't even want to know *how* you know that."

She laughed again. "You can order what you want and then have it sent to me.

That'll protect your identity. I'll even deliver it to you. How's that for friendship?"

I groaned. This idea had sounded much better inside my head.

"Relax, Harp. Gabe will love that you went to so much effort. I'm going to text you the website address. Go and have some fun with it." She cut the call before I could say anything further, and a second later my cell pinged with an incoming message.

I think I died a little inside when I opened the website and saw some of the things they had for sale. While Gabe *had* opened my eyes to trying new things, *this* was a whole new level and my cheeks burned just from reading the descriptions of some of the toys. Twice I closed the site, telling myself I'd just book a table at Joyeuse for his birthday and bring him back here for some private time, only to return to it minutes later to look again.

Gabe's ringtone blaring from my cell made me jump, and I clicked the little x on the website to close it before I answered the call.

"Hey, Frosty." His raspy voice sent a shiver through me. There was something about it that *always* did something to me. "Sorry I didn't call sooner. We got dragged to the studio as soon as the plane landed and I've only just got out."

"That's okay. How was the flight?" I asked, cursing the nervous tremor in my voice. *Stop it! It's not like he could see what you were looking at!* I berated myself.

There was a short silence before he responded. "Are you okay? You sound flustered."

"I'm fine," I squeaked, cleared my throat and tried again. "I'm okay. I've been chatting with Siobhan, that's all."

"If you arrange to go out, make sure you let Remy know. Go to Damnation, that way you can use the VIP room."

"I'm not going out. I'm going to order food and binge watch serial killer documentaries."

He chuckled. "Should I worry about my life expectancy?"

I thought about some of the things I'd seen on the website I'd been browsing. "Maybe. There could be a heart attack in your immediate future. How's your stamina these days?"

"You tell me, Frosty. I seem to last long enough to make you come more than a couple of times." He didn't miss a beat. "Speaking of which, there's something coming for *me* tomorrow. Don't open it until I call." I heard voices in the background, one—I thought it was Seth—calling his name. "I gotta go, babe. I'm not sure how late it's going to be before we get out tonight. Marley's here and Karl—they want to talk about the Black Rosary tour. I'll text you later and call you tomorrow, okay? Love you."

He hung up before I could reply.

I Miss You – Blink 182

Three
Gabe

The meeting with Marley and Karl ran late, and it was almost three in the morning before we rolled back to the hotel. Dex and Luca peeled off to go hunting for willing women. Karl pulled Luca aside, warning him to keep an eye on Dex and make sure he didn't go hunting for dealers as well as women, while Seth followed me to my suite. My best friend had been decidedly out of sorts for the past three weeks. Ever since the graduation we'd attended, in fact. At first, I'd assumed it was because of Dex but then the news had exploded about Seth hooking up with Riley. I could have bugged him to talk to me, but I was aware if I pushed too hard, Seth would lock down. Eventually, if I left him alone, he'd come to me.

He headed directly for the bar in one corner and poured two glasses of bourbon, drained one and refilled it before handing the other to me and flopping down onto the couch with a sigh.

"Ready to talk about it?" I peeled off my jacket and threw it onto the table before joining him.

He slanted a dark look at me. "About what?"

"Whatever crawled up your ass at Riley's graduation and died there." I waved a hand when he opened his mouth to deny it. "Don't fucking do it, Hawkins." I smirked at him over the rim of my glass. "Did you nail her like the reports claim?"

"No, I fucking didn't," he snarled.

"So what *is* your drama?"

"I hooked up with her and she made me think she was twenty-one, and then she took a payout from Karl to stay silent about it. It was all a fucking act to get money out of me." He threw the words at me from between gritted teeth.

"That's not Riley's style." I thought about it for a moment. "She was hooking up with you because she liked you. You're not *that* unbearable to be around, you know."

Seth snorted. "Sure."

"Okay, so let's pretend she did what you think. What are you going to do about it?" I didn't believe for a second Riley had set out to trap Seth—not in the way he was spinning it in his head, anyway—but when Seth set his mind on something, nothing short of a bomb would deviate him from it.

"We need a photographer for the tour."

I arched a brow, immediately connecting the dots. "You can't be serious."

"Why not?"

I shook my head. "I'm not going to stand by and let you hurt her, Seth."

"I won't hurt her ... not physically."

"Just fuck her out of your system," I suggested, taking a sip of my drink.

He ignored my perfectly reasonable suggestion and offered one of his own. "We'll hire her as our photographer and wrap her up in a contract so fucking tight, she won't be able to breathe without our permission."

"And what is that going to achieve, exactly?" He shot me a frustrated look, and I lifted my hands in submission. "Fine. We'll tell Karl tomorrow to hire her." I pointed my glass at him. "But if you fuck this up, I'm not saving you."

"I don't need saving," he muttered, but having got my agreement to hire Riley, he swallowed the rest of his bourbon and rose to his feet. "I'm calling it a night. We need to be at Generation Music by nine. Think you can be ready?"

"I think I'll manage." My reply was dry.

With a final nod, Seth left my suite and I was alone. I tipped my head back against the seat and stared up at the ceiling. Downside of being an insomniac, no one was awake for at least twenty-five percent of the time I was. I idly considered calling Harper but she would be sleeping, and it wasn't fair to wake her up just because *I* wasn't. Instead, I fired off a text telling her I loved her and to watch for the parcel I was having delivered, then grabbed the television remote and channel-surfed until the sun rose.

The interview with Generation Music went the way we expected. There were no surprises and no trick questions. They followed the guidelines we'd laid out—no talking about Harper's kidnapping, my ex-bodyguard, or Seth's short-lived affair with Riley Temple. Afterwards, we went for drinks with friends who lived in Detroit, and our manager, Karl Daniels.

I was listening to Gage Conrad—the lead singer of Jaded Souls, a band we'd often toured with before we hit the big time—telling us about a crazy fan who'd broken into his house *three times*—when my cell vibrated against my thigh. I pulled it out and opened the message, my lips cracking into a grin when I read it.

Frosty: Your package just arrived. What do you want me to do with it?

Oh baby, you have no idea. I laughed to myself.

Me: Put it in the bedroom. DON'T OPEN IT!

I was still smirking down at my cell when fingers snapped in front of my face.

"You're texting Harper, aren't you?" Luca shook his head, rolling his eyes. "You're so fucking whipped."

"Whipping isn't really *my* kink," I dragged my gaze away from my cell. "I've heard you quite like it, though. Didn't you get your ass handed to you a couple of weeks ago in the cages?"

"Like fuck I did," he growled and I laughed.

"Too easy, Luc." I pocketed my cell and reached for my glass, eyeing the singer of *Jaded Souls* over the rim. "You should come and do a gig at Damnation."

Gage smiled. "We might just do that. I've been meaning to come introduce myself to Harper."

"Fuck you, Gage." The last thing I needed was Gage working his magic around Harper.

My friend leered at me. "Sure, but you'll need to wine and dine me first. I'm not cheap."

The disturbing part of that was Gage probably wasn't even joking. He was all about trying everything at least once in his life.

Seth snorted beside me and I turned to look at him, an eyebrow raised in question. "You've finally found someone who's willing to let you into their pants and you're refusing."

I batted my eyelashes at him. "You know I'm only gay for you, Seth."

He shook his head but didn't respond, and the conversation moved on to all things music. By the time we rolled out of the restaurant, it was a little after midnight. I calculated the time difference between Detroit and LA, then pulled out my cell and hit Harper's number as I slipped onto the back seat of the car beside Seth.

"Hey, Frosty," I said when she answered. "Miss me?"

Her soft laugh made my dick twitch. "Hmm, let me think. Do I miss being able to dance around the place naked without some horny guy jumping on me?"

"The answer to that is a resounding *yes*," I prompted, the image of her naked body burning its way into my brain and waking my dick up.

She laughed again but didn't give me what I wanted—an admission that she was missing me. I let it go. I was more than aware that it was her way of showing her independence, proving to herself that she was more than just *Gabe Mercer's girlfriend*. She'd be surprised if she ever realized just how much I needed to hear her tell me she missed me or loved me—those were my own insecurities talking. That little boy who still cowered beneath his father's claims he was unlovable. I *knew* she loved me.

"Gabe?" Her query snapped me back to the present.

"Sorry, babe. The guys were talking. What did you say?" Seth raised an eyebrow beside me at my lie.

"I asked if you knew when you'd be home."

"Not sure. We're here for another day, I think." I shot a questioning look at Seth.

"We're flying back on Thursday." He nodded to confirm it.

"So yeah, another day here, then I'll be home late afternoon the following day," In my mind, I was already working out if I could duck out early and head back to LA.

You Shook Me All Night Long – AC/DC

Four
Harper

The box had been sitting on Gabe's side of the bed for twenty-four hours, driving me insane with curiosity. I knew Gabe was waiting for me to ask what was in it, was banking on the fact I wouldn't be able to resist the temptation, and that alone stopped me from doing just that. It was probably something stupid, something that wasn't worth me obsessing over it. But there it was—a glossy black box that gave nothing away. No company logo, no return address, no hint as to what was inside.

Okay, so *yes*, I'd shaken it to see if I could guess what it was—but there was no movement from inside. Whatever it was, it had been packaged securely. The size or shape didn't even give me a clue. I side-eyed it from where I lay and contemplated beating Gabe over the head with it when he finally arrived home. It would count as just cause, right?

It was most likely something band-related, I told myself. And he'd told me to put it in the bedroom so he could fuck with me. It was something he'd do, *had* done more than once. Yeah, that's what it was. Something to do with the band.

I rolled onto my side, with my back to the box, and flicked through my social media accounts. Since getting back with Gabe, I'd had to lock everything down to private and be very careful on who I added. In fact, Gabe had even gone so far as to make new accounts under fake names for us both, which only had our closest friends connected to them. It was still hard adjusting to the life he lived, especially after everything that had happened, but I was getting there. Gabe's patience with me had been surprising. He'd never been the patient type back when we were young. But he accepted my need to take things slowly, other than insisting I move in with him, anyway. That had been more of a practical decision since I spent more time at his penthouse than I did in the apartment I shared with Siobhan.

What he *didn't* like was the idea of me wanting a job so I could earn my own money. I'd quit the cleaning job I was working when we reconnected because reporters and fans showed up constantly. But I hated *not* doing something with my day. I didn't want to be the girlfriend who sat at home while her boyfriend earned the money and did all the work. It wasn't that he wanted to keep control over me, but he had this crazy idea in his head that everything he'd done had been to make sure *I* lived the perfect life where I didn't have to work or worry. He didn't understand that I needed that independence, that security of having my *own* income. It was the only thing we argued over. And, in a weird way I suppose, it just made me love him more.

My cell screen lit up seconds before the caller ID told me Gabe was calling.

"Hey, Frosty." That deep rasp which never failed to send shivers down my spine sounded out from the speaker. "Missing me?"

"Yeah." I rolled onto my back. "You're still coming home tomorrow, right?"

"I'll *definitely* be home tomorrow." I could hear the smile in his voice. "What are you up to?"

"Just lying on the bed, looking at the band photos Dex posted up."

"Anything incriminating that I should worry about?" He sounded amused.

"Only the shirt Dex is wearing." I laughed. "Where did he get *that* monstrosity from?"

"The purple one?" Gabe chuckled, the warm sound reminding me of nights wrapped in his arms. "It was a bet. Gage was in town and they had some game going on to see who could wear the weirdest clothes and still pull."

I snorted. "Boys!" He waited, knowing I wouldn't be able to help myself. "Who won?"

"Gage."

"Figures." My eyes strayed to the box. *Nope,* I wasn't asking him! "What time will you be landing tomorrow?" I said instead.

"Not sure yet. I might just surprise you."

Wherever he was, I could hear voices in the background, laughter and shouting sounding faintly down the line. "Where are you? Are you with Seth?"

"No, not with Seth. He's being all … well, *Seth-like*. Brooding and shit."

"Over Riley?"

"Over Riley," he agreed. "He'll get over it, eventually." There was a pause. "Did you open that box yet?"

"Of course not."

"Is curiosity eating you alive?"

I sniffed. "Not at all."

"You're such a liar." He chuckled again. "One sec, babe." I heard muffled words and then a door slam. "Okay, I'm back."

"You're in a car?"

"Certainly am. So, do you want to open the box?"

"I thought it was for you." My eyes strayed to where it sat, all black and mysterious.

"It is … but it's for *you* as well. Go ahead, open it."

Now he'd told me to, I found I didn't want to. In fact, I was *nervous* about finding out what was inside.

"I think I'll wait until you're home."

"Just open the box, Frosty." He laughed softly.

Reaching across the bed, I picked it up. "What is it?"

"Open it and find out."

I peeled away the sticky tape holding the lid closed and slowly prised the cardboard up. Inside was a polystyrene container. *No wonder I couldn't hear anything when I shook it.* Wedging a finger between that and the cardboard, I pried it out and stared down at it. It was in two pieces, taped shut with small silver circle stickers on each side. I picked them off and then separated the two sides.

My lips parted, and I gave a surprised gasp. Gabe's laugh was throaty in my ear.

"Wanna have some fun, Frosty?" he whispered.

"Gabe ... that's a ... it's a ... " I couldn't get the words out.

"A vibrator, Harper. It's a sex toy. You know what one of those is ... right?" He was laughing at me; I could hear it in his voice.

"Of course I do, but—"

"I'm not there, so I thought this could be the next best thing until I'm home."

"But—"

"Come on, Frosty," he teased. "Play with me."

I licked my lips, staring down at the vibrator nestled inside its little ... okay, *not so little* container. We'd fooled around with things before. Gabe had a definite food fetish ... Well, a *strawberry* fetish, anyway. He'd used things on me—clamps, ice, handcuffs, *food*—but we'd never played with vibrators before.

I don't even know why I was so shocked by it. I *shouldn't* have been. I should have been more surprised by the fact we *hadn't* used them before now.

"Talk to me, Frosty." His voice snapped me out of my internal monologue. "Don't you like it?"

"I don't ... It's not that. I just ..." I couldn't take my eyes off the damn thing. "Wait ... is this molded off your ... *dick?*"

His laugh was loud and long. "I wondered if you'd notice. Yeah, it is. If we're gonna have toys, there's no way you're fooling around with anything that is bigger than I am."

"You're crazy."

"And yet you love me anyway, and you *are* gonna play for me ... aren't you?"

"Am I?" *Was I?*

"Sure you are. Have you even picked it up yet? It won't bite. Pick it up, see how it feels."

Carefully, I eased the vibrator out of the packaging. It was lighter than I expected, considering the size. There was *no way* I was going to comment on its size to Gabe. His ego was big enough. There was a strawberry motif on the tip, and

I snorted a quiet laugh at that.

"Why don't you give it a test run?" His voice had dropped and I recognized the husky note in it. "You said you're on the bed, didn't you? All alone at home. No one is around to disturb you." His words were soft. "Remember the last time I made you come down the phone line?"

I did. It was hard to forget. It had been just after he bulldozed his way back into my life. He'd taken me to a movie premiere, dropped me home and then called me. He'd whispered dirty things in my ear and watched me from his car when I came.

"No chance of being seen this time, Frosty." His voice caressed me and my body responded to the sound. "Why don't you strip out of your clothes and play with your new strawberry lipstick?"

I choked back a laugh and swallowed. I was no stranger to vibrators. I'd used them before, alone in my bed when I was single, but this felt different.

"It should be all charged up and ready to go. I can talk you through it."

"Are you … " I stopped to clear my throat. "Are you still in the car?"

"The privacy screen is up. No one can hear me, Frosty. I'm going to video call you, and you can show me how much fun you're having."

He wanted me to masturbate for him. I'd done that before—with him beside me on the bed—but never let him record it. The thought of it getting out and being published all over the internet terrified me. But this was a video call. It wasn't being filmed. That made it better … right?

Gabe took the decision out of my hands when the notification of a video call popped up. I hit the accept button and his face filled the screen.

"There you are." He smiled, and I watched as he positioned his cell on the holder fixed to the inside of the car. He leaned back on the seat, arms spread out. "See, I'm all alone back here," he said. "Gonna show me what you've got?"

His smile suggested that he didn't think I'd do it, and bravado immediately kicked in. I reached down and peeled off the t-shirt I was wearing and threw it to one side. Gabe leaned forward, his tongue coming out to sweep over his lips when he realized I wasn't wearing a bra.

"Fuck. I miss you. Find a good position for your cell, so I can see all of you. There's a holder in the top drawer of my dresser. Connect it up and angle the camera at the bed."

I did as he asked, climbing off the bed to find the cell holder. It had a long extendable arm and a clamp. I secured it to the small side-table and checked its position.

"That's good. Now get naked and lie on the bed, Frosty."

I unbuttoned my jeans and dragged them off before climbing back onto the bed.

"You're so fucking beautiful," he whispered. "Cup your breasts. Let me see them properly."

I placed my hands on my breasts and lifted them, rising up on my knees and moving closer to the camera. Gabe's hand dropped down to his jeans while I watched, and I saw him tug down the zipper.

"Pinch your nipples for me."

I caught the sensitive tips between my thumb and finger and pinched slightly.

"Harder, Frosty." His voice was deeper, husky.

I repeated the action, pinched harder, hissed at the sting and heard him groan with appreciation.

"Grab your toy. Turn it on low and run it around your nipples. Tell me how it feels."

I groped behind me for the vibrator, found the switch and flicked it on. A quiet buzzing emitted from it and I could feel it vibrating in my hand.

"There's a remote control with it, which has all the settings on. Start on number one and we'll go through them."

The little controller was flat with push buttons on them—numbered one to nine. I pushed number one and lifted it to my breast to run over my nipples. It felt *nice*, almost like a gentle massage. Something must have shown on my face because Gabe spoke again.

"Jump to number three."

I pushed the button and the vibrations increased. My nipples tightened and I ran the tip of the vibrator across first one, then the other. The sensation was odd but not horrible.

"Lie back on the bed and bring me closer. I want to *see* you better." I reached out and pulled the cell closer to the bed and lay back. "Open your legs, Frosty. Let me see what I'm missing."

Slowly, I let my legs fall open, the vibrator still pressing against my nipple.

"Are you wet? Show me."

One hand dropped, and I opened myself up so he could see the arousal I knew was coating my pussy.

"Fuck," he breathed. "Pinch your nipples again. Twist them and stroke your clit for me. You're so fucking pretty, Harper. I can almost taste you."

I dropped the vibrator onto the mattress beside me and did as he instructed, using one hand to pinch and tug at my nipple while my other hand searched out my clit. My own wetness coated my fingers and I spread my legs wide so he could watch as I stroked myself.

"Get the vibrator, Harper. Press it against your clit. Tell me how it feels."

On the edge of my awareness, I thought he was moving, climbing out of the car, but the vibrator was between my legs and the feeling of it vibrating against my clit splintered any curiosity I had.

"That's it, baby," he whispered. "Does it feel good? Talk to me."

I gave a jerky nod but didn't speak. It *did* feel good. I pressed it harder against me, running the tip around the hood of my clit, coating it in my arousal and then dipping down.

"Do you want it inside you, Frosty? Let me see it fuck you, Harper."

"Gabe." I wasn't protesting his demand. I felt needy, hot. I wanted his hands on me, his *mouth*. I wanted Gabe fucking me, but I pushed it inside, felt the vibrations increase, sending tremors through my body.

"Fuck," he breathed. "Don't come yet. Wait for me, baby."

Perfect Day – Lou Reed

Five

Gabe

It was a good job we lived in the penthouse *and* that it was only accessible by a private elevator because I could hear Harper's moans the moment the doors slid open, and I wasted no time in shucking out of my clothes. Tossing them to the floor, I strode through the apartment. I slowed to a stop when I reached the bedroom, so I could watch the love of my life writhe on the bed while she fucked herself with a vibrator made from a mold of my dick.

Propping a shoulder against the doorframe, I wrapped a hand around my *actual* dick and pumped up and down in time with her movements. Seeing the vibrator sliding in and out of her pussy excited me more than I expected. It was how I imagined it would look when *I* was fucking her, and I squeezed my dick, precum coating the tip and I groaned.

"Fuck, Harper."

She screamed, her hand dropping from the vibrator as she scrambled up the bed and grabbed a sheet to cover herself. I darted forward, grabbing her arm as she lunged for her cell and covered her mouth with my palm to muffle her screams.

"Harper, it's me," I said between laughs. "Baby, open your eyes. Stop yelling, Frosty!" I kept repeating myself until, eventually, my words sunk in and she stopped struggling.

"You fucking *asshole!*" She threw a punch at my face.

I ducked, still laughing, and wrapped an arm around her waist to haul her against me. Once I was certain she wasn't going to punch me again, I rolled so I could settle between her thighs.

"Did you really think I was going to let you play with that thing without me here?" I asked, dipping my head so I could run my tongue over one nipple.

"Don't touch me." She tried to squirm out from beneath me. "You're not supposed to be here until tomorrow."

"Got someone hiding in the closet, Frosty?" I lifted my head and arched a brow while she scowled at me.

"No, but I've got a replica of your dick to keep me happy now, so I don't need to deal with the smart mouth that usually comes attached to it."

Christ, I loved her sass.

"But your pretend dick can't do *all* the things you like," I murmured and proceeded to remind her of all the things the vibrator *couldn't* do but *I* could.

"Want to try something new?" I whispered against her ear a short while later.

She turned her head toward me, her gorgeous lavender eyes still hazy from the orgasms I'd wrung from her body. Kissing my way down her throat, I hooked a hand around her hip and positioned her until she was on her stomach. I ran my hand over her thighs.

"Ass up, face down, Frosty." Leaning over her, I licked a path down her spine while I groped for lube and a condom from the drawer in the nightstand. We didn't always use protection, but for what I had in mind she'd insist on it. I didn't even need to check with her, I just rolled the condom over my dick.

All wrapped up, I slid my rubber-encased dick along her pussy, feeling her twitch.

"Remember when I said I wanted to fuck your ass?" My fingers stroked over the area in question, and I watched her carefully to see how she reacted. "I thought we could do that tonight, and while I'm fucking your ass, *little Gabe* can fuck your pussy. Double-dicked by one man." I squeezed the lube onto my fingers, then slid them backwards to push against that little puckered hole. "Not many women can claim that."

"Gabe." My name was a soft whisper as I eased one finger into her ass carefully, giving her time to adjust to the invasion. When she didn't protest, I pumped it in and out slowly, until her eyes fluttered closed.

I took my time, using the fingers of my other hand to play with her clit while I thrust one, then two, then *three* fingers into her ass. Each time easing out to coat them in more of the lube before going back for more. When a moan escaped her lips, I pulled my fingers free and lined up my dick.

"Ready, Harper?" I whispered, and she nodded.

I moved slowly, easing into her inch by slow, hungry inch until she reached back to claw my thigh.

"Stop teasing me," she hissed.

"Not meaning to," I said around a ragged laugh and slammed the rest of the way in. She cried out and I froze.

"I'm okay, I'm okay," she breathed.

"Want me to stop?"

She shook her head. "No, I need you to …" The words ended in a moan when I began to move.

"Stay with me, Frosty," I muttered when she started pushing back against me, demanding faster … harder. "We're not done yet." Dropping one hand from her hip, I scooped up the vibrator and ran it along her pussy. "Ready?"

With every thrust of my dick in her ass, I pushed the vibrator a little deeper into her pussy. She was panting and mewling beneath me, her hands clutching at my thighs, my wrist, incoherent words spilling from her lips.

I waited until she was on the edge of coming, then flicked the switch, turning it on … and realized my mistake when I felt the vibration hit my dick.

"Jesus Fuck!" I gasped out.

I wrestled for control, failed, and fell headlong into an orgasm that seemed to go on forever. I swear I saw stars. Harper's body jerked and convulsed around me and, *thank fuck*, her own orgasm hit seconds later.

We collapsed to the mattress in a tangle of sweaty limbs, and I carefully eased myself out of her body. With more effort than it should have taken, I rolled onto my back, slid an arm beneath her waist and pulled her against me.

That was my second mistake. The vibrator fell free, dropped between my thighs and buzzed against my balls. I jumped, a ton of four-letter expletives spilling from my lips, way too sensitive to handle that degree of sensation, and grabbed at it. Harper snickered beside me, and I slanted a look down at her while I switched it off and tossed it onto the floor. Her snicker turned into a giggle and before long her entire body was shaking with laughter.

"I'm glad I amuse you," I mock-growled, which just made her laugh harder. "Fine," I grumbled. "I'm going to go clean up, then I'm coming back and *you're* going to tell me how much you missed me." I crawled off the bed, questioned for a second whether my legs would hold me up, and then staggered into the bathroom.

No more than a few minutes later, I'd cleaned up and was climbing back into bed. Harper's arms wrapped around my hips, and she pressed up against my back so she could press a kiss to my shoulder.

"I love you, Gabriel Mercer."

I turned in her arms and brushed my knuckles down her cheek. "Forgive me for scaring you?"

Her lips curved up into a sleepy smile. "Maybe. We'll see." She burrowed closer. "Guess we don't need to go out to celebrate your birthday now, though."

"Oh no, Frosty. You're not getting out of *that.* Tonight was just foreplay ready for the main event."

About The Author

If you are looking for gentle romps through the flowers, with lovers holding hands and never making mistakes, then L. Ann's books are not for you. She doesn't write heroes or heroines, she writes people with baggage, history and problems. Her characters are flawed, they're messy, they make disastrous mistakes that are hard to come back from. Her stories are not sweet or kind, they are dark and, at times, cruel. They deal with uncomfortable subjects and she will not apologize for it. If you like plot twists, characters you don't think you'll ever grow to love but eventually do, sarcasm, dark paths and messy relationships, then come on in. The water may be deep and shark-infested, but she claims to know the way out.

https://www.amazon.com/L-Ann/e/B078RK64FJ

Boss Vibes

Tracie Delaney

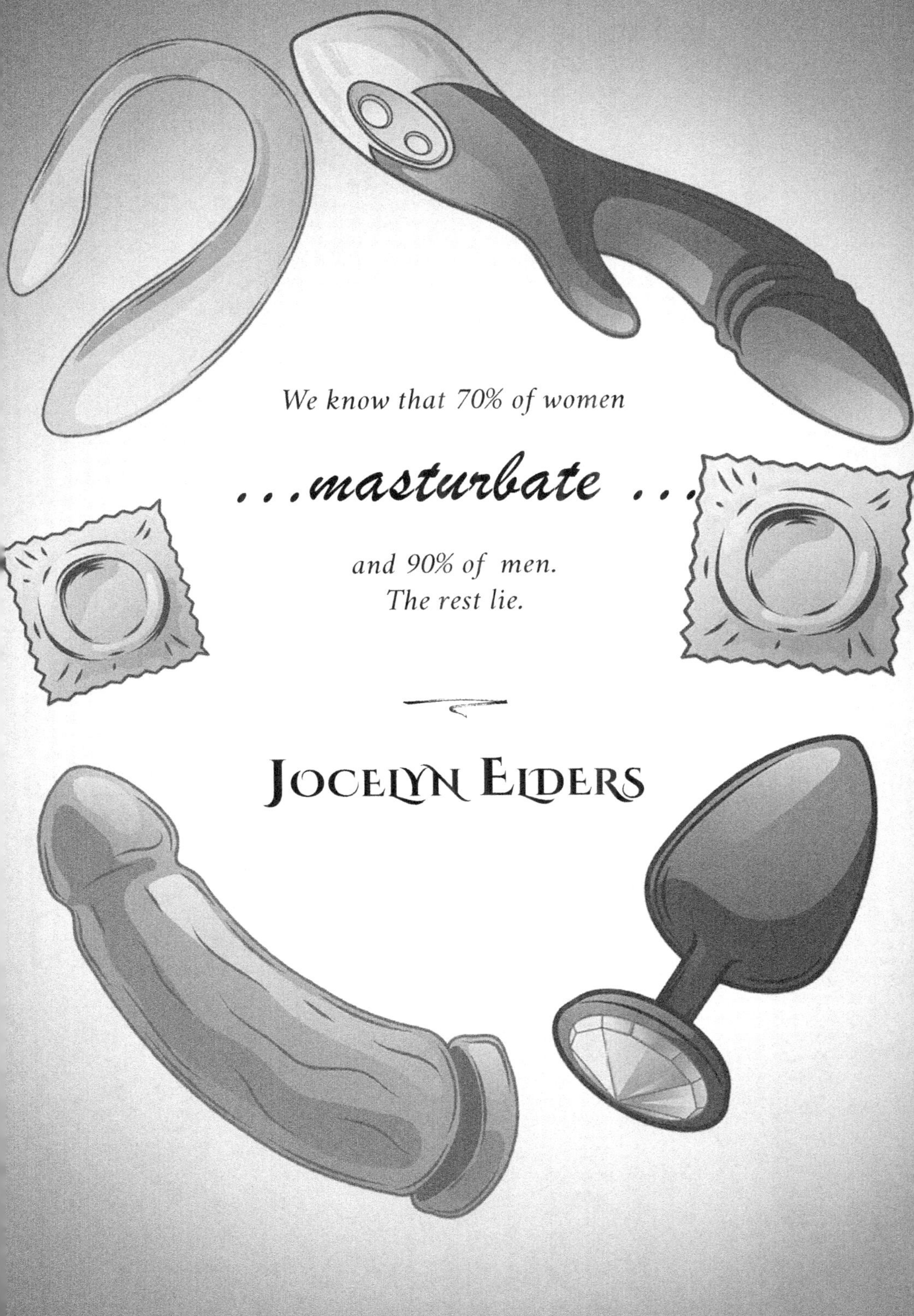
We know that 70% of women
...masturbate ...
and 90% of men.
The rest lie.
Jocelyn Elders

One

Rowan

A terrible screech rang out across the shopping center as I dug my heels into the slippery tiles. Several passersby shot irritated glances my way, as if I'd made some terrible transgression. Ignoring them, I turned my attention to my best friend, Claire, who wore a determined expression mingled with too much mischief for my liking.

"I've told you. I'm not going in there. I mean it."

Claire wrapped her fingers around my wrist, and tugged, almost dislocating my shoulder. Okay, a bit of an exaggeration, but I enjoy embellishing things from time to time. Sue me.

I drove my heels in further and yanked my arm up and backward, dislodging her grip.

Claire pouted and folded her arms across her ample chest. I'd give anything for a rack like Claire's. Sadly, when the day for handing out tits arrived, I didn't get the memo.

"Oh, don't be a daft mare, Row. It'll be fun."

"No, it won't," I insisted. "I've hardly seen you these past few weeks, and this isn't how I planned to spend a rare early finish at work."

"You should ask that boss of yours for a raise. I know you fancy him, but that doesn't mean you should let him take advantage of you."

"He doesn't take advantage," I muttered. "Besides, I'm still on probation for another month, which means I have to work my backside off to prove my worth. You know this job was a step up for me, and I'm determined to make it work. My personal feelings for Grayson have nothing to do with how much effort I put into my career."

"I know that, silly. I just hope he knows how lucky he is to have you, that's all. Now come on. Like you said, you don't get a lot of free time, so let's not waste it."

"What if someone I know sees me?"

"So?" Claire shrugged. "It's not illegal to browse a sex shop."

"Maybe it should be." I glanced over my shoulder. It'd be just my luck for someone from work to amble by the second I walked through the doors. If that bastard, Dave, from IT spotted me, he'd photograph it and shove it onto the home page of the intranet and my mortification would be complete.

"Look." Claire planted both hands on her hips. "If your vajayjay doesn't get some action—battery operated or otherwise—in the not too distant future, you're going to need surgery to open you back up again."

"Claire, for fuck's sake," I hissed. "Keep your bloody voice down."

"No one cares."

"*I* care."

"And that's your problem. If you cared less and fucked more, you might finally jettison that pole shoved up your backside."

"Thanks a bunch, *mate*." I pushed a hefty dose of sarcasm into my tone.

"Babes, you know I love you to death. Tough love. That's what this is. Candles, a bubble bath, and a few orgasms, and you'll feel a lot better. Trust me."

"Fine," I mumbled with another surreptitious sweep of the mall. "Let's get it over with."

Claire grinned triumphantly. She linked her arm through mine—probably to make sure I didn't run—and hauled me through the door.

A couple of mannequins dressed in skimpy black-and-red numbers stood like sentries on either side of the entranceway. Claire stopped to check out the barely there underwear. I hustled farther inside and away from the floor-to-ceiling glass windows where anyone could peer in. Why Claire and I were friends was beyond me. Opposites really did attract, I guess.

"Can I help you?"

Heat rushed to my face as the assistant, a homely-looking woman in her mid-forties, tilted her head to the side. She appeared almost as out of place as me. Still, a job was a job. Everyone had bills to pay.

"First time, dear?"

Kill me. Kill me right this second.

I nodded. Christ, she must think I was mute. Or an idiot. Maybe both.

"Are you after anything in particular?"

Yeah. A way out.

"Um … I … I'm—"

"That's okay." Claire nudged me in the shoulder. "I can take it from here. I'm a pro."

She led me deeper inside the store. Worked for me. Anything that hid me from view got a vote in my book.

"This is a terrible idea," I mumbled as Claire stopped in front of the rows and rows of vibrators and dildos.

"Nonsense," Claire replied. "Which one do you like?"

"Erm, that would be none of them."

"Oh, Row, stop. You're here now. And just think. The sooner you pick one, the faster you get out of here."

"Fine." I snatched up the first one I saw. "How about this?"

Claire gave it a thorough once-over, then picked up a sealed one and read its 'features'.

"Yeah, that's not a bad pick for your first one. It's got several speeds, and a clit stimulator. I'd advise starting on the slowest speed." Claire snorted with laughter. "Or your head will blow off."

"Jesus Christ." I grabbed it from her, then marched over to the checkout and shoved it across the counter. "Can you put this in a bag, please?"

The same woman who'd greeted me earlier winked. "Of course. Excellent choice. You'll have a lot of fun with this."

I prayed for a sinkhole to open right in the middle of the shop and swallow me. I handed over my credit card, winced at the price—damn, they were some expensive orgasms—grabbed the bag, then dashed out of the shop. I made a run for it, only breathing properly when I'd put a good hundred feet between me and the store.

Claire caught up to me, panting.

"Hold up, Usain Bolt. You entering for the next Olympics or something?"

"That was the most embarrassing thing I've ever done in my entire life."

"Oh, please," Claire scoffed. "Everyone goes to sex shops. Everyone masturbates. It's no big deal. Just chill, Row."

She wrestled the bag from my hands and dove inside. The next thing I knew, she had the vibrator out of its packaging.

"What the hell are you doing?"

"Checking it's got the plug thingy to recharge it. Last one I bought it was missing. Pissed me off no end, I can tell you."

"For God's sake, Claire." I yanked the bag back.

The next ten seconds unfolded into a nightmare of epic proportions.

The bag split. The vibrator hit the floor and rolled away, coming to rest in front of a pair of polished black shoes.

I dragged my gaze up. Smart trousers, single-breasted navy-blue suit jacket with one button fastened, a crisp white shirt with silver monochrome cufflinks, and a navy-and-white-striped tie. My eyes traveled farther, meeting a sharp, angular jaw with a dusting of stubble, an aristocratic nose, wide, intelligent brow, glacial-blue eyes, and a head of dark hair styled to perfection. He raised a single eyebrow in query.

"Oops." Claire giggled, bending to pick up the offending item. "Sorry about that, handsome. You got a runaway vibe, Row."

More giggles erupted while I stood there with abject horror splattered all over my face.

No. Please God, no. Don't do this to me.

"Good evening, Rowan."

Claire's head swiveled to him, then me, then back to him.

"Oh, crap. Do you two know each other?"

If I lived to be a hundred, I'd never know how I found my voice, but somehow,

I uttered the awful truth.

"He's my boss."

Two

Rowan

Grabbing the stupid vibrator out of Claire's hand, I shoved it into the bag and fled. My face burned with shame as I stormed through the crowds, vaguely aware of Claire shouting at me to stop. She caught up to me at the east entrance, but instead of an apologetic expression, her face stretched into a shit-eating grin that did nothing to calm the rage warring with sheer humiliation that coursed through me.

"This is all your fault," I snapped. "If you hadn't made me come here and buy this stupid thing, then I wouldn't have to find another job."

Claire's eyebrows shot up in honest surprise. "Another job? Don't be silly. You love that job."

"Did you hear me back there? That was Grayson Brent, my boss. You know, the guy I've spent the last six months swooning over. The same guy who barely notices me other than how well I manage his calendar, how fast I bring him his lunch, and how efficiently I guard him from unwanted visitors."

"Look on the positive side." Claire's grin almost split her face in two. "He's noticed you now."

"Not helping, Claire." I yanked on the door and spilled out into the underground parking garage with Claire hot on my heels.

"Row, stop." She pulled me to a halt. "Where's your sense of humor? You own a vibrator. So what? You're telling me he isn't whacking off on a regular basis?"

"I don't have a clue what he gets up to in his spare time." I ground the words out through clenched teeth.

Claire gave me a playful nudge. "Your most embarrassing moment didn't spend long at number one. Buying a vibrator isn't embarrassing, anyway. Having it spill out of a bag and land at the feet of Mr. Gorgeous, who you've been dreaming about nailing for six months … now *that's* a feat worthy of the number one spot. I can see why you drool over him, though. Talk about boss vibes. I'd do him." She burst into laughter, pointing at the bag containing the offending item. "Boss vibes. Haha. I crack myself up."

I fisted my hands on my hips. "We are no longer friends."

Claire chuckled. "Liar. You'd miss me like hell if I wasn't around. I perk up your life, and you provide some balance in mine. You're stuck with me forever, and you know it."

"Bitch," I muttered.

"Uptight arse."

My lips twitched in the barest hint of a smile that I tried to stop. Too late.

"Aha!" Claire pronounced. "See, you love me." She set off toward the car, throwing a casual. "Dinner's on me," over her shoulder.

"After that disaster, caused by you and your grabby hands, *all* the dinners should be on you."

She threw her hands in the air. "Steady on."

Claire spent the next hour trying to steer the conversation toward Grayson, and coming up with ridiculous schemes of how I might use 'vibrator-gate' as she'd termed it, to my advantage. I tried to head her off, but when diverting her attention proved hopeless, I tuned her out. How would I face Grayson in the office tomorrow?

I wanted to die.

Grayson

Well, that was unexpected.

I'd only stopped by the shopping center to pick up a birthday present for my sister.

I hated shopping, but gift for a family member was the one thing I refused to palm off on my assistant. It occurred to me I should go after Rowan, reassure her that there was no need for embarrassment. But she scarpered so fast, I lost her in the crowds.

Rowan. I almost sighed her name. Five months had passed since she'd started working for me, and in that time, my obsession with her had grown exponentially. Initially, I'd dealt with my attraction to her like a complete prat. Cold, offhand, pushing her harder than I did with many of my other employees. Early starts, late finishes, demanding, overbearing. Downright rude on occasion, almost as if I subconsciously wanted her to quit as a way to solve my little obsession problem. When my unreasonable behavior didn't quash the burn inside me, I'd changed tactics, dating multiple women, all of which made me feel hollow inside and proved how special Rowan was.

The issue I had was that I needed her to make the first move. As CEO and owner of the company, for me to make a pass at my executive assistant was a dumb fuck thing to do. Although I was pretty damn sure she had the hots for me—her covert shy glances and slight tremble whenever our arms or fingers brushed had showed as much—it wasn't beyond the realm of possibility to have read the signs wrong. If I went for it and I was mistaken about a mutual attraction, she could hit me with a sexual harassment suit, and my reputation, as well as that of my company, would be in tatters.

I'd worked too damn hard to allow that to happen over a woman, no matter how much I wanted her. And by God, I wanted her. More than I'd ever wanted any woman in the thirty-two years I'd spent on this planet. I still remembered her interview, and how I'd struggled to concentrate with a dick as stiff as a bat. I prided myself on my professionalism, and I took employee hiring seriously. Recruit an unsuitable one, and with employee rights as tight as they were, you were in for a whole world of pain. Yet with Rowan, I'd spectacularly failed to pay proper attention to her answers, and in the end, I'd asked my COO, Charlotte, to interview her as well. To say Charlotte had thought my request an odd one was an understatement, but luckily, she'd given Rowan the thumbs-up, and two weeks later, Rowan had joined the company on a six-month probationary period.

Turned out she was the best assistant I'd ever had. Hard-working, conscientious, great attention to detail. A real asset to my company, which was another reason I was reticent to ask her out. What if she quit? I'd found a rare gem in her, and I didn't want to lose her.

And just think of the fun we could have with that vibrator.

I couldn't carry on like this. The time had come to drop a few carefully placed hints and hope she found the courage to act first.

THREE

ROWAN

Not a word

Grayson hadn't said a single word about what happened last night. All day I'd been on tenterhooks, waiting for him to bring up the single most embarrassing moment of my life, but other than work talk, it was as if it hadn't happened.

If only…

The door behind me opened, and Grayson appeared with his visitors in tow. Our eyes met, and my heart did a little flip.

"Rowan, would you mind escorting Mr. Devereaux and his colleagues down to reception?"

I stood. "Of course. No problem."

Grayson shook Mr. Devereaux's hand. "Good to see you, Sebastian. I'll have Rowan call your assistant and organize a follow-up meeting in a week. Do you want me to extend that invitation to the rest of the ROGUES board?"

ROGUES was the company that Sebastian Devereaux co-headed with five others. Grayson had been working on a joint venture with them for some time, and the negotiations were nearing the end.

"No." Sebastian paused. "On second thought, I'll ask Ryker if he wants to come. I'll forward him the details if he decides to attend the next meeting."

"Very well."

Sebastian made small talk with me as we rode the elevator to the ground floor. I waited until their car pulled away before returning to my office where I found

Emma, the Chief Operating Officer's assistant, standing by my desk, coat on, handbag over her shoulder.

"A bunch of us are going for a drink. Fancy it?"

"Oh." I glanced at Grayson's closed door. "I'll have to check with Grayson."

"It's six p.m., Rowan. You don't have to ask Grayson's permission to go home when your workday has finished."

"That's easy for you to say. You're not on probation."

Emma inclined her head. "Rowan, you work harder than most people here, apart from the board members. You'll sail through your probation."

"I hope so. It's busy, that's all. What with the ROGUES deal close to being signed." I shot another look at Grayson's door. "I'll give it a miss if it's all the same to you."

She shrugged. "Your call. Just don't burn out."

"I won't. Have fun." I sat at my computer and started work on updates to a commercial contract. Grayson's notes were specific, but there was a lot to get through, and concentration was key to ensuring I didn't make any mistakes. The last stragglers left the office, and an eerie silence descended. Grayson's door remained closed, and only then did it occur to me that he might have left while I was escorting his visitors down to reception. Rising from my chair, I stretched out my back and then rapped lightly on his office door.

"Come in."

So he is still here. I poked my head inside. "I wasn't sure if you'd left already."

He rubbed his eyes, then checked his watch. "I hadn't realized it was so late. What are you still doing here? I'm sure you have other places you'd rather be."

"It's fine. I enjoy being here." I bit down on my bottom lip. "Grayson, about last night. I'm sorry. I'm so embarrassed."

He smiled, pointing his Mont Blanc pen at the chair opposite his desk in an invitation to sit. Willing the heat in my face to bugger off, I took him up on his invitation.

"There really is no need for the embarrassment or an apology."

"I really like working here and I don't want things to be awkward between us."

He set his eyes on me, his gaze intense, unwavering. "I like you working here, too. And there's no awkwardness from my perspective."

Nerve endings in my fingertips tingled, and electricity snapped through the air as we sat in silence. Maybe it was my imagination, but something between us shifted. I didn't dare move in case it broke the spell.

Instead, Grayson broke it. He pushed back his chair and walked to the corner of his office where he kept a decanter of whiskey and a tray of crystal glasses. I took a few deep breaths to slow my thundering heart. I'd been alone with Grayson inside his office many times, but the lack of hustle and bustle on the other side of the door lent itself to a far more intimate and thrilling affair.

Grayson poured two small measures and returned, handing one over to me. Our fingers brushed, and as much as I tried to hide it, I shivered in pleasure. He perched on the edge of his desk, so close I could smell his aftershave and the hint of maleness beneath. I pressed my thighs together, but the pressure did nothing to relieve the growing ache between my legs.

"You're five months into your probation now, Rowan. How do you think it's going?"

"Great. At least I think so. I really enjoy working here." I lowered my gaze, then lifted it again. "Working for you."

He tugged on his bottom lip. *Damn, I'd love to do that with my teeth.*

"Are you happy with my performance?" My voice came out husky, and I cleared my throat.

His gaze lowered to my mouth. "Very."

Oh God. I need a change of underwear. Kiss me. Go on, do it.

He brought the glass to his lips and sipped. I swallowed my disappointment that he'd chosen to put his mouth on the glass instead of me and took a sip of my own. The whiskey burned on its way down, and while I wasn't a fan of hard liquor, it went some way to calming the storm of fiery need scorching my insides.

"Do you own a cocktail dress, Rowan?"

His out-of-the-blue question surprised me. I frowned. "I—um—do I own … own a dress?"

"A cocktail dress," he reiterated.

"I'm not sure. I have a black dress that falls just below my knees, but I wouldn't know whether it fits the description of a cocktail dress."

"I have an account at Harrods." He set his glass on his desk and reached into the inside pocket of his jacket. Opening his wallet, he removed a business card and handed it to me. "Take tomorrow morning off and go to the ladies' department. Ask for Carina and tell her I sent you. She'll make sure you get something suitable."

"But … I …" I smoothed my eyebrow. "Why do I need a dress?"

"Because I need a companion for a dinner tomorrow night, and you're it."

FOUR
ROWAN

I stood back and scrutinized my appearance in my bedroom mirror. Not bad, Rowan. Acceptable. The black number that the woman at Harrods had picked out for me—because I didn't know a cocktail dress from any other kind—accentuated my curves and clung to all the right places. She'd even picked out a pair of heels, a clutch bag, and accessories to complete the ensemble. And Grayson had paid for everything. Lucky for me, given London's skyrocketing cost of living. My salary didn't go very far, even though Grayson paid generously.

He'd blindsided me with the unexpected invitation. I'd been so consumed by desire, so lost in the moment, it hadn't occurred to me to berate him for assuming I was free to attend a dinner at such short notice.

That I had an empty calendar was neither here nor there.

Oh, who are you kidding, Row? I'd have cancelled dinner with the Queen at Buckingham Palace for a chance to spend an evening with Grayson. Not that I'd ever get an invitation to the palace. Even so, it worked as a solid example of just how under Grayson Brent's spell I was.

The question of why he'd invited me ran on a constant loop inside my mind. Why would a man like Grayson—gorgeous, rich, successful—need his executive assistant to attend a dinner as his plus-one? There were tons of women he could have called upon at a moment's notice, yet tonight, I was the female he'd chosen to accompany him. I hoped it wasn't to win a bet or something equally awful. As soon as the thought crept into my mind, I discarded it. Grayson wasn't the kind of man to take part in locker room games. If I had to take a guess, it'd be along the lines of a last-minute change of plans, or the person he'd intended to take had a family emergency and he'd seen me and thought *she'll do.*

I winced. *Time to stop overthinking shit, Row.*

I checked the time. I still had fifteen minutes before my ride came to pick me up. More than enough time for panic to set in. What if I ran out of conversation? Or what if I drank too much wine, lunged at him, and made a huge fool of myself?

Oh God. This was a mistake. Maybe I should call and tell him I was sick, or I'd won the lottery, or aliens had whipped me off to their spaceship, or—

The doorbell rang and I cursed. Whoever Grayson had sent to pick me up, they were early. Crap. Stuffing my phone in my clutch bag, I grabbed my keys and went to answer the door. Except it wasn't my ride waiting on the other side.

"Jesus, Claire, what the hell are you doing here?"

My best friend gave me the once-over and whistled. "You look gorg, babes. I thought I'd pop by and make sure everything is okay before the big date."

"Everything is fine. And it's *not* a date."

She cocked her head to the side. "Well, what would you call it?"

"A convenience."

She snorted. "Whatever. I reckon you have the vibrator to thank for his impromptu and, frankly, overdue invitation."

"Really? How do you figure that?"

She grinned. "It got him to notice you as a sexual being rather than just his overworked assistant."

"You're so full of shit." I gripped her arm and turned her around. "Time to go. I'm being picked up soon."

"Ooh, can I hang around? Wouldn't mind copping another eyeful of Mr. Sexy."

"No, you can't. And you're out of luck, anyway. He's sending someone to pick me up."

"You're kidding? What a jerk."

"He's not a jerk. He's a busy man. And like I said, this isn't a date. Now will you just go?"

I shoved her again, and this time, she headed off, hand in the air as she waved to me.

"Call me tomorrow. I want all the gossip."

She disappeared into the stairwell. Grinning at my madcap friend, I disappeared inside. Seconds later, the bell rang for the second time. If this was Claire again, I'd kill her. I opened the door and sucked in a breath. Instead of the driver I'd expected, Grayson stood in front of me dressed in an impeccable suit, one hand shoved into his trouser pocket.

He ran his gaze over me. My heart stuttered inside my chest. It better not stop. My building didn't have a defibrillator.

"Breathe, Rowan." Another sweep of that gorgeous azure stare followed. "I must send Carina my personal thanks for that dress. She knows how to … accentuate a woman's best assets."

At a lack of an appropriate response, I wet my lips and swallowed. "Shall we go?" Fumbling with my keys, I dropped the damn things, and as I crouched to pick them up, so did Grayson. Our heads clashed.

"Ow."

Grayson chuckled and rubbed his head. "Ow indeed." He wrestled the keys from my grip, helped me to stand, and locked the door, then handed them to me. "Let's head off before there are any more mishaps."

Heat rushed to my face. "Sorry, I'm such a klutz."

"Not to worry."

He stuck out his elbow and, after a moment's hesitation, I linked my arm through his.

A sleek black limousine idled at the curb, and as we approached, a uniformed driver sprang to attention, opening the rear door. Grayson motioned for me to go first. I lowered my head and climbed inside. I swore he hissed through his teeth. Maybe he had a stone in his shoe, or my dress had split wide open as I bent over. I checked for an alfresco situation with a quick swipe over my backside. Phew. All clear.

The car smoothly blended into the busy London traffic. Grayson shifted his body in my direction, his eyes locked on my face. I took up fiddling with the clasp on my clutch bag and racked my brains for a conversation opener. "Where are we going?" I groaned internally at how lame that sounded.

"The Dorchester."

"Oh." I chewed the inside of my cheek. "What's the event?"

"A fundraiser for a charity."

"That's nice."

His lips twitched, and then his phone rang and he cursed. Reaching into his inside pocket, he removed it and glanced at the screen. "Sorry, Rowan, I need to take this."

He put the phone to his ear and spoke in low, rapid tones to the caller. Whoever it was, he clearly didn't want me to overhear their conversation. My stomach hardened, a wave of jealousy that I had absolutely no right to sweeping through me. What if the person on the other end was his original date, and they'd decided they could make it after all? Would he ask the driver to pull over and leave me on the side of the road, or take me home first?

"Sorry about that."

Grayson's apology yanked me from the dark thoughts racing through my mind. I forced a smile.

"No problem."

"I'd switch it off, but unfortunately, a man in my position needs to be contactable."

Oh, so maybe it was a work call after all. I sagged with relief.

"You work too hard. Even CEOs need a break now and then."

He leaned in, his gaze steady. "I solemnly promise that for the rest of the night, you have my undivided attention."

A tremor of desire trickled down my spine, and warmth settled in my stomach. The idea of Grayson's undivided attention was right up there with my most prevalent fantasies.

The car drew to a halt outside The Dorchester. I'd never been lucky enough to visit this hotel, but from what I understood, The Dorchester was synonymous with elegance and luxury. Grayson's driver opened the door, and I got out. Grayson joined me and gave me his arm again. As we were swept along with the other guests, all of whom looked so comfortable in these sumptuous surroundings, my nerves made a comeback.

Several times on the way to the event room, people stopped us, and on each occasion, Grayson introduced me as Rowan.

Not his assistant. Rowan.

I took heart from that. It allowed me to be me, rather than his employee, and I told him as much the first chance I got.

"Tonight, you're definitely not my employee."

I suppressed a shiver of delight, but when he slid his palm across the back of my neck and squeezed, my legs almost buckled. God, his touch did things to me that should be illegal.

A smartly dressed man seated us at a large table with ten other guests. The room itself must have housed at least two hundred people. Ornate chandeliers hung overhead, and expensive art adorned the walls. Dinner was an elaborate affair with seven courses. I didn't know what half of them were, but I devoured every one. Damn, rich people ate well. My signature spag bol dish wouldn't taste half as good now my taste buds had been educated.

Grayson checked in with me now and then, but the other guests monopolized most of his attention. The conversation centered on bonds and yields and a bunch of other things I didn't have enough knowledge to contribute to, leaving little time for small talk.

Solved the problem of running out of things to say, at least.

As the wait staff collected the last of the dinner things, Grayson pushed back his chair.

"Ladies, gentlemen, if you'll excuse us. I promised my date my undivided attention, and with all the business talk this evening, I've let her down badly." He held out his hand to me. "Dance with me, Rowan."

How I stopped my chin from hitting the floor, I'll never know. Date? Dance? Somehow, I rose to my feet without stumbling and folded my palm inside Grayson's.

Was I dreaming? Had I fallen into one of those cheesy princess movies and any second, I'd wake up and plunge right back into the drudgery of everyday life?

He slipped one arm around my waist, his palm low on my back, his fingertips dangerously close to my arse.

"I'm sorry I've been such a dreadful companion this evening. Forgive me?"

I tilted my head back and met his gaze. Sincerity swam in his eyes. Grayson's sharp blue irises were warm and inviting, and a wave of daring came over me.

"Can I ask you a question?" I blurted before I lost my nerve.

"Of course."

"Why did you invite me to come here with you tonight? A successful, handsome man like you isn't short of female company."

"What makes you think that?"

I raised my eyebrows. "Really? Grayson, I'm your assistant. I know you're not short of suitable dates. I'm the one who buys the flowers and the jewelry and sends the Dear John notes to your latest victim."

My lungs flattened, and horror filled my chest.

STFU, Rowan. Jesus, you'll lose your job. "I'm sorry. That came out wrong."

"No, it didn't." Grayson's lips lifted, and his eyes glimmered, but not with irritation. With amusement. And something else, too. Awe, maybe. No, that couldn't be right.

"It came out exactly as you intended. The only reason you apologized was because you're still thinking of me as your boss, and you're worried I might fire you for insubordination."

He leaned in, trailing the tip of his nose down mine.

"I already told you, Rowan. You're not my employee this evening."

I swallowed past a narrow throat and licked my dry lips. "Then what am I?" I rasped.

He traced his tongue on the underside of his teeth and skimmed his eyes over me. "What do you want to be?"

Your lover. Your girlfriend. Hell, I'd settle for your fuck buddy.

"You talk in riddles, you know that?"

A chuckle vibrated through his chest. "And you're a straight shooter. Except, at work, you hold back. You're the consummate professional, if a little... jittery sometimes."

He pressed me closer to him, and his lips went to my ear. "So shoot straight, Rowan. And tell me what you want."

My forehead fell onto his shoulder and, with my stomach tied in knots, I gathered my courage and hoped like hell this didn't blow up in my face.

"You, Grayson. I want you."

FIVE

GRAYSON

Five months. Five long, torturous months I'd waited for Rowan Saunders to tell me how she felt. And finally, *finally* she had. *Now* I could make my move.

I gently cupped her chin and eased her head back, giving her no choice other than to look at me. "It's about goddamn time."

She blinked, opened her mouth to say something, closed it, and blinked again. "Excuse me?"

"You took your time, sweet Rowan." I brushed my lips over hers, wanting to deepen the kiss but forcing restraint. This wasn't the time or the place for our first proper kiss. "I've wanted to tell you how I felt about you for months, but in my position, I couldn't risk it in case you didn't feel the same."

"Wait." She placed the flat of her hand on my chest and shook her head. "I'm confused. You … you … like me?"

"No. I don't like you. I'm crazy about you. Every day I've had to sit there in my office knowing you're on the other side of the wall. I'd have given anything to call you in on some pretext, lock my office door, bend you over my desk, and fuck you until neither of us could see straight." I grinned at her stunned expression. "So 'like' isn't nearly a strong enough word in my book. Blind lust is closer, adoration closer still."

"Oh God." She slipped out of my arms and braced her hands on her knees. "I need a minute."

"Take all the time you need."

She slowly straightened. A delicious blush stole over her cheeks as she spotted a few people at a nearby table had taken an unhealthy interest in us. She moved into my body and tucked her head underneath my chin.

"Tell me when they've stopped staring."

I chuckled. "You really need to learn to care less. I have a speech to make shortly, then what do you say we get the hell out of here?"

She smiled, and I fell, hard. "Sounds like a wonderful idea."

We saw out the rest of the dance and, I'm ashamed to say, I gave an abridged version of my speech, too eager for the real evening to begin. No one seemed to notice, and after the obligatory—and far too long—farewells, we slid into the back of my limousine.

"Where to, Mr. Brent?" my driver asked.

"Home, please." I pressed the button, activating the privacy screen. Waiting to get my hands on Rowan wasn't in the plan.

"You're taking me to your home?"

I arched a brow. "Well, I guess I could ask him to circle the block while I ravaged you on the back seat of my car if you'd rather."

She narrowed her eyes. "Are you teasing me?"

"Would I?" I chuckled, reaching for her. "I can wait until we get home. I'd rather a large bed than a narrow car seat, anyway. Kissing, on the other hand ..."

I cupped her face and angled her exactly how I needed, and closed my mouth over hers. The brief stroke of her lips earlier didn't count. *This,* this right here, was our first kiss, and it stole the very air from my lungs. I pushed her onto her back, my hands roving over her hips, her waist, and the swell of her tits.

We kissed and touched and explored each other's bodies. By the time we stepped inside my private elevator, I was clinging to the edge of my sanity. Years had passed since I'd last dry-humped a girl up against a wall, but with Rowan, I couldn't resist. Months of stifled frustration spilled out in a haze of desire and need and want. We staggered into my bedroom, falling onto the bed in a tangle of legs.

I rolled onto my back, taking Rowan with me. I tugged on the zipper that ran up the back of her dress. When it caught on the runner, I grabbed the two pieces of material and yanked. The dress split wide open.

Rowan gasped. "It's ruined."

"Who cares? It's only a dress."

I wrestled it off of her, tossing it on the floor beside the bed. And then I stared and stared. And stared some more.

"Grayson?" Rowan frowned. "Is everything okay?"

"Christ, Rowan," I croaked. "You're fucking beautiful."

Her cheeks, neck, and chest flushed pink, and she lowered her chin. "I think you had too much wine with dinner."

"It wouldn't matter how much wine I drank, you, Rowan Saunders, are perfect."

I sat up, nose to nose, and kissed her, my mouth and hers moving together perfectly. Flipping her bra clasp, I slid the straps down her arms and threw it on top of her ruined dress, then removed her knickers.

"I need inside you," I mumbled against her lips.

She giggled. "Maybe take your clothes off first."

"Good point." I leaped off the bed and undressed in less than five seconds. Her eyes tracked my every move, and as I peeled off my boxers, she dropped her gaze.

"Do you have protection?"

I reached into the drawer beside my bed and withdrew a ream of condoms, tossing them on the bed beside her.

"You might need permission from your boss to arrive late to work tomorrow."

"Oh, that's a shame." She shot me an impish grin. "He's such a stickler for punctuality."

I tore a condom off the strip, ripped open the packet, and rolled it onto my dick.

"He sounds like a jerk."

Dampening her lips, she fixed her eyes on my groin. "He can be, sometimes." She propped herself up onto her elbows and reached for me. "But don't worry, I can handle him."

"Yeah," I rasped. "You can."

Six

Rowan

I picked up Grayson's arm where he'd wrapped it around my waist, and slipped out of bed. Padding across the room to what I hoped was the bathroom, I pushed on the door.

Result. Found it.

On a bad day, it'd be just my luck to stumble into the closet, trip over a stray shoe, and knock myself out on the clothes rail.

I used the toilet and closed the lid to muffle the flushing sound. Planting my hands on either side of the sink, I checked out my reflection, searching for signs I'd changed. The same old me stared back, but while I might look the same on the outside, everything on the inside had shifted.

Grayson. I'd slept with Grayson. My frigging boss, Grayson Brent. Not just once or twice, but three times.

Three.

And I'd had six orgasms.

See, who needed a vibrator to get their kicks? Not me.

I wrapped my arms over my chest and hugged myself. Not even in my wildest fantasies had I expected the night to end like this when Grayson picked me up from my flat. If I thought about all the wasted months, I could crack both our heads together. I hadn't shown my hand, too scared of cocking up and failing my probation—and he'd been too afraid of a sexual harassment lawsuit to make a move on me.

Pair of dumbasses. That described us perfectly.

And then it hit me. *Fuck.* What if the change in our relationship status meant he didn't want me working for him any longer? I had to work. I needed the money. And I refused to scrounge off Grayson. I paid my own way. My parents had drilled the importance of being financially independent into me, and I agreed with them wholeheartedly. I'd seen too many of my friends rely on a man for money only to see their entire lives wrecked when the relationship ended and they found themselves homeless and penniless.

Maybe he could transfer me to another department? Or use his network to find me a new job. He had a lot of contacts. One of them had to have an opening for an assistant.

"Why are you talking to yourself?"

I clasped a hand to my chest, my heart thumping against my ribcage. "Jesus, Grayson, you scared the hell out of me."

He moved behind me and wrapped his arms around my waist, nestling his chin on my shoulder. "Do you often talk out loud to yourself?"

"Sometimes, when I'm trying to figure things out."

His hands crept up until they cupped my boobs. He rolled my nipples between his thumb and forefinger, and my stomach lurched. I groaned, twisting my head to steal a kiss.

"What are you figuring out?"

"If I still have a job."

He spun me around so fast, I almost lost my balance. Only Grayson's firm hands at my waist kept me upright.

"Why wouldn't you have a job?"

"Well." I shrugged and chewed the inside of my cheek, a habit I often turned to when I felt uncomfortable. "After this. You and me. I thought it might be … awkward to work together."

Grayson's lips curved in a crooked smile. "I can think of at least ten benefits off the bat to having you directly outside my office door." He bent down and sucked on my bottom lip. "And besides, you're the best assistant I've ever had. If you think I'm losing a perfectly good assistant just because we're sleeping together, you're wrong."

I almost sagged in relief, but it was short-lived. "What will everyone say?"

Grayson snorted. "You think I care about idle office gossip?"

"*I* care," I whispered.

Grayson lifted me onto the bathroom counter and eased my thighs apart. Dropping to his knees, he circled my clit with his tongue. "I already told you that you need to learn to care less. Now shut up, woman, and lie back. I have plans for you."

The following morning, I awoke to the sound of the shower running. I rolled over in bed and tucked the covers under my chin. Grayson had the most comfortable bed. His mattress made me feel as if I was lying on the softest, fluffiest cloud, and returning to my lumpy old thing didn't appeal. I thought about jumping into the shower with Grayson, but I didn't feel quite brave enough yet. So much had changed so fast, and my brain was struggling to process it all.

Maybe next time.

Lying here on my own gave me far too much time to think, and the swirl of anxiety I'd felt last night made an unwelcome return. Everyone at Grayson Enterprises knew I had the hots for Grayson. Well, okay, maybe not *everyone*, but enough. Mostly women, too. And one thing women loved was a good old gossip. Except, when you were the subject, it wasn't so much fun anymore. Not that I planned to go bleating to the world and his wife that I'd spent the night in Grayson's bed and, according to him, I'd spend plenty more nights here, too. But office workers could sniff out a story better than most journalists. I'd give it two days before *I* was the story.

I groaned. Whatever Grayson said, I might have to look for another job. It was okay for him, being the boss and all. No one dared giggle behind his back or make fun of him. But me? I was fair game.

Now if Claire was in my shoes, she'd waltz into the office swinging her handbag and announce to everyone that she could "barely walk straight". So many times over the course of our long friendship I'd wished I was more like her, but we were complete opposites. It was one of the things that worked so well for us. She was yin to my yang. I sighed. If it came down to it, I'd have to marshal my inner Claire and front it out.

"You're talking to yourself again."

I raised my eyes to find Grayson, a white towel hanging low on his hips and water trickling between his pecs, standing in the doorway to the bathroom. He rubbed another towel over his wet hair, then tossed it behind him and strolled over to me. As he approached, I reached out and tugged at the towel. It unraveled easily, and I dropped it on the floor.

Hmm, maybe that bravery gene was rallying?

I propped myself up on one elbow. "Want to play hooky?"

His smile came slowly, and his eyes shimmered with devious intent. "I thought you'd never ask."

Seven

Rowan

Over the next few weeks, my fears that I'd become the story of the moment turned out to be unfounded. Grayson and I didn't exactly broadcast our change of status from 'single' to 'in a relationship,' but everyone knew we were seeing each other. Apart from one or two individuals who couldn't help making a snide comment, nearly everyone else told me they were happy for us. Quite a few had mentioned that Grayson appeared more approachable and less hard-nosed businessman since we'd hooked up.

Amazing what sex on the regular did for a man. And a woman. I'd never been happier.

At work, we kept things largely professional, although we'd given in to an odd fumble here and there. And Grayson had been knee-deep in the latter stages of his joint business venture with ROGUES, which had taken up most of his time. Rarely an hour went by when he wasn't in some meeting or other, ironing out the finer details for what appeared to be a lucrative deal for all parties involved.

Claire had drilled for "all the deets" until I'd capitulated and shared enough to satisfy her unrelenting curiosity. Course, if Claire ever told Grayson I'd given her a fair few tidbits that'd make the readers of *Playboy* blush, I'd belt her with that damned vibrator she'd forced on me.

I never had used it. Hadn't needed to. Grayson *never* ran out of batteries or needed a recharge. Maybe I should wrap it up for Claire's birthday. I chuckled to myself. Save me a chunk of cash. And it'd be funny as fuck to watch her face when she opened it.

The intercom on my desk buzzed, and my belly fluttered. I wondered how long that feeling would last. The newness, the insane urge to rip each other's clothes off, to spend lazy Sunday mornings in bed having copious amounts of sex. Hopefully, for a while longer yet.

"Yes, Grayson."

"Come into my office, please, Rowan."

He sounded so formal that a sliver of anxiety trickled down my spine. I stood, smoothed my skirt, and tapped on his door once before entering.

On his desk was a large bottle of champagne, two glasses, and a bowl of strawberries. He gave me a smile that turned my insides to mush, reaching me in two strides. Taking my face in his hands, he kissed me.

"What's this in aid of?" I asked when he let me go.

"I just had confirmation from my lawyer that ROGUES have signed the deal." An enormous grin etched across his face "This is going to be huge for Grayson Enterprises."

I threw my arms around his neck and hugged him. "Oh, Grayson. I'm so thrilled for you. It's what you deserve."

"Thank you for putting up with me these last few weeks," he murmured against my lips.

"Well, you can be pretty tough to take," I teased.

He opened the champagne and poured two glasses, handing one to me. "To success ... and more time for sex."

I widened my eyes. "*More* time? Jesus, Grayson, I'm going to need a rubber ring to sit on."

He pressed a strawberry to my lips, and I bit down on the juicy fruit.

"Let's finish this glass of champagne and then head back to my place."

I frowned, glancing up at the clock on the far wall of his office. "It's only three-thirty."

He gave me a crooked grin. "Benefits of being the boss."

"You might set a bad example to your team."

"That's why we'll sneak out the back way."

Ten minutes later, Grayson and I slipped into his waiting limousine, giggling like a couple of teenagers. We kissed the entire way home, half undressed in the private elevator, and virtually ran to his bedroom, discarding the rest of our clothes on the way.

Lightheaded from the champagne and Grayson's searing kisses, I closed my eyes, angled my hips, and sighed as he slid home.

With smooth strokes, he drove me higher, touching me in just the right way to send me soaring. As I tumbled down into a mind-boggling orgasm that triggered my own personal light show behind my squeezed lids, and caused my toes to curl, Grayson groaned and found his own release.

Rolling to the side, he reached for my hand and knitted our fingers together. Equally breathless, we lay staring at the ceiling and waited for our hearts to slow.

"You and me, Rowan, we're perfect together." He shifted onto his side and stroked his knuckles down my cheek. "I wish we hadn't wasted all that time."

I turned to meet him, nose to nose. "You were too busy with all those other women."

He shook his head. "Since the day you walked into my office, I haven't wanted anyone else."

I frowned. "But the flowers, and the jewelry, and the 'see ya, sweet cheeks' notes you made me send to the women you dated. Are you saying they were fake?"

"No. The women were real. I dated to try to get you out of my head. They were all perfectly nice women, but they did nothing for me. The flowers and gifts were my way of apologizing for wasting their time." He captured my bottom lip and tugged it between his teeth. "You're the only one for me."

"Oh, Grayson."

"Talking of gifts." He reached into his bedside table drawer and fished out a rectangular box. "This is for you. Well, for us, really."

His mischievous grin had me narrowing my eyes in response.

"You're up to no good."

"Just open it." He thrust the package at me.

I sat up in bed, tugged on the silky black ribbon, and opened the box. My mouth dropped open. I stared, and then I laughed.

"Are you kidding me? How did you get a hold of this?" I removed the bright-pink vibrator, the one Claire made me buy, and brandished it at him.

Snickering, he ducked to avoid a bash on the head.

"It seemed such a shame to let it go to waste. Just think of the fun we can have playing with this."

I started it up, and it buzzed. "You charged it?"

"Hell, yeah, I did." He snatched it out of my hands and straddled me.

"Tell me, Grayson." I gasped as he ran the tip of the vibrator around my nipple, causing it to harden. "Did you break into my flat?"

He tapped his nose. "Not sharing. It's good for a relationship to have a little mystery."

"You're a bad, bad man."

"Oh, baby. You have no idea."

About The Author

Tracie is the author of more than twenty-five contemporary romance novels which she writes from her office in the freezing cold North West of England. The office used to be a garage, but, needing somewhere quiet to write, she stole it from her poor, long-suffering husband!

An avid reader for as long as she can remember, Tracie was also a bit of a tomboy back in the day, climbing trees with her trusty Enid Blyton's to read for hours. She'd return home when it was almost dark with a numb bottom and more than a few splinters!

Tracie's books have a common theme of strong women who aren't afraid to go after what they want and alpha males who put up a great fight (which they ultimately lose).

At night she likes to curl up on the sofa with her two furbabies, Murphy & Cooper, and binge-watch Netflix. There may be wine involved.

https://smarturl.it/TracieDelaneyAmazon

All for One

Lily Alexander

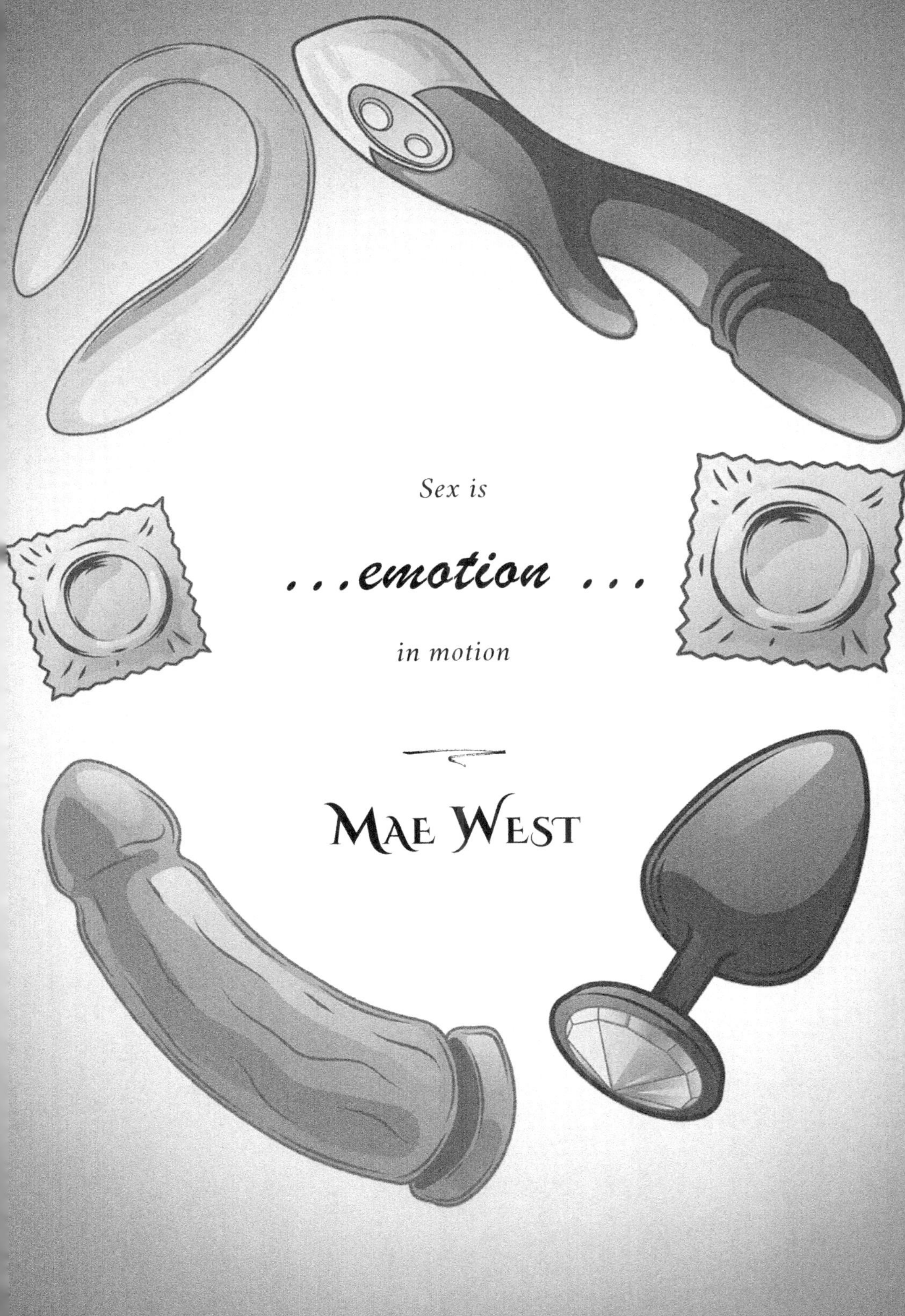
Sex is
...emotion ...
in motion
Mae West

One

Ever

"These things are like crack." Ford popped a donut hole into his mouth as we crossed the parking lot of my apartment complex. One of the newer members of my surf team, he and I had become fast friends thanks to our similar personalities.

"I eat way too many when I'm home." I rubbed a hand over my stomach. I'd only been back a few weeks, but had consumed an embarrassing amount of the fried confection. The crunch of spiced sugar mixed with the tang of apple cider was impossible not to love.

Coffee and donuts from my friend Neil's shop was the traditional breakfast for swag sorting day, so I treated us both to a large latte and bags of the tiny temptations as fuel.

I stopped at my storage locker and pulled out the keys. "You ready for this?"

"Let's go." He set his cup on the cement for a moment, using a tie from his wrist to secure his long curly hair up into a messy bun.

I popped the lock and rolled the door up, exposing boxes stacked over six feet high filling most of the five-by-five space. The limited available floor was littered with envelopes and bubble mailers.

"Jesus," Ford swore, hands on his hips. "I don't get half this much shit when I'm away."

"My fans love me, what can I say."

He snorted as he pulled out my rolling cart. "You don't have *that* many fans. You sure these aren't mostly love notes from that chick you hooked up with in

Mexico? Maybe some panties so you don't forget about her?"

I hurled a bubble envelope at his head, but he caught it with a quick grab.

"Joke all you want, but the big ones are from my sponsors." I rubbed my fingers together, indicating the money I made from them. "And she was freaking *hot*. She can send me panties any day."

"Yeah, yeah. You weren't the only one who got lucky that weekend, old man. But it must be just you old-timers who get all the sponsorships. You need things like joint ointment and vitamin supplements."

"Funny guy! The body only takes so much, kid. Everyone's gotta retire at some point, and it's nice to have some contracts already set when you do. Besides, I mentioned possible retirement *one* time when we were drunk. Quit busting my balls about it, I'm not even thirty yet." Ford smirked as I ranted, amused he'd pushed my buttons. He was only a couple of years younger, after all. "Life after surfing ain't all bad, either. Look at Neil! He's running a donut empire now. You can surf for fun any time you want. It would be nice to not always have a competition coming up. Be home more than I'm away. Don't you ever consider doing something else?"

Ford's head tipped back, his eyes closed. The dreamy grin on his face told me he was picturing himself in the ocean on his board. "Never."

"Your day is coming," I warned as he piled the smaller packages into a laundry basket. I squinted as I stacked a large, heavy box onto the wheeled cart. "What the hell is GVE?"

Ford's mouth twitched. "Who knows? Swag comes from all over."

He wasn't wrong. Shirts, posters, board wax; everything came from different vendors even if they were sent by the same sponsor. It was up to us to give it all out to fans we encountered in public, which was much easier said than done. Hauling around shirts and posters was anything but convenient.

It took a few trips before the little storage room was emptied, and Ford's amusement grew as we organized the boxes in my living room.

"I'm glad you're having such a good time." I used a box knife to cut through the tape. "Here I was worried that you'd be bored."

"It's like Christmas!" He rubbed his hands together as he waited to see what was inside.

We sorted plenty of the usual swag items before I got to the mysterious GVE box. Instead of the normal brown, it was white, with fancy matching paper tape.

When I opened the three-foot cube, I jumped back like something bit me. My foot caught the edge of a box full of shirts and I landed on my ass, plastic boxes full of vibrantly colored silicone spilling onto the floor. Ford had his phone in hand, recording my reaction as he hooted with laughter.

"What the actual fuck?" My eyes scanned over the mass of sex toys. There was every shape, size and purpose accounted for. As I stared in shock, my basset hound, Blaze, ambled by and gave a thoughtful sniff before curling up on the sofa.

"I'm pretty sure the words you're looking for are 'thank you'. So, you're welcome. It was my great pleasure to get that reaction on video." He chortled, wiping the tears from his eyes.

"Ford, why are there dozens of dicks on my floor?"

He shook his head, unable to answer through his laughter. At the same time, my phone rang. I swiped to accept the call from my twin sister.

"Not an awesome time, Es. Can I call you later?" Still stunned, but finally able to move, I sat up, tossing an assortment of vibrators back into the white box. I picked up an item that vaguely resembled a penguin and claimed to be a clitoral massager, chucking it at Ford as my sister spoke.

"I was just checking whether or not I'm still coming over to help tomorrow."

The speaker was up loud enough that Ford heard her, and he snorted a fresh round of chuckles as he started cleaning up the dildo spill.

"That's not the best idea."

"Why not?"

"There's some ... unexpected stuff here." I turned to glare at Ford.

"*You're welcome.*" He tossed a set of anal beads at me, gleefully chirping. "Hi, Esme!"

"Dude, don't talk to her." I scolded, as I batted away the beads.

"Why can't I come over? I can handle Ford. I had to learn to handle all of your surfer friends at one point or another. Sometimes groups of them at one time."

"Jesus Christ, Esme you can't *say* shit like that."

"Oh my God! That's *not* what I meant and you know it."

Ford was having trouble breathing again through his laughter.

"Trust me Es. The guys did something, and now there's a giant box full of sex toys in my living room." I mumbled over the words *sex toys*, trying not to corrupt my twin with the words.

"Blame me, Esme. Your brother was acting like King Dick when we were in Mexico after hitting top three, so we got him a gift!"

My sister cackled on the other end of the phone, clearly not understanding the gravity of the situation. "You are so dramatic, you big baby. How bad could it be?"

"You haven't seen what's in this box, Es. I may never recover from the trauma."

Ford snorted again, closing the box in question.

"Wait, how big are we talking? Can you send me a picture?"

"*Esme.* Stop. I cannot talk about sex toys with my sister. I. Simply. Cannot."

"Dude. Oh damn, this is *way* better than we thought it would be." Ford wiped his eyes with the back of his hand as he sat on the floor, his back against the sofa. His fingers flashed over his phone and I suspected the video was on its way to the entire team. Blaze leaned forward to sniff Ford's ear and Ford obliged him with a head rub.

"You're so ridiculous, Ever. You're a grown man. Don't tell me you've never used any of those before. If you haven't ... well, I feel worse for your girlfriends than I did already. Take the stuff you don't want back. Easy."

"Didn't we agree that we're not going to talk about this?"

"You're right. Go deal with your boxes of grown-up goodies. But for the record? I'm not scared. I'll see you tomorrow. Tell Ford 'bye for me."

"Bye Esme!" Ford called, just to irritate me.

Cringing at my sister's description, I hung up and turned my attention back to my so-called friend. He wore a toothy grin and his light brown eyes twinkled with mirth as he watched me from his spot on the floor.

"Explain." I was fighting not to laugh. The whole situation was ridiculous.

They'd gotten me damn good.

"I'd love to be sorry, but I'm really not." He chuckled, scrunching his face up as he stifled one final burst of laughter. "That night in Mexico when we hung out with that group of girls at the bar? You were a preening bastard with your new rank and prize money." I'd been a peacock about my win. It was my best accomplishment to date. "When you left to hook up with that chick, we found out from her friends where she worked. Sending you a box full of dicks was an idea inspired by tequila. Funny. As. Shit."

"You guys are assholes." I gave in and laughed, which only broadened Ford's smile. "I'm honored, I guess, but what the hell am I supposed to do with all this stuff?"

Ford shook his head. "I dunno man. Keep what you want and try to return the rest?" He echoed my sister's suggestion.

"You guys bought it, so you should get first dibs. Spot anything you like? That confetti sprinkle dong was pretty nice."

"I'm good, man. Thanks though."

Memories of that night in Mexico interrupted my train of thought. They featured the sexy brunette I hit it off right away with at the hotel bar. Her green eyes captivated me from the first moment I'd locked onto them from across the room. We'd been sizzling together, both in and out of the king-sized bed.

"You were super into her." Ford grinned, catching me daydreaming.

"She was hot." I repeated, but I liked her more than I wanted to admit. "You said she worked at this store?"

"Yeah, that's her store. Like I said—you're welcome." Ford nodded my direction.

She and I agreed on no strings and hadn't exchanged any information. No phone numbers, no Instagram accounts, no real names. I'd known her as Jane and she called me Drew. But now? Now, I had a way to find her.

Two

Jaz

The bell over the front door chimed, and a man walked in carrying a large box.

"It's a great day at Good Vibes. How can we help you O today?" I recited the greeting out of reflex, my brain stuttering as I processed what I was seeing.

The tanned Adonis removed the aviators covering his bright blue eyes after setting the box on the counter. His full mouth curled into a sexy smile. A smile I knew. He chuckled, and the rich sound of it made the hair on the back of my neck tingle.

"Oh my God." Memories from a perfect weekend in Mexico rushed in, the sensation I'd gotten from his laugh spreading over my skin, causing goosebumps to rise. "It's *you*." I hated that I sounded breathless.

He crossed his arms, his simple white t-shirt pulling tight across broad shoulders, not at all put off by my brash tone. "You look fantastic." He scanned me from my head to my hip, where the counter interrupted his view. His gaze drifted from my face to the name tag on my left breast more than once. "I honestly didn't think I would ever see you again."

"Yeah, me neither." I leaned into the counter for support, flashes from the beach, the bar, and the bed where we'd spent our short time together crashing through my mind.

"I know, right? Turns out, my friends had other plans." He tapped the box with his fingers. The predatory expression on his handsome face matched the one he'd worn the night he challenged me to body shots.

The surreal feel of the situation made my heart pound. Finding words was difficult. "Oh?"

"They sent me a little surprise. So, I'm here about making a return ... Jaz." He emphasized my name, tasting it. "That's a gorgeous name, by the way. It suits you. So does the teal hair, though you made a great brunette too." His tongue lingered at the corner of his mouth as he grinned at me, and my body, the traitor, responded instantly. It remembered the power that mouth held over me. Seeing him again had never been in the plans. Having him standing in front of me had me completely off balance.

He slid the box toward me. "Oh yeah. I remember this order. Ever, is it?" He nodded. I liked the name. It fit him, but I didn't return the compliment. "*You're* the one who ordered the All for One?"

His brows pulled together. "Sorry, the what?"

"That's the name of the bundle you ordered. It's a collection of our most popular items."

"Ah. Not really, no. Some of the guys thought it would be funny to order it for me and have it waiting when I got home. Your friends leaked where you worked while we were ..." His eyebrow raised, his tongue wetting his lower lip. "... otherwise occupied."

I blushed, remembering how much fun being *occupied* by him had been. "Unfortunately, you're past our thirty-day return window."

His grin slipped, but he rebounded with a charming expression that made my blood pump. "That's too bad. I don't have any use for most of this stuff and my friends already had the fun of recording my reaction as I opened it." Chagrined, he added, "I fell flat on my ass."

I could only blame habit for what came out of my mouth in response. "We do offer product demonstrations if you need a hand figuring anything out."

He chuckled, eyes pinning me in place. "Really? I may take you up on that."

My skin heated. I was headed down a dangerous road, but I couldn't stop myself. "Don't threaten me with a good time."

"Wouldn't dream of it."

Flirting was dangerous. We'd been hotter together than anything I'd ever experienced, but I wasn't sure how we could mesh our one-night-in-Mexico selves with our real lives. Would he even want to? Did I? The possibility shouldn't even exist, but here he was, and he was making me sweat.

"I'm happy to check with my boss if you like?"

"I'd appreciate it." He relaxed a hip against the counter as I moved away, the gravity of him pulling at me as I went.

Taking a deep breath to compose myself, I knocked on the metal doorframe of Gina's office. She peered up at me over the rims of her fuschia reading glasses. She sat behind an ancient computer monitor, mouth pinched. Her tiny office was beyond cramped, the desk and bookshelf both spilling over with paperwork I itched to organize.

"Yes?"

"I have a customer asking about a return." I offered her the paperwork.

Her head shook, nearly dislodging the bright pink glasses from her nose. "We can't take it back, he's almost sixty days out."

"I know, but I promised him I'd check, so here I am." I propped my shoulder against the cool metal door frame as she clicked around on the computer, scowling at the screen.

Gina was well over sixty, still rocking magenta streaks in her cropped silver hair with an attitude to match. Good Vibes was her baby, and I did everything I could to help her keep it going. I knew if I landed the manager position she kept teasing me with, things would run more efficiently.

When she realized I wasn't leaving, she took the glasses off her nose, letting them hang from the pearled chain around her neck. "He's still here?"

"Yes, out front." My body flushed hot. I'd relived the memories of our night together dozens of times, and never guessed I'd see him again. "How many of those All for One bundles have you sold, anyway? I've been here almost three years and never seen one come through before."

Her mouth quirked into a devious grin. "Only the one."

I barked a laugh. "You don't want to lose your unicorn."

"Hell no, I don't. I put that thing on the website as a *joke*. Who, besides *maybe* a brand-new sex dungeon owner orders that many toys in one go? Bottom line, taking back an order of that size would be a nightmare to deal with." Her lips pressed into a thin line. "Give him one of those big gift baskets we keep under the counter. Tell him we'll give him free lifetime lube. But we can't take the product back."

"Alright," I agreed, aware she'd given her final word

My co-worker Amber pulled me aside once I'd left Gina's office. She'd been occupied with another customer when Ever came in, but I'd noticed her wide-eyed expression when she'd spotted him. "Jaz! Do you know who that is? That's Ever Anderson!"

"Should I understand what that means?"

"You don't follow surfing?"

I shook my head. "No, sorry."

Amber's eyes narrowed. "But you *do* know him. You're flushed in the face and not just because he's cute."

"Mexico."

She gasped. "*That's* the guy?"

I shrugged and stepped away, trying to shake the intensity of her stare. Admitting to my co-worker that Ever was the man I got under so I could get over my ex didn't seem like proper workplace etiquette.

"Sorry," I apologized. He smiled, raking me head to toe again. I wondered if he noticed my Good Vibes t-shirt and jeans at all, or if he was picturing me naked. "My boss confirmed, you're too far outside the return window." I reached under the counter. "She said you could have this, though."

He blinked at the collection of lubes and condoms, mouth open. His shock morphed into a feral smile. "Um … thanks?" The glint in his eye signaled that he took the basket as me issuing a challenge. "I appreciate you trying." He put the basket inside the box and tucked in the flaps. His head tipped to the side. "I can't believe it's really you."

The gritty way he said it made me melt. It was impossible to avoid being charmed by a man who looked at me like he was. Like he'd missed me. Like I mattered.

It wasn't hard to remember why I'd fallen into bed with him so easily. He appeared to be everything my ex wasn't. I just wasn't sure if I could trust that.

"Yeah, same."

"Maybe I'll see you around?"

I nodded, unsure what else to say. Shock coated in disappointment that he hadn't asked me out surged through me. He scooped up his box and headed for the door, my emotions unsettled as he went.

Gina appeared at my side, gesturing Amber over from a lingerie display she was resetting with a quick wave of her hand.

"The anniversary event is coming up. Twenty-five is a big year, yes? And we're only a couple of weeks away, so we need to get our asses moving." Amber and I nodded. Promo and decorations had started, but there was still a lot to be done. "I have a friend I've called in a favor with, but I want to make it worth her time."

"Friend?" Amber's eyes widened as Gina's full attention slid her way.

"Yes, Dr. Dorothy Silverton. Heard of her?"

I gasped. "Yes. She's like my idol. Well, her, Dr. Ruth, and Sue Johanson."

Gina's lips twitched. "Well, then come up with a way to get bodies in the door. That may be the push we need to get over this slump. I can't promise a promotion if it does well, but…" She left the idea dangling as she retreated to her office.

Amber and I looked at each other as the door chimed. Ever had disappeared while I was distracted.

He was gone, and I wasn't sure I'd ever see him again, for the second time.

THREE
EVER

"Do you have the packing lists?" My sister handed me coffee and donuts as she pushed past me into my living room.

"Why do you need those?" I was barely conscious and struggling to match her energy.

"Because I need an idea of what I'm dealing with."

I scrounged up as many as I could find from the boxes of swag. Ford and I had moved them all into my guest room once they were opened. Esme did some kind of sorcery that dropped all the information into a program on a tablet while I willed the caffeine and sugar to kick in.

"What do you even do with all this stuff?" She flipped through a stack of shirts to verify sizes before moving on to posters. It would never stop being bizarre that I had stacks of glossy paper with my image on them in my house.

"I'm supposed to take them with me everywhere, give them out when people stop me for a selfie." I wrinkled my nose. "Don't tell my sponsors, but I donate most of them."

"Hmm. What about the *other* box?" She smirked.

"You don't have to worry about that one."

"Oh, I don't mind. In fact, I'd like to see it." Her lips quirked into a grin.

"Why are you like this? Does Cade know?" I immediately regretted asking about her boyfriend when her eyebrow lifted in a taunt. "Shut up. Don't say a word. Forget I asked. It's too damn early."

I was conflicted about giving paperwork with names like *SatisfyHer* and *AssMaster* to my sister, but reluctantly handed it over after depositing my empty donut bag in the trash.

The further down the list she got, the higher her eyebrow climbed. "This is ... eclectic."

"Yep."

"And expensive."

"You have no idea."

"Oh no, I do. It's right here, below the—"

I snatched the paper from her fingers. "*Christ* you're obnoxious."

"Want me to take a few of them off your hands? I will. There are at least four things on that list in my online shopping cart."

"Es. Stop." I pinched the bridge of my nose.

My twin knew exactly how to push my buttons, and loved to do so. I couldn't blame her though. I was the same way. She left the guest room, trailing laughter over my discomfort.

"Oh my God. Where'd you get that? Drop, Blaze. *Drop*."

When I got to the living room, she had my dog cornered against the couch. He had a very generously sized, confetti sprinkled dildo in his mouth. The very one I'd offered Ford. Horrified, I stood with my mouth hanging open as she wrangled the item from my beloved dog. He'd split the box at one corner and spilled a bunch of things out again.

"Aw, come on, B-dog! We talked about this." I shuddered at the way the toy wobbled when Esme snatched it from his mouth.

"Ugh, It's all wet." She sneered in disgust.

"That's what she said," we echoed, meeting one another's eye as we both giggled.

"Seriously, this is gross. You put a bunch of chew marks in it, you beast." She took the destroyed speckled phallus to the kitchen trash and the sink ran as she washed her hands. When she returned, she said, "Well, there's one down. Good boy."

"Don't praise him for that."

Blaze sat between us, glancing back and forth a few times before giving up and lying down.

Esme reached down and patted his head. "Don't listen to him, buddy. You did good. I know you were only trying to help."

I crossed my arms and gave my sister a look expressing my annoyance with her. As usual, she laughed at me.

"What's the plan?" She gestured at the now torn box.

I shook my head. "No idea. I need to call Ford later. It's their fault I'm stuck with all this shit."

She shrugged. "Prank them back. Invite your friends over for a barbecue or something and send them home with a goodie bag. There are whole companies that do nothing but in-home sex toy parties." Her head tilted to the side. "You're doing that thing where you rub your wipeout scar. What are you thinking?"

I dropped my hand away from my chin. "Jaz said they do product demos."

"Jaz?"

I shook my head. I hadn't told my sister about Mexico, and wasn't sure how to explain it. "The lady at the store. Her boss was talking about an anniversary party …" An idea started to form. "I need to talk to the guys."

"Well, have fun with that. I need to get to bed."

"You work later?"

"Yep. O'Malley's tonight. Then dough duty for Neil."

My sister worked a handful of part-time jobs in a dizzying schedule that had her up most nights. My current early morning was her late night. Guilt that I'd kept her busy when she should have been sleeping rushed in. "Sorry Es."

"I'm fine. I still have plenty of time to get a nap in."

"I'm going to regret this." My sister looked perplexed as I covered my eyes with my hands. "You have about thirty seconds, and I *do not* want to know what you take. I'm going to burn the packing list so I can't find out. Ready? Set?"

"Wait! How am I supposed to find the stuff I want that fast?"

"Not my problem. Go!"

My sister squeaked as I counted. The box had already spilled, but she spread the items out as she dug through them.

"This is by far the weirdest Easter egg hunt we've ever done."

"*Never* say that again." Despite myself, I laughed at her ridiculous comment. "In fact, never mention this at all. It didn't happen. Twenty-one, Twenty ..."

"Okay!" she exclaimed as I hit twenty-six.

She helped me clean up all the remaining items into the box, then reached out for a hug.

"Never," I reminded her, eyeballing her large purse.

"Scout's honor." She smirked. "Thanks though."

"Yeah, yeah."

After Esme left, I took a quick shower and called Ford.

"What's up, man? Didn't get enough of me yesterday?"

True to my suspicions, the video of me opening the box of toys was spread far and wide among my friends. There were now dozens of memes and slow-motion gifs of my shocked face and of me falling on my ass. Even I could admit it was hilarious, though I'd had to turn off my text notifications.

"I went to Good Vibes after you left yesterday."

"Oh yeah?" Ford perked up. "How'd that go?"

"She was there."

"Hell yeah! You talked to her?"

"I did. Unfortunately, they can't take any of this stuff back."

"Oh shit." Ford chuckled. "What are you going to do with it all?"

"That's where you come in. You assholes made this mess, now you gotta help me clean it up."

"Fair, fair. You got an idea?"

I grinned. "Very early stages. Think you can help me convince a bunch of the guys to do an event on short notice?"

"These guys are attention whores. I don't think it would be a problem. Are you going to ask her out?"

"Probably. She was shocked to see me, but I've got a plan. Put the word out, would you? Something might be coming together."

"You got it, man."

I relaxed onto the couch, petting Blaze as I formulated a half-baked plan that might both earn me some time with Jaz and allow me to lose some of the contents of that box.

Four

Jaz

"Are you stalking me?" I flung the accusation out, but there was no bite to my words. In fact, I'd been the one doing the stalking. I'd spent hours online researching him once Amber clued me in about who he was.

Ever grinned, glancing down at the bottles of warming massage oil in his hands before setting them back on the shelf and joining me at the counter.

"Not exactly."

I'd been in the back grabbing some extra tissue paper for customer bags. When I came out and found him standing in the lube section, my pulse leaped.

"What can I help you with today? Did you find a use for all your new items?"

"Sadly, no opportunity yet, but. I would be interested in some demonstrations, though." He winked. "I have a proposition for you."

My blood heated at the word. The one he'd made in Mexico had been very mutually beneficial. I could only hope he was about to offer something along the same lines.

"Oh?"

"Would you consider joining me for a coffee later?"

My heart was pounding furiously behind my ribs. The research I'd done online had turned up a shocking lack of skeletons along with plenty of evidence that he was a genuinely wonderful human being. By appearances, Ever was every fantasy I had come to life. Getting the chance to date him was a possibility I'd never dared hope for and I was completely thrown by this new complication.

"I'm … not sure."

His face fell. "Why not?"

"We're not the same people Jane and Drew were."

"Sure, we are."

I shook my head. "We most assuredly are not. You don't know anything about me, Ever. And I don't know anything about you, either. Well, I do *now*, thanks to the internet." He chuckled at my embarrassment over that admission. "We didn't even tell each other our real names. Doesn't that bother you?"

It felt crazy to turn him down, but jumping right back into ... whatever we had, seemed reckless. I itched to tell him the whole truth because otherwise it felt like we were building something on a lie. Besides, weekend flings in other countries were supposed to be nothing more than spicy memories you revisited when you settled back into your regular life and needed somewhere to escape to with your favorite vibrator. If anyone knew about that last part, it was me.

His head tilted and he rubbed his fingertips over a scar on his chin. "Come have coffee with me, Jaz. Let's learn about one another. No strings. We did that part before, right? I bet we can do it again. Better maybe. Longer."

My stomach dipped at his innuendo. "Longer suggests strings," I argued. He pouted, lush mouth turning downward. "Coffee," I said, and his face lit up. "*Just* coffee."

"I have a place. Best donuts you've ever blessed your tongue with. What time are you off?"

Gina appeared at my side, glasses coming off as she inspected him. Aware of her scrutiny, Ever straightened up, but his easy-going smile was undisturbed.

"She was just about to clock out."

My attention snapped to my boss. "No, I wasn't. It's only—"

"You were." The sudden shift of her eyes from him to me made me flinch.

Unsure of Gina's motives, I went to clock out as she stood at the counter. Amber was still with a customer, but sent a panicked glance my way.

"Let's go." I forced a tight smile as I walked past my boss and Ever, striding toward the front door.

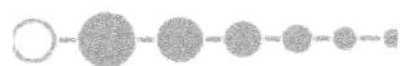

I wasn't sure how my day had taken such a turn, but soon we were seated at a cute bistro table with a paper boat full of tiny donuts covered in cinnamon sugar between us.

"Sorry. Can you say that again?" I'd been distracted by the playful curve of his mouth and the unique shade of his eyes.

"When I was leaving the other day, I heard your boss mention an anniversary sale. I might be able to help with that. So, I called her earlier." He placed his elbow on the table and leaned toward me. His proximity made my pulse pound in my throat. "Since I can't return my order, I was considering donating them to the cause. That way I can …" He waved his hand, trying to pluck a word from the air. "Pare down my now extensive collection, and you'll have plenty of your most popular items available to give demonstrations with." He grinned and my stomach dipped. This thoughtful man made me weak. It was a wonderful thing while on vacation, but felt dangerous now. "Is that something you can help with?"

"You want to get rid of some of the stuff you bought. By giving it back to the store?"

"To use as demo units and door prizes." He smiled, proud of himself. "The stuff is already paid for. I don't have any use for it. Well, most of it." He gave me an exaggerated wink.

"I … I'm not sure I understand why you need the store. You could just give everything away, right? What's in it for you?"

"Well, for starters, I convinced you to come to coffee with me."

I narrowed my eyes, which only served to amuse him.

"Look, I'm trying to help. I didn't mean to eavesdrop, but I have friends who owe me a favor. That means there are at least half a dozen athletic men with their own built-in fanbase who don't have any qualms about running around shirtless. That might be helpful if you're trying to draw a crowd."

"We don't want to get cited by the city for nudity. But if they're the friends from Mexico, I can confirm they're hot." I drowned a sigh with a sip of coffee. All in all, it was a good offer. I considered logistics as I nibbled on a donut hole.

"Ouch. You wound me," he teased, hand over his heart.

"Don't be dramatic, pretty boy. You know you're cute. I did go to *your* room that night, didn't I?"

His boyish grin was infectious. "You did." His tongue swept his teeth and my whole body went hot.

I cleared my throat, trying to focus. "Can they help with advertising? Like, would they be willing to share around social media so their fans spread the word?"

He reached for his phone. "I don't see why not, but I'll double-check." Ever's mouth puckered to one side when he focused on something. I found myself staring, remembering the warmth of his kiss. I pressed my fingertips to my lips, trying to remove the tingle.

"We could put up posters, too. The best kind of advertising is usually word of mouth."

"The demos would be the big draw, I'm guessing." He grinned at me and I melted a little. This man couldn't help but radiate charm. "*I'm* certainly looking forward to them. Plus, the doctor your boss mentioned seems like a big deal too."

I was cautiously excited about the idea, despite how bizarre it was. His friends really could be the pull we needed.

"What did Gina say?"

His smile was victorious. "She sent you off to have coffee with me, didn't she?"

I gasped, stunned by the scheming they'd done. "Seriously?"

Ever leaned in, hands around his coffee cup. "Don't blame her. It's my fault. I wanted to spend some time with you. When you're ready, I'd love to take you to dinner. Maybe back to my place for a private demo on a few things I'm curious about. But you're not ready for that."

I swallowed heavily, suddenly very warm. "No?"

He shook his head. "Nope. I have to convince you that being real-life Ever and Jaz isn't a problem." His voice dropped, and my blood surged. "Even though I'm sure you remember how fucking *good* we were together."

I absolutely did. Even though I knew it was ridiculous, disappointment swamped me. "Oh."

"It's okay." He winked, leaning away. "I'm a patient man. I'm an expert at waiting for the perfect wave."

I squirmed in my seat, itching to get everything out in the open. Damn his perfect face and charm, anyway. And was he calling me perfect?

"What happens if I tell you why I hooked up with you, and you don't feel the same way as you do now?"

"You mean it wasn't my skill at body shots?" he teased, but shrugged, seeing how serious I was. "I can't imagine what you could tell me that would scare me off."

My pulse pounded in my throat. Honesty was the best policy, but that didn't make it easy.

"You were a rebound. I was trying to get over someone. So, I got under you."

Ever blinked once, a wolfish grin spreading over his mouth. "That's it?"

I recoiled from the unexpected response. "What do you mean, *that's it*? I used you. You don't care?"

"Nah. I'm glad I could be there in your time of need. Did it work?"

I gaped at him. "You're serious."

"As a heart attack." He reached across the table, folding my fingers into his. "Jaz. I don't care. I'm kind of flattered, in fact. Knowing that doesn't change anything for me."

"I ..." words failed me.

"Did it work though?"

His hopeful expression made me laugh. "Yes, it worked."

"Excellent."

"How about if this works out, I owe *you* dinner." It was the best offer I could think of.

Ever licked his lips in anticipation. "Deal."

FIVE

EVER

"Thanks for coming by! If you're ready, Amber will take care of you. Don't forget to take a bag on your way out, complimentary door prize." I handed off autographed shirts to a young couple who'd collected an armful of items while walking around the store. I was on one end of the long checkout counter, with Amber manning the register on the other.

Seven of my teammates showed up to support the cause. Three of them weren't even involved in the prank, but wanted to help anyway. There was something to be said about good friends and the prospect of women and free vibrators, I suppose.

Neil donated coffee and donuts, and we all autographed shirts until we couldn't hold a marker any longer. They'd done their part and then some by spreading the word too. We were pumped to find a line of customers down the block before Good Vibes even opened for the day.

Gina doled out assignments to us all as she prepared to open the doors. "Lose the shirts and grab some toys. Aim for things you can figure out how to use, would you? You three are on line duty. You two, man the doors. No more than 20 people in at a time or it'll get too crowded."

Nobody was going to argue with her, so we were all walking around in our board shorts and flip-flops, hands, and pockets full of gadgets. A couple of guys found the novelty items from the store's display and were hauling around comically large dildos, giggling like they were twelve. Jaz had a bunch of my items at her table and the rest put into brightly colored paper bags with tissue for use as door prizes.

Dr. Dorothy Silverton was drawing a crowd on her own, signing books and even her own customized line of toys. As a sexologist and a well-renowned sex educator, her well of knowledge was deep. Jaz was completely enamored by her. Gina was sitting at Dr. Silverton's table, managing all the items people were asking to be signed.

In the days leading up to the event, Jaz and I spent quite a bit of time together at the store, planning, and I learned that she wanted to do something similar to the woman nicknamed Aunt Dottie. Jaz's heart was in helping people find sexual gratification, and that was a passion I could get behind one thousand percent. From what I remembered about our time in Mexico, and from seeing her around the store, she was well on her way already.

"This is great, right?" Amber asked during a lull at the checkout counter. Both Jaz's and Dr. Silverton's tables were busy, but the rest of the group wasn't quite done shopping yet.

"I wasn't sure what to expect, to be honest."

"Did your friends know what they were signing up for? There are so many people." Her eyes were wide as she assessed the line still running along the front of the building.

"Honestly? I'm not sure. But we're all attention-loving guys. They heard adoring fans and free stuff at my expense, and that was all they needed."

"It's so exciting, right? People are buying things that will improve their sex lives and getting to meet their favorite surfers. It's a weird combination, but it works." She'd seen enough of me lately that she'd gotten over her initial shyness. She was a pretty big surf fan, and I was worried she might pass out when I introduced her to Ford.

"You mind if I take a quick break?" I asked.

"Sure, go ahead."

I stepped out from behind the counter and weaved my way to the station in the center of the store where Jaz was manning a table. She had an array of toys spread across the top and was available for people to ask her questions or get a quick demonstration of things they were interested in. She was in her element and watching her show her expertise was unexpectedly sexy.

I lingered near a display of bondage equipment as she finished up showing a couple of women how the vibrator shaped like a penguin worked. It wasn't at all what I'd expected from how it looked in the package. Jaz's hair was braided back away from her face, the teal shade a perfect match for the Good Vibes logo on her white t-shirt. She was gorgeous, and I couldn't wait to claim my dinner date.

"Ever? Would you mind?"

"Sorry?" I hadn't been paying attention to what she was saying, and blinked, realizing that the eyes of the group were focused on me.

"Can I get your help for a few minutes?"

"Oh, sure." I glanced back at Amber, who was managing both my shirts and the register with ease. Putting on a grin, I approached the table, unsure what I'd managed to get myself into.

"Placement is important. This is a clitoral stimulator, so unless you line up the opening with the target, not much is going to happen." She took my hand and applied the beak of the penguin to the pad of my finger. "Then turn it on, and adjust your suction levels." Small puffs of air pulled at my fingertip, and as the audience looked on, Jaz turned it up. "This one has fifteen settings, but depending on the series you can get anywhere from nine to twenty. We also have one with an internal vibe as well."

"Oh my God," I muttered, unsure if the sensation was nice or just odd.

"Nice to know it works," one of the ladies joked, and the whole group laughed.

"I can say from personal experience, it works very well." Jaz winked at them and I suddenly had difficulty breathing. Walking was out of the question for at least a few minutes, and I was sweating. Jaz turned off the vibe, returning my hand to me. "Thanks for your help."

"My pleasure."

"Can you do Thumper?" one of the customers requested.

"Oh, that's a good one. Can you hand me that pink rabbit please?" Jaz asked me.

My cheeks flushed as I reached for the magenta vibrator with short prongs on the front of it. I didn't leave, however, because she didn't take it from me. Instead, she pointed out important features while I held it. I shifted my weight from foot to foot, moderately uncomfortable as she started her explanation.

"Rabbits are one of our most popular items, but this one is special." Jaz pressed a button, and the item hummed. My discomfort grew in direct proportion to my fascination with what I was holding. "Like most, both the bunny ears and internal part vibrate, but this one …" She pressed another button and I damn near dropped it. " …has independent controls for both parts." The third press of the button activated a feature that had me coughing over a laugh. "Plus, both the head and ears rotate for maximum stimulation."

Jaz gave me a saucy wink as she took the item from my hands and answered a few more questions as I stood there speechless. I was torn between embarrassment and amazement. Ford, the eternal troublemaker he was, was giving me a thumbs up from a few steps away, having recorded the entire thing. Again.

I gave him the finger, heading outside to check on the guys and catch my breath. They were masters at managing crowds and were giving it their all. I reminded everyone waiting to pick up a signed shirt and door prize as I walked up and down the line. Ford followed me and was juggling dildos to keep them entertained.

Before returning to my post at the checkout counter, I took in the organized chaos. My friends were now doing long-range, two-person juggling with the novelty-sized cocks and the crowd outside was only growing. Through the window, I could see Jaz holding a set of handcuffs and a riding crop. Gina was smiling as she helped Dorothy autograph a bullet vibrator.

All in all, it wasn't a bad way to spend a Saturday.

Gina smiled at us all, and not in her usual scary way.

After sending the volunteers home with her profound thanks, a gift card, and a couple of things from my stash, she addressed the handful of us that remained.

"You did good today, boys and girls." Her right eyebrow lifted as she pulled off the store's copy of the register tape. By the time she got to five arm-spans worth of paper, her eyes were wide. By ten, Jaz had covered her mouth with a hand and

Amber looked like she might pass out. "We didn't have any door prizes or shirts left either," Gina grunted, staring at the paper closely. "Wait. Who the hell bought an All for One?"

Amber raised her hand. "It was Dr. Silverton."

"Seriously?" Gina blinked.

"Yes. She said she wanted one of everything for her collection."

"Well. I'll have to send her a bottle of wine or something, then." She turned her steely gaze to Jaz. "You and I need to have a chat on Monday."

"Really?" Jaz gasped.

"You bet. This was well executed. You deserve that promotion. Now get the hell out of here, all of you."

I hung around so I could walk Jaz to the parking lot, but found Ford waiting outside the front door.

"What are you still doing here?"

He grinned at me. "I'm taking Amber for a drink."

"I'm …" I shook my head. "Honestly? I'm not surprised."

"You don't have to worry about me, Ev. You know I'll treat her right."

"I do." I offered him my knuckles and he bumped them with his fist. "Thanks for all your help today."

"You bet. Least I could do, right?"

"Something like that."

Amber slipped out the door, blushing when she spotted me.

"Have fun, you two."

"We will!" Ford waved and wrapped an arm around her shoulders as they walked down the block.

"Well, that was a day." Jaz sighed, joining me outside. "You hungry?" Her green eyes sparkled, making my blood stir.

"Starved."

"I've got a bargain to uphold then." Her smile was bright. "Your choice, my treat."

She didn't have to tell me twice, and the pleasure was all mine.

Six

Jaz

Ever drove us to a cute Irish pub near the beach called O'Malley's where his sister happened to be our waitress. I was a little embarrassed to already be getting the family meet-and-greet, but she was sweet.

"Let me know if you need anything." Esme delivered our food and went to help a nearby table.

"Are you two close in age?" I asked.

"Twins." I could tell Ever adored his sister from the sparkle in his eye. "I'm older."

"Only by six minutes!" Esme called over her shoulder on her way back inside, having heard him.

I laughed, enjoying their cute interaction.

We small-talked as I worked my way through a delicious cottage pie and he enthusiastically destroyed a mountain of fish and chips. In Mexico, we'd flirted, drank, then fell into bed, all without pressure or expectations. Now that we were doing ... whatever this was, I was in knots.

Ever gave me a grin that made me melt, briefly wrapping his fingers around mine on the tabletop after passing me the salt. The feel of his skin made my heart race.

Dinner stretched into dessert, and dessert into coffee with whiskey. A pleasant, warm sensation filled my gut as we continued to chat. The abrupt realization that I was genuinely enjoying his company without the distraction of friends, or the expectation that we were going to end the night getting sweaty shook me. I *liked* him. I wanted him, as badly as I had in Mexico. And there was nothing in my way except *me*.

"You alright?"

"I'm perfect."

"That's my line," he teased.

"Ever?"

"Uh-huh." He stuffed a wad of cash into the leather check booklet. I was fairly certain his sister would be annoyed by his generous tip, but it was an adorable gesture.

"Take me home?"

His eyes snapped to mine, his whole body still. "Is something wrong?"

I laughed. Clearly, I was off my game. "No, not at all. I want you to take me *home*, Ever. Your place, my place ..." I raised an eyebrow, trying to express my meaning.

He swallowed, Adam's apple bobbing. "Don't get me wrong, I'd love nothing more, but are you sure?"

I understood his subtext. He only drank one cup of whiskey-heavy coffee to my two, but I had all my faculties about me. "I'd like you to take me to bed. Please."

He folded my hand in his and ushered me to his car. Tension stretched between us as he sped us toward his apartment.

"Oh damn." Key in the door, he paused.

"What's wrong?"

"I have a dog. I need to take him out. You're not allergic, are you?"

I laughed at him. "No, not allergic, and I'm in no rush. What kind?"

He beamed. "Basset. His name is Blaze." The door swung open, and a low howl greeted us. "Come on boy, let's go." Ever snatched a leash off a hook next to the door and clipped it to the collar of the stout dog.

"He's so cute!" I squatted down, letting the hound sniff my knuckles. I got a droopy-eyed lick as a reward.

"We'll be right back. Make yourself at home."

Ever dashed down the flight of stairs with Blaze toddling behind him. I wandered around his living room. The basket of lube and condoms sat on his coffee table which made me giggle. There were a handful of vibrator boxes in there too. I'd strongly suspected he would keep some and was not disappointed in his choices.

"Sorry about that," he panted, hanging up the leash and his jacket when they got back from their quick walk.

"No problem."

I stood and he peered over my shoulder toward the table. "What are you looking at?"

"Seeing what you kept for yourself."

His expression turned hungry. "Yeah? How did I do?"

"Some of my favorites. Would you care for a private demonstration?"

"Hell yes."

Ever's fingers sank into my hair, pushing the bits that had fallen out of my braid away from my face as he leaned in to press a deep kiss on my mouth. He drank me in, then gentled the pressure, lifting his lips away only to press them gently again at each corner. Our breath mingled as he stared intently into my eyes. I saw his mouth twitch with a smirk just before he devoured me.

Angling my head just how he wanted, he pressed his lips greedily into mine, tongue nudging them apart. His groan rumbled through me as we tasted one another. My body lit up at his touch and heat flooded between my thighs as his lips worked mine. The tang of whiskey filled my senses as he dipped and flicked, removing my doubts with his talented mouth.

"Fuck, I missed you."

"Me too." I angled my head up to steal another kiss. "Bedroom?" I prompted.

Without hesitating, Ever lifted me tossing me over his shoulder before marching toward the bedroom. With his free hand, he planted a solid smack on one cheek and I yelped in surprise.

"Those gadgets better not require charging."

I laughed. "I remember how you do things. We've got time." I squealed as he flipped me over and I bounced off a mattress.

"Hell yeah, we do."

Through the blinds, a streetlamp cast a golden glow across us as we took turns stripping each other down. There was some cautious exploration as we remembered how to touch, nibble, and caress. My body recalled everything and then some, tensing as it craved his touch. His fingertips skated down the planes of my stomach, then my thighs, stopping just before reaching the place I needed them most.

"Please, Ever." I found myself pleading with him, which only made him grin.

"We have time, remember?"

He chuckled at my impatient groan and proceeded to use that warm, talented mouth to taste every inch of me he could reach, driving me to frenzied heights before using his fingers, then the toys. I was only allowed to touch him for brief moments. While I appreciated how devoted he was to his ministrations, I was getting frustrated.

When he finally pressed his body into mine, he sighed my name into the column of my throat. Inner walls clenching, I called his name out as we rocked together in a rhythm wholly our own. As he moved inside me, my body tensed and I climaxed with an intensity my body had never found with anyone else.

By the time we ran out of ways to please one another, the light streaming in the window was from the sun, and we were both exhausted. I thanked the universe for sending this man back to me, even when I wasn't sure I deserved him.

Epilogue

Ever

The palm trees, beach, and the resort were all virtually unchanged since the evening I agreed to a night with no strings with a gorgeous, green-eyed woman.

Two full years after that chance meeting, here we were, about to enjoy tacos and margaritas at the bar where we'd first met. All because my friends pulled a prank that landed me with a massive box full of sex toys and a way to find my dream woman again.

Jaz was a vision in a lime bikini, swinging in the hammock outside the patio door of our cabana with her arms over her head. The oval-shaped rock I'd put on her finger a few weeks ago sparkled in the late afternoon sun.

I had my surfboard tucked under my arm and my girl waiting for me in paradise. Everything was perfect.

I leaned down to kiss her before grabbing a towel and rubbing it over my wet hair. The sweet smile that took over her face when she saw me never failed to make my blood warm.

"It's so weird how it all looks the same."

"All of it?" I glanced down at myself.

"Most of it." She playfully poked a finger into my abs.

"So rude," I accused, Jaz squealing as I maneuvered myself into the hammock on top of her.

"You're all wet! And we're going to flip this thing … Drew."

"Should have thought of that before, *Jane*."

My fingers danced along her ribs as she squirmed underneath me. As usual, it only took a few moments before our play turned heated. The tickles turned into slow glides as I melded my mouth to hers. My fingertips dipped under the ties of her bikini top on the upward strokes, my thumbs the bottoms as I swept back down.

"That doing something for you?" Her green eyes were glassy with need as she stared into mine. "The names? Role-playing isn't something we've tried since we first met, and it wasn't exactly intentional then."

"Nah." I traced her full bottom lip with a thumb. "I prefer you as Jaz. I like the bright hair and knowing how you take your coffee." I nipped at her lips, balancing the hammock with my bodyweight as I untied her suit string at the hip. "I love how you sound when you laugh so hard you can't breathe. How you spoil Blaze with extra treats when you think I'm not watching. The little dance you do after I feed you when you're grumpy." I dipped for a kiss and she dodged.

"Are you saying I get hangry?"

"Not out loud. I value my life."

I pressed her further into the netting as I maneuvered both of our bottoms out of the way. She breathed my name as I pushed into her warmth, hands cupping her hips, rocking at an angle that sent sparks into my blood. I was impressed we hadn't twisted out of the hanging net and ended up on the tile floor.

I lost all sense of space and time as her hips rose to meet mine. She used my shoulder to stifle her moans, salt from the air clinging to my lips as I suckled on her collarbone, release chasing hotly down my spine as she trembled underneath me.

The hammock swung gently as we clung to one another, remembering how to breathe as the rush subsided. The sound of waves hitting the shore lulled me further into relaxation.

"Drinks?" I prompted, aware that if we continued to lay there we wouldn't move. I carefully stood before helping her out of the net's cradle.

"And tacos. All the tacos," she confirmed.

"Naturally."

"I need a quick shower, though."

"That makes two of us." It might be a while before we finally made it to dinner.

This woman was everything I hadn't known I was looking for, and I hoped to have a fling with her in Mexico every chance I got for the rest of our lives.

About The Author

Lily is a Colorado native enjoying the fantastic climate of Southern California with her family and cranky cat after surviving more than a decade in hot, humid places where hurricanes get their own season and Winter is a myth.

The written word is her favorite thing. Reading or writing; she doesn't discriminate. Left to her own devices she can read a book a day—a good happily ever after is a powerful drug!

An only child, she grew up inventing elaborate stories for her dolls to act out. She started word processing on a computer around age 10 and never looked back. After suffering the heartbreak of catastrophic drive failure a regrettable number of times, she has finally learned to back things up appropriately and often.

http://www.authorlilyalexander.com/

The Life and Vibes of Jessica Van Horne

Emma Jayne Mills

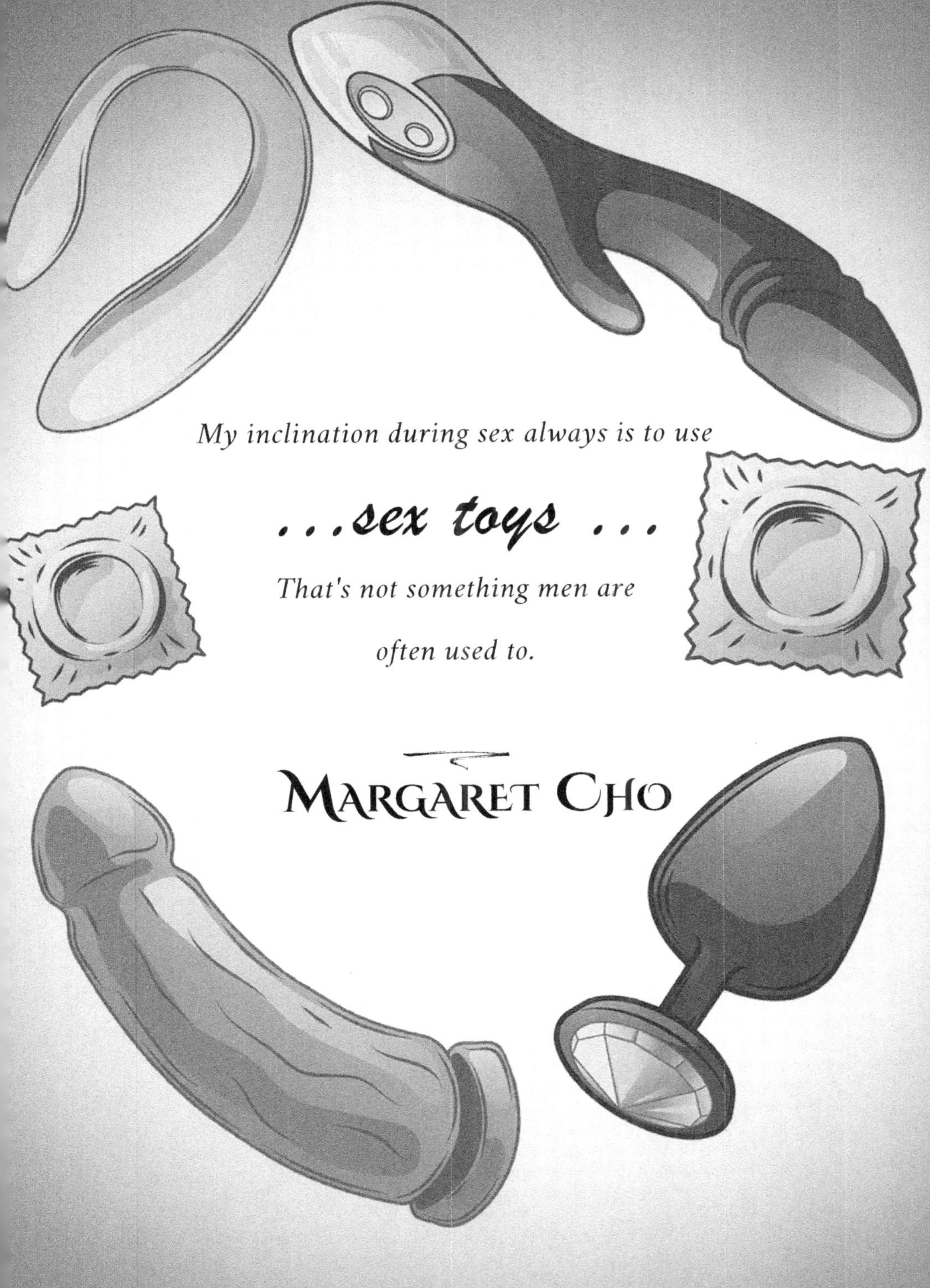

My inclination during sex always is to use
...sex toys ...
That's not something men are
often used to.
Margaret Cho

One

"Fuck!"

The back of my head hits the pillow and heaven surrounds me. You know the feeling. It starts as a tickle, a stirring tease to get you in the mood. Light touches and smooth caresses that pump the blood and build the anticipation. Then the soft touch is gone and every move is full of need, pushing you closer to the edge.

I guide him inside, that fullness bringing a satisfied smile to my face. This is how it should feel. One thrust, a twist, deeper, harder. I cry out, lifting my hips to meet each push. I don't know how it's happening but every spot is being hit at once. The sensations are almost too much. Almost. That delicious expectancy builds. My pleasure has never been pulled from so deeply within me. This one is a keeper.

Black flecked with gold paints the inside of my eyelids and I can no longer lift my body off the bed. My nipples are hard as rocks. The wave is reaching breaking point. It comes from my toes, tearing up my legs, over my hips and into my centre all at once.

"Uh! Oh! Ah!" I'm certain the entire street can hear my cries but I couldn't care less. Nothing has ever felt like this. "Yes! Oh, fuck! Yes!"

Sweat breaks out all over my body. I collapse, shaking and sated, on the wrinkled sheets. My heavy breaths fill the empty air and I smile.

"You're a keeper." My words are no more than a murmur, breathless and hoarse to the big boy lying beside me on the bed. "No man has ever done that to me. Bonus points for the lack of awkward after sex cuddling, as always."

Reaching out with a shaky hand to the bedside table, I grab the stop watch to time my recovery. I won't be sneaking away for a quickie with this one, but my readers need the details.

My name is Jessica Van Horne and I am a sex toy reviewer.

No, it's not fake or a pen name. It's my real name. I was born with it and honestly, what else was I supposed to do with a name like that? Become a nun? Sex really was my only career choice. So, I named my column on the website for the UK's leading sex toy manufacturer "Jessica Van Horne: No man required" and embraced my destiny.

I bloody love my job. Let's look at the pro's; I get paid to orgasm. Fairly sure hookers don't even get that every time. I work from home. No office drama or gossip mongers. The best thing though, no boss breathing down my neck. I only see her once a week. She's somewhat of a recluse. But, hey, as the woman who designed the country's biggest selling vibrator, she's probably the only person on earth who understands my life. Sex toy reviewer isn't something I find translates to real world relationships well. I mean, picture it ...

Hot blokie approaches, "Hi, I'm Gilbert (What? It's a name), I'm an *insert trade of choice here. Builder, investment banker, racing driver, whatever.*"

Then comes the expectant silence while he waits for my answer. Can you hear it? Think about it for a second. There it is.

"Hi, I'm Jessica Van Horne. I fuck myself with vibrators daily and write reviews on them so other women can have mind blowing orgasms too."

It's all downhill from there.

Not only does my name make me sound like a Bond bunny, but he immediately thinks I'm an easy lay because I've gone straight in with the sex talk. Only, it's not your regular sex talk, it's the "you will never match up to my vibrator," sex talk. If that isn't enough, and we by some miracle, make it as far as the bedroom, you know he's waiting for my review when the deed is done. If I rate him, it goes one of two ways.

He's offended and spends the rest of his life celibate because he feels ill-equipped to satisfy any woman again. I live with the guilt of creating a hormonal wreck who can't hold down a functioning relationship and sending him out into the world.

His ego balloons to the point where his head may actually implode. I live with the guilt of creating a manwhore of the worst kind and sending him out to harass women everywhere.

If I don't rate him, well, it's the same scenario only messier. At least with option two more women get orgasms. Either way, I never see him again. Anyway, that was my long-winded way of telling you I'm single. I stay single as a public service for the reasons listed above. Nobody wants those men, do they? I'll stick to big rubber dicks, thanks.

Right, time to work. I start with a quick mental body check. My breathing has returned to normal, my throat is dry but not sore, my legs are steady enough to walk. I click the button on the stop watch and glance at it. Four whole minutes have passed since the "O" hit. I'll have to check my notes, but this may be a new record.

With a contented sigh, I push off the bed, grab my robe and head to the kitchen. It's past seven and I fully intend to indulge in at least two glasses of the bottle of Chardonnay that's sitting in my fridge. Just as soon as I ring for pizza. Orgasming is hungry work.

The light from the fridge casts a menacing glow over the envelope I've been ignoring. It sits on the kitchen counter, daring me to open it. I know what's inside, I'm not ready to face it yet. I grab the wine and shove the letter in the drawer with the others. My hamster, Rupert, stops stuffing his face and looks up at me with his beady little eyes.

I point at him. "Don't look at me like that."

Two

I threw my coffee up when I read the letter this morning. It's a sin to waste good coffee. Stupid thing is notice of a rent increase on my flat and there's no way I can pay it. The thing about me is, I'm shit with money. I don't live an extravagant lifestyle. I do value my free time though, so I work enough to cover my basic needs and no more. The problem is my work no longer covers those needs.

It's Wednesday, my review just went live and it's time for my weekly meeting at the offices of Afternoon Delights. I shove the letter of impending doom into the pit of despair at the back of my mind and lean my head to the left, avoiding the scowling eyes of the secretary, to peer into my boss, Cathy's, office.

Cathy laughs and leans over a man's shoulder. A shuffle of his chair lets her see the screen he's looking at. I've never seen him before but whoever he is, he's taken my mind off the letter. It really should be illegal to look that good in a suit. Flopping into the seat the secretary pointed to, I relax and do some discreet drooling. Listen, just because I don't want a man doesn't mean I can't appreciate a fine specimen when I see one.

With the help of the open door, I can just about hear Cathy's voice. "Some like it fast and furious, I'm a long and slow kinda girl. I want my pleasure to be drawn out. Pull that orgasm from me kicking and screaming and leave me quivering on the bed. Show me the stars. I haven't climaxed properly unless my legs are numb, my throat is sore from screaming and my head is spinning. Take me to fever pitch or lose me forever."

"Bollocks!" I cover my face with my hands before anyone sees the blush. They're reading my article.

"She just gets better and better," the man rumbles. I tuck my chin into my chest while the corners of my mouth stretch into a smile.

"This purple bad boy simply has to be ridden to be believed." Cathy laughs at the words on the screen. The man murmurs something I don't catch. Cathy laughs again, slaps his shoulder, and keeps reading. "This baby is so good, I'm going to throw my rules out the window and say if any man can satisfy me in the way the Tantalising Tingler can, I'll marry him on the spot. Are you up to the challenge?"

I lower my hands and drag in a breath. This is good. They like my words. Common sense attempts to stamp out the flames of the imposter syndrome that sets in while I wait. My hormones, meanwhile, have zero common sense. They're distracted by the man with Cathy. His voice alone makes me feel things I have no business feeling. His eyes leave the screen and find mine. Oh, shit! He caught me. I check my chin with a swift wipe of my hand, thankfully it's drool free. A smile twitches on his lips and he pushes the chair out from the desk to stand.

Cathy looks up, waves and gestures for me to enter the office. I stand, smoothing out the non-existent wrinkles in my clothes and walk towards the open door.

"Jess." Cathy greets me with a hug. "Have you met my brother, Calvin?"

"No." I smile into his deep brown eyes and thank the Goddess in charge of making hot men that he isn't Cathy's husband.

"I've been enjoying your articles for months. You have a way with words." Calvin extends a hand to me.

When his fingers close around mine, I let the sigh I was holding in escape. Only it's not a sigh. It's a lust filled moan. Spontaneous combustion would be a blessing right now. He ignores my embarrassment and rubs his thumb over my hand, gently tugging me closer. I stumble the step he wants me to take, almost colliding with him and faceplanting on his chest. Oh, but what a chest it would be to faceplant into.

Cathy chatters away about something but I'm not listening and I don't think Calvin is either. We're standing too close. I need to look away, rescue my hand, but I don't. I'm anchored in his orbit. Taken prisoner by the dimple in his chin, eyes that forget to tell his mouth he's smiling and the confidence that oozes from him. Run, save yourselves, there's no way out for me.

"Great article this month." Cathy's voice finally breaks me out of my Calvin shaped jail and my hand slips from his to hang, lost and alone, at my side.

"Thanks." I will myself to get a grip. Okay, he's good looking. That doesn't mean I have to lose my mind over him.

"Thanks for coming in today, Jess. Calvin works closely with our P.R team and we have something we'd like to discuss with you." Cathy leads us to a seating area at one side of the office with sofas and a coffee table. It's homely and welcoming, which is good because I don't need help in making this situation more uncomfortable. She gets straight to business. "Until now, Afternoon Delights has focused predominantly on the single woman, but we want to open up our range to couples."

My mind races ahead, full throttle. I'm single. I'm not in a position to test and review couple's sex toys. I'm getting fired. "I see."

Calvin sits beside me. I can smell his aftershave, feel the warmth of his thigh against mine. I swear he just inched closer. "You have to keep moving in this business. Especially with all the romance authors opening the world's eyes to the sex toy industry."

"Romance authors?" I tilt my head to frown at him.

"They can be very influential." His mouth quirks in an almost there smile, the eyes are all over it though.

"We have to give the public what they want." Cathy opens a copy of the company's catalogue and turns it to face me. "We want to expand on your favourite products. Imagine using them with a partner."

"Well, I can look, but shouldn't you be talking to a couple for this?"

"Your reviews get more hits than anything else on our website. We're asking you." Calvin's deep voice is heavy next to my ear.

I flick through the designs with a shaky hand; whips, ball gags and nipple clamps adorn the pages, among other things. Romance authors, I get it now. "People are reading about this stuff and becoming more adventurous."

"Exactly. We're not the first company to enter this side of the market, so we need to stand out." Calvin's leg moves against mine as he turns his body to face me.

"How much more satisfying could they be with a partner?"

"They're pretty damn satisfying as they are." I clamp my lips together before I can shove my foot any further into my mouth.

"I can see that from your reviews." Calvin reaches up to open the top button on his shirt and loosens his tie. Interesting. Not that I am. Interested, that is. Sometimes this girl needs a face in mind while she's getting herself off. That's all.

"I'll see what I can come up with but I call the column no man required because it's true." I shrug and Calvin looks at me as though he's trying to piece together a puzzle.

"I have faith in you. Here's your next assignment. I can't wait to see what you make of this one." Cathy hands me a fancy paper bag with the company's logo on. "I know I already said it, but your article really was fantastic this month. You just keep getting better."

"Thanks." I glance at Calvin and stand. His eyes are setting fire to my loins and I have to leave before I strip off and offer myself to him on a platter.

"I loved the part where you set the challenge. I'm not sure if you know what you've let yourself in for, promising to marry any man who can satisfy you in the same way as the Tantalising Tingler." Cathy laughs. "You might want to move house or you'll be inundated with marriage proposals."

"I doubt that." The polite laughter dies and I fill the silence with a typically British, "Right."

"We'll talk again next week, when you've had chance to think about what we discussed." Cathy smiles and goes back to her pile of papers.

"Nice to meet you, Mr Dean." I almost fall over my own feet in my haste to the door.

"I'll see you out." He's behind me by the time we reach the exit, close enough for me to feel his presence but not quite touching. I tense, pulling my shoulders back and wondering if he can hear the hammering in my chest. His next words give me more tingles than any battery powered dick has ever managed. "Challenge accepted, Jessie."

Oh, fuck!

THREE

Jessica's perfect man walks into a bar …

Thirty seconds ago, Calvin Dean slid onto the bar stool next to mine and ordered, "two of what she's drinking," with a sideways nod in my direction. I'm now sitting here dying inside while the barman prepares the drinks. Feigning bravado, I turn my head towards Calvin and stare. I'm aiming for the classic, "how dare you assume you can buy me a drink," stare. The not very covert slide of my eyes over his body tells him I'm too curious to pull it off though.

My freak alert beacon is flashing bright red for danger but my eyes can't keep their mitts off this man. You bet your crotchless knickers I'm ogling him. There's no way he doesn't feel violated by my eyes right now and I don't care, not even a little bit. I'm collecting material for the wank bank. Yes, women have them too.

"Hello again." He leans forward, letting his breath brush my cheek.

Stomach muscles clenching, I meet his eyes, leaning to one side to avoid the intrusion. "Excuse me?"

"I'm not a game player, Jessie. Let's not do that."

Holy clit tingles, his voice. "Not a game player, I see. So, perhaps you're a stalker?"

The drinks are set down on the bar. My eyes dart a glance at the landlord, Mick, who is watching from the end of the bar. He sends a questioning look my way. Calvin is hot but this is odd.

"Night, Mick." I push up from the bar stool.

"Do you need one of the fellas to walk you home, lass?" Mick's eyes now narrow at Calvin and out of the blue, I realise I don't want that icy glare on the man beside me.

"Can I buy you a drink?" Calvin shoots blind into the void I've put between us.

"Apparently, you already did."

An uneasy laugh coughs from his chest. "Sorry, I'm coming across as aggressive and it's unsettling you. Will you grant me the time it takes to have one drink? Let me convince you I'm just a bloke in a pub who wants to share his time with a beautiful woman."

My eyes roll and flit to Mick for reassurance. He grins and winks, relaxing again. One barely there nod later, I'm back on the stool and Calvin is occupying the one next to me. He reaches for the drink in front of him and takes a sip. His face screws up in disgust and he gags.

"What is this?" His wide-eyed disgust makes me laugh and I relax.

"Malibu and coke. I'm cursed with a sweet tooth."

"That's disgusting."

"Hey, no hating the Malibu. It's tropical. We can all use a bit of tropical in this town."

"Ain't that the truth." While we laugh away our awkward start, Mick wanders over with a bottle of Whiskey and a glass. He sets it on the bar and pours a double then slides it over to Calvin. At Calvin's curious look he says, "You look like a whiskey man."

"Thanks, I am." Calvin samples the new drink and smiles. "That's better."

"So?" I want his story.

"I just moved into town a few weeks ago." Bullshit! You don't move into this town without being seen, let alone go undiscovered for weeks. I know at least three people whose radar he would have hit if he was new in town. "Thought it was time to venture out and make friends with the locals."

"Lucky locals."

"Lucky me. To have found one I already know." Has he superglued my eyes to his somehow? I can't look away.

Mick's conspiratorial looks aren't helping. He should not be supporting this. My raging hormones are supplying all the encouragement Calvin Dean needs, thank you very much. They're like a team of cheerleaders in heat, throwing their pompoms at him in a frenzy of teenage hysteria. Any second now, I'll be doing cartwheels and getting the pub goers to spell out his name. Give me a C!

He's not gorgeous. It's the Malibu making me see things I want. He's tall and there's a stack of toned muscle stretching the material of the shirt he wears. Rolled up sleeves and an undone top button give away the fact he came here from the office. The same office I met him in a few hours ago. Dark hair is swept back from his face and he has lips that I want wrapped around my nipples. It's the Malibu, I tell you. If I take him home, he'll be ninety and bald by morning. Nope, I'll stick with Percy the Pussy Pounder, thank you very much. Which reminds me, I must replenish my battery supply.

My mind wanders back to his comment this morning, challenge accepted. It was arrogant and should have been a turn off but it excited me. I can't bring my rum fogged mind to give a hoot that he's my boss's brother either. I reach for my drink. Our eyes meet over the glass and I'm propelled into a vision of tangled sheets, sweaty, writhing bodies, and mind-blowing orgasms. He looks like the kind of man who can play a woman's body to perfection.

Before I know it, we're three drinks in and flirting like crazy. That's when his smile captures me. I lean in when he does, his hair brushing against my forehead. "If we keep drinking, I don't know how much of a gentleman I can be."

"Gentlemen are overrated," I slur through a giggle. Men in general are overrated, I don't say.

"You deserve more than a one-night stand." His words stun me.

I'm gaping. Mouth opening and closing like a goldfish. "Who said anything about a one-night stand?"

"Exactly." Getting to his feet, he takes his wallet from his pocket and slides several notes over the bar to Mick. There's a silent exchange between them, a language only men understand. Mick, a man of few words, nods and moves along the bar to serve someone else. Calvin turns to me. "I'll walk you home."

"Oh." I slither off the barstool, certain I must resemble a conga eel in heels. "I can find my way."

"I'm sure you can." He offers his arm to me. "Humour me, Jessie."

I like the way he calls me Jessie and my hand, burrowed into the crook of his arm, is warm and cosy. Neither me nor my hand want this walk to end. Tragically, I live less than fifty steps from the pub's front door.

"This is me." I stagger to a halt at a door between two shop fronts, my breath painting the frosty air white. My stomach is tumbling. Everything I'm feeling is against my rules. Jessica Van Horne: no man required. A kiss isn't the same though, is it? One kiss. I can get the rest from The Grinder, who is currently waiting in my bedside drawer. "Why did you come here tonight, Calvin?"

"Despite the way it looks, I didn't come looking for you. I came for a drink. I stayed because you intrigue me. I want to know the woman behind the words that make me laugh every week." Lord, help me! I can't handle sweet. He takes my hand from his arm, tangling his fingers in mine. "Until next time, Jessie."

He leans in. I push up onto tip toes, close my eyes, pucker my lips, the world stops spinning and nothing happens. I peel my eyelids open to find him smiling down at me. With a tilt of my head, I narrow my eyes. He lets out a quiet laugh and pecks the softest kiss to my cheek. My cheek? What is this, the eighteen hundreds? Eat my tonsils, you sexy beast!

"Right." I let out a long breath. Keys tugged from pocket, I stumble the two steps to the door and open it, wondering what the hell is going on.

"You set a challenge, Jessie. I accepted it." Calvin's deep timber reverberates against my back. I stall. He's close. So close. His darkly stubbled chin appears in my peripheral and his eyes are undressing me, caressing my neck, moving lower, over my collar bone. "Goodnight." The whisper of his lips strokes my ear lobe, sending a luscious shiver down my spine. He hasn't touched me but I'm trembling like he just ate me alive.

"Night, Calvin," I manage to whisper.

The cold of the night hits my back. I don't turn around. I don't want the disappointment of seeing an empty street. I simply go inside and shut out the world. The back of the door supports me while I fumble for the switch and flick on the lamp. Rupert watches me from his cage in the corner.

I glare at him. "Shut up!"

FOUR

The knock at the door causes my heart to leap into my throat. I groan and toss the vibrating mean machine onto the bed, where it bounces a couple of times before lying abandoned on the sheet. Pitiful thing looks lost, he didn't get to prove his worth. "I'll be back, Brigadier Buzz!"

Grabbing my robe from the back of the door, I rush to shove my arms into the sleeves and tie the belt at the waist. "This better not be one of your jokes, Vinnie!" It's not Vinnie.

Calvin Dean's glorious form fills my doorway. "Vinnie?" He raises an eyebrow.

"My neighbour." I frown at him. His eyes travel over me. I follow them, looking down to realise my robe is gaping open. The girls are practically waving at him. Come on in, get a good look. We honk if you squeeze. Traitorous beasts! I tug the material over my chest and cross my arms. "Can I help you?"

He holds aloft a brown paper bag and a bottle of wine and does the eye smiling thing. "I brought lunch."

"Did we make some kind of arrangement I was too drunk to remember?" I was in the middle of a review and I didn't get to finish. Irritated is not a big enough word for what I'm feeling right now.

"I'm wooing you, Jessie." He glides past me and into my flat, a light kiss to my forehead as he passes.

"Wooing me?" I whisper and stare at his back.

He sets the bag on the kitchen counter. "I imagine the work I … Cathy has you doing can be demanding. The body needs fuel, am I right?"

He's inserting himself into my life uninvited and there isn't an argument in the world I want to throw at him. Besides, I'm hungry. "I'll get dressed."

"Not on my account." He shrugs off his suit jacket, draping it over the back of a chair as though he's done it thousands of times. Then he undoes the buttons on his shirt cuffs and rolls up his sleeves, never once taking his eyes off me. I will not fall for this man's fuck me tricks. Nope. Not me. "Did I interrupt a review?"

"Yes." Why bother lying? He knows what I do.

"And you're frustrated because you didn't get to finish." A smile plays on his lips. "I'd be happy to wait while you wrap things up."

Don't tempt me, I think. Out loud, I answer, "I'm good," and grab two wine glasses from the cupboard. I set them on the counter and fish the corkscrew from a nearby drawer, sliding it towards him. He opens and pours the wine, alcohol free because he's driving, while I distract my disloyal eyes from the obscene amount of arm porn he's displaying and peek inside the bag. My mouth waters. There's a freshly baked loaf of artisan bread, it smells divine. I pull out cured meats, several kinds of cheese, grapes, and a jar of chilli jam. Either Calvin Dean has done this before or he's been spying on me because this is my favourite kind of food.

"I remembered your sweet tooth." He pauses to watch me empty the bag.

I dig deeper, finding the lemon cheesecake he's referring to. Boy did good. "Cheesecake is my favourite." When he puffs his chest out like he brought home a hunting trophy, I can't help laughing.

We sit on the rug in the living room to eat, picnic style. He stretches out his long legs and leans back on his elbows. Calvin fills this small space. It should feel cramped, but it's oddly comfortable. Before I know it we've been volleying questions back and forth for an hour.

"Favourite band?"

"Kiss!"

"Kiss?" I look up from where I'm rolling a grape around my plate, surprised by his answer. "You don't look like a Kiss fan."

"Should I be wearing face paint? Platform boots and a studded lycra jump suit?"

"Well, that would be quite a sight." Slashed to the waist, washboard abs on display. I could live with the make-up and lycra.

"Never judge a man by his suit." He points at me. "It's what's underneath that counts."

"Flirt!" Laughter comes easily with Calvin, I find.

"Guilty!"

"Okay, favourite colour?"

He frowns. "It's my turn to ask."

"Purple."

"I wasn't going to ask that."

I shrug. "My turn, favourite colour?"

He laughs and shakes his head at me. "Green."

"What?" I screw up my face at his answer. "Nobody likes green. They're always the last sweet left in the bag."

"Green is the colour of spring. Spring brings new beginnings, lighter times. Hope." He looks up, locking our eyes.

"Cricket pitches are green. I like cricket."

"My garden is big enough for a cricket pitch. We could have a company team." He confesses he bought a house in Frost Ford months ago but hasn't moved in. That's where he was last night before he came in the pub. "It's too big for one person."

"So, where do you live?"

"In a flat over the offices of Afternoon Delights."

"You live where you work?"

"So do you." He gestures to my tiny living room with a lift of one hand.

"Living where you work and working from home are not the same thing." I take a sip of my wine. "Besides, where else could I do this job?"

"It would be an entirely different job if you did it anywhere else." He leans towards me, lifting one hand to tuck a strand of hair behind my ear. "You are a temptation, Jessie."

"I offered to get dressed," I remind him.

His hand moves down, caressing my neck and one finger tracks the opening of my robe. He doesn't reach beneath or even attempt to peep at the girls, but the suggestion is enough to heat the air between us. "A gentleman would have let you."

"We already discussed my thoughts on gentlemen," I whisper as his lips draw near. This is where you kiss me, dimples!

"Why do you think a vibrator can replace a man?" He's suddenly serious and leans back. Damn tease!

I blink away my frustration. "Men are generally disappointing."

"In what way?"

"Well, there's the after sex awkwardness. You don't know if you'll see each other again. He says he'll call, he doesn't. If he does, you spend a few weeks going out but the romance fades. The initial thrill is gone and you're stuck in a relationship that doesn't fulfil either of your needs."

"You speak from experience."

"You don't get to thirty-two without it."

"True." He nods. "With me, relationships don't work because women see the suit, a fancy car, a decent job, assume a hefty bank balance and start hearing wedding bells."

"You don't want to get married?"

"Yes, to the right woman." While he mulls over what he wants to say, I wish I could read minds because I need to know what's making him smile the way he is. "Sex is more than carnal desire though. What about emotions, affection, support, love?"

"None of them add to my pleasure."

"Because you've never had a man who could provide those things."

"You think you're that man?"

"Are you willing to find out?"

I nod because I want more of this. More spur of the moment lunches, more searching conversations, more laughter. Just more of him.

FIVE

For two weeks, the letters and answer phone messages from my landlord piled up while I let myself get lost in Calvin. I don't know why I thought I could ignore them. I'm in my kitchen taking a phone call from a man who has every right to be pissed off with me. Mr Rogers recently decided he wants to sell the flat and was prepared to give me first refusal. It's money I don't have though.

"Mr Rogers, I simply cannot do it. I appreciate the offer, I really do. It's just not within my means right now."

"It's going on the market today, Ms Van Horne. You can stay at your current rent until it sells. I'll warn you though, there has been interest in it. I felt it only fair to give you first refusal, despite the fact you ignored my letters."

"And I'm grateful for that. Again, I apologise." I hang up and turn to see Calvin standing in the doorway, forgetting I'd left it on the latch for him. Hands in pockets, he gives me an expectant look. I plaster on a smile, drop the phone on the table and peck a kiss on his lips, we've moved on from cheeks, as I walk past him but he's no fool.

"Jessie." He's on my heels, a hand on my elbow.

I hold his gaze to let him know I have this handled. Ha! "Distract me."

"Show me what you're working on this week." His eyes sparkle with the dare. I'm wearing my robe again, it's a dead giveaway.

I return his look with a devious one and stand, holding out my hand to him. "Challenge accepted."

In the bedroom, I lean against the desk and press the switch on my laptop. The screen lights up with a half-written article that I gesture for him to read, knowing full well this isn't what he meant. He grins and unplugs the laptop, lifting it and taking it to the bed. He shoves Heart Stopper, my latest assignment, aside and gets comfortable, propping himself up on the pillows, legs crossed at the ankles, with the laptop resting on his lap. He pats the space beside him and I climb on while he starts to read aloud.

"Jessica Van Horne: No Man required." He gives me a sideways glance.

I nudge his shoulder with mine. "Just read, Mr Smug!"

There's a lingering moment, we can't tear our eyes away from each other. A thousand words are unspoken in that look. We're coming to an understanding that this is the beginning of something. It's new and exciting. I didn't know I was looking for it but the promise that it could become something very real is there. I won't fuck it up by telling him my problems and looking like another gold digger. I don't know how much money Calvin has, but it's significantly more than me.

He licks his lips and starts reading. "First impressions? Well, ladies, this one is a beauty. You don't want to keep the Heart Stopper hidden in a drawer beside your bed with your other battery-operated boyfriends. With his heart shaped tip and rose gold collar, he begs to be displayed. Place him proudly on your antique Welsh dresser, alongside the Victorian dinner service you inherited from Great Granny. I'm kidding. Don't do that. Not unless you live alone and never have visitors."

Laughing, he looks at me. "You're wasted on our website, Jessie."

"I like my job." It just doesn't pay the bills.

He sets the laptop on the bedside table and turns to me. "What are your dreams?"

"Career wise?" He nods. "I always wanted to be a magazine editor when I was growing up."

"What happened?"

"I travelled, did the back packing around Europe thing. Then took whatever jobs I could get to pay the rent."

"And now?"

"Life takes us in other directions, dreams get left behind." I smile.

"Never let go of your dreams, Jessie."

"What about you? Tell me yours."

"To make money." He laughs but quickly grows serious. "We didn't have much growing up. I decided to make sure we never wanted for anything again."

"Are you a partner in the company then?"

He looks at me for a long moment. "Cathy is the face, I take care of the business side."

"It must be nice not to have to worry about money."

"It has its perks."

"And its downside?"

"All the money in the world means nothing without someone to share it with." His lips brush mine in the lightest of kisses. I lean in, craving what he is only too happy to oblige. I smooth a hand along his arm, to his shoulder and then his neck, letting my fingers explore, while his find my hips and pull me closer.

Pulling back, my hands dance over the material of my robe and I tug the belt, undoing the tie. The knot slips easily and he bites his lip as I push the material from my shoulders, exposing the girls to his hungry gaze. With his eyes on me, I can take on the world.

He looks at the vibrator laying between us. A thrill goes through me, he wants a one-woman show. I never knew being watched could be such a turn on. Something about showing Calvin this part of me is exciting.

I pick up Heart Stopper, grateful I got as far as playing with the settings earlier. Watching me figure out how a vibrating dick with a heart shaped tip works would be an instant mood killer. Easing back on the bed, I part my legs and his groan, accompanied by his body shifting, is the sexiest sound I've ever heard.

I reach down, the way I would if I were working, and drag my fingers through my folds. I'm already wet, but I linger there, putting on a show of pinching my clit between two fingers and bucking my hips when the heat pools in my centre. I circle my thumb over the little gem and let out a gasp.

"Fuck, Jessie."

Tracing Heart Stopper's bulbous tip along my pussy has him leaning back to adjust himself. I flick the button on the toy and it buzzes to life. The tip circles on this one and I know it's going to feel amazing inside me but I need the tease first.

I reach up with one hand, keeping the momentum going with Heart Stopper, and suck my fingers into my mouth. With my forefinger, I track a circle around one hard nipple and Calvin rewards me with another moan. His reactions build with mine, his voice becoming rougher, more a growl than a moan. My eyes close and I push Heart Stopper into me, lifting my hips to take the unusual shape.

The bed dips and my stomach tumbles. If he touches me, I'll gush on impact. There's a pause in both our breaths, our movements still. Then he's at my ear, whispering, "Show me, Jessie."

My heart flutters and I squeal, pushing the toy deeper and flicking the switch to make the tip rotate. "Oh!"

He still hasn't touched me. His presence is enough. "More. I want all those noises. Don't hold back."

Heart Stopper hits my g spot on every other cycle. The pressure is borderline torture. With each move I almost tumble into my orgasm, then it's ripped away from me with the next. I grab my breast with my whole hand, wanting it to be Calvin's fingers, wanting from him what I'm giving myself. I need his hands on me, his skin on mine. The thought, not the toy, is what takes me to my peak. My moan is long, drawn out and guttural. My juices coat the vibrator, heated cum spilling over my fingers. Stars paint the inside of my eyelids and my head spins.

Heart Stopper is snatched from my fingers and my eyes fly open. Calvin's hooded gaze meets mine as he licks the heart at the tip of the vibrator. It's enough to have my stomach clenching with the need to feel his tongue on me.

Heart Stopper is cast aside and Calvin leans over me, one hand braced on the bed beside my head. "Jessie Van Horne, you will be the death of me." He crashes his lips into mine, pushing his tongue between them so I can taste myself on him. My hands are in his hair, gripping, pulling him closer. I want him on top of me, his bodyweight pinning me to the bed, his hips pushing my legs apart. He obliges, climbing over me and settling in like he belongs there. Maybe he does.

"Calvin." His name is a needful plea.

"We need to stop." He draws back. I don't think I've ever been looked at the way Calvin Dean looks at me.

Wait, what? "Stop?"

"If we don't, I'm going to devour you right here."

"I have zero issues with that."

He laughs, shifting on the bed and pulling me into his arms, my head resting on his fully clothed chest. "Emotions, feelings, remember?"

"My emotions are pretty strong, right now," I argue, getting comfortable.

"Patience." He pulls a blanket over us. We're back to the gentleman thing and disappointment settles in my gut. He kisses my forehead. "Thank you."

"For what?"

"For sharing this with me."

My good mood returns. "I'm glad you enjoyed the show."

"I've never been so hard in my life."

"I can still help with that."

"Soon." He squeezes my shoulder. "I still have a point to prove."

"I think we're well past that stage."

He settles on the pillow and holds me close, drawing gentle fingers through my hair. "You claim you don't need a man because you have the toys. I'm going to give you everything a sex toy can't."

He already is. No! No man required. That's my motto. It doesn't matter if Calvin is chipping away at it every day. It's mine and I'm keeping it. Maybe.

SIX

Cathy is setting out a display of sex toys on the coffee table in her office when we arrive. A month has passed since our initial meeting. We've had several more, during which we've discussed and designed a new range for couples. One that Calvin and I have spent many an afternoon brainstorming ideas for. That new range is in production and another line arrived this morning. All I'm saying is, sex toy design is fun.

A giddy assortment of dildos, vibrating rings, and nipple clamps is on display. My heart races in my chest. With those toys and this man, I could have so much fun. He's sitting next to me. His leg rests against mine, his body heat seeping through my jeans and warming its way up my thigh to the top of my legs. I will not clench. I will not clench.

I clench.

"Oh, God!" The blush burning my cheeks betrays my feelings. Calvin chuckles quietly, he didn't miss the clench.

"Pardon?" Cathy looks up, eyes bouncing between the two of us.

"Oh, wow!" I exclaim with more excitement than necessary and reach out to pluck the nearest object from the table. It just happens to be a huge pink dick with those tiny bunny ears attached.

"I know." Cathy's eyes glint. "Those ears."

"Genius!"

"Can't replace a tongue though," Calvin whispers when Cathy walks away.

"Ooh, tongue shaped vibe. There's an idea."

"That would be hideous!"

Cathy is oblivious, wandering away to open another box and rummage around inside while we giggle like children at my idea. Something was set free in me that first afternoon we spent together and Calvin has been watching me work ever since, never once touching me, let alone using his tongue. He's a damn tease but I can't deny I'm loving every second.

Cathy comes back to the table and takes a seat opposite. "This is our latest line, as I said."

Calvin leans back and crosses one leg over the other, his hand sliding over the leather seat and coming to rest on the small of my back. I squirm. "I can see these things pleasing the ladies."

His fingers slip over the exposed skin where my shirt has ridden up. "No emotion though. Connection, that's what's missing."

I pick up a bullet shaped toy and twirl it between my fingers. "Trust me, you can become emotionally attached to one of these bad boys."

"That sounds like another challenge," he murmurs for my ears only. I don't look at him. If I do I might strip off and make him watch how I get attached.

The rest of the meeting is surprisingly professional and doesn't descend into the torrid sex marathon on the desk that I'm definitely not envisioning. Calvin remains close, his finger trailing a hot path across my bare skin, but we discuss sex toys like adults and come up with a running order for each one to be featured on the website.

"I don't know how much you two have discussed about the couple's toys so far." Cathy flits a knowing look between us. "Calvin's products are aimed at women, predominantly single women. As you know, we aim to change that."

"Calvin's products?" Cathy's skin turns beet red and I snap my head to the left to face the man next to me.

He lets out a long breath, his palm, flat on my back, burns a hole in my skin. "Jessie, there's something you should know."

I've already jumped to the right conclusion though. Money was his goal. Cathy always seems to take a step back when he's around. It makes perfect sense that he would be the owner of the company. Calvin Dean is my boss. "Why?"

"Not because I don't trust you, Jessie. Don't think that." How does he already know what I'm thinking all the time? Because he's wormed his way into my life and he knows me, that's how. But that's also what hurts. I've laid myself bare to him, in more ways than one, over the last few weeks and he couldn't trust me with this. "I had every intention of telling you."

"When?" I struggle to muster more than one word responses.

There's a moment's pause while Cathy excuses herself. Calvin reaches for my hand. I snatch it away. He's nothing if not persistent and reaches again, this time holding it in both of his and shifting so he can see my face.

"Afternoon Delights is, for the public, owned by Catherine Myers, aka my sister. When I set up the company, following a drunken conversation with Cathy and her husband, Will, I decided that mine was not the face a company aimed at women's pleasure needed. Enter Cathy, elegant and approachable, someone for women to relate to. She became the outward face of the company. My identity has remained secret."

"Afternoon Delights." I don't know why I repeat the name. Maybe because it's become a symbol of our relationship. One that began with a series of lunchtime trysts and developed over the last few weeks into something deeper.

"It sounded better than Dean's Dildos!" He laughs. It's an almost defeated sound and I hate it. It doesn't suit him. "Look, as long as we're doing this—" He stalls in his flow and I snap my eyes to his. "I'm not the only one with a secret, am I?"

My stomach drops. "What are you talking about?"

"The letters you shove in the kitchen drawer and pretend don't exist. The phone calls you've been avoiding."

"You went through my mail?" My voice is almost a shriek.

"I want to help, Jessie. I intended to tell you everything today, but then Cathy called to say the new products had arrived."

"Can you just stop talking for a second?" He does, but his eyes are on me.

I want to kill him. Or at the very least, break his legs. I'd throw him out the window but it's only a two-storey building and he's huge. There's no way I could lift him.

"I have to go." I pull my hands from his, refusing to look at him. I don't answer when he calls my name. I've never left a place so quickly. In my rear-view mirror, he's standing on the steps of the building, hands shoved in pockets, watching me drive away with a look of despair on his face.

"Fucking men!" I smack a hand on the steering wheel and shake out the pain. Tears sting the corners of my eyes. It's the ache in my hand, nothing whatsoever to do with the realisation I'd been taken in by him.

I'm an idiot!

Seven

The boxes are packed. Rupert stares at me from his cage. In a few days we'll be back with my parents like the loser I am. Calvin Dean has called every day, countless times. I've ignored him and his messages just like I ignored the letters. You'd think I'd learn. He's currently sitting on my doorstep, where he's been all evening, just like every night since I discovered his secret identity.

"Don't look at me like that, Rupert." I sigh and rest my chin in my hands. The hamster stares at me with big, round eyes. "I know, I probably should hear him out, but he lied to me. I understand why. He doesn't want another gold digger. I just don't know how we come back from that." Rupert nibbles on a seed. "Yes, I know I shouldn't have let him get close. You don't need to tell me that."

I pour a glass of wine, letting the liquid reach the very top of the glass, then I bend to suck it up. "The thing is, Rupert, I shouldn't have fallen for it in the first place. No man required. That's just how my life is. I was a fool to think it could be different with him."

Rupert lets out a series of squeaks. "Well, of course you like him. He feeds you leftover spaghetti." I take a gulp of my wine. "That's not a reason to fall in love with the man, you know?" Rupert squeaks again, a huff in hamster. "You're wrong. I do not love him!" Another squeak. "I am most certainly not in denial, Rupert!"

Calvin's body shifts against the outside of the door. "Are you ever going away?" I mumble to myself.

"You should listen to Rupert," comes the muffled reply.

Lifting the wine glass, I creep to the door and sit with my back against it. My desire to be close to this man hasn't disappeared in any way.

"Rupert talks a lot of shit!" I mutter. "He's a bad influence too."

"How so?"

"He talked me into opening a second bottle and now I'm weak."

"You are anything but weak, Jessie." His normally sexy husk is filled with pain. "I'm truly sorry."

There's a pause while I finish my wine. "I need the bottle for this." I stand to get the bottle from the kitchen and return to my spot on the floor, imagining us sitting back-to-back, the door between us.

"For the record, I never thought you were a gold digger."

"So, why lie?"

"I've kept my identity secret for so long, I suppose I wasn't sure how to tell you."

"Hi, I'm Calvin Dean and I'm your boss." I deepen my voice to imitate him then lift the bottle to my lips and drink. "Or, you know, hey, Jessie, Cathy isn't really your boss, I am. Or even, want to fuck, Jessie? By the way, I'm your boss."

"We haven't fucked yet," he points out.

I roll my eyes at Rupert. "Hey, Jessie, I plan on seducing you, but first you should know, I'm your boss." More wine passes my lips. "Yo! Jessie, you know all those rubber dicks you're letting me watch you use? Well, those are my dicks!"

"Yo?" It's a crime how much I like the sound of his laugh.

"Sup, Jessie, it's Tuesday and I'm your boss!"

"Yeah, any of those would have done it."

"I can keep going," I offer with sarcasm.

Silence, then just as I'm about to speak, he says, "Sup, Jessie I'm your boss and I'm falling in love with you."

"Shit! How do I respond to that?"

"You could open the door and let me in."

"Did I say that out loud?"

"You did." He laughs again.

When I open the door his hair is a mess, his suit crumpled and he looks like he hasn't slept in days. He probably hasn't because he's spent days on my doorstep. "Yo!"

"Sup?" I point to my hamster. "For the record, I'm onto you two. I know you were conspiring against me."

His eyes move over my shoulder to Rupert. "Thanks for having my back, furball."

"I'm scared," I admit and he links our hands. "I'm a mess. My life is falling apart. I show the world this put together woman and it's not who I am. I can barely pay my rent."

"I'm scared too." I look into his eyes with a question in mine. "I've never let anyone into my life before. Not like this. You and Cathy are the only people who know who I am. Fear is a good thing though."

"How?"

"We were both hiding from something, now we have no choice but to face those things. I have nothing left to hide and neither do you."

"How are you single?"

"Am I single, Jessie?"

We move at the same time, hands grasping, mouths clashing. Calvin Dean is falling in love with me and I can't think of a single reason not to believe him. Nothing else matters. Just him and me in my tiny flat, ripping each other's clothes off.

His musk invades my senses and this time, I'm getting all of him. No watching, no secrets, just two people making love. Our bodies are quickly naked, where the clothes went is irrelevant, and he is lifting me. I wrap my legs around his waist, letting him carry me to the bedroom. When he lays me on the bed, I get my first look at him in all his glory and gasp.

"I know, it's not what your used to," he quips with a mischievous grin. "This one isn't made of rubber and comes with a set of bollocks. Look, they even swing." He swivels his hips and a loud cackle bursts from me. "No batteries required!"

"I might need a demonstration." I giggle.

He climbs over me. His knees not needing to push my legs apart to make room for him, they're already wide and begging. I'm an insatiable slut for this man and he still hasn't touched me properly.

As if hearing my thoughts, he lowers himself over me and covers my neck in kisses, working his way lower, over both breasts, tongue circling, teeth nipping.

My skin pebbles under his touch and I feel him grow hard against my leg. I lift my hips, whimpering my need. He laughs and continues his descent. I'm not getting the D until he tastes me in the way he's wanted to for weeks.

His taunting builds. When his tongue finally licks the path I want it to, I let out a scream, clutching his hair in my fingers and pulling. The vibration of his moan tickles and I almost overflow right then. But he stops, lifting his eyes to mine, looking like a crocodile in the water. What? He does. A damn sexy crocodile, too. Wait, let's not descend into bestiality. Eyes on me, he flattens his tongue against me and licks the length of my lips, dipping the tip of his tongue between them to tease my nub.

"Calvin." I've never been so needy. He's reducing me to an emotional wreck and I'm loving every delicious second.

Finally, moving back up my body, he's ready to give me the good stuff. Not that it hasn't been good up to now, but I'm primed and ready to explode. I need to be fucked. Thankfully, one of us is thinking straight and he sheaths the beast before entry.

Lining himself up against me he drags the tip through my wet folds and I throw my head back, screaming, "No more teasing, Calvin, I need you inside me!"

"Jesus, Jessie, keep talking like that and I'll be done before we start!"

"Don't you dare!" I reach down and circle his length with my hand. "Hmm, now that's a toy this girl could get used to."

"Fuck!" He thrusts his hips and buries himself deep. My legs are pushed wider under his weight, his toned arms resting either side of my head. I turn to kiss his bicep and wrap my legs around his hips.

He's been paying attention to the way I please myself and it shows. He knows exactly how to move, where to touch, when to slow down and when to speed up. It's my turn to get to know him. I slide my hands over his shoulders, down his back, to the pert bulge of his arse. How can a man have such a peach? I squeeze and he pushes into me with a moan. I let my hands roam his body and he comes alive under their demand.

It's with my fingers in his hair that we both begin to come undone. He pushes deeper. Each grind of his hips rubs delicious friction against my clit, pulling the pleasure from me. His lips, buried in my neck, place a kiss there before he lifts his head to look at me. Eyes locked, the emotion of the moment threatens to overwhelm. My heart is wide open and my very soul is joining itself to this man. He knows my hopes, my fears. This connection is so much more than carnal pleasure and on a whole other level than anything I've felt with a toy. Calvin Dean has broken me open. Pulled my feelings from me and taught me how to accept his. We fall into the abyss together, tumbling to the climax as one. Our bodies still as our pleasure ripples through us. Legs entwined, hearts pounding, hips joined and lips tenderly kissing.

"No toys required." He drops next to me.

"We don't need them." I squirm to settle in his embrace.

"Well, maybe sometimes," he teases. "Because I never realised watching was my kink."

"I never realised being watched was mine." I roll on my side and look at him.

"I believe this makes me the winner of your challenge," he says as we lie in the afterglow. "You'll need to make an announcement in your next article."

"You do understand that I didn't issue that challenge seriously?"

"I was always going to seek you out, Jessie. Your challenge just gave me the opportunity."

"This falling in love thing works both ways, just so you know." I place a kiss to his chest.

"Thank fuck for that."

Eight

"I just remembered, there's something I need to take care of at the house. Will you come with me?" Calvin is standing in the kitchen with a set of keys in his hand.

I have packing to do because as good as it was, one night of sex doesn't change my living situation, but he's looking at me as though this is something he really needs. "Okay."

Calvin's house is set back from the others on the street, almost making it seem part of the forest behind it. His car sits in the driveway, which is unusual because he normally parks it outside my flat when he's in town.

"I've been spending some time here recently," he says when I spot the car.

"Finally going to move in?"

"That depends." He unlocks the door.

Inside is an exhibit of solid wood floors, original ceiling beams and bare stone walls. The furniture is rustic, minimal fuss and a huge fireplace provides the centre piece of the room. I walk around the hearth, trailing a hand over the brick. "This is stunning."

"This room is the reason I bought the place." He shoves his hands in his pockets and watches me with a smile.

Full length windows on one wall overlook the dark green of the forest that surrounds Frost Ford. "We could be in the middle of nowhere here."

"Peaceful, isn't it?" His hands slide around my waist and I lean back against him.

"Hmm." I lift my chin and beg a kiss. He never refuses.

"Move in with me, Jessie."

My hearts stops and a gulp gets stuck in my throat. I turn to face him. "What?"

"I'm serious." He cups my cheeks, refusing to let me put space between us. "You need somewhere to live and I don't want to be here with anyone else."

"No, Calvin." I lay my hands on his chest. "This is my problem to solve."

"It doesn't have to be. Don't you see what I've been trying to do all this time? Let me in, Jessie. Let me give you the support a partner can give you."

"Then give me a raise. Let me pay my own way. Asking me to move in with you isn't supporting me, it's fixing my problems."

"You've got your raise and a promotion."

"What?"

His smile is a mile wide. "I want you to be the editor of Afternoon Delight's new couple's health magazine."

I'm sure my eyes are bulging from my head. I must look like a frog on steroids. "Are you serious?"

"Of course." He leans in to kiss me. "The company needed a new angle, this is it. The job is yours. You earned it."

My heart is punching a hole in my chest. "I don't know what to say."

"Say you'll move in with me. I don't want to fix your problems. I want to give you the tools to fix them yourself, while also trying to move our relationship to the next level. If the last month has taught me anything, it's that I want a life with you, Jessie."

"What if I'm just after your money?"

"You're not."

"What makes you so sure?"

"This isn't about what I think, is it?"

"What do you mean?"

"The money thing is your issue. I know you're not interested in my bank balance."

"Everyone else will think it."

"Who else and why do they matter?" He sighs, laying his hands on my hips. "If you want to live alone, I'll help you find somewhere. But will you at least think about moving in here with me?"

"If I say no?"

"This place will remain empty until you change your mind. I'm not letting you walk away from me again, Jessie. I won't live here without you."

"What if I don't want to live here?"

He laughs because he knows I'm all out of shitty arguments. "We'll sell it and choose a place together."

I lay my palms on his chest. "You're so certain we belong together."

"Aren't you?" The dare flashes in his eyes, the same one from that first afternoon we spent together. In the seconds it takes me to answer, I realise Calvin has done exactly what he set out to do. He has shown me that I needed a partner, not a sex toy.

"Challenge accepted, Calvin Dean."

About The Author

Emma had a dream. It took a long time to realise that dream.

When it finally happened, it came via a career as a pre-school teacher, becoming a Mum of three, and 15 years as an army wife, following her husband from posting to posting across the UK and Europe while he served his country. She and her family have now left the army bubble and settled in their forever home of Spain.

In between masquerading as a domestic goddess and drinking gallons of sangria in the name of staying cool she has, at last, sat down and listened to the voices in her head.

Emma writes strong female leads who enjoy running in circles around the men who turn to mush for them. Her books can be dark and twisty, with bloodshed before the happy ever after, but she'll get you there. Eventually.

https://www.amazon.com/Emma-Jayne-Mills/e/B077JYXR85

Hollywood & Vibe

Fancy Roberts

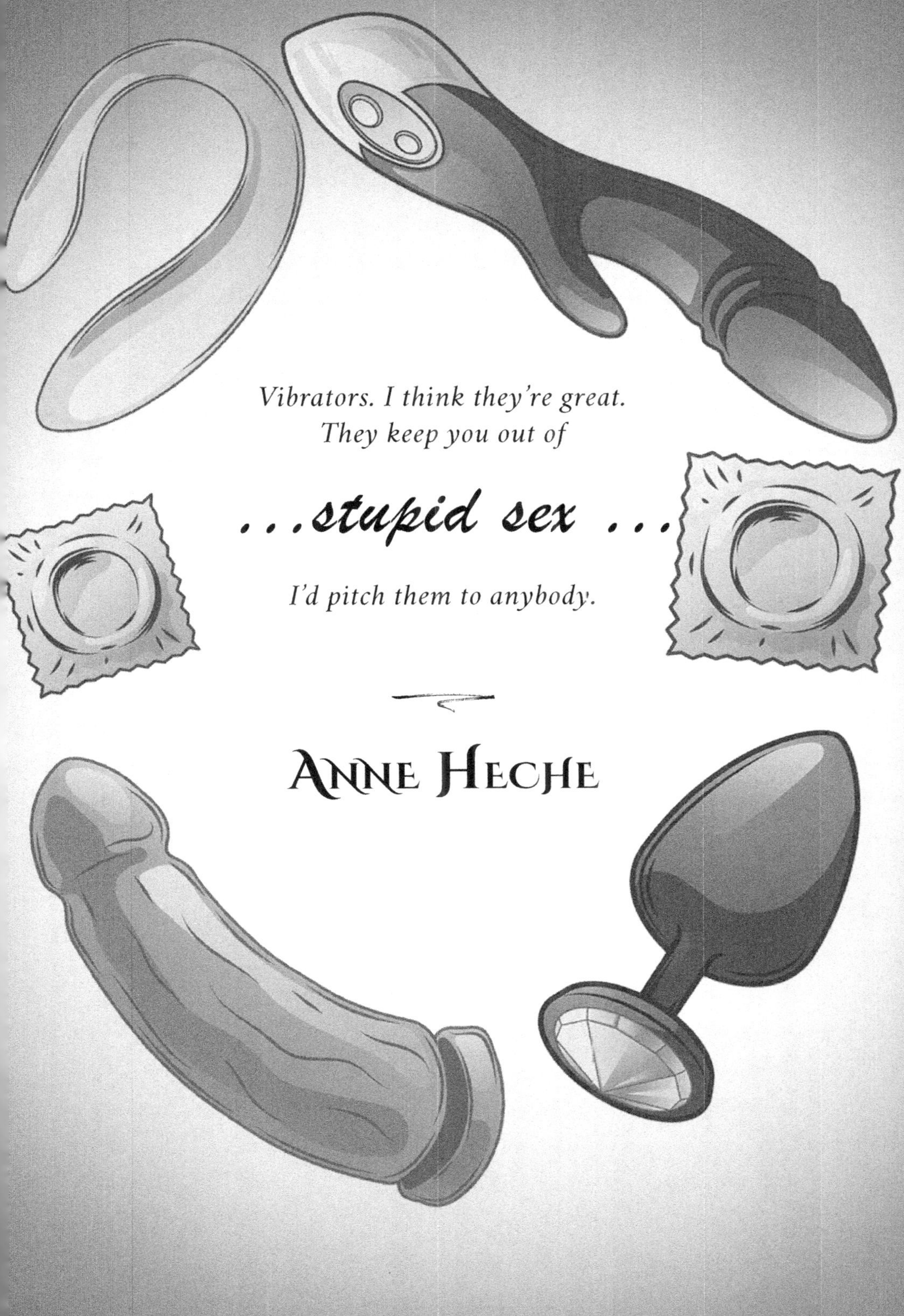

Vibrators. I think they're great.
They keep you out of

...*stupid sex* ...

I'd pitch them to anybody.

Anne Heche

One

Casey

"When I regret this in the morning, please remind me that I was fully sober when I made this decision." My stomach rumbles, full of rice, beans and hole-in-the-wall carnitas goodness. "God, I miss good Mexican food."

"You should be home more often then." Garrett's eyes twinkle as he looks me over from head to toe. I stretch my arms over my head and lean back in the chair, groaning in satisfaction.

"You know, some people would say it was weird that I flew all the way to Los Angeles to eat cheap tacos with an ex, but I would argue it was one hundred percent worth it."

"An advantage of being the star of the movie, I suppose?" Garrett teases. "Did they really charter a plane from bum-fuck Montana just so you could have the tacos you wanted?"

"A plane was chartered and I got the tacos I wanted." I wink. "Take that however you want. But truthfully, I have a meeting tomorrow morning and they needed my fine ass here in person." I eye Garrett as he leans back in his chair, mimicking my pose. His green eyes have been impossible to resist since we were kids, and his artfully messy brown hair has my fingers itching to tug on those strands. Heat washes through me and I allow a little of it to creep into my eyes, where I know he can see it. Garrett and I may have enough history for a ten-hour Ken Burns documentary, but the one place we never had problems was in the bedroom. Despite everything we've been through, he's one of the few people in the world I trust. And we still can't keep our hands off each other.

"Well..." His eyes rake over every inch of my exposed skin in the short sundress I'm wearing. "I guess that makes me one lucky bastard." Garrett's lower lip catches between his teeth and the lust in my eyes is mirrored in his. He pushes back from the table, drops a bill on it, and reaches out to take my hand. "Not to sound like a cliche, but ...Do you want to get out of here?"

"Aye, aye, Captain." I giggle as he takes my hand to pull me out of my seat. It's been years since he was cast in that superhero movie and I still laugh every damn time. I follow him out of the little restaurant, hanging back so I can admire the view. Damn, that truly is America's ass.

"I know you're staring."

"We both know you love it."

We weave our way through the restaurant to the back door, hightailing it out before we're recognized. Pushing open the back door, the black town car the studio loaned me for the night is waiting, with another one parked right behind it.

Just as well they're parked out back. Nothing screams "hey, someone important is here!" like two unmarked cars. But this is LA, everyone is *someone* here. My theory is that it's the traffic—we all want to be important enough to not have to deal with it.

Guess what?

Even Casey Sutton, America's Sweetheart, Precocious-Child-Star-turned-Serious-Actress, gets stuck in traffic.

Well, my driver gets stuck in traffic.

I shoot a grin at Garrett. "Wanna reduce your carbon footprint?"

He growls at my use of our old code, eyes glinting. Back in the day, when he and I had been co-stars on the same werewolf teen drama, we'd share a limo or a car in the name of reducing our greenhouse gas emissions.

We also had a lot of sex in the back of those shared limos.

"Anything for the environment."

Laughing, I slide into the back of the car, my bare legs sticking to the leather, Garrett right behind me. I hit the privacy button as Garrett's hands slide around my waist, hauling me onto his lap.

He buries his face in my neck. "I missed how good you smell." His words tickle my skin, his lips following. Pressing hot kisses along my jaw to my ear, he takes the lobe between his teeth, pinching, while his hands slide up my thighs, my thin cotton sundress sliding up to my hips. The familiar shape of his erection presses against me, reminding me of how good we are together. When we're not fighting.

I grind my hips, like scratching an itch, the relief of it flooding through me. "Just tonight, right? This doesn't mean anything." I moan, determined to believe the words this time. They're the same words I say every time I see this man. Maybe one day I'll mean them.

"Just tonight, like always." He groans as I press down harder, my hands sliding up to cup the back of his head the way I know he likes. "Casey …" His words are hardly more than a breath. I dig my thumbs into his neck, taking the weight of his head in my hands. Boneless, Garrett sinks back into the leather seat, arms flopped on the bench, at my mercy. "Ugh. Damn it Case, how do you do that?"

"It's like riding a bike, babe. I know all your secrets." I lean in close, taking my turn to trace his jaw with my lips. His stubble is rough and I relish the tingle telling me I'll still feel the mark tomorrow morning. How is it possible I forget how good he feels? How our bodies know each other inside out?

The car stops and starts as we make our way through downtown LA to the hotel, Garrett and I making out like teenagers the entire way. Just like we did when we were hormone-riddled adolescents. If all those tourists milling around the corner of Hollywood and Vine knew what was happening in the back seat as we crawl past them, America would lose its collective mind.

As tempting as it is to strip right there in the back of the car, we've both had too many close calls with the paparazzi to risk it. If this was Rosco, my personal driver, I'd consider it. But he's taking a well-earned vacation back in Montana and I hadn't wanted to cut it short for one impromptu trip.

There's probably already some asshole with a photo of us from the restaurant that'll end up on TMZ tomorrow with the headline, "America's Sweethearts Sweet

On Each Other Again?" or some bullshit like that. Why everyone is so obsessed with us getting back together is beyond me. As far as the public knows, we dated for a year almost ten years ago, that's it. But America can't let it go. The scandal that caused our breakup back then has something to do with it. Hollywood loves a good comeback story, right?

The fact that every time we see each other we end up in bed together might suggest the public is on to something. But neither of us would ever admit it.

There's a knock on the privacy screen as the car stops again. "Ms. Sutton? We've arrived. I pulled up to the back entrance, I assumed you didn't want to go through the front together." The driver's voice pulls me from my exploration of Garrett's shoulders.

"Thank you." I peer out the window, there's no one around, just the private elevator to the hotel. Not trusting someone isn't hiding, I step out first so I can check. "Coast is clear." I reach back for Garrett's hand and we dash to the elevator door, giggling like kids.

Inside the elevator, we behave, aware of the security cameras always watching. With his baseball cap pulled low over his eyes, Garrett keeps his head down and his hands to himself. I wish we had the luxury of not caring, but that ship sailed for both of us before we'd even gone through puberty.

"So, what's the movie they need your fine ass here for?" Garrett's voice is rough with need which has me pressing my thighs together, an ache forming low in the pit of my stomach. Dry humping him while we made out in the car was not enough, a taste of what I know it's like to be with him. It's never enough.

Despite how full my belly is from dinner, I'm ravenous.

"It's a biopic on Betty Dodson." If Garrett thinks talking about work will help me keep my hands to myself, for once he's wrong.

"Who?" He rocks back on his heels, hands jammed in his pockets, as the numbers go up.

I don't have time to answer before the elevator stops and the doors slide open. The hallway is empty as he follows me to my room, his eyes burning into my back as I lead the way. "She was a feminist in the seventies who taught women how to masturbate." I keep my voice down as we walk, distracting myself so I can keep my hands off the solid chest and shoulders I know are hiding beneath the soft t-shirt he's wearing.

I fumble with the keycard, almost dropping it when Garrett steps up close behind me, his warmth enveloping me, the familiar scent of his cologne both comforting and driving a sharp ache through my core. I miss that scent. I miss having my pillows and sheets smell like him.

Finally, I manage to get the door unlocked and we tumble inside. The second we're away from prying eyes, Garrett's hands are on me. My back hits the door, Garrett's lips already on mine. He kisses me like I'm the air he needs. It's tender, soft, and I can't take it. I don't want this Garrett. This Garrett is too precious, will drag up all those pesky feelings I was determined not to have tonight. Soft Garrett is my undoing.

I nip at his bottom lip instead, my hands sliding under his shirt, pushing it up so I can get my greedy hands on his body. He's even more built than the last time I saw him, the body of a god among men. The ridges of his abs and hard outline of his pecs under my fingers are almost enough to distract me from the way his fingers are exploring my torso. He may only pretend to be a superhero on the big screen, but none of the muscles every woman in America drools over are CGI.

Grinning, I pull back from the kiss so I can pull his shirt over his head. "Looking for the zipper?" I have to keep things light. I'm leaving tomorrow night. Playing up my teasing words, I stretch my arms above my head, bracing them against the door. "Happy hunting."

With a growl, Garrett crowds me, his hands sliding up my arms to twine his fingers in mine, pinning them to the door. "Still a fucking tease, huh Casey? I don't have anywhere else to be." He leans in close, his whispered words vibrating against my ear, sending waves of pure lust shivering down my spine. "I can do this all night." He makes his point by dragging that firm, talented tongue of his down my skin. Goosebumps cover my body, and I don't stop my gasp when he bites down on that magic spot where my neck and shoulder meet.

I jerk my arms down, but he shakes his head, lips caressing my collarbone.

"Stay." That commanding tone? That's the real secret to Garrett Garland's success. He holds both my wrists in one hand while the other drops to my chin, angling my face up towards him. "I haven't seen you in over a year Case, I'm taking my fucking time. Do Not. Move." Each word is punctuated with a roll of his hips against mine. The fabric of his jeans pushes my dress up with the movement, baring my thighs to the friction he's creating between us.

Did I mention we both got our breakout roles as kids playing dancers? The things this man can do with his body are positively unfair. Dropping to his knees, Garrett kisses his way up my thighs, his head disappearing under my dress so all I can do is *feel*. I close my eyes, head back against the door as he works his way up. The anticipation of not knowing fills me. "Oh! Yes." The word hisses out of me as Garrett presses an open-mouthed kiss to my core, over my silk thong. The heat of his mouth through the fabric has my already wet panties soaked.

Teasing me with his tongue, Garrett traces the edge of the fabric, from the waistband down to where I'm aching for him, first on one side, then on the other—never quite touching me where I need him most. The bastard knows exactly what he's doing, and I'm torn between taking my hand and shoving his face into me or wallowing in the tension he's building.

Garrett's hands slide up the back of my thighs to squeeze my ass, his tongue and lips still teasing me. Without missing a beat, he slides my thong down my legs, stuffing it in his back pocket. "Mmmmm, hello old friend." His breath against my bare lips spirals me even higher.

"Not old …definitely a friend. She missed you too." My head thumps against the door as my hips jerk forward, searching for a way to get that magic tongue where I need it. Instead of doing what I want—because why would he?—Garrett pulls his head out from under my dress. I glare at him for abandoning his post but he smirks back, those famous green eyes of his never leaving mine.

He holds my gaze as he pushes upright, not like a normal human. Nope. Garrett slides his chest up my body, his hands touching every inch of my skin from my calves to my shoulder blades, his hips rolling against mine. Because when Garrett does something he *does* it. God, I want him to do me.

Two

Garrett

All we need is Ginuwine's *Pony* to play in the background and this private performance of *Magic Mike* would be complete. But that's old news, we did that the night of the premier years ago.

Casey's breathy giggle turns to a moan as I press my hips into hers. I need this woman and I need her now. My dick aches and twitches against her stomach, demanding to be allowed to join the fun. Her sweet pussy is his favorite companion.

Picking her up, her legs wrapping around my hips, I walk us to the bed. I'm about to drop her on it so I can strip that damned dress off her when a familiar black silicone shape catches my eye. "Is that what I think it is?"

"Is what?" Casey's big brown eyes dart around the room.

I set her down, then point to the rather large, black vibrator laying on the bed. "Did you bring a *vibrator* with you on an overnight work trip? Damn Casey, I didn't realize you were so hard up out there in Montana." Struggling not to chuckle, I opt to toe off my shoes and unbutton my jeans.

"Fuck." Casey flops back on the bed, one arm thrown over her face. "Jesus Christ, I'm glad it was you I brought back to the room. I forgot I left it out."

The idea that she might have brought someone else back here rips a growl from deep inside me, my fingers stilling on the zipper of my jeans. Fuck that.

Casey Sutton belongs to me, like I belong to her. It doesn't matter that we haven't been able to make a real relationship work between us—Hollywood executives, her mother, and the paparazzi saw to that. But deep in our souls, since we were kids chasing each other around a TV soundstage, we've been a team. Casey

Sutton and Garrett Garland—Hollywood's "It" Couple. Cassette. I'm pretty sure the pair of us keep the gossip rags in business.

I eye the vibrator on the bed. The vibrator I gave her. It had been a promotional item from the same movie we'd celebrated together two years ago. We'd made good use of it that night. I'm torn between satisfaction at knowing she's made use of it since that night and raging at the thought of anyone except me having the pleasure of making Casey orgasm. Even an inanimate object.

I know it's stupid, but I can't help myself. "Why do you have a vibrator with you, Casey?"

"It's dumb."

"It's dumb that you can't go one night without getting off? You realize I jack off at least once a day, right?" I abandon getting undressed and climb onto the bed, straddling her hips. I'm too curious to let it go without getting to the bottom of this. Besides, we have all night to get to the good stuff.

Casey peeks at me from under her arms and I circle my hips against hers, mostly to make her laugh, but damn it feels good. "Promise you won't laugh?" The vulnerability in her eyes tugs at something in me. Not many people get to see this side of Casey.

"I'll do my best. But I may not be able to help myself." I wink. A patented Garrett Garland wink. I know it doesn't work on her, she knows me too well to be swayed by my flirting, but it makes her laugh which is what I wanted anyways. Sex with Casey may be amazing, but her laughter is pure heaven.

She sits up, leaning back on her elbows so she can look me in the eye. "Betty Dodson, that woman I told you about? She used to have these group masturbation workshops for women. They'd use vibrators and practice giving themselves orgasms."

Damn, that's crazy.

Casey laughs at the expression on my face. "I know, it's bonkers, right? But also, she is so cool. I've been doing research on her for months. Seriously, Garrett, she's amazing."

"So, you brought the vibrator so you could get into character? Are you auditioning? Or did they already offer you the part?" Garrett Jr. is so confused by this conversation—the idea of Casey using the vibrator I gave her sends blood rushing to his head. But the idea of her having to audition for a part like this—the thought of some asshole director making her "prove" she can pull this part off—makes him shrivel up in my jeans.

Casey must see something in my expression because her eyes narrow at me. "I'm *producing* the movie. The vibrator was in case of emergency."

My eyebrows shoot up at her words.

Her expression softens and she shrugs. "I don't know why I brought it. I knew we were having dinner, but I didn't—" She bites her lip and closes her eyes.

Not looking at me, Casey keeps talking. "I wasn't counting on …this … happening. Last time we saw each other …"

Last time we'd seen each other our coffee date had been interrupted by fans wanting to know if we were back together. When we denied it, one of them threw herself in my lap, nearly unzipping my jeans in the middle of the coffee shop. To say it put a damper on our evening was an understatement. We've been in touch over the last year, but I don't think it's been a coincidence I haven't seen her in person.

Instead of letting her flounder for words, I lean down and capture her lips with mine. "We don't need to talk about it now." I work her dress up around her waist. Sitting up, I reach over and grab the vibrator. "Maybe he can play too." I kiss her again, swallowing her protests.

Casey guides my hand to her side. I wrap my hands around her rib cage, thumbs brushing the underside of her breasts. The zipper of her dress brushes against my hand. "Ah, found it." I lean down, one arm braced on the bed beside her head, nibbling along her collarbones while my free hand works the zipper down. I sit up so I can pull the dress off her.

She doesn't speak, just slides her hands along my torso, kissing the tattoo of an old-school Walkman on my ribs. Cassette. The stupid name the media dubbed us, but it became our own private joke, the tattoo a reminder of the girl who knows me better than anyone, even if life fucks us over every time we try to be together. "Jesus, Casey. How are you more beautiful every damn time I see you?"

She's always been slender, but ten years as Hollywood's Girl-Next-Door means her body is a work of art. I drink her in, studying to see if anything has changed in the year since I've seen her. Her breasts are still the same perfect handful they've always been, her curves toned and firm. Like me, part of her job is to look good. I spend hours a day working out, Casey is no less dedicated. It sucks, but it's part of the job.

"Garrett," Casey whispers. "I need you." She slides her hands into my hair, pulling me to her. I revel in the tug of her fingers as I pay homage to the masterpiece in front of me. I go back to the breasts I wasn't able to appreciate earlier, pulling the tip of one nipple between my teeth before closing my lips over it. Casey moans as I swirl my tongue and suck it to a peak. My hand runs along the soft skin of her stomach, seeking her other nipple, plucking it between my fingers once I find it.

My hips roll against hers of their own accord as I take my time, giving each of her tits the attention it deserves. "So beautiful." I whisper the words over and over between kisses.

Her hands glide down my back, kneading and pulling at me as I draw pleasure from her. "Oh god, Garrett. I forgot …I forgot how good that was." Her voice is quiet, as if she doesn't know she's saying it out loud. I hum against her skin, pressing open-mouth kisses along her taut abdomen.

Patting the bed beside me, my hand finds what it was looking for. I flip the switch, letting Garrett the Third, yes that the vibrator's name now, buzz in my hand. As I make my way down to her hip, to the apex of her thighs, I touch the vibrator to one of the nipples I just left, still shiny from my mouth. Casey's moan is music to my ears.

Giving in to my need to taste her, I take her sweetness in my mouth. Working my tongue against her clit, I side one finger inside her. I can't help the groan that escapes me at the taste of her, the warmth of her. The way she feels and tastes like everything I've ever wanted.

I slip another finger inside her, pumping my hand while my tongue works her fast then slow and the vibrator does his magic. Her moans and wordless exclamations pitch higher, telling me she's close. I pull away, running the vibrator down her belly to touch it to her clit, my fingers still pumping inside her.

"Garrett! So close." Casey writhes beneath me, her hips bucking from the added stimulation. It only takes a few more moments before she comes, her walls tightening around my fingers as she collapses back on the bed.

I pull the vibrator away, giving her a moment to rest while I dispose of my jeans and boxers. "Am I correct in guessing that you brought Garrett the Third along in case you ended up alone in your bed tonight? Baby, I'm hurt you didn't think I'd take care of you."

Breathless laughter rings out from Casey as I crawl back on the bed with her. "Garrett the Third?"

"Is he, or is he not, the same size as me?" I lay next to her on the bed, hauling her over to straddle my hips. My cock is still rock hard, jutting up between us. Casey wraps a hand around it, picking up the vibrator with the other. Grinning, she holds the vibrator up next to my dick. When it's obvious they're the same size, she bites her bottom lip and rocks her hips, grinding her clit against me.

"I don't know if they really compare—Garrett the Third is so smooth. And he vibrates. Can you vibrate?" Her cocky smirk pulls a growl from deep in my chest. "Oooo, so close." Fucking tease.

"You think I can't make you feel as good? There's a reason I named him 'the Third.' Third-rate compared to the real deal."

"I call bullshit. Maybe I'll ask Chad if he can vibrate." She doesn't stop pumping her hand up and down my cock, even as we talk. He's weeping for her, a drop of pre-cum glistening at the tip.

I dig my fingers into her hips and nod my chin in the vibrator's direction. "Don't. You. Dare. You're not going anywhere near that asshole's tiny dick." I thrust my hips up to punctuate each of my words. We're edging towards dangerous territory and she knows it. Chad Wilson, her current co-star, happened to be my co-star in said male-stripper movie. There's no love lost between us, partly because he's a slimy Hollywood douche, and partly because he won't stop asking Casey out.

Casey leans down to kiss me, her tongue sliding across mine until I can't remember what I was getting worked up about. "Hmmm, you don't quite vibrate, but I think you'll do. For now."

"No more talking." My last word ends in a gasp as Casey slides back on my thighs and, without warning, takes me in her mouth. "Fuuuuck, babe." I feel more than see her smile as my hips lift up off the bed. She's always loved being able to bring me to my knees like this.

She pulls up far enough to tap my leg and ask, "Condom?"

"In my wallet." She doesn't let up, her hot mouth working up and down my cock as she digs my wallet out of my jeans.

I'm lost in the perfection of her as she rips the packet. When she rolls the condom on before lowering herself onto me I lose all sense of time and place. There's just her and me, the rest of the world be damned.

She rides me slow and lazy, her hips rocking and circling above me. The orgasm building at the base of my spine wants me to grab her by the hips and slam into her, but I wait, biding my time. Closing my eyes, I recite lines from old movies in my head, distracting myself enough to let Casey take her time.

"Oh fuck," I grind out at the buzzing sensation at the base of my cock. I push up on my elbows. The most beautiful woman in the world is riding me, her head thrown back in ecstasy, her nails digging into my thighs as she touches the vibrator to her clit.

"Casey, baby, I'm going to come." My words are a growl.

"Then come. Come with me." Casey cries out as she tightens around me. Between her and the buzz of the vibrator, my own orgasm hits me like a freight train, racing down my spine. I empty myself, ripping the vibrator from her hand so I can pull her to me. Our mouths meet in a clash of tongues and lips.

"How do you do that?" I murmur against her once I've come back to earth.

"Do what?" Her coy smile doesn't hide the real question in her eyes.

"Get hotter every time? It's been ten years and I swear to God every time we're together is better than the last." I say all this between sweeps of my tongue against hers. I've loved Casey Sutton since we were kids, and I always will. Why aren't we together again? I ask myself the same question every damn time.

And every time I have to remind myself of the same answer.

Because I fucked it up.

THREE

CASEY

I sign my name with a flourish, crossing the "T's" in my last name like I'm slicing through the paper. Putting my autograph to something has never felt as good as this moment. The executives across the table from me flash their crocodile teeth, thinking they have any say in my movie.

Let them try. I've got enough money to throw at this to make their lives miserable if they cross me, and they know it. Maybe I'm extra sassy because I woke up this morning to another round of amazing sex with Garrett, but for the first time in my life I'm going to be the one in charge. No one is going to get to tell me what to do, who to be seen with, who *not* to be seen with.

"Gentleman, if we're done?" I push back from the table.

A weasel-faced man on the left clears his throat before I can walk away. "Ms. Sutton, before you go. We'd like to know if the rumors are true."

"Which one?" I sneer. "That my genius little brother is really my son? That I have a pain-killer addiction, or that I'm part of a cult and that's why I've been in Montana?" Those were just from this week. "You can see the one about me gaining fifty pounds and hiding away at a weight loss camp isn't true." I wave a hand up and down my body. Considering how much work I put into keeping a camera-ready physique, those are the ones that hit the secret, soft center of me the hardest.

The doughy Boomer next to him leers at me, raking his eyes across my body. I wait for him to make it up to my face before flipping him off. He coughs and averts his eyes. "Besides, why does it matter? I'm not in front of the camera for this one." Instead of leaning my hands down on the table the way a man would, giving them all a look down my shirt, I cross my arms over my chest, planting my feet wide, my heels giving me a few extra inches.

Weasel-face is the one who answers. "That you and Garrett Garland are back together. We would prefer if your relationship status could stay out of the papers. This movie is going to be controversial enough."

"I'm sorry, what the fuck?"

Doughy slides his phone across the table, a picture of Garrett on the street in front of my hotel splashed across the screen. "He was spotted this morning."

Shit.

"Garrett Garland is my good friend. I will not apologize for that. What we do is no one's business. Last time I checked we were adults, not the underage teenagers everyone seems to think we still are."

"His past ..."

"Is in the past. For starters, the whole ...lawsuit." I dare anyone to contradict me with a raised eyebrow. When no one does I continue speaking. "Was concocted by my darling mother and my former agent. You should know better than to bring it up. Besides, the charges were dropped—because they were ridiculous. Secondly, he's been sober for years."

"We're putting a lot of trust in you. This is your first time producing and you know this movie is going to draw a lot of criticism. It's about masturbation, for fuck's sake, Casey. You have to be squeaky clean, not give the paps any ammunition." Weasel-face doesn't let it go.

I know what they're going to say, but I ask anyway. I want them to say the words. So I can walk out of here and know exactly what I'm ignoring. "What are you saying?"

"We're asking you not to have any contact with Garrett."

"Not going to happen." I stalk to the door and wrench it open.

I seethe over their request the whole drive to the airport, the traffic giving me plenty of time to stew. How dare they tell me who I can and cannot spend time with. Who the fuck do they think they are?

My mother? Who took it upon herself to sign contracts for me to endorse everything from cereal to cars—that I wasn't even old enough to drive—and then stole half of the money from me?

Or my former agent, who not only was sleeping with my mom, but is the one who discovered a newly-eighteen Garrett and still-seventeen-year-old me in the back seat of a limo and concocted the accusations that ripped us apart? Sending Garrett on the path of self-destruction he's spent the last three years dragging himself out of.

Garrett.

There was something different about him last night. A tenderness in his touch I haven't felt for years. He hid it well, but glimmers of the Garrett I used to know kept peeking out. I itch to send him a message, but that would be breaking the rules. No sweet texts the day after.

I've been keeping my feelings for him locked down tight for years. Pretended to enjoy our trysts, always reminding us both that they don't mean anything—when in truth they meant *everything.* At first, he was so shattered by the accusations leveled against him that I did it to keep my own heart safe. The drugs, the drinking—they made him cruel. Seeing him back then was a way for both of us to get back at the people who had come between us, we didn't care that each time we both left a little more broken.

It would be impossible to recapture the wonder of the years we spent together as teens. We were so innocent back then, believing loving each other was enough, that nothing could come between us.

Ten years, a couple of stints in rehab—his in public, mine in private—and here we are. Maybe once I'm back in LA there can be more. Less acting, more reality.

I dig for my phone in my purse and shut it off, not trusting myself to resist temptation. Instead, I pull out my script and attempt to learn my lines for tomorrow. Only one month left to wrap up my current project, then I'm the one in charge.

By the time I land back in Montana I've gotten myself under control. I don't have the luxury of wallowing in my emotions right now, I have a movie to shoot. I don't turn my phone back on until I'm in the car being driven back to my temporary

Montana home. A barrage of emails and messages greet me, but there's only one that catches my eye.

Garrett: Sorry about the paps this morning, I thought I was home free.

Garrett: A little birdie told me the execs don't want you to be seen with me anymore.

Me: Did the same birdie tell you I told them to go fuck themselves? They can't tell me who to see.

It doesn't take long for Garrett to respond.

Garrett: Don't take a hit for me Case, it's not worth it.

How does this man not see he is worth everything to me? That I would drop everything to be with him if he asked? All these years, I've been waiting for him to come back to me. Even though the idea of it is terrifying, he knows exactly how to hurt me, I still love him. I always will.

Maybe I'm a better actress than everyone thinks I am.

I can't formulate an answer before the driver pulls up outside the cabin I've been calling mine for the last three months. The rustic log cabin isn't exactly my style, but the privacy can't be beat. The only other soul within a two mile radius of me is Rosco, my driver/security, the rest of the cast and crew are holed up on a ranch a few miles away.

I wait to respond to Garrett until I'm inside, my bag dumped out on the floor.

Me: You're my best friend. They can't tell me not to see you. I'll toss a "fuck off" to whomever I please.

I pull out a pair of cozy flannel pajamas, not the sexy kind, before I gather up my dirty clothes from the trip and toss them in the laundry for someone to pick up tomorrow. That damn vibrator falls out, nearly crushing my toe, so I toss it on the bed next to my phone.

Something starts buzzing against the blankets. Assuming I accidentally turned it on, I'm surprised to see it's Garrett video calling. He never calls the day after we see each other. Never.

Curious, I swipe to answer.

"Hey butt-face." Those green eyes are hypnotizing even through my tiny phone screen.

"Hey poop-head." My heart thumps at his use of our nicknames from the characters we played on that first TV show together. "I'm sure no one's told them to fuck off in at least a week. They were due."

His laugh is low and rumbling, before he sobers. "Casey Marie Sutton. Don't risk shit like that for me. It's not worth it." What he really means is that he thinks *he's* not worth it. I sit down on the edge of my bed, toeing off my shoes.

"Garrett Frederick Garland. You have been my best friend since you found me crying behind a fake staircase when we were eleven. You couldn't tell me what to do then, and you can't tell me what to do now."

His eyes crinkle as he smiles. "You've always been a stubborn pain in the ass. I'll never forget the look on that director's face. What was his name?"

"Shayne Melville. He was asking for it. Who the hell asks an eleven-year-old to act sexy?" I'd dumped his coffee in his lap, covering up my utter mortification behind righteous anger, then booked it off the set. The whole shoot had to be halted while they looked for me. Garrett had been the one to find me, curled up behind a set piece on the sound stage next door, crying hysterically, convinced I was going to be fired.

Garrett chuckles again at the memory. "They should have known what they were getting into with the pair of us, huh?" We'd been double trouble from that day on. Always getting into mischief together, daring each other and our cast mates to do more and more ridiculous stunts. Growing up the child stars of a hit sitcom, we'd shared the same weird life growing up. It was a bond no one else would ever understand.

We'd shared a lot of firsts. First awards show. First run in with a crazy fan. First morning talk show appearances. Garrett had been my first kiss, on screen and off.

"So, to what do I owe the pleasure? Besides useless warnings to behave?" I wanted to get away from reminiscing, from words that will make me miss him. I put the phone down on the bed so I can change into my flannel pajamas.

"I can't call just because I want to? What if I said I missed you already?"

"Garrett ..." I warned, not meaning it. I finish buttoning the top before picking the phone back up and crawling onto my bed, my body exhausted from the long day.

The screen spun for a second before his face came back into view, his head resting on his pillow, mirroring me. "Casey ..." He cleared his throat and the phone dipped, granting me a momentary view of his sculpted chest. I bit my bottom lip, trying to hide the shot of lust it sent straight to my core. "Look, I thought ...I don't know."

There's a long silence before he speaks again. "You're almost done shooting right?"

I nod, keeping silent. A tiny spark of hope ignites in my chest.

"And then you're going to be in LA for the foreseeable future? This biopic is the next thing on your calendar, right? I don't have any shoots out of town for a while. What if we ...?"

I need to make sure I'm not wishing for things that will never be. "Are you saying you want to see me when I'm home? You know I'll always want to hang out."

He brings the phone closer to his face, to the sculpted work of art that has dozens of Instagram fan accounts dedicated to it. "Casey. I want to take you out on a real date. I'm tired of watching you walk away from me. Of being the one to walk away from you."

Why couldn't he have said this last night?

"Don't you think we're going to hurt each other again?" I whisper the words into the dark of my cabin. "Isn't what we have now safer? Last time we tried ..."

Garret growls. "Last time we tried being together, I was still using, and you had just left that toxic douchebag. Neither of us were healthy, and you know it." His voice softens. That had been a few years ago, two weeks of constant sex and fighting had been enough to prove that as powerful as our chemistry is, we weren't ready. "But babe. That was years ago. We've both put in the work. And last night ... last night was different. You felt it too, I know you did."

He's not wrong. Over dinner he'd told me about the therapist he's been seeing for the last year. It's not the first therapist he's seen, but it sounds like he's found someone he really clicks with. In every word of our conversation he was different, a lightness had come back into his life. In between our standard outrageous flirting, we'd shared truths and apologies that were years overdue. But we've always been like that, able to flip from serious to ridiculous in the space of a sentence.

"I'm in Montana for another month, Garrett."

Almost as if he'd been waiting for my objections, Garett answers immediately. "What's a month when we've been waiting for each other for years? Maybe it's better this way. You know how it is when we see each other, Case. It's fuck first, ask questions later." He grins to take the sting out of his words, and I can't help giggling. It's true.

His next words have me choking on that giggle. "Besides, you have Garrett the Third with you. Not quite as good as the original, but he'll do for a proxy."

I flip the covers over my head, hiding my burning cheeks from him. I don't know why his words have me so flustered, I'm no prude. Maybe it's the emotion behind them, that for the first time in years this is more than just scratching an itch. "Cas-ey." His quiet sing-song has me peeking back out. "Where is Garrett the Third?" There's an edge to his question.

I push down the covers and grab the vibrator. "Right here." A trickle of heat runs through me at the idea. After last night, I know that the vibrator is the same length and width of the real Garrett. I run my fingers over it, imagining it's him.

"Already on the bed, huh?" He flashes his Hollywood smirk at me.

"Yeah well, he almost broke my toe earlier. I'm not sure he deserves to be rewarded right now." I glare at the offending silicone, giving it a hard poke.

There's a rustling noise on the speaker and Garrett disappears for a second before coming back into view. "Well now, we can't have that. He'll need to apologize. Thoroughly." There's movement on the bed as he talks.

"Are you ..."

"Take your pajamas off, Casey." The command in his voice silences my objections. This isn't Garrett my childhood partner-in-crime, this is Garrett Garland, sexiest man alive. Seriously, he's been on the cover at least three times.

So instead of giving him attitude, I do what he says. On my terms. I flip on the bedside lamp so he can see, then stand up, propping my phone on the nightstand. "Give me one second." I tap a few buttons to turn on some music. I debate between going old or new school for a second, but settle on something that's not going to ruin the moment. The hard beat of The Arctic Monkeys *Do I Wanna Know?* breaks the silence of my cabin.

"Christ, woman. You'll be the death of me." His words are encouragement to keep going. He's not the only one of us that can do sinful things with their body.

He's angled his phone so I can see his chest but no lower, just the steady movement of his arm stroking himself while I tease. My hands tap against my hip bones as I dance, a sultry, smooth, rolling through my spine. I run my hands up the sides of my waist, twisting my hips from side to side and piling my hair up in my arms. My face hidden before I let it drop, cascading down my back.

"Casey."

I ignore him, lost in moving my body. Reminding myself of how it felt last night when we were together. I'm sliding my hands inside the front of my flannel pants when Garrett's strained voice cuts through.

"Casey. Baby, don't be cruel. Lose the clothes."

I freeze, fingers centimeters away from touching myself. "Were you getting lonely over there?" My teasing words light a fire in his eyes. Instead of torturing him anymore, I hook my thumbs over the waistband of my pants and push them down, leaving me in the button down top. It shouldn't be sexy, but the hem brushing against the bare skin of my hips and pussy is turning me on more than I could have imagined.

I keep teasing him, unbuttoning the top and dropping it to the floor while I dance, dragging it out for as long as I can stand it. Garrett watches, rapt, his arm moving the whole time. "Wish you were here." My words are a whisper as I sit on the bed, bringing the phone with me as the song ends.

"Grab the vibrator Casey. I want to watch you."

"Maybe I want to watch you, too. You've been keeping the goods out of sight."

Garrett doesn't answer, just moves the phone so I can see the hard length of his cock gripped in his fist.

"Is your proxy allowed to join the party now?" I ask, reaching for the vibrator.

At his nod, I flip it on and touch it to my inner thigh, a moan escaping me at the sensation.

"Yes baby. Are you thinking of me? Imagining that's my tongue on your skin, tasting you? You taste like heaven." Garrett's words are spinning me higher as I drag the vibrator to the apex of my thighs. "Let me see." Garrett's "please," is more of a grunt, but I let my knees fall open anyway, letting him see how turned on I am.

My eyes never leave his as I work the vibrator, running it up and down my slit until I can't take it a second later. His expressive face is glued to my hand and the vibrator. His tongue darts out to lick his lip before his bottom lip rolls between his teeth as I slide the vibrator inside of me. I work it in long strokes that match the rhythm of his own hand on his cock.

We're both moaning and whispering incoherent endearments, working ourselves up and egging each other on. "Garrett, I'm so close. I need you." My hips buck as I slip the silicone I wish was his tongue across my clit, so sensitive it's almost painful.

"I'm almost there, baby. Touch your tits for me. Tell me how it feels."

In my desperation to fall over the edge, I claw at my breast, rolling and plucking at the pink tip. "It feels so good. I wish it was you though, your teeth, on me."

I keep working the vibrator while I drag my nails across my torso. I remind myself not to leave any marks that might be visible tomorrow when I shoot. "Garrett, I'm coming. Come with me, babe." My orgasm hits me fast and so hard I see black for a second. I catch Garrett's groan as he comes too, emptying himself on his glorious abs and chest.

"Fuck, Casey. That was …" Garrett flops back on his bed, the pillows and blanket obscuring him from my view for a second.

I curl up onto my side so I can watch him. His chest is rising and falling, breathing hard. I pat Garrett the Third with a silent thank you for a job well done.

"Will you make it a month without giving yourself a heart attack?" I tease. Not looking at the screen, Garrett flips me the bird, making me laugh. "Glad to know you haven't changed that much after all."

"Gimme a second, babe. I can't feel my legs."

FOUR

GARRETT

Click

"Garrett! Is it true that you and Casey Sutton are back together?"

Click

"Garland! Garrett! What about the rumor she's been seen cozying up to Chad Wilson? Is she cheating on you already?"

Click

"What does her mother think about you and Casey dating again?"

Click

Click

Click

"Garrett! Garrett!"

I tune out the hounding and the words meant to get a reaction out of me and slide into the back seat of the car waiting for me. The buzz of my phone is almost drowned out by the cacophony of paparazzi. Surprised at the name on the caller ID, I answer. "Teddy?"

"Garrett." Casey's younger brother growls my name.

"How the hell did you get this number?" No one has this number except my inner circle. I don't give it out to anyone. "Did Casey give it to you? Is she okay?"

"Genius computer hacker, remember?" The smirk in Teddy's voice is audible. That little fucker. He's about to graduate from MIT and already has a bidding war from some venture capitalists on the program he created for his senior thesis.

"Casey's fine, as far as I know. Why? Should I be concerned?"

I fidget in my seat as the driver turns onto the freeway. "No reason that I know of." Since Casey cut ties with their mother over the false accusations against me, Teddy is the only family she has and they're tight. He and I have never been super close, understandable after the way I treated his sister before I got clean, but I've always liked him.

"You want to tell me why I keep getting news alerts about you guys? Casey told me you two were 'seeing where things went' but I don't trust you. Last time you did this she spent months crying over you and refusing to say your name. Do you know how hard it is to avoid your handsome fucking face? It was torture, for both of us."

"Teddy, I swear, it's different this time." The dirty, run-down buildings of the LA outskirts flash past my window.

"I'm pretty sure you said that last time too. What is different this time, man? You know Casey. She's not as tough as she looks. She puts on that 'I don't give a shit' front to hide her squishy, soft center. But she has no defenses against you and you know it."

He's right. "I know. I know all the ways I can hurt her, the same way she can hurt me too. But we've been taking it slow."

Teddy snorts and I grin.

"Well, we've been trying. Her being in another state helped." There was no way I could have gone to visit her without every pap in the western United States finding out, so we've been limited to phone and video chats. It's been hard, but worth it to force ourselves to slow down. "Listen, Teddy. I get it. But I love your sister. I've always loved her. I've been sober for three years now. Did she tell you I've been in therapy?"

"Yeah, she did." There's still doubt in Teddy's voice but less than a moment ago.

"Listen, I give you permission to kick my ass the next time I screw up, but I swear to you it's different—it's real—this time." A sign for the airport flashes overhead. "Teddy, I gotta go."

"I'm holding you to that. Give her a hug for me, I assume you're picking her up at the airport?"

"Yes I am. Will do." I hang up and tuck my phone back in my pocket, fixing the baseball cap and sunglasses I pretend will hide me from the prying eyes of the public. Meeting her here like this is a risk, but I can't wait another second to see her.

The car pulls around to a smaller, private entrance where the chartered plane is going to land. She flew back with some of her co-stars and crew. I climb out and lean against the car, waiting for the glint of dark hair I've been missing. Chad Wilson jerks his chin at me as he walks past to his own car.

"Hey man, you picking up Casey?"

"Yup." I don't take my eyes off the group of people descending the stairs of the plane. Chad doesn't walk off like I expected. I eye him over the top of my aviators. "You got something you need to say?"

"We had dinner one time because neither of us could stand being holed up in our cabins one more night. She was telling me about you the whole time."

He's nervous. I can't blame him. Last time he took Casey out to dinner I'd shown up, more than a little drunk, and given him a black eye. I take momentary pleasure in the way he shifts his weight from foot to foot. In another life, without the pressure of Hollywood, we could have been friends. Maybe we still can be. He and Casey are, and I'm man enough to be fine with it.

It's past time for me to make the first move. I extend a hand to Chad. "Nah, we're cool. I trust her."

Slim arms wrap around my waist from behind as Chad shakes my hand. "You have no idea how much that means to me." Casey's words send my heart thumping in my chest. After all the fights, the harsh words between us, our past threatening to ruin everything, something so simple as those words means more to the pair of us than anyone will ever know.

"I think that's my cue to exit." Chad tosses a wave and jogs off to the car waiting for him behind mine.

I pull Casey in front of me and wrap her up in my arms. "I missed you." I dive in for a kiss, her lips yielding and soft under mine. "Should we go home?"

"You are my home." Casey sighs against me, her words sending my heart soaring. Finally. I'm going to do everything possible to deserve this girl. "But sure, let's go to my place. Garrett the Third is ready for a vacation, he's been clocking in a lot of overtime this month."

Epilogue

Click

"Casey! Is it true you and Garrett are on the verge of divorce?"

I roll my eyes, taking another few steps down the red carpet. They were so desperate for us to get back together, now that we're a boring married couple all they want is the divorce. There's no winning, so we just ignore them.

Click

"Casey! Over here!"

I turn my head to smile for the cameraman calling my name.

"Have you seen the pictures of Garrett at The Green Room? Is he using again?"

I scowl, my stomach threatening to empty itself for a second, before the feeling passes.

"Garrett is fine." It's all I can bring myself to say without cursing. I take another few steps down the gauntlet, my long silver dress trailing behind me.

Click

Click

"Casey!" I stop, letting Garrett catch up.

"What happened?" I lean close so he can kiss my cheek. His hand on my hip is warm and comforting through the fabric of my dress. We pause and smile, working the crowd without paying attention.

"I had a minor malfunction."

"What does that mean," I whisper through my smile. "Are you okay?"

Garrett's hand drifts across my belly, still flat but not for much longer, and he smiles. "I'm great, babe. But Marcia pointed out the can of ginger ale I slipped in my pocket for you looked a little suspect."

I whirl to face him, laughter bubbling up inside me. "You'd do that for me?"

"Casey Marie Sutton Garland." Garrett pulls me close, and I grab him by the lapels of his tux. "I'd do anything for you. And Garrett Junior."

I smack his chest. "We are not calling *her* Garrett Junior."

"Well, we can't call him Garrett the Third." Garrett waggles his eyebrows at me and I laugh, ignoring the flurry of clicks and shouts behind me.

"Why do I put up with you?" I gasp as he spins me to face the cameras waiting for us, wrapping one hand around my waist and pulling me against his side.

He leans down to whisper in my ear. "I don't know, but I'm sure glad you do."

About The Author

Fancy Roberts likes her heroes how she likes her coffee—hot, strong, and at least twice a day. Classy on the outside and sassy on the inside, Fancy loves nothing more than to drop a well-timed profanity and tell a sexy story.

Just like her, Fancy's heroines are more than meets the eye and give as good as they get. The road to their happily ever after may be rocky, but she promises everyone gets what they deserve in the end.

Besides, who doesn't love a woman who orders a whiskey, neat, then tells you a dirty joke while wearing a twinset and pearls?

https://www.amazon.com/Fancy-Roberts/e/B0979KCDHW

Mercy's Chase

Claire Marta

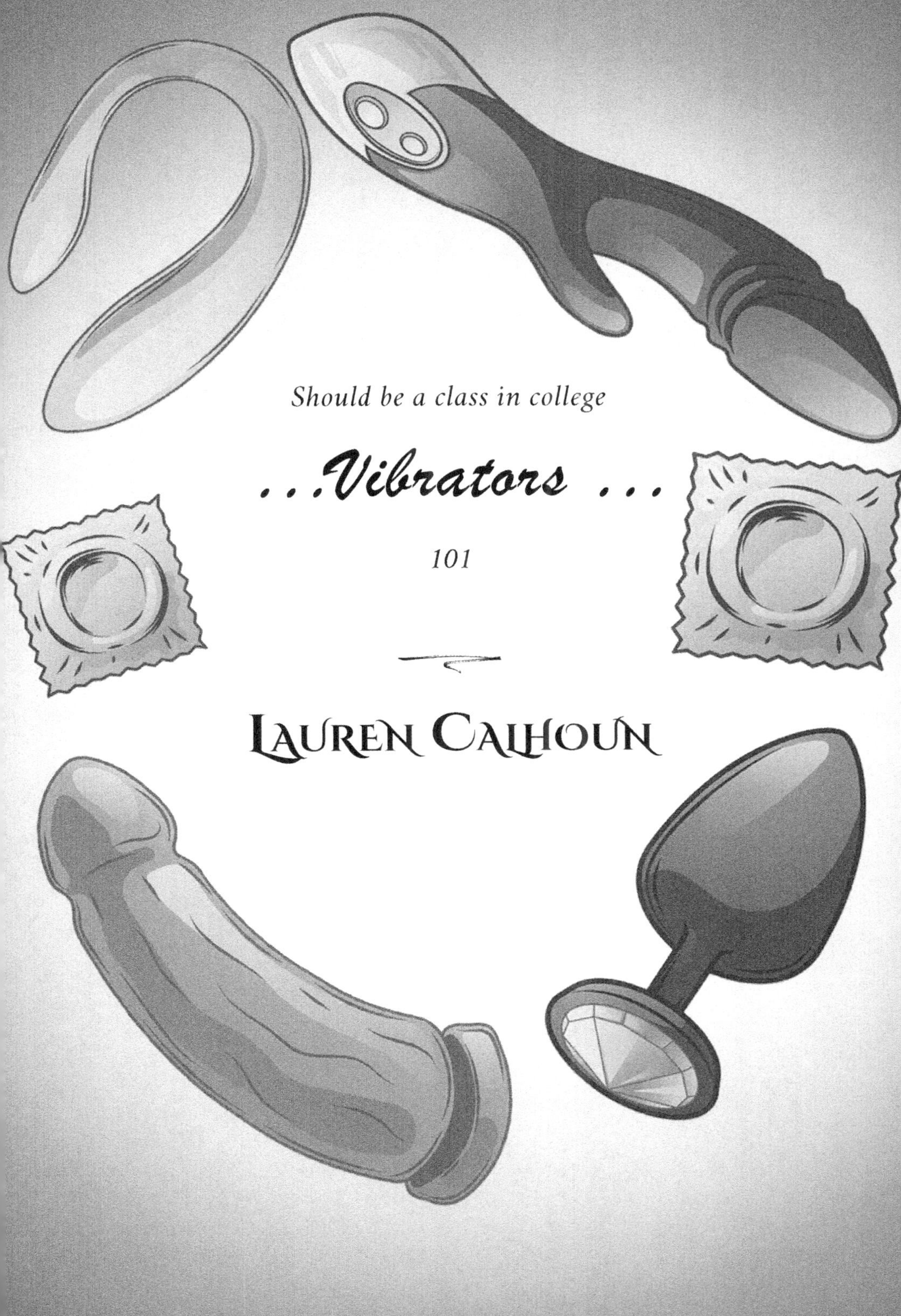

Should be a class in college

...Vibrators ...

101

Lauren Calhoun

One

Mercy

Mercy Williams had only entered the raffle to help out the animal shelter. The thought of all those poor helpless cats and dogs made her heart all fuzzy and warm. Who would have known she'd actually win first prize?

Gnawing on her lip, she wondered what the heck she should do with the golden ticket in her hand. An all-inclusive three evenings to a very exclusive London kink club was something she'd only dreamt about. Mostly in the privacy of her bedroom with her nose buried in one of her romance books and her hand between her legs while she read the steamy bits. The kind of stories her best friend Wilder always teased her about.

All the kink she'd obsessed over in secret from the pages of her favorite novels. For three evenings, she had a chance to explore, be someone she'd always dreamed of being. She could sexually experiment where a safeword could protect her if her courage ebbed.

Stuffing the ticket back into the envelope, she placed it in her bag. It was lunchtime, and like every Wednesday, she was waiting in her car outside Wilder's work. They always ate together on this day, frequenting the same place they'd found the first day they'd met. With her assistant running the flower shop she owned while she was out, she had nothing to worry about. Vanessa was a sweetheart and was more than happy to do it.

Her thoughts were cut off when the car door opened, and Wilder slid into the passenger seat. "Hey."

With thick blond hair, broad-shoulders, and a lean-hipped body set off by the faded jeans and black shirt he was dressed in, he could easily grace the cover of magazines with his good looks.

"You ready to eat?" She was distracted by the cloud of cologne that surrounded him. Something popular, she guessed. He was always following the latest fashion and fads.

Clicking on his seatbelt, he turned clear green eyes her way. "Let's go. I'm starving! By the way, your order came in."

In the process of maneuvering the car out onto the road, Mercy widened her eyes and shot him a look. "Oh ...you have it with you?"

Wilder was already in the process of tugging it out of his backpack. "You paid for it, so I thought it would save you a trip coming into the shop."

To her relief, he kept the box the vibrator came encased in within the conspicuous pink plastic bag as he twisted and dropped it onto the backseat.

"That's so sweet of you."

"Next week is the anniversary of when we first met," Wilder reminded her. "We should do something to celebrate it."

Mercy bit her lip as she concentrated on driving. "I haven't forgotten."

"I still remember when I found you browsing through the dildos and vibrators in the shop. You didn't know where to look when I walked around the corner, and you were holding that twelve-inch monster in your hand." His chuckle was warm with amusement. "I've never seen anyone go that shade of red before."

Mercy rolled her eyes, still embarrassed after all this time. "I just wasn't expecting anyone to stroll up and give me assistance. I told you it was my first time in that kind of shop."

"Then you started stuttering," Wilder continued with a grin.

"Until you broke the tension with the lamest joke I'd ever heard." Her lips twitched, and before she knew it, she was smiling back.

That was the moment things had clicked between them. They'd been best friends ever since. Mercy had had a secret crush on him for the last few years. Not that he ever noticed. Wilder was clueless when it came to how she felt about him, and Mercy wished she was brave enough to change that. She was frightened of destroying their friendship or making things awkward.

"How's work?" She wanted to steer the conversation onto safer ground.

"Same as usual. How are things with you?" He returned his attention to the road.

"Stacy and Owen finally got engaged." She was unable to contain her squeal of happiness for her housemate. "I was starting to think he was never going to have the courage. Debbie didn't look all that thrilled, but I guess she's probably worried about us finding another housemate when Stacy moves out."

It had been the three of them for the last year. Mercy had grown close to Stacy, but Debbie was a little more reserved. Although she joined in on pizza night and girls' nights out, she was the quietest of them.

Wilder hummed in agreement. "I'm sure it's just that. Tell Stacy congratulations from me when you see her tonight."

As Mercy focused on the road, they fell into a companionable silence. By the time they reached the restaurant. she was feeling a little more relaxed. With her bag safely over her shoulder, she locked up her car and accompanied him into the restaurant.

The waitress greeted them with a smile and showed them to their regular table. Slipping off her bag, Mercy placed it on the seat between her and Wilder, who seated himself on her right. It was already busy, the tables bustling with the lunchtime crowd. The warm April weather had coaxed people outside to enjoy the sunshine, filling the cafes and bistros with hungry customers.

"French toast and a tea, please," Mercy told the hovering waitress.

"I'll have a bacon sandwich and a coffee, thanks," Wilder added as the woman jotted the order on her notepad. Done, she slipped away, skirting past the tables and heading for the kitchen.

Twisting in his seat to face Mercy, Wilder threw his arm over the back of his chair. "So, are we on for Friday night like usual? It's lady's choice for movie night."

"I...can't this week," Mercy confessed.

His eyebrow arched. "A hot date?"

"Of course not." Heat rose in her cheeks. "I just have somewhere else to be."

And that was all she was going to tell him. Mercy wasn't about to blab that she'd won the ticket. Not everyone would be thrilled about it, and she didn't want anyone's censorship or disapproval of her choices. If she wasn't so attracted to Wilder, she might have confided in him. He knew about the toys she bought from his shop, but the thought of admitting she was going to a kink club almost crippled her with embarrassment.

Their waitress reappeared with a crammed tray. Sliding the drinks onto the table, she placed their plates in front of them with a flourish. Mercy's stomach rumbled at the sight of her food, reminding her she hadn't had breakfast. Picking up the pot of maple syrup, she doused her puffy buttered French toast with it.

"Do you want toast with that?" Wilder chuckled as he watched her.

Mercy scrunched up her face. "You're so funny."

"What's this?"

The odd change of his tone had her looking toward him. Rather than tucking into his sandwich, he was holding her golden ticket between two fingers. Cursing inwardly at her bag for not having a zipper, she realized he must have plucked it up from where it was poking out of the envelope.

"It's nothing." She tried to grab it, but he swivelled away from her in his chair.

Wilder inspected the words printed neatly on the front of the gold card. "You know this is an underground kink club, right?"

"Yes, I know." Mercy snatched it back and stuffed it in her bag, her cheeks hot with embarrassment that they might be overheard. "I thought I might go see what the fuss is about since I won a trip there. How do you know about it?"

"I work in a sex shop. We know a lot of things," he reminded her. "You aren't actually thinking of going, are you?"

She sliced her French toast into chunks. "Of course! Why not?"

Wilder shrugged. "I just never thought it was something you were interested in, that's all."

"Well, Friday night, I'll be seeing what all the fuss is about. If it's not all it's cracked up to be, I'll probably be home in bed by eleven and not bother with the two other evenings."

Popping a piece of food into her mouth, she focused on chewing, hoping to end the conversation. No one was going to talk her out of it. Just two more days, and she'd be stepping through the club's doors. Mercy wasn't sure if she should be elated or terrified. She guessed time would tell.

Two
Wilder

Wilder couldn't keep from staring at the dollop of syrup that clung to Mercy's mouth. It was all he could do to stop himself from leaning over and licking her lips. Instead, he spent the next few torturous minutes watching her consume her meal. By the time she'd finished, he was so fucking hard he could barely think straight.

With her long, blonde honey-colored hair and freckle-kissed nose, there was something innocently sweet about her. One glance at those baby blue eyes and her hourglass curves, and Wilder knew where he was going to be Friday night.

Mercy Williams was going to a kink club. Not just any club, but Blaine's. Wilder wasn't sure if he should be happy or worried. Blaine Wallace was one of his closest friends. They'd practically grown up together as their fathers had been business partners and even now had business dealings. Wilder provided Blaine with sex toys for his club. He also held one of the exclusive memberships for it, which cost a fortune.

He sighed.

Not that Mercy knew any of that. She thought he was a shop assistant, with no inkling that he was actually the multi-billion-dollar owner of the highly successful chain. He knew he should have come clean long ago, but fear at scaring her off had held his tongue. The moment he'd seen her in one of his shops, he'd been intrigued by her. Face a bright shade of red, there had been a shy innocence about her. Pretending to be what she thought he was had been easier. Mercy had opened up to him in a way he was certain she wouldn't have if he'd told her the truth, sure she'd feel intimidated. It hadn't taken him long to realise he was head over heels in love with her. Now he was stuck in the lie. For two years, he'd kept up the pretense, only digging the hole he was in deeper.

The fact that Wilder was a Dominant also held him back. He enjoyed sex and kink. The path of dark desires he craved wasn't for sweet, innocent Mercy.

Since meeting her, he'd turned to others to drown out his attraction to her. He never kept a submissive for long and had certainly never collared any. But being with them had never extinguished the yearning he had for this woman.

Despite the books she'd read, he was sure Mercy would go running the second she learned of his needs. So here he sat, friend-zoned, eating lunch with her week after week. In control and confident with everything else in his life, he was a fucking coward around this woman.

"You're quiet," she observed, jolting him out of his thoughts.

A sheen of syrup was coating her lips again, sending Wilder's imagination wild with all the other ways he could use it to bring her pleasure. God, he'd give anything to see those lips wrapped around his cock.

Slapping himself mentally, he reined in his raging libido. "Just thinking about work stuff. That's all."

"Anything I can help with?"

Wilder shook his head. "Not this time."

She was always good as a sounding board when he had ideas for new sex toys. Part of his latest line had been created from conversations with her. Mercy had no idea how helpful she'd been with some of his hottest new items. Even the vibrator she'd ordered was one of the things she'd helped him create. Wilder had gotten a kick out of bringing it to her today when he'd seen her order online. He could only imagine her delight when she used it this evening, spread out alone on her big bed.

Letting his knowledge of the club slide for now, Wilder steered the conversation into safer waters. Mainly food and the books she was reading. If she was stepping into his world, then he wanted to know what was fueling it. What fantasies did Mercy have? What was she searching for?

By the time she dropped him off, he had the threads of a plan sewn together. One he couldn't wait to carry out. All he needed to do was get it all in motion.

"I'll text you later," she called to him with a huge, sunny smile, out of the car window.

Giving her a wave, he watched her join the flow of traffic and disappear down the road. The second she vanished, the smile slid from his face. Heading along the street, he made his way to the usual rendezvous point, knowing Smithy would be waiting.

Fishing out his phone, Wilder hit speed dial. "Debbie? Cancel all my afternoon appointments. I won't be in the office for the rest of the day."

"Yes, sir," his personal assistant purred. "Is there anything else I can do for you?"

"No, I'll see you tomorrow." Before she could find an excuse to stay on the line, Wilder cut the call.

It had been his idea to place her in Mercy's home. She'd been more than willing to keep an eye on her for him. The problem was, it hadn't been until recently that he'd seen how clingy and possessive she had become of him. She'd started with little jabs and lies about her housemate that she thought Wilder would gobble up. He hadn't, of course. Wilder knew jealousy when he saw it. Debbie was a problem he was going to have to deal with.

Reaching the silver Mercedes, he greeted the heavy-set, muscled man leaning against it with a nod. "Sorry I'm a little late, Smithy. We lost track of time."

His driver smiled. "Did you have a good lunch date, sir?"

"Yes, thank you."

"Back to the office?" Smithy opened the rear door for him.

"Not today." Wilder slipped into the expensive leather interior. "Give me a minute, and I'll let you know where we're going."

"As you wish, sir." Slamming the door closed, his driver rounded the vehicle to the driver's side.

Pulling up his friend's number, Wilder made the call. "Blaine, we need to talk."

He was answered by a yawn, then a sleep-edged voice. "I have time now if you swing by the loft."

"I'll be there in thirty minutes."

"Good. Gives me time to drink my weight in coffee." Blaine chuckled before hanging up.

Shaking his head in amusement, Wilder informed Smithy where they needed to go. With time to kill, he pulled up a web search and explored the books Mercy had mentioned she was reading. The storylines were varied, but the theme was the same. An alpha male who took charge. Roleplay, spanking, forced orgasms, orgasm denial, and a whole host of other kinks he'd never dreamt she'd be interested in. How serious was she? Reading about something and reality didn't always measure up. Would she really be brave enough to delve into these waters, or would she be frightened off? It was something Wilder wanted to learn, and Friday night couldn't come quick enough.

THREE

MERCY

Releasing a sigh of relief, Mercy glanced up from the desk full of consent forms. She'd had no idea there would be so many to sign. Her list of hard and soft limits had been filled out and whisked away. She guessed the staff was finding her a suitable Dominant for the evening. One who wouldn't be too hard on her, she hoped. At least for tonight. Mercy still wasn't sure if she was doing the right thing but she refused to chicken out. This might be the only chance she ever got to experience such a place. She wasn't about to pass it up.

Kelly, who'd been assigned to her when she first arrived, was waiting with a patient smile.

The beautiful redhead was tall and well-dressed, her voice holding only a trace of her American accent. "Perfect! Now Mercy, if you'd like to come with me? We have something for you to wear."

Mercy wiped her damp palms on her denim-clad thighs. She should have realized that jeans and the pretty pink top she was wearing weren't going to do. Oh god, what would they make her wear? An image of a gimp mask and latex suit danced through her head. Trying not to panic, Mercy obediently rose and followed Kelly across the elegant office.

She could always say no, she reasoned. Nothing was stopping her from walking out whenever she wanted. Kelly had assured her she was safe. With the safeword she'd picked out, she could stop this at any time.

The woman showed her to an ensuite, halting at the door to remove something from the bag she was carrying.

Mercy blinked at the scrap of material held out to her with the tags still on, indicating it was new. "Is that … a gold bikini?"

"Yes, it's what you're required to wear for this evening," Kelly replied calmly. "You'll need to wear a mask like the rest of the patrons as we have an event in progress. That's also in the bag. Put your things inside it, and I'll make sure they remain safe. Take your time, and when you're ready, I'll be waiting out here to take you onto the main floor."

She handed it over to Mercy, who took it in a shaking hand. "Thank you."

Stepping through the door, she closed it behind her and was delighted to find a stylish ensuite. She guessed they were keeping her away from the regular changing facilities because she wasn't a member. Like Cinderella, she had a limited amount of time. This wouldn't end on the stroke of midnight but in three days.

Discarding her street clothes, she left them piled on a chair and slipped into the outfit that had been chosen for her. The skimpy bikini left little to the imagination. Mercy was far from having the perfect body. When she did go swimming, she wore a bathing suit that was a lot less revealing. The scraps of material—if they could even be called that—barely contained her boobs but were enough to cover her nipples. The bottoms shielded her groin from view, but the back was a piece of thin cloth wedged between her ass cheeks.

Trying not to overthink things, she found the bag and tugged out the mask. Gold to match her outfit, it had small black horns curling from the top like a deer. Judging by the detail and craftmanship, Mercy was sure it was expensive.

She slipped it over her face and tied the black ribbon behind her head to keep it in place. Viewing herself in the full-length mirror, Mercy didn't recognize herself at all. With her hair like burnished gold cascading down her shoulders, the color of the bikini complemented her pale skin. She looked ethereal, otherworldly.

"You can do this," she told herself quietly. "Just don't be too self-conscious and try to relax."

Pep-talk over, she gathered her things, pushed them down into the bag, and padded barefoot out to where Kelly was waiting. The other woman gave a nod of approval when she saw her, accepting the bag and taking charge of her possessions.

"Master Blaine is waiting to meet you." Kelly guided her from the office and out into a corridor. "He'll be instructing you in what happens next."

Anticipation darted through Mercy. Squashing the nervous jitters, she accompanied her chaperone until they reached a pair of black ebony doors. When she entered the main room of the club, her eyes rounded with awe.

People flowed around them wearing an assortment of animal masks. Lions, swans, rabbits, wolves, she could see them all, but Mercy appeared to be the only deer. Where some members were dressed as scantily as she was, others wore a lot more clothing. The main part of the club reminded her of a spacious ballroom. Around it, individuals were taking part in public scenes. There were stocks, St Andrew's crosses, and strange-looking benches adorned with belt-like restraints. Some of them she'd read about in her BDSM romance novels, but others were a mystery to her.

Sensing eyes on her, she sliced a look around. A dark-haired man was sauntering toward them. his long legs encased in leather trousers, his muscular chest bare and covered in tattoos. He wore a tiger mask, his brown eyes gleaming warmly through the eye slits with predatory interest. Every move he made spoke of grace and elegance.

"Master Blaine, I have our guest here for you," Kelly introduced politely when he reached them. "Mercy, this is the man in charge of everything."

The owner of the club swept Mercy with an appreciative look from head to foot. "Mercy, congratulations on winning the ticket. I hope we can make your three evenings here with us as enjoyable and memorable as possible."

"Oh, I'm sure you will," she replied, going for cool confidence but her voice betraying an audible shakiness.

Giving Kelly a dismissive nod of thanks, Blaine laced Mercy's arm gently through his and led her across the room. "Breathe. There's nothing to be nervous about. You have your safeword should you need it. If you use it, everything happening will stop, and I promise you'll be whisked safely home."

Grateful for the reassurance, she walked with him, aware of the glances of others as they passed. "Thank you, Sir."

"This evening, you are the golden hind. A very lovely and elusive creature that I think is fitting for your first time here."

Movement caught her eye, a flash of blond hair snagging her attention. Craning her neck, Mercy spied a familiar-looking man through the crowd. She couldn't see his face with the black panther mask obscuring his features, but there was something about the way he moved that sparked recognition.

"Oh my god, is that Lance Arthurs?" she whispered, leaning in toward her host in unbidden excitement. "I thought he was in Vegas!"

The famous magician was known worldwide for his stage shows and television series. Handsome, adventurous, he'd left a string of broken hearts in his wake from what she'd heard.

"Lance is one of our members," Master Blaine confided in a raspy murmur. "Whenever he's in London, he enjoys an evening of entertainment at the club." He motioned at someone in the crowd. "I think it's time we start your evening properly. You have a lot to fit into the three days you are here, and you also agreed to wear a training collar."

The people around them parted, and a man emerged. Tall, muscular, and athletic, his ash-blond hair slicked back and controlled. Just like Blaine, he was topless, and a pair of black leather trousers hugged his lean legs. A bear mask hid his features from view, but his searing stare burned into hers from the eye slits. She was being stripped bare with the intensity of his turbulent green eyes as they flayed her alive. There was a palpable presence about him. It made part of her want to run and hide while another side of her was wet from thinking about what he might do to her. Finding it difficult to breathe under such a force, all she could do was helplessly watch him get closer.

"Master Brutus will be seeing to your needs this evening." Placing a calming hand on her shoulder, Blaine bent his head and brushed her earlobe with his lips, stealing her attention back. "Then perhaps we can have a drink afterward?"

Mercy felt a blush heat her cheeks beneath the mask in response to the sexy smile Master Blaine gave. "Yes, Sir. Thank you, I'd like that."

"Then I'll see you later and leave you in his capable hands." He sounded almost reluctant to leave her when he stepped away.

Master Brutus took his place. Holding up the inch wide black leather collar with its gleaming chrome D-ring, he also let her see the leash. Allowing her to stare at it for only a moment, he then secured it carefully around her neck.

Mercy shivered at the brush of his fingers against her skin. The unfamiliar weight and tightness of the collar gave her a stab of unease. When he clipped the leash to the ring, she visibly gulped with apprehension. She'd agreed to this, wanting to know what it was like, and now she knew.

Unable to stop herself, Mercy glanced up at Master Brutus. His mere presence was like molten chaos to her senses. The way he stood before her, his whole bearing screamed Dom. Mercy just hoped she was going to be able to handle everything he threw at her. It was one thing reading about this kind of thing. Experiencing it was quite another.

FOUR
WILDER

Wilder surveyed his submissive for the evening through the eye slits of his mask. He took in the cling of the gold bikini bottoms, the slender hips, up to the swell of her perfect breasts contained by the two triangles of material. He'd known she was beautiful, but seeing her like this, in the outfit he'd requested, almost brought him to his knees. Wilder hadn't been able to get the idea of seeing her in it out of his mind after he'd introduced her to Star Wars on one of their movie nights. Tonight, his sweet little innocent would be his 'slave girl'.

Mercy had requested no penetration. No impact play. No humiliation. Her list of limits was extensive, but she'd left him with a few things to work with. Wilder could tell she was curious and wanting to dip her toes in the shallows of the lifestyle rather than plunge straight into the deep end. He was proud that she at least had good sense. If she didn't balk after tonight, he had two more potential evenings to show her what he craved.

Not that Mercy would know it was him. Wilder was ready to keep up the pretense of being just another Dom in the club's employ. She'd be safe with him, and he wouldn't have to go out of his mind imagining her with someone else.

It had taken some convincing to get Blaine to agree. For some reason, he had been reluctant to hand over control. Now Wilder could see why. His friend was interested in Mercy too. He hadn't missed the glint of lust in the other man's eyes.

Irritation that she'd agreed to have a drink with his friend after their session annoyed him, but he refused to let it sour his mood.

"Come," he growled out softly, disguising his voice enough she wouldn't recognise it. With a yank of the leash, he reinforced his command.

Mercy resisted for a second, a flash of panic in her big blue eyes before it was gone. Wilder spared himself only a small pang of worry. She wanted this. If she didn't, she wouldn't have come here tonight. He had to stay in his role as her Dom. One slip and she might figure out who he was—something he couldn't afford to let happen.

Wilder led her through the room, a sense of pride and protectiveness puffing out his chest when he saw the covert looks of jealousy from the other Doms and Dommes. They could see what a stunning beauty she was. A fresh canvas to teach and mold.

"What's your safeword?" he questioned as they reached a door that led to the private playrooms.

"Pickles," Mercy replied meekly, her eyes lowered to the floor.

Wilder's lips twitched in a smile, amused she was using food. "We will use green for 'okay' and orange for 'give me a moment'. Do you think you can remember that, slave?"

"Yes, Sir."

He felt like pinching himself when he heard her say that word. This had to be a dream. Any moment, he was going to wake up, and Mercy would be gone, leaving him in tangled sheets and longing.

Having his private playroom prepared, Wilder knew they would not be disturbed. No one else used it. When he was here, it was his domain.

Guiding her along the corridor, past door after door, he didn't stop until they reached the one at the end. Opening it, he tugged on the leash, showing her inside. The walls were painted cream, and a range of equipment sat within it. A large four-poster bed with black silk sheets. A St Andrew's cross. Near a metal dog crate in one corner loomed wooden pillories.

Wilder wanted to put them all to use, but tonight he had to ease her into things. He could sense her trepidation, feel it in the slight hesitation as she shuffled in after him without an ounce of confidence.

"This is my playroom," Wilder explained to her gruffly. "I'm going to tie you up, but if you feel uncomfortable, tell me. What color are you right now?"

"Green, Sir," Mercy replied, the tone of her voice conveying her anxiousness. "I…I don't mind being tied up."

Leading her toward the metal cross, he knew it was sturdy enough to keep her in place for what he intended. Clicking off the leash, he motioned silently for Mercy to stand in front of the piece of equipment. Once she was in place, he touched her shoulder, guiding her back against the metal frame.

Wilder took her arm, lifting it out to shackle it in place. He repeated the action with her right before dropping into a crouch and nudging her feet apart. Once he was satisfied with the distance, he shackled them too.

A tiny whimper escaped from Mercy's lips. Eyes huge and glittering in the slits of her mask, her uncertainty at what was happening became more evident. Wilder softened, his Dom side craving her submission, but the love he felt for her made him want to alleviate her fears.

"Still green?" Rising, he stroked his hand down her body from her shoulder to the curve of her hip in a gesture meant to soothe her.

"Yes." Mercy nodded with a sigh. "They must have told you this is my first time. I'm just really nervous."

"That's understandable," he replied. "Just remember to tell me if you want me to stop."

The urge to clamp those magnificent tits of hers was strong, but Wilder resisted.

Patience. All in good time.

If not tonight, then he had two more evenings to play with her. He was yet to gauge how much pain she could take. If she wasn't into that kind of thing, he wasn't going to push her, even if he craved it. He would see to Mercy's fantasies and needs. Allow himself to enjoy these stolen moments before she went back to her life. He'd remain her best friend, resigning these memories to his spank bank.

Wilder's gaze devoured her body, memorizing every fine detail from the graceful curve of her neck to the small scar on her knee. The pale expanse of her creamy skin begged for his hands, teeth, and implements to brand her as his. Mercy was perfection.

Tearing his attention away from her, he focused on the task at hand. Spread out on the surface of the table near the wall was an assortment of sex toys. The magic wand with its silicone head was perfect for clit stimulation. With its variation in intensity and vibration patterns, it was one of his biggest sellers. Next in line was a smaller blue vibrator. Its contoured shape fit over the clit and gave a pulsing suction sensation.

He could feel her watching him as he reached for the third vibrator he'd laid out. It was the same model she'd bought online a few days ago. Where the one he'd given her in her car was pink, this one was purple.

Hooking the material of her bikini bottoms with a finger, he pulled it to one side. A blonde thatch of curls greeted his gaze as Mercy froze in shock.

"What color are you now?" Wilder questioned.

"Gre ...green," she stuttered, peering down at him.

Wilder switched on the vibrator as she watched. Its soft buzz filled the air, and he savored her sharp gasp of surprise when he caressed her between the legs with the bulbous end of it. Mercy grew wetter within minutes, her hips moving restlessly as he settled it against her clit.

With a press of a button, he notched it up to the next level. Lips parting, the noise that left her throat was more of a strangled moan than a cry. A pretty flush stained her throat and chest. She was so responsive, she'd orgasm quickly.

Mercy gave a garbled moan, her body arching away from the cross before she went slack.

"Well done, slave. Your first one of many this evening," Wilder rumbled, giving her a second to recover before he found her clit again with the buzzing vibrator.

That snapped her out of her languid state. Eyes shooting wide, they latched onto his masked face. "More?"

Instead of answering her, he increased the sex toy to another level. Mercy's thighs twitched in response, her mouth becoming a perfect O. Bound as she was, she had no escape. Hearing her high, breathy pleas to stop, he reminded her if she wanted it to end, all she needed to do was say her safeword.

She didn't, though. Mercy was enjoying what was happening. From the way she responded, Wilder could see she was getting off on being held captive and helpless. He happily led her from orgasm to orgasm, leashing the desire to bury himself balls-deep inside her every time she fell apart with the pleasure he was giving her.

After six forced orgasms, he swapped to the magic wand. Carefully rearranging her bikini bottoms, he lined the bulky rubberized tennis-ball head up between her legs over the cloth. As far as Wilder knew, this would be the first experience Mercy had with a wand, and he didn't want to overwhelm her with its effectiveness too quickly.

The second it made contact, she jerked in reaction. As the vibration worked its magic, she didn't last long. Howling at the top of her voice, she came hard and violently. Wilder swore he could almost see her having an out-of-body experience as she hit a peak with an intensity that made her expression twist in indescribable ecstasy. As the sadist in him rose, he kept it pressed tight to her pussy, wringing every last drop of pleasure from her. When her moans shifted to whimpers and her muscles shook uncontrollably from the orgasms, he finally showed her pity.

The muskiness of her arousal was pungent in the air, and from the fine sheen of sweat coating her skin, he'd given her a night to remember. Noticing the glazed, dreamy look in her lovely blue eyes, Wilder smirked. He'd bet anything that tonight he'd gotten Mercy hooked. If she didn't roll back into the club tomorrow evening like he expected, he'd be surprised. One way or another, he was determined to find out. The only Dom his sweet innocent would be playing with was him. Wilder was going to ensure it for the next few days at least.

FIVE

MERCY

It was midnight, and Mercy hadn't been home long. Still high from the events of the evening, she was having a hard time finding sleep. Master Brutus had been amazing, making her orgasm over and over until she'd begged him to stop. Never in her life had she orgasmed like that. The sheer intensity of it all had blown her away. He must have been a sadist because he'd showed her no pity, making her come more times than she could count before relenting.

Afterward, he'd carried her to a chair, and they'd cuddled. He'd fed her bites of chocolate in silence and given her sips of water. Mercy had enjoyed being curled up on his lap, his strong hand stroking her back while his other had gently squeezed her left buttock. It made her wonder if he'd been testing the firmness. Seeing what he had to work with if he got the chance to spank her.

When aftercare had finished, she'd joined Master Blaine at the bar for a glass of champagne. Mercy had felt positively decadent and naughty, still floating on post-orgasmic bliss and drunk on the atmosphere of the club. Sitting at his private table, she'd been able to observe the public scenes going on around her. Some had made her squirm in her seat with arousal, and others she found a little alarming. She'd been aware of Master Brutus close behind her the whole time like a shadow.

The soft ping of her phone interrupted her spinning thoughts. Groping for it on her bedside table, she peered at the message glowing brightly on the screen.

Wilder – *Are you ok? Did you get home safely?*

Yes. She typed, touched he was checking up on her before adding, *And I'm going back tomorrow.*

Holding her breath, she waited for his reply and expected disapproval. When a simple ok, sleep well appeared, she felt a little disappointed. What had she been expecting? For Wilder to tell her he cared and not to go? She'd been daydreaming about them getting together way too long. Maybe it was time to work Wilder Chase out of her system. Time at the club might just allow her to do that, especially under the expert hands of Master Brutus.

Exhaustion finally catching up with her, she fell into a deep, dreamless sleep. She almost missed the piercing shrill of her alarm clock when it went off in the morning. Mercy woke with an odd new blooming of fragile excitement she couldn't shake.

She spent the day at the flower shop, preparing bouquets for a wedding with her assistant. Despite keeping busy, her thoughts were lost in delicious memories of the night before and daydreams of what was yet to come. What would Master Brutus do to her this evening? More forced orgasms, or had something even more devious been planned for her?

By the time the evening came around and she presented herself at the club, Mercy was practically thrumming with expectation. Kelly greeted her at the door, the poised, sophisticated redhead showing her to the fancy office where she was once more made to change. This time her bikini was silver, but it came without a mask.

"You go straight to Master Brutus's room tonight," her chaperone told her, escorting her from the office once she was changed.

Kelly's heels clicked along the marble floor while Mercy's bare feet moved soundlessly. Heart hammering in her chest and blood pounding in her ears, she followed the other woman meekly. Her mouth had gone dry, and as they approached the door to the Dom's domain, her footsteps slowed to a shuffle.

Noticing her reluctance, Kelly petted her arm reassuringly, giving her a look of sympathy. "If you need a moment, you don't have to go in straight away. I can get you some water if you want. I know how scary it can be when you first step into this lifestyle."

Mercy offered her a shy smile. "Thank you. Honestly, though, I'm not sure I'll go beyond the three nights here."

The other woman laughed softly. "You'll have to let me know if that's still true by the end of your time here."

Glancing at the door again, Mercy drew in a steadying breath. "I can do this."

"Remember, you can safeword at any time," Kelly reminded her kindly. "If you want things to stop, use it."

"I won't forget," she promised, raising her chin to hold her head up high. "I'd better go in before he comes searching for me."

"Probably best." Her chaperone smirked. "The things he can do with a crop would make you wet and your bottom red. Master Brutus has a fondness for punishing naughty slaves."

Spurred on by her words, Mercy quickly knocked on the door and slipped inside when she heard a gruff voice calling her to enter. Her temporary Master stood waiting for her, bare-chested as before, black leather sheathing his legs. The bear mask he'd worn last night was over his face, keeping his features a mystery.

As she shut the door behind her, he came prowling toward her with all the grace of a hungry jungle cat.

Master Brutus's eyes glinted with cold promise. "Good evening, slave. On the bed. Now."

Mercy shivered at the low gravelly command, something about his voice stirring in her thoughts. It sounded familiar. Before she could think more about it, a hard swat of his hand on her ass got her moving. Scrambling across the room, she crawled onto the huge mattress and lay down.

SIX

WILDER

Possessiveness raced through Wilder's veins as he watched his little innocent make herself comfortable on top of the king-sized bed. Against the black silken bedcover, her blonde hair shone like spun gold, skin pale and pearly, while anxiousness danced in her blue eyes.

His gaze lingered on the smoothness of her shoulders, narrow waist, and curvy hips. How submissive was Mercy in nature? It was a burning question he wanted to find out. He had plenty of implements, both big and small, to tease and torment her. He'd enjoyed having her bound to the St Andrew's cross the previous evening. The innocuous dog cage sat in one corner next to the chest where he stored toys and boxes of condoms, all waiting to be used.

Mercy's eyes would see too much if he left them out.

The conqueror in him was ready to claim what was his. He'd spent all day living and breathing in eagerness of this evening, and finally, she was his again. He hadn't been able to fucking focus on anything else.

Fishing out the silky, black scarf from his pocket, he let Mercy see it. With measured steps, Wilder strode to join her. Mounting the mattress on his knees, he loomed over his timid slave. He didn't miss the worry and excitement shimmering in her gaze as it locked with his. Covering her eyes with the blindfold, he tied it securely behind her head. When he was certain that Mercy could no longer see, Wilder rid himself of his mask.

"How are you feeling?" he questioned softly.

"Green," she replied with more confidence than the night before.

"I'm going to tie you up again tonight. Remember, any worries, just say your safeword. and I'll stop."

Reaching for the tethers on either side of the bed, he secured her wrists and ankles, leaving her spread-eagled. Wilder knew from the way her body remained tense and alert that she was overthinking what might happen.

Mercy's breath was harsh, aroused, on the very edge of anxiety. "Master Brutus?"

"Settle, slave." With gentle fingers, he undid the ties of her bikini top and stripped her of it. "Color?"

"Green" came her breathy response.

God, her breasts. They were even more flawless than he'd imagined. Wilder couldn't stop himself from exploring the softness, cupping them, fondling and stroking her nipples into hard peaks. Mercy's tiny whimpers made him grin. Finding the pot of maple syrup he'd left ready on a table beside the bed, he dipped his fingers into the sweet, golden, viscous liquid.

"Taste," he ordered roughly as he began to paint Mercy's lips.

They parted prettily, her pink tongue darting out to lick, and she moaned softly when she recognized what it was. Her groans continued as he trailed a sticky finger down her neck and along her collarbone. With deft strokes, he painted her breasts and nipples with swirling lines.

Arching her spine, Mercy responded beautifully to his teasing, biting her lower lip when he tweaked the aroused peaks but went no further in playing with her.

Displaying patience he barely held in check, Wilder ringed her belly button with syrup. He was tempted to rip off her bikini bottoms and decorate her pussy but thought better of it. The sensual spell he'd woven between them was something he didn't want to break. If she became uncomfortable and safeworded, he'd lose his time with her. It wasn't something he was willing to let happen.

Discarding the pot, he crawled onto the bed beside her. Mercy's head moved on the pillow, feeling the dip of the mattress from his weight. Not wanting to startle her, Wilder gently caressed her cheek before bending to lap at the path of syrup he'd left along her neck. With soft, wet, suckling kisses, he followed the route he'd left toward her collarbone.

Mercy mewled, writhing in excitement when he reached her breasts. Fingers clenching and unclenching uselessly in the shackles that bound her wrists, there was nothing she could do to stop him. Not unless she said her safeword, and so far, she hadn't.

Her cries turned ragged when he moved on across the flat planes of her stomach. Sucking gently at the stickiness ringing her belly button, he tongued the center, making her giggle.

"Fuck, I knew this was going to be as good as I imagined," he muttered out loud.

When she tensed, he realised his mistake in not disguising his voice.

"Wilder?" Mercy asked in small, hesitant bewilderment.

Knowing he'd been caught, he released a harsh breath before tugging up her blindfold. Dark thick eyelashes blinking rapidly, her baby blue orbs settled on his face. The shock he saw was swiftly replaced with confusion and embarrassment.

Sitting back on his heels on the mattress, he gave her a wry smile. "It's okay, Mercy. You're safe with me."

"But you! We ..." Her mouth opened and closed in growing panic, as if she was having a hard time processing what she was seeing. "Oh, my god! I let you do all those things to me! What the hell are you even doing here? Is this some kind of cruel joke? I'm never going to forgive you!"

Still tethered to the bed with the restraints, she tugged at them in desperation. Seeing her alarm, he quickly undid them, setting her free.

"Did you really think I was going to let someone else do all these things to you?" Wilder growled angrily, unhappy at her reaction. "God damn it, Mercy, I wasn't going to stand by and watch that happen. Do you know how insane it would have made me?"

Bringing her legs quickly up, she hugged her knees protectively into her chest, eyeing him warily. "Why would it drive you insane?"

"Because I'm in love with you," he blurted out, knowing he'd come this far, and things had already changed between them. There was no going back to before. Not now. Not ever. "I have been for over a year and a half now."

"You're in love with me?" Mercy echoed, her expression holding disbelief at his confession.

"Is that so hard to believe?"

"Yes!" She wouldn't meet his eyes. "I mean, you're Wilder Chase, gorgeous, funny, smart. You don't fall in love with girls like me."

"Why not?" He frowned.

"Well, for one thing, I'm not beautiful." Mercy's voice was wistful and tinged with envy.

Unable to stand the distance between them anymore, he wrapped his arms around her, drawing her to him. She shuddered at the contact, her nipples crushed against the haven of his bare chest.

"You're more than beautiful," he told her. "You, Mercy Williams, are sweet and kind. I've been mooning over you all this time. Every time you ordered a new toy from the shop, I'd fantasize about you using it. I even used the same kind of vibrator on you last night that you bought last week. You'd be crazy not to see we're meant for each other."

Mercy tilted her face up to his, her brow furrowed in a frown. "You have?"

Wilder smiled. "Yes, my little vanilla girl, I have."

She gave a small huff. "You have a lot of explaining to do."

"I know, and I'll tell you everything," he promised, angling his head down to hers. "Later."

"What are you doing?"

"I'm trying to seduce you." Mouth finding hers, Wilder kissed her with his heart on his lips.

Mercy allowed the kiss before pulling away. "Oh, is this what you call it?"

She didn't resist when he drew her down onto the bed and pressed his length against her body.

"Are you trying to bruise my ego?" he joked softly.

"Did you set this all up from the start?" she questioned, suspicion lacing her tone.

Wilder dragged a hand through his hair. "No ...I didn't even know you'd won the ticket until I saw it in your bag on Wednesday. Then I had to scramble to get myself here when you turned up yesterday."

Mercy's hand crept up his arm, her fingertips dancing over the muscles of his biceps. "Are we still master and submissive? I mean ...we're still in the club."

"No, sweetheart. Right now, we're just a boy and a girl. I'm hoping you see me as more than just a friend." His hands stroking, caressing, they lingered on each curve and contour, learning every inch of her through his fingertips. "Nothing is going to happen unless you want it to. Tell me to stop, and I will. If you don't feel anything for me, then I will walk away now."

She sucked in a breath when he cupped the side of her jaw. "Why are you staring at my mouth?"

"Because I'd really like to kiss you again," he admitted with a flare of hope. She hadn't rejected him, and he'd like to do more if she permitted.

In answer, she touched her lips to his, exploring gently. Unable to remain passive, Wilder snaked his tongue inside her mouth when it opened for him, deepening the kiss. Mercy ran her hands down his back, across his leather-clad buttocks to his flanks.

"I love you, too," she whispered shyly, her lips meeting his over and over.

Her words had Wilder's heart leaping up into his throat and the last of his control shredding. "I need to claim you. Make you mine. Say yes."

"Yes." Her soft, keening moan was his undoing.

Shedding his leather trousers, he removed the triangle of cloth from between her legs. With her bikini bottoms gone, he had access to exactly where he wanted. Sliding a hand down, he parted her thighs, seeking her wet heat. Touching delicately at first, he deepened the caress, watching her quiver under his teasing.

Mercy's blue eyes clouded with excitement as they remained locked onto him. The breath caught in her throat, body tensing with a building orgasm. Abandoning his toying, he ignored her cry of loss to open the drawer of the bedside table. Grabbing a foiled packet, he tore the corner and quickly sheathed his cock with the condom. Wilder growled in triumph as he moved to cover his body with hers.

Her sob of pleasure as he thrust into her was followed by a gasp when he rammed into her over and over. Wilder could not be gentle. Not with this woman who'd driven him crazy for so long.

There was no hesitation when she wound her arms around his neck and her slender legs lifted to bind him closer. Fisting her hair, he pinned her head on the pillow, forcing her to arch her neck. Bringing his mouth to her neck, he bit down hard on the place where it met her shoulder.

It elicited a squeak which morphed into a long-drawn-out moan as she shuddered beneath him. Wilder was determined to brand her in some way. Leave a visible mark on her for others to see. The Dom inside him demanded it, and so did the caveman he was being.

"I want to own you," he snarled as he nipped at her earlobe. "It's the only thing I've been thinking about since we met."

Mercy was taking the punishing pace of his passion for her, and there was no way Wilder could hold himself back. Still inside her, he swept her up until she was straddling his lap while he knelt on the mattress. Hands spread wide on her hips, he smoothly lifted her up and down on the length of his cock.

"Wilder!" Her harsh cry sounded lost and high.

"I want to mark every piece of you so that every Dom and Domme in this place knows you're mine." He dipped his head until his mouth found her right breast. Licking, sucking, and then biting down on her nipple, he tugged it between his teeth.

Words spilled from Mercy's mouth, more gibberish then a scream as an orgasm rocked through her. Wilder roared in triumph, feeling her pussy spasming around his dick. He'd wanted to last longer. Next time, he promised himself feverishly., still riding the high of their frenzied coupling, he came harder than he ever had before. He clung to her when she went limp in his arms, still buried deep inside her and not ready to let her go. Realising she wasn't moving, he discovered she'd passed out.

"Hey, vanilla," Wilder crooned softly in concern, already liking the little nickname for her. "You still with me?"

Eyelashes flickering, her dazed eyes opened to find his. "I feel a little light-headed."

"Don't worry, I've got you." Releasing her, he laid Mercy gently on the bed and stretched out beside her.

"We need to talk," she murmured, words slurred with tiredness.

"And we will," he assured her. "Soon. Right now, I want to enjoy this moment."

Tugging the black satin sheets up over their bodies, Wilder grinned at the warm, fuzzy feeling inside his chest. He wanted to rush out to the bar and grab a bottle of champagne for them to make a toast with.

There were so many things he still needed to tell her. Hidden truths about his life she didn't yet know. Wilder knew she'd be angry with him at first, but eventually, she'd forgive him. They had tomorrow to talk. Really talk. For now, he was happy to hold the woman he loved in his arms.

ABOUT THE AUTHOR

Claire is a Brit living in Italy and a lover of all things supernatural. When she's not writing she's a mum, avid reader and enjoys having adventures with her family. She writes deliciously addictive Paranormal Romance books with twists, packed with darkness with plenty of steam. You can find Claire and her books on her page!

https://www.facebook.com/groups/898725670258533/

The Vibrator Virgin

K Elise Hoffman

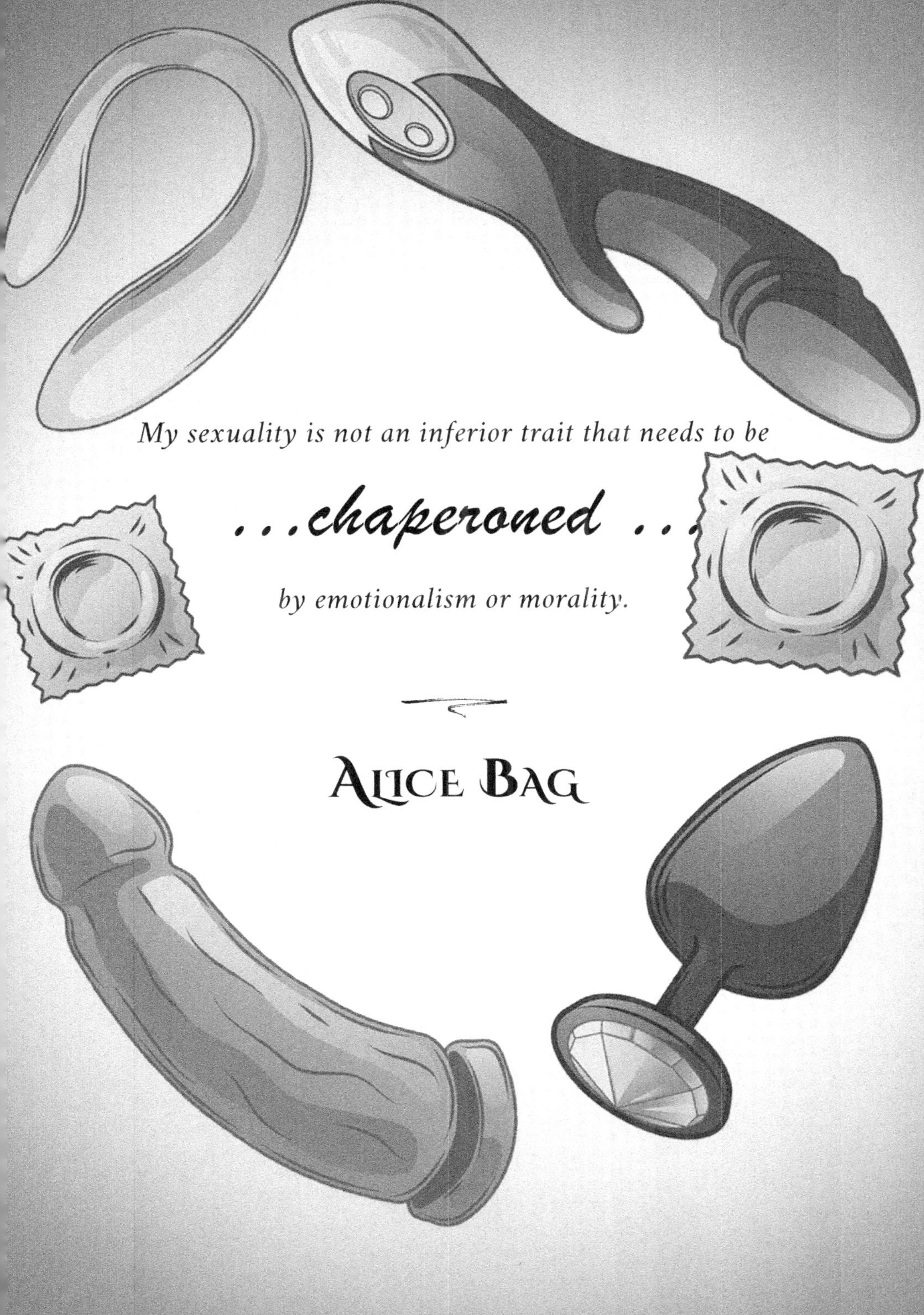

My sexuality is not an inferior trait that needs to be
...chaperoned ...
by emotionalism or morality.
ALICE BAG

One

The Store

"Can I help you ladies find anything today? Looking for something particularly special? I have buy one get one free on stockings, and tights, as well as three for ten dollars on all thongs, and G-strings. Twenty percent off bridal lingerie, and five dollars off select toys."

When we walked into the boutique we had to show our IDs to prove we were adults. The lady, an older woman sporting bifocal glasses and crow's feet, took each card in turn. She checked our dates of birth and scrutinized our faces, memorizing details. The intensity made me want to confess to every wrong thing I'd ever done, up to and including stealing ball point pens from work. Sucking her teeth, she handed them back like she thought we might have pulled one over on her.

Without warning she flashed a smile belonging in a toothpaste commercial, turning into a peppy customer service rep. The change nearly gave me whiplash, but Megan took it in stride, lighting up like a Christmas tree.

"Oh my gosh! Yes! I need something for my honeymoon. I'm getting married in two weeks, and my friend ..." She dragged me from my spot where I was rooted like a damn oak just behind her. " ... Needs some foundation garments for her bridesmaid dress."

My cheeks flushed as the saleswoman turned her sharp gaze to me. I quailed under the pressure.

"Perfect. My name is Mindy, I own the Knock Out Boutique, and I will be delighted to help you find everything you need today, Megan and Darcy."

Megan gave a hop on her toes as she clapped her hands together and squealed.

I couldn't blame her, she was getting married. People in love are weird.

"Why don't you head on over to the bridal corner." She addressed Megan, who was the more comfortable of us. "And I'll take *you* ..." She nodded to me. " ... Over to our foundation garments. What kind of dress will you be wearing? Do you have a picture?" She steered me toward the opposite side of the store while my best friend shot toward the bridal section.

"Uh, yeah." As I followed her to our destination I reached for my phone, pausing at a half wall display of sex toys and vibrators.

Now, I'm not a prude. I'm not a virgin. But it had been a *while*. I'm busy! So sue me! I have plans. I'm finishing my business degree, then I'm going to take the world by storm and become the greatest ... something ... ever.

Alright, I had a vague notion of plans, but they kept me occupied and I hadn't had a date in a couple of years. However, I've never had *help* in the bedroom during my dry spell. I'm perfectly capable of achieving climax with nothing more than what the good Lord gave me. So, this display was intimidating.

Mindy stopped and turned to me to see what had caught my eye.

A knowing glint lit those flinty eyes. "Ah, are you in need of something a little extra today? If you don't want to share your intentions with your friend, I can help you choose something and wrap it up for you before she sees anything?"

"W-what?" I was shocked back to reality. "I don't—that is, I wasn't! I mean—"

Mindy gave a good-natured chuckle. "I see, never had one before?"

Way to play it cool Darcy! Could a person die of embarrassment?

She tapped the side of her nose. "I understand. *If* you're interested in trying something new, I wouldn't recommend any of these. These are for people who want a little flash in the bedroom. They're meant to be shared with someone. They can be used solo, of course, but I think you might want something a little more ... discreet?"

My body must have taken over because I found myself nodding without meaning to. Evidently my libido wasn't satisfied with my solo ministrations after all.

Traitorous body!

"Come with me." She leaned toward me, then cocked her head toward a separate room toward the back of the shop.

My feet followed as I puzzled over what the hell was happening. I was here for a strapless bra and maybe some Spanx. I was not here for—for *that*.

As we entered the room, my jaw hit the floor. Four solid walls filled corner to corner with sex toys of every kind. So many options available there was nary an inch of space between the packages. Inexperienced as I was, it was overwhelming.

As I turned to bolt out of the room, *and the shop*, leaving my friend to do whatever she needed to do—Mindy whipped out a hand. Her iron grip latched onto my upper arm and halted my momentum. Who knew such a seemingly sweet, if somewhat daunting, older lady was so strong?

"Now, now, settle down, sweetheart." She dragged me further into the room. "It's nothing to be afraid of, or *ashamed* of. Let's find something for you to try, and if you don't find it enhances your experiences I'll refund your money. You don't even have to return it to me. In fact nothing in this room is returnable anyway, but for *you* I will make the exception of giving a refund if you aren't completely ... *satisfied*."

Uncomfortable didn't begin to describe how I was feeling in that moment. I don't talk about this stuff with my best friend, let alone some over-the-hill stranger. Weren't older women supposed to be conservative about this stuff? Wasn't her generation part of the whole making up benign names for things that were perceived as sexual? Like "the one-eyed snake" and a woman's "cave of wonders"?

I couldn't speak as she led me around the room and I was sweating from the blush that took over my entire body.

She stopped in front of a grouping of necklaces with long, and stylish pendants in different metal finishes. I screwed up my face in confusion, which brought out a genuine smile from her.

"Exactly. *You* don't even know what they are, do you?"

"Well, it's a necklace. I just thought you were here to show me ... you know ... other *things*." I found my voice again.

"Oh, but you see, this *is* one of those 'other things', as you say. This pendant is a vibrator you can wear around your neck. It's a beautiful, sophisticated piece of jewelry as well as an intimate companion to keep with you for whenever your body starts to beg for attention. It hides in plain sight!"

My eyes widened at the prospect. *Orgasm on the go?*

"Why would I need a portable orgasm machine?"

"Oh, honey. Bless your heart. We'll work on that. Let's move on, shall we?" She didn't let me respond before she was showing me something else.

Work on what now? I'm pretty sure orgasms are for private time, not for public experience on-the-go!

"What about this one? Perfect for your nightstand or to keep in your purse. It looks like it could be a tube of mascara, or some other cosmetic, and yet it has powerful vibration and several different pattern settings to suit your mood."

She handed me the box so I could investigate. The box was light, the packaging sleek and alluring. I couldn't help but turn it over in my hands to see the description on the back.

Five-hour battery life? USB rechargeable. "Wife loves it, I got three more just in case"? Oh my ...

Mindy gave a satisfied nod when I didn't hand it back to her right away. "Let's ring that up for you before your friend finishes shopping. We can take it out of the box, and you can stash it in your purse. She'll never know."

With a wink she took me to the register, and I paid for my new item in a daze. She put the toy in a satin drawstring bag with its charger, and a small bottle of lubricant. I kept turning my head to be sure Megan didn't surface from her shopping excursion, then stuffed it into my purse as soon as Mindy handed me the bag. She chuckled then took me to a much more conservative part of the boutique to find the garments I had actually come for.

Once our shopping was finished Megan headed out to the car, but Mindy stopped me just before I dashed through the door.

"Remember if you aren't happy with it, just come back for a refund." She nodded at my purse with a cunning grin.

I swallowed hard and left without a word.

Two

Vibrator Virgin

When we got back to our apartment building, Megan was so excited she followed me into mine. She had the apartment two doors down and we spent as much time together in one apartment or the other we may as well have lived together. However, when Megan started hooking up with Cole it became clear that having a separate living situation was ideal to avoid any awkward moments.

I liked Cole, but seeing his bare ass was not on my bucket list.

I was excited that, rather than moving to a new place, Cole was going to move in with her after the wedding. So, my best friend and I would still be close. I think she might have bribed him into the deal with sexual favors, but we had a strict "don't ask, don't tell" policy when it came to sex.

Well, except for today. She was so over the moon about her impending wedding she was parading her purchases in front of me like sex talk was normal for us.

"I *love* this one!" She pulled out some strappy contraption that had barely enough lace to cover the important bits.

"Oh my god, Meg! Your boobs won't even fit in that." I laughed. It was true, she was well endowed, and this thing barely had enough to cover *my* meager assets.

"Well, it's not like it will be covering them for long anyway. I'm pretty sure Cole will like all of this better on the floor than he will on me." She giggled.

I rolled my eyes. "Then what's the point? You spent, like, five hundred dollars in that store on scraps of lace he's just going to tear off you a second and a half after he sees you in it."

"Ugh, you're the worst." She gave an exasperated sigh as she stuffed the fabric back into the bag and pulled out a pink satin baby doll. "First of all, it makes *me* feel sexy. It's a great confidence booster when I'm feeling frumpy and gross. Not that Cole cares. When I had the flu a couple months ago, he admitted it was killing him not being able to bone me. That was while I had snot running down my face, and I couldn't keep down liquids. Guys are so weird."

I cringed. "TMI Meg! Ew!"

She giggled at my discomfort. "You are *such* a prude. None of my other—non-best friends, by the way—have any problem talking about sex."

"I am NOT a prude! I've had sex! I have orgasms, I just don't like to *talk* about it. It's private. I like to keep it private."

"Anyway." She batted my outburst away in a motion that said, *yeah, yeah, we've heard it before.* "The second reason is it makes him feel special. I went out of my way to be his ultimate fantasy. Guys appreciate that stuff. It makes them feel like they could have anything they want. Namely us ... naked, and writhing beneath them." Her grin was wicked, knowing I would squirm at the statement. I didn't disappoint.

"Okay, okay, stop now! I haven't had enough to drink to deal with your twitter-pated commentary." I poured a glass of wine.

"I need one of those too, please!"

I poured a second and handed her the glass as I sat on the opposite end of the couch from her. This was our routine. Sit on the couch, feet propped up on the cushions next to each other's hips, and talk nonsense ... or deep thoughts, until we were both a little more than buzzed, feeling relaxed and comfortable.

I was desperate for that feeling of relaxation. The whole experience with Mindy was unsettling, and this conversation was no better.

My mind drifted to my purse where my new 'package' was waiting to be broken in. I was surprised at how much I wanted to get my BFF out of the apartment so I could take it for a spin. Mindy seemed certain I would be satisfied with my purchase, and I was curious on what the fuss was about.

Still, I wasn't about to deny my friend the time she needed to be exuberant about her upcoming matrimonial bliss. I put those thoughts aside to give her my full attention. It wasn't every day someone you cared about was getting married to the love of their life.

"Down to brass tacks." Megan had spent an hour talking about random wedding stuff, decorations, cake flavors, blah, blah, blah. We'd been through all of it more than once over the last couple days, not to mention the last few months as she was working on all of it. But the repetition put her nerves at ease. Talking through it all helped her cement she had everything covered.

I leaned over and put my wine glass down, hugging a throw pillow to my chest. I gave her a quirky salute to let her know she had my undivided focus.

"Cole's best man is coming in tomorrow, and the rehearsal dinner is next week. I'd like you to meet him before then. *Maybe* because I'm a little nervous about meeting him myself."

"Why are you nervous? He'll love you."

Megan is amazing, practically a magnet of positivity. Seeing her lacking confidence was weird to say the least.

"He's the person Cole cares the most about. They're all but brothers, but they ended up in different cities when they were kids. They stayed tight, but it's been sort of a long-distance thing for most of their lives. They visit each other as often as they can, but I've still never met the guy. I hear plenty about him, he sounds like he's nice enough but ..." She bit her lips and gazed down at her empty glass. "I guess I'm scared that if he *doesn't* like me, it will change Cole's mind and he'll realize I was never good enough for him, and call the whole thing off."

I put my pillow aside and leaned forward to wrap her up in my arms.

"That is beyond ridiculous."

A sob escaped her. The stress of everything was getting to her. She had been hiding it behind staying ludicrously busy with wedding details, and now this tiny insecurity was breaking everything down.

"Listen, he is going to love you. There is *no doubt*." I held her at arm's length so I could force her to meet my eyes. "You are an amazing woman. Cole wouldn't go for just anybody. For instance, I never would have stood a chance with him."

Megan giggled.

"Cole and I get along, but we're totally different people. He picked you for a reason. His best friend is going to see you together and *know* this is a match made in heaven. Stop freaking yourself out about it. It's going to be better than fine. It's going to be incredible."

She took a deep breath and wiped a few stray tears from her face. "Okay." A smile tipped her lips up. "But I still want you to meet him with me. You'll be walking with him at the ceremony, and doing all the best-friends-of-the-couple stuff together. I don't want you to be uncomfortable. I don't know what I'll do if you are, but I'll figure something out so you don't have to hang around him."

"It'll be fine. It's only for a little while. Besides, if he and Cole get together as seldom as you say they do, I'll never see him again anyway."

"True."

"What's his name?"

"Ender." There was a strange quirk to her features, like it was the weirdest name she had ever heard."Ender? What the hell kind of name is that?" I laughed.

"I know right? Cole says his dad was seriously into sci-fi lit and named him after the main character in a book."

"Well, to each their own, I guess."

After a few minutes of idle chit-chat about the rehearsal dinner Megan took her leave.

I washed out our used wine glasses, placing them in the drying wrack, then braced my hands against the countertop as I eyed my purse sitting there where I plopped it down after we got back.

I went back and forth in my mind about using it. What could be the big deal? What's so much better about a battery-operated toy compared to my own hands? There's no way it could be that impressive, especially not so much I'll want to *keep it in my purse* to use when I'm not at home.

I cringed at the thought.

Okay, fine. You never know unless you try, right?

I grabbed the satin bag out of my purse and headed toward my room, hoping it was one of those things that had a little bit of charge already, enough to at least try it. Since I was sure it wasn't going to be that impressive, I wasn't too bothered with the longevity of the device before giving it a full charge.

Taking the wand out of the bag I dropped it on my duvet and stared at it for a moment, intimidated by the little device. Stripping out of my clothes, I eyed it like it might jump up and bite me.

Once I was comfortable under the covers of my bed, I picked it up and found the little power button, pressing it down for three seconds until it started buzzing.

So far, I was as unimpressed as I imagined I would be: it didn't seem very powerful. I switched it back off deciding it was a lost cause, dropping it down beside my thigh on top of the covers. I slipped my hand under the privacy of the blankets, moving in a slow caress over my breasts, tweaking each nipple before moving down my stomach toward the heat pooling between my thighs.

I pictured my favorite sexy scene from the romance novel I had already devoured yesterday. It had several scintillating scenes of an alpha male stripping the heroine out of her clothing and pounding her against a wall. Despite the tight control I had on my life, I craved a man in charge.

A moment later my fingers were slick with my arousal, sliding over my clit and back again, sometimes dipping down inside. As the scene played out in my mind and my fingers did their work, my breath quickened, the pressure built, and then ... I was *stuck*.

I worked my body more aggressively chasing that high, but somewhere in the back of my mind I was still wondering about the toy lying next to me on the bed. A part of me was still curious, and it was keeping me from sweet release.

Aggravated, I abandoned my efforts and reached for the device, pressing the button with more force than necessary until the buzz started and I thrust my hand back under the covers.

The moment the wand caressed that sensitive bundle of nerves, I knew just how wrong I was about it. A jolt of pleasure zinged through me like a bolt of lightning and I squeaked at the sensation. The sound quickly became a moan of ecstasy as I moved the wand back and forth.

Since when do I moan?

In seconds I was flying over the edge in the best orgasm of my life, panting, *gasping* for air as I fisted the sheets and threw the vibrator from me when the explosion wracked my body.

Holy hell! I've been missing out!

As soon as I recovered my senses enough to move, I dug out the charger from the little bag and plugged in my *new* best friend.

Sorry, Meg.

Three
Act Natural

The next day as I walked to my second class I got a text.

Megan: Early dinner tonight with Cole and Ender?

I bit my lip as I considered it. I was nervous about meeting him, too. I didn't see the need to get cozy with him, and what if *he* was the one uncomfortable with *me*? Wouldn't it be better to have left it off until we had to meet at the rehearsal? But this isn't about me. It's all for Meg, because I loved her, and this was important to her.

Me: Of course! Where and when?

I texted back after a deep breath.

Megan: Crab Shack at 5pm, be there or be square!

Doubtless she would be with Cole long before five rolled around, so I'd need to make my way there on my own. That would give me plenty of time to psych myself up to meet the new person.

I hate meeting new people. I grimaced.

I spent most of the day wondering what this Ender person looked and sounded like. Stressing over whether he would like me at all. Just because Megan did, didn't mean this random guy would.

Once in my apartment I went through my wardrobe trying to find the perfect outfit. The Crab Shack was by no means a place of high standards. It was a shorts and tank top kind of place. Still, I felt like a dress was in order.

I settled on a yellow sundress with ruffles on the hem of the short skirt, the top was an off the shoulder style. I laid it out on the bed along with a pair of red peep-toe pumps and my favorite lacy cheeky panties from Victoria's Secret. I'd need the confidence boost, and pretty undies always do the trick.

I hopped in the shower, daydreaming about what he might be like, what he might sound like when he laughed. *Does he laugh? Crap, what if he's super serious?*

I wondered what he smelled like, something heady like lumberjacks in the woods.

Or B.O.! Lumberjacks do a lot of sweating Darcy! Maybe he smells super gross.

I guessed what he looked like, tall, dark, and handsome. The typical romance novel cover model.

Or a troll. What if he has warts? On his face? What if he's super hairy as well as stinky, and you have to walk with him down the aisle?

By the time I got out of the shower I was more stressed than I had been when I went into it.

I took extra time doing my makeup so I had something else to focus on, putting extra care into my eyes so they would pop. That meant dramatic eyeliner. I usually went for massive amounts of color in my eyeshadow, but since I planned to wing this bitch like she was flying over the Pacific Ocean, I ditched the brighter palette.

However, unable to completely forgo some real color I picked out the perfect red lip stain to match my killer heels. The crimson popped against my chocolate tresses that I let cascade over my bare shoulders.

I. Look. Fierce.

Feeling more confident I pulled on my dress and my heels, then looked at the clock. I still had an hour before we were supposed to meet at the restaurant, and it would only take half an hour to get there.

Well damn. I hate waiting.

Miffed by my poor timing, which only gave me the chance to crawl back into my head and worry over this introduction, I collapsed on my bed. My anxiety ramping up again.

I found my mind straying to my new BFF, the subtle little toy plugged in beneath my nightstand. A little release might help to cool my nerves. Besides, now I knew what to expect I could draw things out a little more, really enjoy it. It was worth a shot, right?

It took very little convincing to strip out of my cheeky panties and lie on my bed with wand in hand. And I *did* take my time.

It was like I was discovering my body all over again with this little device. I went slow as I touched and stroked against the sensitive skin and nerves at my core. I tried different pressures, and managed to work my way through all the different settings offered until I found the one I liked best. It was a slow pulse that grew in intensity and then dropped off, taking me to edge and then leaving off just to build me up again.

When my release finally came, it was even better than what I experienced the night before, and I discovered I had rather ruined my dress for the night. A large wet spot decorated the fabric, a souvenir of my escapade. I only had about ten minutes before I had to leave. I jerked the dress off and washed my magic wand of pure bliss, cleaned up, and rummaged through my closet again.

I landed on a navy-blue crepe dress that hit just above the knee and had a plunging halter neckline. A cream-colored ribbon wound around the waist to tie in a bow at the back. It was light and pretty, and even more perfect than the yellow dress had been. How had I not seen it before?

A knock sounded at the door just as I finished tying the bow and I jumped out of my skin, as though my body feared someone would know what I had just been doing.

I shook my head at myself and peeked through the peep hole of my door. A man was outside, looking away from the door so I couldn't see his face.

"Hello?"

His head whipped around to the door. It was hard to tell through the fish-eye distortion of the peep hole, but he looked handsome. *What is a hot guy doing at my door?*

"Uh, yeah, hi. I'm looking for Darcy? Is this the right apartment?" His baritone voice reverberated through the door.

I was even more confused. "Who is asking?"

He reached a hand to scratch at the back of his neck, his eyebrows quirked like he was embarrassed.

"Uh, Ender? I'm Ender. I'm her best friend's fiancé's best man?"

What the fuck? I jumped back from the door, my flushed skin heating even more. *Holy hell! He's hot! He's ... why is he* here?

"Darcy? That is you, right?"

My breath came too fast and a wave of lightheadedness crashed into me. My epic orgasm was now backfiring in a huge way. Did I look like was just doing ... *that?* I had planned on having a half hour to settle down again and be ready to meet this guy and he was here? *And he's gorgeous?!* Why hadn't I made Megan show me a picture last night?

Get a grip, Darcy. He's just a guy. Totally normal, run of the mill guy. Chill out! Act natural.

I took a slow deep breath, smoothed out my hair and tugged my dress straight, then opened the door with an abrupt jerk. I lost control of the swing and it flew out of my hand, banging into the bumper on the wall with a loud thud. As it bounced back, a hand struck out to catch it before it could do any more damage.

"Whoa, you o ..." His voice drifted off at the end as though he had forgotten what he was asking as his eyes met mine.

I couldn't breathe at all. I was caught in his gray-blue gaze. He was half leaning in through the doorway with his hand stretched out against the door that tried to kill the wall. As he straightened up he took a half step inside, his frame commandeering the space like he was made to be there.

He was tall, alright, over six foot, with broad shoulders, and his torso slimming into a narrow waist. Think Chris Evans, but a little leaner build, not quite so bulky. Don't get me wrong, there was a *lot* of muscle there. It was roping over his forearms, defining his pecs, and I'm sure there *had* to be that perfect V every woman dreams about beneath his belt. He had dark blonde hair in a cut that was longer on top and styled just enough to look like it *wasn't* styled. His nose was straight, and his lips were the kind of full that beg to be nipped at during a long, leisurely make out session.

He was wearing an aquamarine polo that complimented his bronze skin. The top buttons undone just enough to see the dip at the base of his throat. The shirt was tight over his frame, but I was not complaining, and he was wearing formfitting jeans in a dark wash, and … flip flops? Okay, I wasn't ready for that, but it worked.

Even as I soaked in all the glory that was *Ender*, his eyes were roaming over me. Every nerve ending was on fire as his gaze raked over my body until his pewter-blues came to rest on my lips, slightly parted in my shock.

"Hi."

I swallowed hard, not sure my voice would operate any better than his just had. "I'm Darcy."

He just nodded, his eyes still caught on my lips. He pointed to his chest. "Ender Collins."

"I thought I was meeting you at the restaurant." I sounded accusatory. *Nice Darcy.*

Ender gave his head a slight shake and blinked a few times before meeting my eyes.

"Right. Yeah. Cole and Megan went ahead to grab a table and I offered to come pick you up. They're all mushy and I'd rather meet you alone than be their third wheel, you know? Megan said she would text you to let you know. She didn't do that?"

My brows pulled together in confusion, and I turned to grab my phone off the counter where I left it after getting home. Sure enough, there was a text from my friend. It had come just as I was beginning to try out my new toy. The buzzing of the one having been much more captivating than the buzzing of the other.

"I guess I didn't hear it go off while I was …" I cleared my throat awkwardly. "Getting ready."

"You look amazing." He snapped his mouth shut like he hadn't meant to say it.

I couldn't help but smile. At least I wasn't the only one off kilter here. Besides, I *did* look amazing, and I wasn't ashamed to admit it in this instance since I stood in front of Adonis himself. Thank goodness I put in the extra effort instead of just a tank top and shorts like I would normally wear to The Crab Shack.

"Thank you. I like your shirt, the color really pops with your eyes."

"Thanks." His smile was wide and genuine, all pearly white teeth, and … oh my sweet great aunt's fluffy golden pancakes—*are those dimples?* I think my ovaries exploded. "If you're ready, my car is just outside."

I nodded in a mild daze and grabbed my purse, dropped my phone in the bottom and somehow – on the third try – managed to lock the door. Then followed him outside where he gallantly opened the door for me as I stepped into his car, and off we went.

Four

Dinner and Dessert

The ride to the restaurant was uneventful. I was quiet and shy, even when I wasn't sharing close space with the most attractive man I'd ever seen outside of a magazine. He tried to keep up a steady stream of non-threatening chit-chat.

"How long have you known Megan?"

"It feels like forever. We bonded in second grade over our love of Penguins. Happy Feet had come out that year and we were both obsessed. We both had penguin *everything,* and we started taking tap dance lessons together. We were both terrible at it, so that didn't last long." I had forgotten about the tap lessons. Our parents pulled us out of those because we spent most of the time giggling together over our missteps rather than actually making an effort." Megan said you and Cole have been best friends since you were kids too, right?"

He nodded as he signaled his next turn. "That's right. My Dad was in the military and Cole's parents were supportive while he was away. We managed to stay in one place longer than most active families do, but eventually we had to move. I spent all my summers with him and his folks. The school year sucked, but summer was something I always looked forward to. He's the one friend I made and managed to keep. Now we're really good at the long distance bromance thing." He threw a quirky grin in my direction.

I couldn't help but laugh a little. "You know, that's a problem."

He tensed up.

"There's this perfect word for guys who love each other but aren't *in love* with each other. But chicks don't have anything like that. 'Sismance' just doesn't have the same kind of ring to it."

He barked out a laugh. "You're right. It doesn't quite roll off the tongue. Is that what you and Megan have, a sismance? Chickmance, maybe?"

"Yeah, but I don't think chickmance is an improvement."

"If it makes you feel any better, women get chick flicks and men don't have an equivalent. Bro flicks doesn't work there so well."

"Fair point. I guess I can give you the bromance moniker then." I chuckled.

"I appreciate it. Very generous of you." With that he gave me a wink and my face flushed again.

When we parked at The Crab Shack, I went to open my door and Ender reached across to keep it shut. "I got it." He went around to open it for me from the outside.

"Thank you."

"I think I like you, Darcy." He offered his arm like some southern gentleman.

I couldn't resist winding my hand into the crook of his elbow, letting him lead me up the steps of the restaurant where Megan and Cole were waiting for us.

Cole wasn't paying attention, but Megan zeroed in on us, her face lighting up. I could practically see the delighted squeal building up in her body. She wasn't just happy to see *me* right now, she was excited to see me on the arm of Ender. She was already beginning to plan my wedding to this man I hardly knew, and I wondered if maybe I misunderstood her true intentions in getting me to meet Ender ... and why she might have so readily given him the thumbs up to pick me up from my apartment.

Once we were at their level she ran up to hug me, as Ender and Cole exchanged the guy version of the same thing with hard thumps on one another's backs. It was easy to see the deep affection between them in the gesture.

"Darcy!" Megan was squealing now. "I'm so excited you're here! How was the drive? How is Ender?" She gushed in an undertone so the boys couldn't quite catch what she said. I was pretty sure they knew what was going on anyway. They weren't stupid.

"Meg, please." I gritted my teeth behind a smile. "Not now. It's fine, everything is fine."

She lifted an eyebrow in disbelief. "That little stroll looked like it was more than just *fine*. He's cute right?"

"Megan! Stop it! He's *right there*, you know."

She giggled, and turned back to wrap an arm around her future husband.

We stood around and chatted until our table was ready. Ender offered his arm again when the hostess came to seat us, going as far as to pull my chair out for me at the table, and sat across from me while Megan took the seat next to me.

I thought chivalry was dead, but Ender was showing up every man I had ever met. Including Cole.

We all ordered, then bantered about our fondest memories of our respective best friends. We laughed at our many shenanigans, then reminisced on all the times we thought we were so cool and grown up, only to find out we were definitely not.

As the evening wore on, Ender paid more and more attention to me, his eyes seeming to linger just a little too long at points in our conversation. He helped me crack a tough crab leg and offered me the rest of his butter when he finished with his plate.

If there was one solid way to a girl's heart, it was butter. He may as well have proposed right there. I would have said yes.

Megan's eyes were on us throughout the evening as well. She appeared to be analyzing every move he made, every smile I sent his way, and the tonality of each and every comment we exchanged. In between her sleuthing she was playing footsie with Cole under the table. Cole couldn't seem to stop himself from reaching across the table to hold her hand between bites from his meal.

The whole thing was just romantic and mushy. I couldn't help but laugh at the situation I had found myself in. This had *never* been my thing. I didn't do romance, long lingering touches, fawning gazes, and butterflies in my tummy. Yet, I was in the middle of it, and wanting it all. Ender and I may not have been touching, but his eyes suggested he wanted to reach for my hand the same way Cole was for Megan's. I wished he would.

After our meal we ended up leaving with different partners than we arrived with. I was disappointed I was going home with Megan rather than Ender, who was taking Cole with him back to his apartment. He gave me a warm hug, bordering on an embrace. A look crossing his features as he stepped away said he wanted to say, or do, something more. He didn't, and I missed his warmth after the hug ended.

In the car Megan started in on me and I put a hand up to stop her.

"Not right now, okay?" I laughed to take the sting out of it. "I just want to enjoy this for now. You can drill me about everything later. Yes, I like him. Yes, he's gorgeous. That's all I'm saying for now."

She gave me a knowing, sly smile, then mimed zipping her lips, but she still grinned the whole drive home.

Back in my apartment I shucked off my heels, the grin splitting my face making my cheeks ache but I couldn't stop smiling. I went into the bathroom and took off my makeup, managing to force seriousness long enough to get the foundation out of my laugh lines.

I tossed my dress into the dirty laundry pile and picked out a set of thin satin pajamas, button-down collared shirt and frilly shorts I only wore when feeling feminine. I replayed every single moment from the evening in my head. My memory of it didn't do his perfect dimples justice, or the fine edge of his jaw, the unique storm cloud blue of his eyes, but Ender took up every square inch of real estate in my mind.

I could practically feel his arms as they wrapped around me for a short moment, which stretched out in my thoughts as though it lasted for hours rather than seconds. I had been pressed against his chest, able to feel the pull and release of his muscles as he moved, his chin briefly resting on top of my head. He smelled like fresh linen with a bright citrus top note, just enough to make the scent a little sweet, and still masculine.

I remembered how his hands cracked the crab legs, his corded forearms working as he snapped them open to get at the meat inside. His long fingers dripping with butter ... the way he sucked each one into his mouth to lick it off when he was finished. I was surprised to find that in my reverie of all things Ender, my hands had undone the buttons of my top of their own accord, and my fingers stroked over my taught nipples.

Ravenous for release, I reached for my magic wand. I left it in the bathroom and never put it back. But there was something else in the satin bag when I grabbed for it.

I pulled out another device, shaped much like my wand, but this one had a small hole shaped like a suction cup, just large enough I could press my pinky finger into it. Attached to the device was a note:

On the house. This is just a "tester", come see me for a better model. –Mindy

I wasn't sure whether this was sweet or creepy. She must have slipped it in while I was being paranoid about Megan seeing me make my purchase, and I somehow missed it when I pulled out the wand last night. I was also not sure what this was. Obviously it went *down there,* but what did it do?

I pressed my finger to the little button on the opposite side of the hole for a few seconds until it started up. My brows pulled together at the odd sound of air puffing out of the hole, and I pressed my pinky finger to it and giggled a bit at the sucking sensation that pulled at the tip.

Oh I see. I grinned and bit my lip. *Mindy hasn't steered me wrong yet.*

I should have been embarrassed to be thinking of Ender as this new delightful device found its way beneath my shorts and onto my clit. But the sensation that took over was so tantalizing his image was soon scrubbed from my consciousness as I fell into the throws of an awe-inspiring climax.

Once I finished, I could scarcely remember my own name, let alone *his,* and I felt no guilt whatsoever in finding such a satisfying release.

I take it all back. Megan, nor the wand, nor this fabulous new toy are my best friend anymore. My best friend is Mindy. Mindy knows *things, and she's discreet about it. I may be in love with Mindy.*

In the morning I called the Knock Out Boutique, Mindy answered on the second ring.

"Knock Out Boutique this is Mindy, how may I bring your fantasy to reality today?"

I stifled a laugh at the introduction. That could be taken the wrong way.

"Hi Mindy. My name is Darcy, I came into your shop the other day with my friend?" I slapped my hand to my forehead for sounding like an idiot at asking a question as though I didn't know whether I'd been there or not.

"Oh yes! Darcy! Darling, how are you? Are you satisfied with your purchase?" At this point it was like she was that one weird Aunt most people have who is super eccentric but everyone loves because she's weird. Or was that Uncles? Whatever.

"Yes, that's why I was calling. I just want to say thank you for introducing me to something new, and for the extra gift you left in the bag. You really didn't have to do that. I'd be happy to come and pay for it."

"Did you enjoy it?" There was a knowing lilt to her voice.

"Yes. Yes, I did." My face was flaming and I was glad we were not having this conversation in person.

"Then there is no need. I remember being new to pleasure toys. I wish I had had someone to give that kind of gift to me and show me there was no shame in it so I could have enjoyed it for more of my life." She laughed. "I don't want you to miss out like I did. Come in any time you want to try something new. I'll be glad to help you."

"Thank you so much, Mindy. "

I could almost hear her smiling as she clicked off, and I made a vow to go back to her shop soon and buy everything she showed me.

FIVE
TOY VS TONGUE

As the rehearsal dinner approached I stayed busy with finalizing plans for the Bachelorette Party which was happening the day after rehearsal, and coaching Meg through all her anxiety while dodging talk about Ender as much as possible.

I hadn't seen him again since our initial introduction and dinner, but Megan wouldn't stop talking about him. He and Cole had been out prepping for the wedding, going to Tuxedo fittings and running all the errands Megan sent their way. All the while she was insisting *he* couldn't stop asking about *me*. Which I found hard to believe. Even the guys I had dated in the past hadn't been *that* interested.

Still, Megan kept badgering me about him.

"You said you liked him, though right?" We were at the church getting ready for the rehearsal dinner.

"Yes, Meg! I liked him! He was nice, he was gorgeous, what more do you want from me?"

"How about I give him your phone number? Cole says he keeps asking if you've said anything about him and all I can give him is you thought he was *nice*, which is the lamest compliment ever, by the way. If he has your number, he can ask you himself. And you can go on a date. And get married. And have babies." She was serious about the potential outcome.

"First." I hold up a finger before straightening a table cloth. "I am not getting married. You are. Second, I do not want babies *any* time soon, that's why I have an IUD even though I haven't hooked up with anyone in—"

"In two *years*."

I pointed at her in acknowledgement of her accuracy.

"Third, I don't think I want to be with a guy long distance. I like living here and I would never expect someone to move here just to be with me. That's ridiculous."

She placed floral center pieces down a long table. "About that. Ender had an interview for a job in town this week at..." She was cut off as the door to the dining hall opened with a gust.

"The men have arrived!" An insanely happy, almost giddy, Cole walked in carrying a box full of china. Ender was close on his heels, his eyes finding me. A broad smile lit up his features and he sent me a wink. The shy smile that graced my face was automatic.

Megan dropped her centerpiece haphazardly and rushed to throw her arms around Cole as he plopped the box down on the table with a clatter of porcelain. His mouth crushed to hers as he picked her up, her toes swinging off the ground.

"Ugh, you guys, get a room!"

Cole broke away long enough to give me a cocky grin. "Soon enough, Darcy, you're going to be yelling for us to get a building instead."

"Ew!" I laughed, picked up a folded napkin, and threw it at his face.

Then Ender was by my side helping me with the place settings, bumping my shoulder or making little comments under his breath about the lovebirds. It was all innocent, but when I met his eyes there was something more there. A hunger. The look raised goosebumps on my skin and caused a simmering heat to build in my center.

My gaze lingered on his lips during dinner as he gave his speech to party. He was seated across from me again, and every once in a while his toes pressed on the tops of my shoes under the table, a discreet signal a more primal part of my mind understood. Soon, I was returning the gesture, slipping my feet out of my heels to run my toes over the top of his flip-flop clad feet or against his ankles. I could have sworn he shivered once from the contact. When he met my gaze afterward, he was biting his lip as he grinned at me, heat ever more present in his look.

When our speeches were done and the guests were gone, we shooed Megan and

Cole off home while we cleaned up. For the most part we worked in silence. The quiet was heavy and building in pressure like a volcano about to erupt. Electricity crackled between us every time we passed one another as we packed up tablecloths, and loaded dishes into dishwashers. Every touch was "accidental", virtuous enough, but laden with promise for later.

By the time we were finished, I was already breathless and needy. He walked me to my car and leaned forward as though to open the door for me, instead pressing my back to the vehicle, caging me between his arms and kissing me with all the pent-up energy we had held onto the entire night.

His tongue slid over mine, tangling, heady. A quiet moan slipped from my throat, and he broke away, brushing his nose against mine.

"Can I come to your place?" His voice was rough and deep, and still every bit the gentleman. His intention was clear, if he came to my place things were going to get serious, but he wouldn't hold a grudge if I decided to back out. As much as he had just taken charge, he wanted to know I was okay with it.

Unable to find my voice I just nodded.

He leaned his forehead against mine, a harsh breath gusting from his already swollen lips.

"I'll follow you. Drive safe, huh? Wouldn't want something to happen to you before I can get a real taste of you."

I made record time getting back to the apartment, and he was on my tail the whole way. I could barely get the key into the lock on the door because he was behind me, sweeping my hair aside and trailing hot kisses down my neck and over my shoulder, moving the strap of my dress aside for uninterrupted access to my skin.

We stumbled into the apartment. I dropped my keys and purse on the floor because I missed my counter as I also reached to pull his shirt up. We left a trail of clothing in our wake as we made our way to my bedroom. With my dress off and my bra coming undone he snatched me up into his arms. Pressing me to the wall and pinning me there with his hips, his mouth devoured every inch of my skin, and his hands brushed over my breasts.

My hands were in his hair, clawing at his shoulders, too frantic to land anywhere for long. *Good lord it has been too long, and it has never* ever *been like this.* I pulled his face back up to mine so I could kiss him, sucking his bottom lip into my mouth and giving it a nip that elicited a deep, rumbling growl from his chest.

He snatched me off the wall and managed to toss me onto my bed. Finding the lamp on the bedside table he flicked it on muttering about being "damned if he wouldn't see every inch" of me.

When the light came on, he paused, his eyes having caught on something…

More specifically, and to my horror, having caught on the secret gift Mindy had left me and which I had forgotten to put back into its bag after I used it last.

My hands flew to cover my face in my embarrassment as he picked it up with curiosity. A low chuckle met my ears, and his weight shifted next to me as he stretched out on the bed. He pulled one hand from my face. He was smiling devilishly at me.

"I happen to know what this is." The wicked smile widened. "Is this your favorite?"

I couldn't answer. There's no way I could answer that question. The answer, of course, being *YES*. He chuckled again when my face—no, my entire body flushed tomato red.

"You remember before we left I said I wanted a real taste of you?"

I nodded.

"I meant it. I'm willing to bet I can make you forget you ever enjoyed using this." His eyes were a deep pool of sinful promises. He tossed the toy aside and proceeded, with maddening slowness, to kiss and lick his way over my body making me forget my humiliation. Paying delicate attention to each breast, one hand glided down my stomach to my panties where he tugged them down my hips as his mouth followed the path of his hand. Once he had them off, he flicked them to the side with a smirk.

He was kneeling at the edge of my bed. Curling his strong hands around my thighs he dragged my hips to the edge, in front of his face. He hooked my knees over his shoulders, kissing his way up the inside of my thighs as he did. He pressed a hand to my stomach to hold me in place, the other hand still hooked around my left thigh, keeping me right where he wanted me.

In one long, slow stroke his tongue made a path up my center, stopping to tease my clit for a too brief moment before plunging it deep inside me. As my back arched, his hand pressed me back down, and his admonishment rumbled in my core as he devoured me like a last meal. It was nearly enough to send me over the edge then and there.

His attention to detail was striking. Even in my hazy sex fueled sensibility I was aware of how intentional he was being. A few strokes deep within, then slow circles around my clit, a gentle nip, a hard suck. His timing perfect to keep my body buzzing on the edge of explosive release. Even with his hand heavy on my stomach, and vise like grip around my thigh I couldn't keep from writhing around him. I was making the most mortifying sounds, little squeaks and yips, low guttural moans and muffled screams. It just propelled him on in his quest to convince me his tongue was more effective than my toy.

"Are you ready?" He barely broke contact with my pussy before diving into it again with ferocity.

I couldn't speak, I was too concerned about what would come out of my mouth if I opened it. I nodded in an erratic motion that might have looked more like I was having a seizure. His chuckle vibrated low in my core.

"Come for me." He growled, then latched his lips around my clit and sucked *hard.*

A primordial detonation of color blinded all awareness for an extended, euphoric moment hanging in a rip of the space-time continuum he'd created in my body. Concussive shockwaves wracked my limbs as I came down off the high. All the while he was kissing his way back up my body until he was lying next to me again.

He caressed every curve, every goose fleshed patch of skin, every line of my face. Those gentle caresses caused a little convulsion to take me each time, and a light buzzing thrummed in my extremities like I was connected to a live wire.

When I managed to open my eyes, my system settling, he was smiling at me with his head propped against his hand. He'd managed to get out of his underwear, likely while I was blacked out by my orgasm. He leaned forward and kissed the tip of my nose.

"Still need your toy? Or will having me around instead suffice?" He knew damn well what my answer would be.

"If you're sticking around, I'll dump that thing down the garbage disposal."

"Good. I'd like to do that to you some more." His hard length pressed against me. "But there are other things I'd like to do first if you've come back down to earth again?"

A throaty giggle escaped me. "What do you have in mind?"

He didn't bother answering with words. Turned out, he was a man who knew actions spoke louder. And trust me, we were loud.

Epilogue

The week of the wedding Ender landed a job with the same architectural firm Cole worked for. Since Cole was no longer in need of his apartment, and the landlord hadn't found a new tenant, Ender took over his lease and started making plans to ship his belongings. Once the wedding was over he was going to dash back to get his things packed.

It's been six months since then, and it only took a few dates before we officially became a couple. He was amazing. Charismatic and funny, and an absolute ace in the sack. But he made me feel like a better version of myself. His confidence had bled into me, and I was taking opportunities I never even dreamed of as I applied for jobs managing marketing strategies. He had been constantly encouraging me, and pushing me onward.

Now he was on his way back from his third consult with a building company, and he asked me to pick him up from the airport. As soon as he folded his tall frame into my little sedan he leaned over the center console to kiss me, threading long fingers into my hair. The feeling was exquisite. Every look and touch from him was like electricity coursing through my veins, sparking over my nerve endings.

A slow smile spread over my face when he pulled back to look at me. I couldn't help the glow I was feeling as the freaking pterodactyls bounced around in my tummy. Butterflies were for losers who had never been kissed by Ender Collins.

"Thanks for picking me up. I missed you." He brushed his nose against mine before leaning back. "Do you mind if we stop somewhere real quick?"

"No problem."

He gave me an address and I pulled out into traffic. We didn't say anything as we made our way there, and the car was full of nervous anticipation. Out of the corner of my eye I saw his fingers knotted together in his lap, knuckles white. As we rounded the last corner heading to a tall, pristine apartment complex I caught him rummaging through is carry-on between his feet.

"What's this?" I asked when I put the car in park.

"I'll show you."

I waited patiently as he rounded the car to open my door, something I'd become used to over our short courtship. He took my hand, threading our fingers together and led me into the building.

This place was pretty high class, way above my current living conditions. He led me to an elevator and after a quiet ride to the tenth floor we exited to a foyer that had double doors on either side of its expanse. Only two sets of double doors were found in the vast foyer, one on each side, number 1001 on the left and 1002 on the right. Taking out a key, Ender unlocked the left doors and swung them open wide for me to step through.

My jaw hit the floor in shock. It was an open floor plan with all the top line amenities, and it was mostly furnished with brand new furniture. It was gorgeous.

"What do you think?" His hands were stuffed down in his pockets as he looked at me.

"Like it? Ender, this is amazing! What is going on?"

"Well, Cole and I landed a huge deal with the building company I just met with. It's enough for us to start our own business. More than enough actually. And we have another company that wants our designs. He and Megan are moving into the apartment across from here."

I was stunned. How could I not have known this? Megan is my best friend and she hadn't told me? What the hell?

"Hey, don't freak out yet. I made Meg promise not to say anything. She's been bursting at the seams though. She helped me pick out some of the furniture because I wanted to make sure I got things you would like. I wanted to make a place for you that you'd love."

"I don't think I quite understand." My head was starting to go a bit fuzzy as my subconcious started to draw conclusions my concious mind was unable to grasp. While I was trying to wrap my head around this bombshell I hadn't noticed him take something from his pocket.

"This is the other part of the surprise. I know we haven't been together for very long, but I just ... *know*."

He stepped closer to me, not quite making eye contact as he fiddled with a little black box in one hand

"I never expected to find someone like you, Darcy. You came out of nowhere. Cole and I talked that night, that *first* night after dinner at the crab shack. I told him what I thought about you, that instant magnetic attraction. He set up an interview for me, and I knew I had to land that job. I *had* to be close to you. I couldn't let you get away. We decided that once I got the job we would start putting together a plan to form a company, and once we had a good start ... I could do this."

His tongue swept out over his lips as he knelt before me.

"I know deep in my bones I want to spend my life with you. You're it for me, Darcy. You make me want to be a better person. You build me up and support every whim I have. Even more than that, you let me support you, too. You've shown yourself to be a perfect a partner. You're beautiful, intelligent, and the most enrapturing woman I've ever known. Will you marry me?"

My mouth was dry and my throat parched. I could hardly take in what he was saying. Thankfully the subconscious part of my brain was still functioning. That part was doing the happy dance my body was currently incapable of enacting due to shock. I felt a tear slip down my face as I managed to swallow.

"You really mean that?" I couldn't believe this was happening, but a smile was creeping up my cheeks.

"Without a doubt or hesitation." He opened the top of the box to reveal a single carat, princess cut diamond solitaire.

"Absolutely yes." I wrapped my arms around his neck and kissed him senseless while joyful tears slid down my cheeks.

And that's how we started our happily ever after.

About The Author

K Elise Hoffman is a lover of books, cats, coffee, and colorful hair (which changes frequently). She is new to this thing called story writing, but determined to reach for the literary stars. When she's not at the keyboard she is chasing around her miniature clones, narrating audio books for other authors kind enough to entrust their creation to her, and reading as much as possible while snuggled up with one, or more, of her four cats. You can connect with her in various places like Facebook, Instagram, and TikTok via the tag @bookishlybye

http://www.facebook.com/bookishlybye

The Sponsors

Rae B. Lake

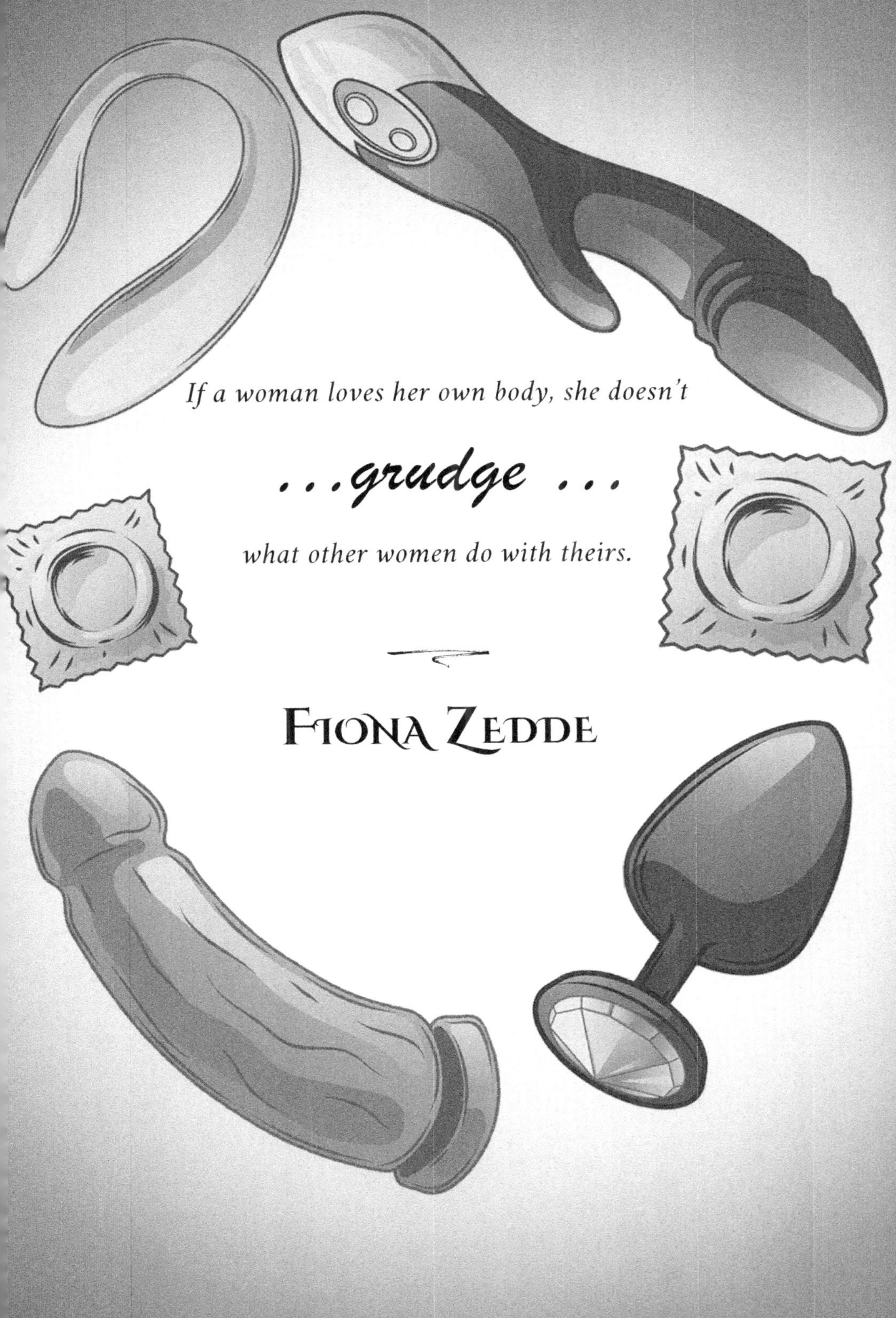
If a woman loves her own body, she doesn't
...grudge ...
what other women do with theirs.
FIONA ZEDDE

One

Perla

"Once you sign this contract, you belong to us for the night."

My eyes drift over the words again. I never thought I'd be in a predicament like this. My life revolves around cars and engines. Now I'm in a room with three brothers who want to have their way with me, and I'm actually entertaining the idea.

When I woke up this morning, this is not how I thought my night would end.

Eight Hours Earlier

"Perla, you don't understand. It's not like I have a choice. I already lost. I can't get the money anywhere else!" Tammy screams in my face before she turns and barges into her room, closing the door behind her.

"Are you fucking kidding me? You have the nerve to be upset with *me* when you're the one who lost our house gambling? I don't know what you have to do, but you're going to head down to that casino and tell them that the deal is off." I push my way into her room, not giving a shit about the boundaries she's trying to set.

My sister exploded my world in a matter of minutes. I work hard to provide for my siblings, and thankfully, my mother left us the family home. Imagine my surprise when I come home for lunch to find my sister boxing up our fucking stuff. She has gambled her entire paycheck away. Then, because she was *so* sure she'd come out a winner, she decided to place a seventy-five thousand dollar bet on a card game, using our house as collateral.

"Perla, these aren't the type of people you can just say, 'Hey, the deal is off.' It

I slam my hand on her oak dresser—the one that's been in the same spot her entire life. "Then *make* it work like that!" Knickknacks and makeup skitter to the floor from the force of my blow.

Teresa glares at me for a second before she falls onto her bed and weeps. "Perla, I don't know what to do. They'll *kill* me; these people are no joke. I *tried* to find a different way."

I don't want to feel sorry for her, but she's my kid sister, and even though she fucked up, I still love her. I don't want her to hurt like this. "What people are you talking about? Is it the fucking mob or something like that?"

"No. Worse." She wipes the tears from her eyes and stares up at me.

"What the fuck is worse than the mob?" My eyebrows jump to my hairline.

"Motorcycle club," she replies.

I've seen a few clubs around town, but I don't know much about them. If Teresa's saying they're worse than the mob, then I have to believe her. "They're coming today?"

Teresa already has half of our house packed in totes and garbage bags, and I rack my brain for a solution to this mess.

"Yeah, Bones said I need to be out before four this afternoon."

Spearing my hands through my hair, I glance over at the clock, and it's almost two. "Would he come over earlier if you called him?"

"Why the *hell* would I do that? He'll see I'm not even close to finishing up." Her gaze darts around the room, and she picks up another bag to continue packing.

"I need to have a talk with him—there has to be a way we can work *something* out."

I want to give her a little bit of hope. If we're forced to leave this house, we'll have nowhere to go.

Even if she can't find a way, *I* have to.

It's up to me now.

Two loud motorcycles pull into my driveway, and my heart jumps into my throat.

I've seen a lot of bikers driving around town, but I guess I never got a good look at them. These bastards are scary looking. Both wear leather vests with various patches on them. The largest emblem on the back is a set of wings with skulls inside, and under it reads, "Wings of Diablo MC, New Orleans Chapter."

"That's them," my sister tells me. "The one with all the scars is Bones, and the bigger one is Pirate."

I tilt my head in Teresa's direction. "Really? *That's* their names?"

"Maybe they use fake names, so they don't get caught by the cops or something like that." Teresa shrugs her shoulders and moves farther behind me, as if my body will hide her. Even at twenty years old, Teresa is still looking to me for protection.

A heavy knock sounds at the door. "Go on to your room. Let me talk to them on my—" She's already backing up before I even have a chance to finish the sentence.

"Are you sure?" Her eyes are wide, and I can tell she's scared.

"Yeah," I nod, "go on."

I head to the door and take a deep breath to steady myself before I open it. I don't want them to see how scared I am, but I've never had to deal with anything like this in my life.

The second the door opens, the pair stroll in without the slightest hesitation, as if they know the house is already theirs.

"Doesn't seem like you did much clearing out," Pirate, the larger one, remarks.

"We can just toss it," Bones tells him.

Neither of them have yet to address me. Scary or not, there is no excuse for bad manners.

Stabbing my hands on my hips, I narrow my eyes. "Excuse me? You *do* realize you are in *my* home and have yet to speak to me."

The men turn and fix menacing stares on me. But I refuse to back down.

"I see." Pirate smirks. "I'm sorry, I was under the impression that you were calling us here to get the transfer over with. Is there something *else* we need to discuss?" He saunters over to me. "Like, you having our money?"

I stare at him defiantly. "I don't have it."

"Then we have nothing to talk about." The large man turns away from me to examine more of the house.

Darting around his frame, I stand in front of him. "The *hell* we don't." My hand shoots up, and I press it to his chest. The other man, Bones, takes a step in my direction, and by the look in his eyes, he's clearly ready to do some physical harm. I drop my hand from Pirate's chest. "Look, I don't know what my sister did, or how the hell a bet like this can even be made, but this house is all I have. I have to take care of her *and* my little brother, not to mention myself. There has to be another way. There must be a way for us to come up with the money, if you give me a chance." The words race out of my mouth—they're panicked, but this is an intense situation.

"How old is your little brother?" Bones asks.

Letting out a breath, I answer, "He's seven."

"Ya'll don't have any family in the area?" He arches a brow. "Where are your parents?"

"They died. We have nothing. I barely make ends meet as it is. I work at a small auto parts shop—"

"You're a mechanic?" Their eyes pop wide in surprise.

I hate that just because I have the typical blonde hair, blue eyes, and big tits, they assume I don't like to get my hands dirty. "Yeah, I work on domestic engines."

They glance at each other, what seems to be a secret look passing between them.

"Look, your sister owes us seventy-five thousand dollars. It's not something we can just let go." Pirate picks up one of the doilies sitting on the side table by the phone. "But since it's not just your sister we're kicking out, there may be a way you can make the money, if you want to."

I bite my lip for a second and scan the room. I'll do whatever it takes to keep this place, but if it's something that will land me in jail, I'll definitely have a serious problem with it. "Will I be doing anything illegal?"

"No, it's not illegal," Pirate replies, "but it *is* frowned on."

"Fine, what is it?" I offer them a seat, and they go over the *one* option I've never in my life thought I'd even consider.

Payment for sexual favors.

Two

Perla

Bones and Pirate agree to hold off on kicking us out of the house if I look into the sponsorship program they offer to a select few individuals. Apparently, the Gold Wings Casino has quite a few high-rolling clients. Some of which might be willing to help me out of the predicament I'm in. My sister isn't a candidate for their special program, because she uses recreational drugs. Another secret I hadn't been aware of before this shitshow went down.

I, on the other hand, am as clean as a fucking whistle. I barely even drink alcohol. Although the two of them try to convince me that it isn't prostitution, I know what I'm getting into. If this is the only way I'm going to be able to keep my home, then I guess I'm going to have to walk down this seedy road.

The two of them explain that there's a two-fold interview process. Part one: I don't get to see the sponsors, but they'll be able to see me. This is where they'll decide if they like my appearance. The second part of the process is, if the sponsors choose me, I'll be able to discuss exactly what they're interested in and sign all the appropriate paperwork. It's all very technical, and apparently, a lucrative business for the casino as well.

The other part of the deal is that I'll have to work as an on-call mechanic for their MC. It's a paid gig, so I have no problem with it.

I'm to show up at the casino at nine this evening in semi-formal attire. Dress to impress. I put on my little black dress, four-inch black heels, and blow-dry my hair. I don't waste much energy on my makeup—my natural look usually gets more attention than I can handle.

My sister owes *seventy-five thousand dollars.* The number alone seems astronomical. I don't know how much money these people have, but I'm sure I'll have to do some mind-boggling shit if it's going to be worth that kind of cash.

When I walk into the small area where Pirate instructed me to meet him, there are four other women. One of them is dripping in diamonds. Her dress appears to be made of rhinestones and barely covers her ass. Her hair is styled in big fluffy waves that cascade down her back. She shoots a catty glance in my direction, but I shift my gaze away. I'm not here to fight her or anyone else. I just hope there's someone that likes what they see in me enough to be a sponsor. Even if it's not the entire amount owed, maybe it'll be enough to hold off Pirate and Bones from taking the house.

A man walks into the room wearing a Wings of Diablo vest—the same as Pirate and Bones. This guy says his name is Shyne. His smile is easy, and he's not hard on the eyes, either. I'm more at ease, which is probably why he's here, and *not* Bones, who looks like he could melt the skin from your face with just one glare.

"Ladies, it's very nice to see you this evening. We have a few sponsors ready to meet you, so I'd like to get this underway. First let me ask—do we have any new people here tonight?"

I raise my hand. I'm the only one who does. *Oh, shit.*

"Figures." The woman in the rhinestone dress scoffs under her breath.

I squint my eyes, and peer in her direction. I may not be here for a fight, but I won't back down from one if she chooses to start some shit.

"Okay, no problem. I'll run down what you're to expect this evening, and what we're trying to achieve." Shyne nods at me before he explains in more detail what Pirate and Bones told me earlier. "You are not forced to do anything, but if you don't complete the tasks, the contracts will be void and you will not be paid.

"The usual requests from the sponsors are men or women to spend weeks with them in distant lands—some just want to act out incredible fantasies. Others just want a good fuck. Either way, the expectations will be known before anything is signed."

After he explains everything, I nod and tell him I understand. Shyne gives us all a form to fill out, which includes personal information along the lines of the date of my last period. A few photos are taken, then we're shuffled into another room behind a one-way mirror so the sponsors can get a good look at what they're getting for their money.

THREE

MARCUS

"This is ridiculous. The last two times we tried this, it turned out to be shit." Malcolm sits back in his chair and downs another shot of whiskey.

"I know, but how many women do you know who would be open to being with all three of us with no strings attached? This is the only way to do it without any blowback. We've got too many acquisitions to have some woman going to the press about our kinks." I pour my own glass of whiskey and take a seat next to him.

This sponsorship program that the Wings of Diablo MC offers through the Gold Wings Casino is a gift and a curse to my brothers and me. We have a specific need most women either don't understand or can't seem to come to grips with.

Mathew, Malcolm, and I are brothers—each of us less than eighteen months apart. We grew up on a small island in the Caribbean, with parents more concerned about the social class of the people we hung around with than their moral compasses. The three of us grew up sharing a lot, including our women. When we were younger, it was easier to find a girl that didn't mind having fun with us. Though now that we're grown and the CEOs of one of the fastest growing acquisitions and merger companies in the western hemisphere, it's a bit harder. Everyone either wants to change us, marry us off, or destroy us. This sponsorship program is the only way we have been able to find women who fit all of our criteria, and still keep it out of the public eye. The only problem is the past two women we've chosen to sponsor have come up lacking in one way or another.

"Malcolm, take it easy. You know the last two times it only turned out bad, because you were such an asshole to them." Mathew chuckles at our brother while he scrolls through his phone.

My brothers and I are in a room waiting for our first glimpse at the candidates. There is a one-way mirror on one wall where we'll be able to see them, but they won't be able to see us. I'm assuming there are other sponsors, but I've never seen them. The Wings take great care to make sure each sponsor is set up in their own room, completely separate from the others.

"Here we go." Mathew puts his phone away as a bright light illuminates the stage, and the women make their way into the space, each of them fitted with a number for identification.

"That one." The words are out of my mouth before number seven can fully get into my line of sight. It's almost impossible to choose someone based on looks alone when you have such an outrageous lifestyle for them to adjust to. But something about number seven screams strength and rebellion.

"Which?" Mathew asks, glancing over my shoulder, trying to figure out who I'm talking about.

"Number seven." Malcolm's voice is deep and husky.

"You see that, too?" I shoot him a glance over my shoulder, only to see him focused on the gorgeous woman in the black dress and dirty-blonde hair. Number seven.

"Fuck yes."

"Oh." Mathew finally catches on. "Oh, yeah, I'm going to have fun with her."

He's on board. All that's left is to make sure our offer is good enough for her to sign on with us. She may be just what we're looking for physically, but that doesn't mean we're what *she's* looking for. It isn't normal for us to cater to what a woman needs, but I have to talk to Shyne or Pirate about what this one needs, so we can make her an offer she can't refuse.

FOUR

PERLA

Three offers come my way. One is for thirty thousand dollars, which is far less than what I need. The other is for a hundred thousand dollars, but it's for an ongoing tryst—again *not* what I'm looking for. Finally, there is another for ninety thousand dollars. With the twenty percent charge the Wings take as a fee, this would be almost enough for me to pay off the debt. The caveat with this offer is that though it's for one night, it's also with three men.

I'm sitting across from Shyne in a waiting room, discussing my options. "They *all* want to be with me? The three of them?"

"If that's what the paperwork says, then yes." Shyne's waiting on me to choose an offer to move forward. He shoots me a smile, but I can tell by the heavy sighs, I'm starting to get on his nerves. I've asked questions about every part of the contract, probably more than he's used to.

I've never been with more than one man at a time, but I can't lie and say I'm not interested. *How will that even work?* Will they just lay there, and expect me to please them? Are they into each other and want me to watch? It's intriguing to say the least.

"If I choose this one, is it set in stone? What if I don't like it?"

He shrugs. "Like I said, in the beginning, no one will force you to do anything you don't want to, but if you back out, you don't get paid."

I gnaw on the inside of my mouth. I need that money. "Okay, this one." I hand over the offer from the trio. He initials a few places before grabbing my hand and leading me toward a different room.

"Where are we going?" My palms are sweaty and my pulse thunders in my ears. God, this is the worst fucking idea I've ever had.

"You have to meet with them. If they're good to go, and all the paperwork is signed, that's it." Shyne opens a door and ushers me inside.

My mouth drops open as I get a good look at the three men I'm supposed to spend a night with. I expected them to be old or ugly in some way, not so aesthetically pleasing. *Damn*. I couldn't have been more wrong.

These men are drop-dead gorgeous. They aren't triplets, but I can tell they're brothers. All three of them have ink-black hair and gray eyes. Two of them have what looks to be a few days' worth of scruff on their face, while the other is clean-shaven.

"Perla, these men have put in a request to sponsor you." Shyne gestures to each of them as he introduces us. "Malcolm Curran, Mathew Curran, and Marcus Curran. Gentlemen, this is Ms. Perla Gats."

"Perla." The man Shyne introduced as Mathew walks up and grips my hand. He kisses my knuckles, and I can't help but giggle. It's cute.

I take a seat in the one single chair, while two of them sit on the couch on the opposite side. Marcus stands behind it. I direct my attention to Shyne, who's standing by the door.

"Please, feel comfortable to speak freely among yourselves." Shyne pulls out his phone, ignoring us, but not leaving the room.

"Do you do things like this often?" Malcolm is the first to speak. His mouth is set in a tight line, and his gaze makes me a bit uncomfortable, as if in my mind, I know he's dangerous.

I shake my head. "No, I've never done anything like this."

He strokes his chin, seeming to study my expression. "Why now?"

"Does it matter? Either you like me, or you don't." I shrug and immediately regret it. I'm supposed to be impressing them. I don't think giving them attitude is the right way to go.

"It matters," the one introduced as Marcus says, leaning forward. "We like to know what kind of person we're getting involved with."

I figure it's best to be honest and give him a straight answer. "My sister owes a substantial amount of money, and this is the only way for me to get it."

They share a look among each other before they continue talking. Their questions range from when my last sexual partner was, to if I'm open to the use of different types of sexual apparatuses. I've used the occasional vibrator. Only from the way they're talking about it, I'm starting to believe that this is more than just your normal ten-speed bullet from the sex store.

"How do you feel about being with all of us at the same time?" Marcus asks from behind the couch.

I can tell them that I'm a hundred percent cool with it, but that will be a lie. "I'll be honest, I'm scared. I'm not used to doing anything like this."

"I swear to you, nothing will happen that you don't want to. It's an intense experience, but one that will be pleasurable for all of us." Mathew's voice is smooth. It feels like silk wrapping around my doubts and concerns.

It's crazy and even dangerous, but also exhilarating. *Fuck it. You only live once, right?*

Heaving out a breath, I agree, "Okay, I'm willing to give it a try."

They smile and sign the paperwork.

"So do we do this here or . . .?" I direct my attention to Shyne who's still ignoring us.

"Here? Oh, no, sweetheart." Marcus is the one to speak up. "We'll have our fun tomorrow night." He stands and brings the contract back to me with a pen. "Once you sign this contract, you belong to us for the night."

My eyes scan the words on the papers for what feels like the millionth time, before settling on the agreed upon amount—ninety thousand dollars.

I shake away my apprehension, press the pen to the dotted line, and sign. I look up at the men before I mutter a soft prayer that I haven't just made the worst decision of my life.

FIVE

PERLA

The small house where I'm to meet the Curran brothers is located in the center of the French Quarter. I'm happy it's in a more populated part of town, but also a bit apprehensive. What if someone sees me walking in? Will they know what I'm doing there?

"Stop it. No one knows why you're here," I mutter under my breath, lifting my hand and pressing the bell. I did tell Teresa what I'm going to do, but as per the Nondisclosure agreement I signed, I couldn't tell her where, or with who. She only knows that if I don't come home, the bikers from the Wings of Diablo MC know where I am.

The door opens, and Mathew's there with a glass of wine in his hand.

"Perla, welcome." He stands back to let me in. As I make my way inside, both Malcolm and Marcus are there waiting for me to come in as well. Marcus steps forward, and takes my light jacket, as Mathew hands me the glass of wine.

"It's white. I hope that's okay with you?" Marcus indicates the wine Mathew just gave me.

"Um, yes, that's fine. Thank you." My eyes cut over to Malcolm who's still standing back, while his brothers tend to me. I let my gaze roam over him, but he doesn't look away. I wonder if he knows how intimidating he is. "You do a lot of staring. Are you trying to scare me off?"

He crosses his arms and arches an eyebrow. "If you're that easily scared off, then perhaps you're not the one for us."

"Malcolm!" Marcus hisses at him.

"It's fine." I walk past the two of them and toward Malcolm. "I've already told you I'm scared. I'm doing my best, but you seem intent on trying to make me feel as if you don't want me to stay. Just let me know, and I'll leave. I'll find a different way to get what I need." The words that come out of my mouth sound strong, but on the inside, I feel like I may turn to mush at any second.

Malcolm glares a second more before the corner of his mouth inches up in a slight smirk. "We wouldn't want that now, would we?" He lifts his hand, and I grasp it, then he turns and leads me down a long hallway. His brothers follow behind, as my heels click against the hardwood floor. The walls are lined with artwork and books, and the house itself has somewhat of a homey feel to it.

"Do the three of you live here?" I'm doing my best not to fall into an awkward silence.

"No," Marcus answers. "We live separately but use this place for our joint pursuits."

Malcolm shows me into a large dining area where a cherry wood table takes up a large portion of the space. Soft candlelight bathes the room as the smell of a rich culinary feast wafts up my nose. It reminds me of the tables you would see at large family dinners. There is food from one end to the other. Desserts, meats, and different side dishes, not to mention at least three different types of wine.

"How many people are we feeding?" Surely, this can't all be for me.

"We weren't sure what you would like," Mathew says. "We wanted to make sure you're comfortable."

"Making sure I keep my strength up," I quip.

Marcus and Mathew chuckle, while Malcom says, "Without a doubt."

We sit down for a meal, and if I don't think of how I'm about to have sex with these gorgeous men tonight, it almost feels somewhat normal talking to them.

I learn that Malcolm is the lead lawyer for Curran Enterprises, while Marcus runs the public relations department, and Mathew is the head of acquisitions. They don't tell me much about their work, but from what they do share, and the way they banter with each other, I can tell they're quite passionate about it.

Dinner is over quicker than I would have imagined, and as I push my plate away and fiddle with my second glass of wine, my pulse quickens. It's time for me to work for my money.

"Are you done with your meal?" Mathew asks from the opposite side of the table.

"Yes." I meet his gaze from above the rim of my wineglass. "I guess we should get this over with."

Mathew tsks and walks over to where I am, then grabs my hand, taking my glass, and helps me out of the chair. "I hope you don't truly feel that way. Yes, this night is about our needs and wants, but most, if not all of them revolve around pleasuring you. I'm quite confident this won't be a night you just want to get over with."

My lips part as Mathew leans in and kisses me on the side of my mouth, brushing his lips against mine. "Come, let us show you all the fun we have planned for tonight."

Like a puppy on a leash, I follow obediently behind Mathew, this time Marcus and Malcolm bringing up the rear.

I don't know what I expected when he opens up the double doors that lead into the massive bedroom, but I'm not expecting this.

Six

Perla

The room is massive, a fireplace roars on one side, and on the other, is a large, king-size, four-poster raised bed. The windows are covered by layers of black-out curtains, and the only light in the room comes from the fire. A small sitting area furnished with two lounge chairs and a dark-brown chaise decorate the far side of the room. I can also see the very edges of an en suite bathroom. If it in any way matches the rest of the room, I'm sure it'll be the most extravagant bathroom I've ever seen.

Next to the platform the bed sits on is a large table, and that's where my attention lands.

"Oh, um, wow." I don't move a muscle as my common sense and my sex drive war inside of me. On the table is every type of sex toy I've ever seen, even some I haven't. This is fucking *crazy*. I'm not prepared for this at all. Yeah, I have my vibrator under my mattress at home, but that small pink device is *nothing* compared to these. Though I'm petrified, my panties are already drenched from how turned on I am.

"Please, feel free to look at anything, touch, ask questions." Mathew steps to the side so I can move farther into the room.

I nod and walk over to the table. There are dildos, butt plugs, nipple clamps, vibrators, whips, handcuffs, and everything in between. Among the more interesting pieces on the table are a pair of what looks like latex gloves. I run a hand over them and feel that the fingers are all lined with some type of device.

Mathew smirks at my raised brow. "Those vibrate."

"Vibrate?" My voice squeaks out. "That seems like it would be too much." I swallow and move away.

"On the contrary, when used correctly it can be just right," Marcus says from behind me as he wraps an arm around my waist.

"We have pretty much anything you could want to use here. But if you would allow, I'd love to see you come while I use this." Mathew picks up the glove and slips it on his hand.

"O … okay." I take a deep breath and lean back into Marcus' grasp.

Malcom steps in front of me and grabs my chin. "Relax, Perla, let us take care of you."

I nod, and he leans forward to kiss me. It doesn't take long before my body completely submits to his attention. Malcolm is the most intense of the three brothers, and his kissing is no different. His hands cup my face as his tongue pushes and plunges into my mouth. A gasp escapes me as he pulls me closer to him, and I feel the distinct outline of his cock through his pants. He grinds against me and a deep ache pulses through my core.

"Malcolm, share," Marcus says from behind me. I'm so consumed by Malcolm's hot kisses, I almost forgot about the other two men I'll be pleasing tonight. My hair is pushed to the side before Marcus sucks and kisses up my neck and near the shell of my ear. He presses himself against my ass, and my hips rock back and forth against both of them. I let out a moan as they work me over.

"Fuck, you're so sexy," Mathew says from the side. I move my face away from Malcolm, but he doesn't miss a beat as he kisses and sucks down the opposite side of my neck. "Her dress, Marcus," Mathew orders his brother, and sure enough, Marcus pulls the zipper at my back until they both move away and lift the light-blue dress over my head.

A click precedes a low buzzing filtering through the room. Mathew rubs a slick liquid on the glove and moves closer to me. Marcus unhooks my bra, and Malcolm quickly pulls down my panties.

"Oh, God, is this really happening?" I can't believe I've managed to get myself into this.

"If you want us to stop, you have to say." Malcolm stands to his full height and peers down at me.

"No, I want it … More." They've barely touched me and already I feel so needy. I wrap my arms around Malcolm's neck and kiss him. Instead of standing in front of me, Malcolm moves to the side, allowing Mathew to move in closer. Marcus resumes his spot behind me, kissing my neck, but this time, his hands knead my ass.

My head leans back as Malcolm bends to lick and suck on my nipples.

"Mmm, that feels so good," I groan as I thread a hand in Malcolm's thick hair and snake my other hand around to Marcus who's grinding his thick cock against my bare ass. The feel of the cloth of his pants is heightening my arousal.

Mathew leans in and whispers in my ear. "That's it, Perla, just let yourself go. We've been dying to please you all day." His words are sure and clear, the gritty sound of his voice calling to my inner vixen like a fucking siren. He places the hand with the vibrating glove on my neck, and I jump at the sudden sensation. It's not too much like I'd first assumed. It's a deep vibration, just enough to make me want more. "We've been thinking about how you would look as we make you come over and over again," Mathew continues as he trails his gloved hand down my chest, pausing at my breast for a second, then moving down my midsection.

Marcus picks up whispering sweet nothings on the other side. "As we fuck you while you scream out our names."

Mathew's gloved hand makes its way down to my wet pussy at the same time as Malcolm raises up from his position worshiping my tits. He grabs my chin, and rubs his thumb over my lips, before slipping the pad of it into my mouth. His clear gray eyes lock on mine. "As we stuff every one of your holes with our cocks, and watch you love every fucking second of it."

Mathew rubs a vibrating finger over my clit, and my knees shake from the intensity of the pleasure exploding throughout my body.

"Mmm …" My mouth latches onto Malcolm's thumb and I suck hard. Mathew rubs that amazing vibrating glove against my pussy again, the deep sensation rolling through my body, causing me to cry out in need. Marcus kisses down my back and I feel something wet in my crack. His finger massages the tight ring, and I clench up. "We want to take you at the same time, but you need to prep a bit. Relax, we know what we're doing."

"I've only …" My mind is going a million miles a minute, and it's hard for me to formulate the right words. "Only once before." I try to let him know I'm not very experienced. Marcus continues massaging while Malcolm goes back and forth between sucking and nipping at my nipples.

My thighs squeeze together, but Marcus spreads them with his knee. I turn my head when something hard and thick presses into my ass—a butt plug. I gasp at how easily it slides in. I wait for the pain, but there is none.

"Oh, shit, you took it. Fuck. I can't wait." Marcus looks up into my face, I assume to wait for me to complain, but it feels good. "Matty, now. Make her fucking come now."

Mathew presses his hand harder against my pussy and slides two fingers inside my slick opening. The heel of the glove vibrates faster than the fingers, and bright lights flash behind my eyelids as Mathew finger fucks me.

"Oh, fuck. Mmm," I moan as a barrage of the most intense sensations I've ever felt rocket through me. The walls of my pussy clamp down hard on Mathew's hand. I grab onto Malcolm and hold on as Mathew massages me through my orgasm, while Marcus plays with the butt plug at the same time. "God, it's so fucking intense," I whimper and writhe, trying to get away from the overwhelming pleasure. I attack Malcom's mouth, crazed with need. He groans and pulls his shirt off. Just as that wave comes to an end, Mathew presses the heel of the glove hard against my clit, spurring me into another orgasm. I scream loud and drop my head onto Malcolm's broad chest. The light smattering of hair tickles my nose as I bite down on his pec and continue to moan.

He grips me hard as a powerful groan slips from between his lips.

"Bed. Oh, *please*. I can't take it. I'm going to fall." My legs are like limp noodles, ready to give out at any second.

Malcolm takes charge, moving Mathew's hand, and lifts me up before rushing me to the bed.

I lay there with nothing on, a butt plug in my ass, my clit still throbbing from the two massive orgasms I've just had, and my own arousal dripping down my leg.

"I knew you would be fucking perfect. So damn sexy," Marcus says as he and his brothers quickly get rid of the rest of their clothes.

Mathew pulls off the glove and tosses it on the side of the bed. I remind myself to ask him what that's called at the end of all this. I'm going to need one to add to my handy pink vibrator.

When they've managed to get out of their pants and underwear, I second-guess what I've signed up for.

Each one of them is bigger than any man I've ever been with, and they expect me to take all three at once.

"Boys, she looks worried," Marcus teases me as he moves closer to the bed.

"Fuck yeah, I'm worried. Your dicks are the size of baseball bats." I lean up on my elbows so I can get a good view of the three of them.

"If you want to stop, say that shit now. Don't fuck around," Malcolm growls as he stands next to the bed.

I swallow down my fear—I want to do this. I'm more turned on than I've ever been, but I don't know how I'll manage. I'll have to attack this the same way I've dealt with every other problem I've had in my life: head-on.

I scoot to the side of the bed, raising up on my knees. "Sounds like you want me to stop? Like you're searching for a way to get me to tap out? Is that your plan, Malcolm?" I grab his cock and lick the underside of it. His eyes roll back, and he moans.

"Shit no." Malcolm grips the back of my head and presses the tip of his dick against my lips. I take as much of him as I can. Then I pull Marcus on the bed with me. Next, I reach for Mathew, and do my best to jerk him off.

The crinkle of foil sounds from behind me, and a condom wrapper is dropped to the side where I can see. I let Malcolm pop out of my mouth when Marcus presses into me. "My God." It's so much, but so good at the same time.

"Holy hell, she's so tight." Marcus grunts as he plunges into me. The feel of him thrusting in and out of my soaking-wet pussy sends me into overdrive. The brothers take it as a personal challenge to turn me into a quivering pile of ecstasy.

Malcolm's the hardest to take, as he's the biggest. Yet, he makes sure I'm okay, and seems to love to see me come more than he's interested in fucking for his own pleasure. Mathew's the opposite of his normal mannerisms. When it's his turn to slide into my pussy, he fucks hard and handles me roughly, pulling my head back by my hair and holding it down on his brother's dick as he rails into me. Marcus, I have to say, is the most skilled, the most in tune with my body.

"You ready for all of us?" Mathew asks as he pulls out of my mouth, sweat causing his abs and chest to glisten.

"All?" I'm so deep into my lust-fueled adventure, I forgot that was the end goal. They all want to fuck me at the same time.

"Yeah, I think you're ready. We're going to pop at any fucking minute. I want it to be deep inside of you." Malcolm grunts as he pulls himself out of me.

The butt plug has been in this entire time, but that was a small thing compared to any one of their dicks.

Marcus kisses up the side of my neck. "Tell me what you're thinking. Your whole body just got stiff."

"I don't know if you're all going to fit. I want to try, but I don't even know how."

Malcolm presses a few soft kisses up my back before he gets to my ear on the other side. "You don't have to do anything, Perla. Let us take care of you. All you're required to do is feel good."

"Who do you want to fuck your ass?" Mathew asks.

I point to Marcus, needing someone who really knows what my body is saying.

"Okay, I'll take your mouth, because I'm way too close." Mathew grits through his teeth as he squeezes his dick.

"Come, lay on top of me." Malcolm lays flat on the bed and pulls me on top of him. He slides inside of me, and Mathew kneels on the other side where my head is. I reach up to get a grip on Mathew, but he moves back.

"No, wait. I want to see your face as they stretch you open."

I can't even stop the lazy smile that inches up my face.

"Relax, babe, I got you," Marcus says as something cool drops on my ass.

Malcolm caresses my hair and kisses the top of my head. For someone who's such a hard ass, it's such a nurturing feeling to have him holding me like this. Marcus slowly pulls out the butt plug, and my hips move on their own against Malcolm.

He moans and leans his head back before he looks at me. "Bad girl, be still."

Before my ass can even get used to being without the plug, Marcus is pressing his hard and much-larger cock into me.

I do my best to relax all of my muscles, but with me being already full with Malcolm, trying to take Marcus is right at the edge of impossible.

I claw my fingers into Malcolm's arm, but he doesn't complain. A deep guttural moan leaves my mouth, and just as I'm about to tell Marcus I can't go on, I feel him slide in.

"Oh, fuck, I'm so full." I'm scared to move. I whimper as both my ass and pussy feel like they're being stretched to the extreme. All this and neither one of them have even moved yet.

"Fucking hell, look at her face. I'm going to remember this shit forever." Mathew speaks up, and when I open my eyes to look at him, there's an expression of complete awe on his face. My entire body is trembling as I do my best to get used to the feeling.

"Perla, babe, do you want me to stop? I can pull out." Marcus grunts out from behind me.

"Don't you fucking pull out."

The three of them laugh at me.

"Yes, ma'am." Marcus moves back and forth. After a few seconds, Malcolm joins in the motion.

The brothers are kissing and touching me. It feels like the three of them are cocooning me. I don't know where I stop and where they begin. The sounds that are coming out of my mouth would be embarrassing to me on any other day, but right now, all I can focus on is how good they're making me feel.

"I'm done. I can't hold back anymore." Mathew inches closer to the bed, and

I turn my head to take him into my mouth. I'm not doing any work besides not clenching my jaw. I scream with Mathew deep in my mouth, Marcus in my ass, and Malcolm pounding away at my pussy. My orgasm builds to an unbearable pressure. Since I'm so full, there is no way for my body to brace against what's to come. I climax hard, and my eyes roll up into my head. Mathew is the first to blow his load, a deep grunt and moan, followed by a spurt of hot liquid down my throat. Next is Marcus who roars and slams into me one final time as his cock pulses his release into the condom. Malcolm is the last to finish, cradling me like a doll against his chest as he pistons up into me using his powerful hips. I cry out into his neck as he clutches me hard and finally growls out his own orgasm.

The four of us lay there gasping for breath and letting our bodies return to a state of normal.

Marcus rolls off me, and I roll off Malcolm. Mathew flops down at the foot of the bed, his arms entwining with my legs.

I'm so drained, I can barely keep my eyes open.

I chuckle and feel my body drifting off to sleep.

"Something funny?" Malcolm says from my side, with one arm draped over my midsection, while Marcus has a hand on my hip.

"Best. Job. Ever." I tilt my head to the side with a smile.

The three of them snicker until those snickers become full-on laughter. I snuggle into the lush mattress and just let sleep take me.

SEVEN

PERLA

I wake up the next morning to Mathew kissing my neck.

"Oh, crap." I jump up, and my body reminds me I had the most intense sexual experience I've ever had in my life just a few hours ago. I hiss out in pain as I slow down.

"Easy, Perla," Marcus says from where he's sitting by the fireplace. The fire is out and there's a small table with what looks like coffee and breakfast food.

"Sorry, I didn't mean to sleep so long." I run a hand through my hair and search the room for my clothes.

"I picked up a few things for you this morning," Malcolm says. "I hope you don't mind. I didn't think you'd want to leave wearing the same clothes from yesterday." Malcolm sits next to me on the bed and pulls out a skirt and shirt outfit he bought. The tags are still on the clothing.

Giving him a grateful smile, I meet his gaze. "You didn't have to do that for me."

"We wanted to."

Mathew walks over with a cup of coffee. "Do you need anything? Are you hungry?"

I grab the cup from him and take a sip, and it goes down smoothly. I carry the clothing Malcolm brought for me into the lavish bathroom. Taking a quick shower, I stretch the deep ache in my muscles from overuse. When I exit the bathroom, we sit down and eat together. The conversation is easy, and I'm completely relaxed with them. So relaxed in fact, I don't even realize I've stayed with them clear into the afternoon. I remember I have a car coming in for a tune-up that I need to be at the shop for.

"Boys ..." I glance between the three of them. "I think it's time for this fantasy to come to an end. I have to work."

"Are you sure?" Mathew leans forward in his chair. "I mean, you can't take the day off?"

"I can't." Part of me wants to offer them my phone number, or some way to get in contact with me, but I know it's against the rules. It's one of the many itemized guidelines I signed off on. They wanted this to be a one-time thing. No strings attached. When I signed, I was sure one night would be more than enough. Now I'm not so sure. "You boys sure know how to show a girl a good time."

"We try." Marcus gets up from his seat and reaches for my hand. I let him help me up, and the four of us walk toward the front door of the house. Malcolm gives me a bag with the clothes I wore yesterday. The brothers line up in front of me, and I take my time saying my goodbyes.

I start with Mathew, the first of them to make me feel at ease. "Thank you for a wonderful evening." I lean up and kiss him goodbye. His hands caress my hips softly before we pull away from each other.

I move on to Marcus. "Best experience of my life." I wrap my arms around his neck and press a kiss to his lips as well.

"Our pleasure," he replies before he lets me move on to Malcolm.

"And you," I wrap my arms around the gruff man's neck, "are nothing but a big old teddy bear." I press a soft kiss to his lips, but I should've known a soft kiss wouldn't be enough for him. Malcolm threads his fingers in my hair and ravages my mouth.

"Bro, if you don't stop, we're all going to get worked up again," Marcus says from beside him.

I push away and hold onto Malcolm's arms as I catch my breath.

"Bye, boys. Be good." I give them a bright smile before I take the bag and walk out the door, leaving the three men behind.

I rush to my car and scream in excitement when I get inside. I can't believe I've done something like this. It all feels like a dream, but that deep ache inside lets me know last night was all reality.

Eight

Perla

I get back to my house, and Teresa runs out to meet me the second my car stops in the driveway.

"Oh, my God. Are you okay? I was so worried. I didn't know if I should call the cops or not. I even went over to the Wings clubhouse, but Pirate wouldn't tell me anything. Only that you were having a good time."

"Where's Deacon?" I gaze toward the house to make sure Teresa knew enough to pick up our little brother from school.

"I got him. He's taking a nap." Teresa grabs my arm and turns me back to her. "Perla, are you all right?"

Visions of the night before rush through my mind, and a slight smirk lifts the corner of my mouth. "Yes, I'm fine."

"What about the bet? How much do we owe?" Teresa wrings her hands in front of her stomach.

I rub the back of my neck. "I think, three thousand more?" I say it more like a question because I'm not quite sure of the exact number.

Her eyes pop open. "What, that's all? What the hell did they have you do? Did you rob a bank? What the hell, Perla?"

"Don't worry about what I had to do. No, I didn't rob a bank." I push past her and into the house so I can get ready for work. Teresa follows behind me, still trying to figure out what happened the night before. Another rule on the contract was I couldn't divulge any information about what happened between the four of us.

"Well, if it were that easy, we can do it—"

I cut her off before she even has the chance to finish that sentence. "No! Do you hear me? I will not be doing this again to bail you out of whatever fucked-up gambling debt you have. Either you learn how to control yourself, or you're on your own from here on out." I get in her face and snarl down at her. I want her to see how serious I am. "And if I ever find out that you put my and our brother's livelihood in jeopardy again, I promise I will fucking disown you. You understand, Teresa?"

She nods her head, but I'm not satisfied. I want to hear the words. "I said, do you understand?"

"Yes, I understand, Perla. Never again."

Her face falls, but I don't have time to coddle her right now. I have a job to get to.

An hour later I'm elbow-deep in engine oil. The memories of the night before are still heavy on my mind, but slowly fading into the background that is my life.

"Perla, you have a customer here to see you," Lenny, the owner of the shop, shouts out. I'm just a junior worker at the shop. I do the grunt work most of the time, even though I know more about cars than half the men in here. I'm a woman, therefore I don't fit in. I don't have any assigned customers, either.

I grab the rag from my back pocket and wipe some of the gunk from my hands before I walk over to the main office. Sitting in one of the chairs is Bones. He gets up and strolls over to me when I come in.

My heart races as I think back on what could have happened. Did I do something wrong? Did the boys not enjoy themselves? Is he here about the remaining three thousand on the debt owed?

"I'm sorry. I was going to bring you the rest of the money when I got off work."

Bones eyes me up and down. "Well, fuck me, you really are a mechanic. I thought for sure that was a lie."

I grit my teeth and force myself not to say anything too sarcastic. "No, I have no reason to lie to anyone."

"Good, that's what I like to hear." He reaches into his pocket and pulls out a thick envelope and hands it to me.

In it is a large wad of cash. "Wow, what's this? I don't understand."

"Your sponsor opted to add a tip onto the agreed upon payment. They were very pleased."

My mouth drops open, and I can't help the excitement that bubbles through me. This is more than enough to set Teresa, Deacon, and I up with a little nest egg, so we don't have to worry about living paycheck to paycheck.

I count off the three thousand I still owe on Teresa's debt, but Bones stops me before I can hand it to him.

"Your sister's debt is paid in full." He nods once as he walks by me toward the exit.

"Hey, can you do me a favor? I don't know if you can note it somewhere, but if my sister ever comes back to the club and tries to put her house up as collateral, deny her. She's a grown woman, and I can't stop her from making stupid decisions with her life, but I'd prefer if we were never in this situation again."

"I'll make sure to note it. Though ..." He hesitates before he turns back in my direction. "If you ever need to make use of our sponsor program again, you only need to speak with Pirate or myself, and we can get you right in."

An idea springs to the front of my mind. Will they be there? I'd be open to having my mind blown by the Curran men again, and this could be the perfect way to get in contact with them.

I shake the thought out of my head. It was a great night—one I'll never forget—but I can't allow myself to get used to that sort of treatment.

"Thanks, but I don't think I'll be in need of *those* particular services again."

"If you say so." Bones shrugs and heads out of the office.

The Curran brothers will be my one naughty secret, but I'll never see them again. I can't.

EPILOGUE

MARCUS

"I can't stand this. It's been a month already. Why don't we just pick another girl and move on."

"What other girl do you want, Mathew?" Malcolm snaps. "Show me one of these candidates that can hold a candle to Perla."

"What can we do? You want us to keep coming back, hoping she shows up?" Mathew snaps right back.

"Hey! Stop the shit—the both of you." I fall onto the chair and rub at my temples.

She's destroyed us.

Ever since our one night with Perla, she's all we can think about. Sure, we've had women in the past make repeat appearances, but none of them have had us at each other's throats like Perla. Each one of us are pent up and needy for her. After the first week, we reached out to Pirate about getting her to come back in, but of course, he hit us with the bullshit agreement we all signed. The only way we're getting her again is if she shows up and accepts our offer. We've been here every week looking for her.

"Malcom, I don't want to admit it either," I say, "but Matty may be right. We might have to give her up."

"If you want to give her up, by all means, do that. I won't complain if you want to leave her all for me."

Jealousy boils to the surface of my skin, and I jump out of the chair, darting in his direction. "You *asshole*. You didn't even think she was for us." I've never been jealous of sharing my woman with my brothers, but one mention of someone taking Perla for themselves has me rethinking any idea about giving up the search.

"That was before, Marcus, but since we've had her." He leans his head back and groans. "I'm not stupid enough to think we're going to find someone more compatible, more open, fuck, more trainable than Perla. She's everything we want, and I'm not going to give up on her because you two can't see the long game."

"The long game? What the hell long game are you talking about?" Mathew asks.

As the youngest, sometimes it takes him a little longer to catch on to what Malcolm and I know. We might not be twins, but there are times it feels like Malcolm and I share a brain.

"The long game is keeping Perla, exclusively and permanently," I reply. Just the idea of her at our beck and call is enough to get me through another two months of waiting.

She's the one for us.

I know it.

PERLA

I've done my best to put the boys out of my mind, but after a month of doing everything I can to distract myself, my body is still aching for them. The smile on Pirate's face when I walk in asking about the sponsor program is comical to say the least. He and Bones have been taking bets about when I'd return.

I guess he won.

I sign the contracts in the appropriate places and wait for Shyne to instruct us to walk through the room with the one-way mirrors. I can't be sure that the boys will be here today. Shyne isn't allowed to tell me, but when I get an offer for a night with three men, I know it's them.

"This one." I hand the offer back to Shyne without even reading through it.

"Are you sure? This other one is quite lucrative." Shyne tries to draw my attention to one of the other offers on the table.

"No." I shake my head. "This one."

"As you wish. Right this way." He gestures out of the space, leads me to one of the back rooms, and opens the door.

Malcolm, Marcus, and Mathew are there with their model good looks, staring at me like they've just won the best prize.

Mathew and Marcus smile when I step in the room. Malcolm just glares at me.

"Hey, boys."

Mathew leans forward in his chair. "Thank fuck."

"Perla, I'm so happy to see you." Marcus smiles at me.

My eyes slide over to Malcolm, and I raise an eyebrow at him, waiting for him to address me.

He walks over to me and leans down so his large frame is hovering over me. I have to crane my head back so I can stare up at him.

"Mr. Curran," Shyne says from the door. Clearly, this is not the usual protocol. I put my hand up to tell him I'm okay.

"You have something to say, Malcolm?" My voice is breathy.

"Where the fuck have you been?" he growls as a slight smirk inches up the corner of his mouth.

"I thought I would make you boys wait a little."

"Too long. We've waited too long." He brings his lips to mine, kissing me deep enough to make my toes curl. Other hands touch me. Both Marcus and Mathew are joining us.

"Guys, at least sign the paperwork first. Y'all going to get me in trouble," Shyne says from the door.

Ready to have the Curran brothers take me back to ecstasy, I hold my hand out for the contract. "Where do I sign?"

THE SPONSORS

About The Author

Rae is a daydreamer, nurse, bookworm, nature enthusiast, wife, momma, animal activist, and optimist. She has lived her entire life in NYC and loves to travel with her family. She writes about flawed bad boy alphas who fall hard for their women. There is always angst, drama, and steam in whatever she writes. When she is not working as a nurse in her community, she can either be found reading, writing, or taking a walk while listening to music. She has been writing books in her mind for as long as she can remember but decided that maybe there were others out in the world that would find joy in the words she would put down on the page.

https://www.subscribepage.com/raeblake

BUZZ BREAK

IVY NELSON

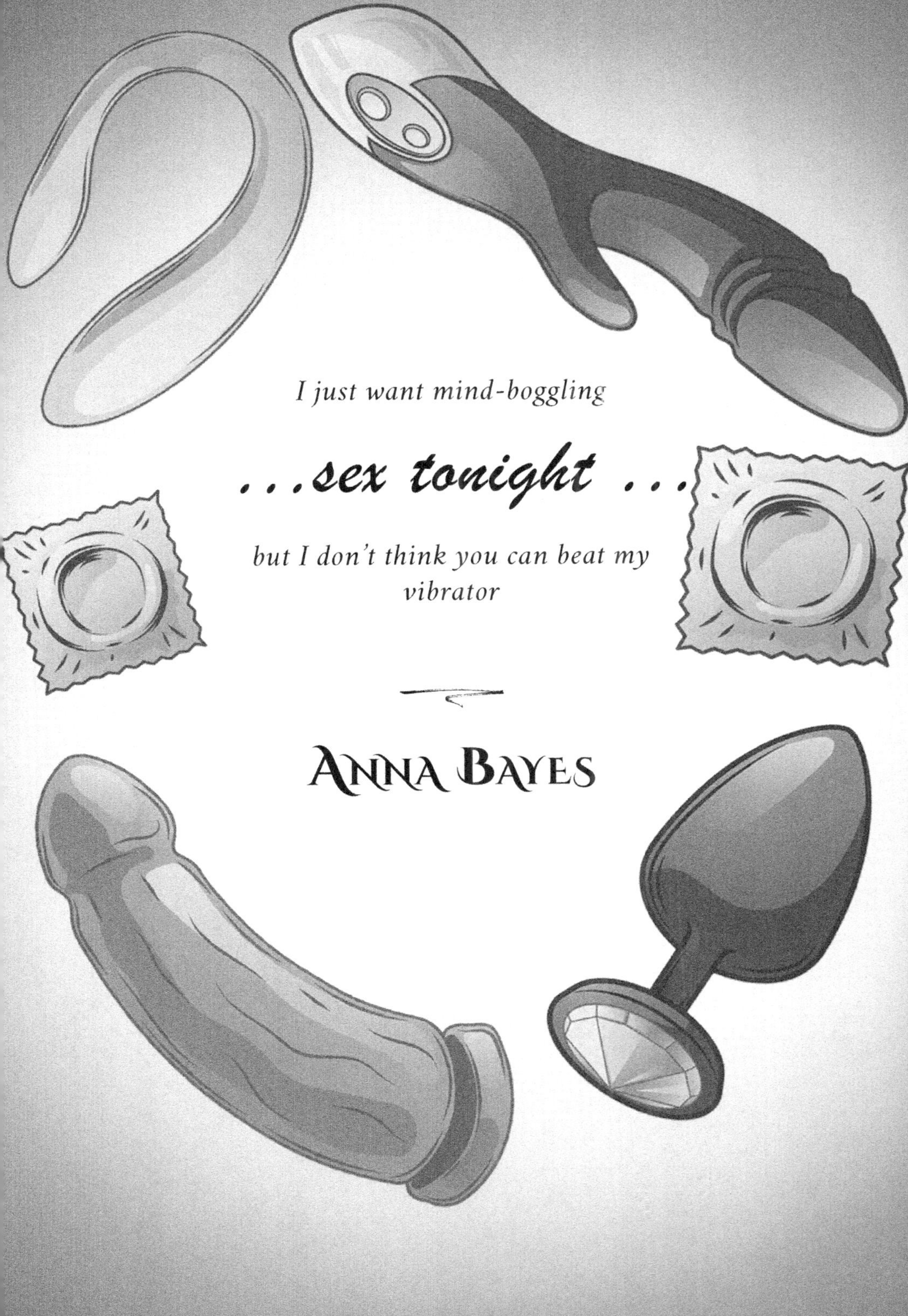

I just want mind-boggling

...sex tonight ...

but I don't think you can beat my vibrator

ANNA BAYES

One

"Carter's thick cock slid inside her. Finally, thought Jayla as she reveled in the feeling of being taken by him after so many days of the teasing and torment he'd called her punishment."

Melody Warren slipped her headphones off and took a deep breath as she eyed the vibrator charging in the corner of her office. She'd been recording the smutty audiobook all morning and needed a buzz break. There was time.

Snatching the toy off her desk, she headed for the sofa along the other wall. She pushed down her pajama bottoms and let them pool at her feet. Her panties joined them. She laid on the couch to give her aching pussy some much needed attention. Sometimes, she preferred to use her fingers. It took longer, but the orgasm was always super intense. Today, though, she was on a deadline and her trusty Rabbit would get her to that ultimate climax a lot faster. So would thoughts of the hero in this story hovering over her, getting ready to put his cock inside her. Her pussy clenched and a moan escaped as she imagined the character and pressed the buzzing toy to her already throbbing clit.

"Fuck." She turned up the speed and lifted her hips to get a better angle. The scene rolled through her mind, and she writhed on the sofa.

"Yeah, that's it. You're almost there." Her voice strained with need as she coaxed herself closer to the brink.

The orgasm shook her, and she fell back against the couch, letting the vibrator drop to the ground.

When her breathing returned to normal, she sat up and dragged a hand through her long red hair.

"Much better." Energized, she stood. Pulling on her panties and pajama bottoms she headed for the bathroom, where she cleaned up her toy and set it on its charger on her desk.

Back at the recording station, she picked up her phone, scrolling through notifications before getting back to work. There was a text from someone she didn't recognize.

Hey, my name is Ian. I'm editing the audio for Captured By Carter. Janet has a family emergency. The client is asking for the files sooner so if you send me whatever files you've already recorded, I can work on them.

She scowled. Clients weren't supposed to be able to just move deadlines up. At least not her freelance clients. Now that she worked for a production company on top of her individual clients, some things were more complicated, and she didn't have as much control. She was free to refuse any project she wasn't interested in and had even negotiated right of first refusal into her own contract with the company. The upside to the company was they provided in-house editing and mastering so she didn't have to contract out or do it herself. It was handled. All she had to focus on was getting the voices right.

With the deadline now two weeks sooner than before, Melody set up to start recording the next chapter. She frowned at the screen. It was still recording from her previous session. Then a slow smile formed. That meant it probably caught her little buzz break. She pulled out her phone and opened up her *SexyTime* app and tapped out a message to her followers.

I've got an extra little audio treat for all my supporters later tonight so if you want to hear what it sounds like when I'm thinking about you make sure you subscribe to my exclusive content.

She set the phone aside and settled in to work for the rest of the afternoon. Later, when she was preparing the audio to send to the editor, she would strip out the extra stuff and post it behind the paywall of her *SexyTime* account. She'd started doing digital sex work a year ago as an outlet for some of her own sexual desires, and it had turned into a nice little side hustle. Guys liked her red hair and bubbly personality and they tipped her to do the easiest things on camera. The majority of it didn't even involve nudity. And it was low pressure so on the days when her plate was full with narrating or her anxiety made her not want to talk to anyone, she could just not open the app.

There were only a few chapters left to record, and Melody was able to get through all of them before her voice was done for the day. Now she just had to spend some time preparing the files to upload and send to Ian. She'd tried to find out what kind of producer he was based on the limited information she had but hadn't found anything useful. As she was trimming the excess recording from where she accidentally left it running, her friend Jasper called.

"Hey, honey a bunch of us are going to the bar tonight to kick off the weekend. Want to join?"

"Margaritas sound perfect. What time?"

"Whenever. I'll probably be there by five because I'm thirsty but Marc and Kathy both work until seven."

Melody glanced at the clock in the corner of the computer screen. It was four-thirty in the afternoon.

"OK. I've got to finish up some work on some audio files and then I'll head that way so you're not drinking alone."

When she ended the call, she finished renaming the files she was working on and dropped them all into the work cloud the studio set up for her and sent Ian a text to tell him he could start working on them whenever he wanted.

Ian Summerlin sat in his office at Paradise Studios listening to the audio files for *Captured By Carter*. It had been a while since he took on a project himself, but Melody's voice had caught his attention when she first joined the company a few months ago. So when the previous editor had a family emergency, he jumped at the opportunity to work with her. He just needed to knock some of the dust off his editing skills. Being in charge of the entire company meant that a lot of his knowledge went unused, but he still had what it took to produce a high-quality audiobook. Melody was a good narrator with a wide range of voices to offer their clients, and she didn't sound too breathy when she read the dirty scenes. But damn if she didn't sound horny and hot. He was a consummate professional at work, but that didn't stop his dick from reacting to the sultry sounds playing in his ear.

Chapter eighteen ended, and he clicked over to the next one. Instead of the audio for chapter nineteen playing, there was a long silence. Figuring she'd pressed record but had her mic muted or something, he moved his cursor to the fast forward button, intent on skipping ahead. But whimpers and moans froze his hand. This was not in the book. He turned the volume up but paused it a split second later. Surely, she hadn't meant to record herself masturbating. And it would make him an asshole to sit there and listen. Then again, maybe she was an exhibitionist who got off on that sort of thing. Though, when she recorded this audio, she thought she was still working with Janet. She could be a lesbian or bisexual, but somehow, he knew this had been accidental. He did his best to put the little cries of pleasure out of his mind as he moved on to another chapter after dragging the non-book audio into the trash

But now it was impossible to hear her seductive voice reading the dirty book without picturing her masturbating to the content.

He stood and stretched, trying to give himself a break. Then he sat down and headed for Audible, where he looked for other books Melody had narrated before she joined his production company. They were all spicy, kinky even. Without thinking, he put them all in his cart and checked out. Before he could stop himself, he put her name in a search engine. Her Instagram popped up first, and he scrolled through her pictures. The majority were marketing images of the books she'd done or books she'd read and enjoyed. But then he found the selfie of the gorgeous redhead with glasses and pale skin.

His dick stood at attention. He needed to know more about this girl, and he felt like such a creep for that. Should he tell her what she did, or just let it be and find some other excuse to talk to her?

He smacked his palm against his forehead. "Quit being a lizard brain, Ian."

His smart watch buzzed, and he glanced at it before hitting play on chapter twenty.

`You know you miss this.`

The watch told him an image was part of the message. He didn't even have to open it to know the photo was of Chelsea in some state of undress. Sure, she was hot, but that was where the positive traits stopped. He considered telling her she was fired for being inappropriate at work, but Chelsea was vindictive, and he didn't want to fire her until he had a better reason than sending naked pictures to her ex-boyfriend. Chelsea would get bored soon and move on to someone else.

Ian smirked as he thought about moving on from Chelsea with a pretty, red haired narrator.

Two

"No, no, no," Melody stared at the message from a subscriber on *SexyTime* as her face grew hotter.

Hey beautiful. Thanks for the special audio surprise but I'm not sure I understand what it's supposed to be. Are you sure you uploaded the right thing? It sounds like you're reading a story or something.

Had she accidentally mixed up the files when she was sending audio to the producer? Her stomach turned as anxiety sent her pulse racing. Fuck. Because of her embarrassment, she couldn't even make herself sit down at the computer and look. But she did press play on the file she'd uploaded to *SexyTime*. Sure enough, there she was reading chapter nineteen of *Captured By Carter*. And it wasn't even a particularly sexy chapter. Well, there went her narrator career. If she really did send a clip of herself masturbating to the editor, there was no way she didn't get fired. Right? At least she had her freelance clients to fall back on.

Her mind raced with a thousand different thoughts as she paced her small living room. Her phone rang and she looked at the screen with one eye shut, half convinced it was going to be the studio calling to say they were terminating her contract. But it was Jasper so she blew out a long breath and answered.

"Hey hot stuff."

"I thought you were meeting me for margaritas."

She pressed her free hand to her forehead. "I was. Fuck. I'm sorry. I don't know if I can make it. I'm kind of dealing with something right now. Let me finish this and I'll let you know if I can come."

"You OK? You sound like you're panicked."

Jasper knew her well. "I am. I might have fucked up a work thing and I'm a mess."

"Everyone makes mistakes. I'm sure you're overthinking like you do. Come out for drinks. We'll give you a pep talk or you'll get drunk and forget about it."

When the call ended, she forced herself to go to the computer and check the files. Somehow, she'd mixed up the labels when she was preparing everything to send. Heat crept up her neck again.

With trembling hands, she picked up her phone and opened the text thread with Ian. It took four drafts, but when she was OK with the message, she squeezed her eyes shut and pressed send.

Hey Ian, I hope you haven't gotten too far into Captured by Carter. There's a giant mistake in the file for chapter nineteen. I'm going to upload a new version for you to edit. If you could just ignore the original one I sent, that would be great. No need to even listen to it.

Her phone rang a few minutes later, and she jumped, knocking it off the desk. The number was unfamiliar, so she let it go to voicemail. There was no way her anxiety was going to let her talk to a stranger right now.

The voicemail icon popped up in the corner of her screen. Curiosity won out, and she tapped it.

A velvet voice that poured over her like melted wax came through the speaker.

"Melody, it's Ian Su … It's Ian from the studio. I wanted to put your fears at ease. The file has been deleted. No one else will hear it."

Her face burned like she'd stuck it in an oven, and she nearly hung up. But his voice was captivating, and the phone stayed glued to her ear.

"I wrestled with whether to even tell you about it, but then I saw your email. I get it if you're embarrassed, but I need to know you're OK to continue working with me on this, and you're not beating yourself up for this. Please call me back."

"Nope, nope, nope. That's not happening." She was not talking to him on the damn phone. Not when he had a voice that sounded like sin. Now she wondered if he'd ever done any narrating himself.

"Stop it, Mel. You will not obsess over him."

She thought about sending him another text but decided against it and instead sent a text to Jasper to see if anyone else had showed up at the bar. If she didn't get out of the house, she would spend the night an anxious wreck. When Jasper sent back a photo of her friends gathered around a table with drinks, she grabbed her keys and left.

As she got to the bar, her phone buzzed. It was a text.

`This is Ian. Please just tell me you're OK.`

She shoved the phone in her purse and made a beeline for the table her friends occupied.

"Yay. Melody is here!" They stood, and everyone exchanged hugs and kisses on the cheek before someone shoved a glass in her hand. She took a long drink of the margarita that seemed to be mostly tequila.

"Did one of you sleep with the bartender or something?" she asked, feeling more in her element now that she was with friends.

One of the girls shrugged and winked at her. "Or something."

Melody laughed and tipped the glass back again. If she drank enough, the embarrassing memories would go away. Or at least seem less embarrassing.

After her third drink, she looked at her phone again. There was only one more missed call. At least Ian wasn't blowing up her phone. It was sweet that he was worried about her. Wasn't it?

She found his text and tapped out a reply.

`I'm OK. Just embarrassed and hoping you're telling the truth when you say you deleted it.`

Her phone rang less than thirty seconds after she hit send.

"Fuck. It's him."

"What was that, honey?" Jasper asked.

She shook her head and hovered a thumb over the ignore call button.

"Damn it. Fine, he's already heard me come anyway." She stepped away and tapped the green phone icon instead.

"Melody?" that smooth as silk voice asked.

"And you must be Ian."

"Where are you? It sounds like a good time."

"I'm at Freddy's and it's always a good time when I'm involved." She let out an alcohol fueled giggle.

"Sounds like someone has had a few drinks. Let's talk tomorrow instead."

Melody frowned. Why couldn't they talk now? "You could come drink with me."

He laughed. "I would, but considering everything that has transpired between us today, it would look like I'm taking advantage of you. I would much rather have your consent the next time I hear you come. How about dinner tomorrow night? My treat."

Her stomach did flips, and her pussy clenched at his bold declaration. If there were any questions about whether he'd heard her recording, they were gone. She should refuse his invitation. They were co-workers. "Tomorrow works."

"Wonderful. Text me your address. I'll pick you up at seven."

"OK." She couldn't find more words.

"I look forward to it. And make sure you drink some water before bed, Melody. Wouldn't want you to wake up with a headache and an excuse to cancel dinner."

She damn near whimpered at the sound of her name on his lips. The way he said it sent tendrils of lust through her system. She was going to be reaching for the vibrator when she got home.

Three

Ian parked in front of Melody's building and stepped out of his Honda Civic. He'd chosen the car because it was new, but not flashy. Judging from the neighborhood Melody lived in, and the bar she was in last night, she might not appreciate flashy. And he wasn't sure he was ready to out himself as the head of the company just yet.

He tried to ignore the voice in his head telling him the choice was a bad one. He would tell her before the night was over. If she didn't recognize him first.

When he knocked on her door, she opened it so fast she had to have been waiting for him.

"Ian?" She looked him up and down.

"That's me. You're Melody, I hope."

She nodded and stood back. "Come in. I just need a minute."

He stepped inside and watched with amusement as she ran to her couch and picked up two jackets and held them up to his shirt.

"I wasn't sure what kind of dinner we were having, so I have two choices. Casual or nice. But now I still don't know because you're dressed in between."

He pointed at the peach denim jacket. "I like that one."

She set the other aside and slipped the peach one on. "And you're sure denim isn't too casual?"

He offered her his arm. "Not at all."

She flashed a shy smile as she tucked her hand into the crook of his elbow and followed him out the door. They stopped long enough for Melody to lock her front door, then made their way downstairs to the car, where he opened her door for her.

"Where are we going?" she asked as he started the car.

"There's a quiet little place I like to go on the weekends. They have a bit of everything, but the chef's specialty is comfort food."

"Sounds delicious. Quiet sounds good after last night."

"Too many margaritas?" He winked as he turned the key and put the car in reverse.

"Something like that."

He pulled out of the parking lot.

"Nervous?"

"Very. Aren't you?"

He shrugged. "Maybe a little, but first dates are exciting, don't you think?"

"Date? Is that what this is?" She sounded horrified.

He reached for her hand. "I would like to think so."

"You set up your own blind date?"

He laughed as the light changed and he eased forward. "I guess I did. That hadn't occurred to me. How does that make you feel?"

"Weird. Especially given the thing that brought us here."

"How about we pretend that didn't happen and start over. We can even invent an imaginary mutual friend who set us up on this date. Then we have someone to hate if it's a disaster."

Her laughter was like music filling the car. He'd broken a barrier between them. Now to make her see she had nothing to be embarrassed by.

"So we don't need to talk about how unprofessional that was? I'm terrified it's going to wind up on the boss's computer and I'm going to get fired."

Did he tell her? Something told him if he revealed who he was right then, she would jump from the moving car.

"I don't think you have to worry about that." It was the truth.

"How far away is this place?"

"About twenty minutes. We have plenty of time to get the basics out of the way."

"Like what?"

"The usual. Where we're from, what we studied in college, favorite books to read. All those mundane questions. Then we can talk about the good stuff over food."

"Books are the best stuff," she said.

"It is how we make our living so I guess I can see that."

He peppered her with questions as he drove them to the small, out-of-the-way restaurant owned by a friend. He'd already been assured they had a table in a secluded area with plenty of privacy.

She seemed to relax as he ticked off the traditional first date questions and even started asking questions of her own. Ian found her easy to talk to and liked the way she laughed often, but not so much that it was annoying.

He pulled into the parking lot of the restaurant, and Melody's eyes widened. "Do you know how hard it is to get a reservation here?"

Ian laughed. "I'm lucky enough to be friends with the executive chef. I may have pulled a string or two."

Inside, they were led to a corner away from the other patrons, and Ian ordered them a bottle of wine and a sampling of appetizers.

When they were alone, he leaned forward with his hands folded together and elbows resting on the table.

"So, Melody, tell me what got you started reading dirty books out loud?"

Melody's face heated at the question. She wasn't ashamed of her job, but it was still unnerving to have it put that way. And the way his eyes never left hers and his voice never wavered as he asked made her squirm even more.

"I've read them for years for myself and I love listening to audiobooks. The corporate office I worked in a year ago downsized, and I got laid off. A friend of mine in the theater industry suggested I try it. They knew of a couple of independent authors looking for inexpensive narrators, so I auditioned and got the jobs. I haven't looked back since. Now I feel like I have my dream job and I've never been so grateful to get laid off in my life."

Melody relaxed as she talked about a thing, she was passionate about. Ian had been doing his best to put her at ease all night, but she hadn't expected him to be quite so stunning when he showed up at her door. She could barely form a coherent sentence in her mind. Somehow, she managed not to make a fool of herself so far.

"And do you always gravitate to steamy books?"

Her face grew hot again, but she gave a firm nod. There was nothing to be ashamed of in her reading choices. That had never been a problem for her. But something about the way he asked, and the look in his eyes, unnerved her.

"Have you ever done any narrating?" she asked. "You have the voice for it."

His smile lit up the dark restaurant, and it held a hint of wickedness in it that sent little tendrils of need roiling through her.

"I was already an ace at the editing and producing side of things before the popularity of male narrators reading erotic tales started. I've thought about dipping my toes into the performance side of it. Especially if I could do a duet with someone like you." He winked and pressed a finger to his lips as he glanced to his right. The server approached with their wine.

They stayed silent while he poured, and Melody fidgeted with the edge of the white tablecloth until they were alone again.

"And the subject matter of the books ..." Ian trailed off as he lifted his glass and tasted the wine. "Are you drawn to kink themes for a reason?"

"Are you asking if I'm kinky?"

He shrugged. "Seems like a legitimate question. Forward perhaps, but I like to get straight to the heart of things. I'm drawn to kink themes in literature because I enjoy it in real life. I enjoy hearing what draws others to these themes as well."

Her mouth formed an O as she contemplated her answer.

"I've had a few experiences with past partners. I'm ... interested in the lifestyle. They are the books I'm most attracted to, and it's what I choose to read in my free time. Do you like other kinds of erotica?"

"I enjoy all manner of erotic literature. But BDSM speaks to me the most. I prefer lived experience over fiction, though."

He lifted one eyebrow and gave her a seductive smile. The voice, the smile, the sinful expression. It was a heady combination, and way sexier than any book she'd narrated. Ian was going to be a part of her fantasies for a long time.

"I know we said we wouldn't talk about it, but I can't get the sound of you out of my head," he admitted.

She bit her lip and twisted the stem of the wine glass between her fingers.

"I … I don't know how to respond to that. It feels like an invasion of privacy, but I did it to myself so I don't blame you. And I'm … intrigued by the way it almost excites me that someone heard that."

"Sounds like you have an exhibitionist streak. That could explain why you're so great at narrating these kinds of books."

Melody took a long drink. Her hand trembled, so she tightened her grip on the glass.

"I hadn't thought of it like that before." Ian wasn't wrong. Her exhibitionist streak was also why she enjoyed dabbling in sex work.

He reached across the table and picked up her hand when she set the wine down.

"Tell me if my questions make you uncomfortable. I'm a pervert, but I'm a polite perv and I never want to make anyone squirm in a bad way. We can talk about whatever you want."

He squeezed her hand and the sensation that jolted through her almost had her pulling her hand away. But she loved the way his skin felt on hers, so she returned the squeeze.

"I appreciate your honesty. I've never thought of myself as a perv before, but I'm not ashamed of my sexual appetite. Even if I get nervous talking about it with you."

"Just tell me if I cross a line. I'm very attracted to you, Melody."

"Ditto."

He laughed. "So succinct. Here's a fun exercise. Are there scenes you've narrated that you want to act out?"

Melody lifted her eyebrows and blew out a breath. "Oh boy. Too many to count. Umm … the one I was recording before the incident that got us talking is a good example."

"The incident? You make it sound so ominous."

She laughed and realized she wasn't turning beet red anymore. Progress, right?

His presence was larger than life and she wondered how someone personable ended up on the backside of the production process. He was far too charismatic to be stuck behind a screen editing other people's words. She would make it her mission to get him into a recording booth. His delicious voice deserved to be shared.

"Where did your head go just now?"

She grinned. "I was just thinking about how you need to get in front of a microphone. Your voice ... it's intoxicating."

"I'll keep that in mind, Melody."

The meal continued that way for the rest of the night. Ian would ask inquisitive questions and Melody found the voice to answer them despite her nerves. He would pause every few questions to see if she had questions of her own, but she found it easier to repeat his questions back to him since his were so good. The meal was exquisite and his voice seductive. Her libido was on high alert by the time they were finishing dessert.

"I'm going to be blunt, Melody. I want to see you again, and I *really* want to hear you again. Only this time I want you to know I'm listening."

His words damn near melted the ice cream on her spoon, and she set the utensil back in the bowl.

"I rarely do sex on the first date."

Ian gave her a slow smile. "I'm not talking about sex. I'm talking about dropping you off at home and having you call me."

Her mouth went dry, and she reached for the almost empty wine glass.

"Is this where I've overstepped?" he asked, still holding her hand.

She gave him a jerky shake of her head. "Not at all. In fact, I think we should head home now."

Four

Ian sat in his car and watched Melody prepare to get out. His cock was raging hard as he imagined the phone call she'd promised him. Through the entire meal he hadn't been able to get the sound of her coming, or the possibility of hearing it again, out of his head.

"You'll have to call me. I'm too chicken to do it myself."

Ian gave her an understanding nod. "How much time should I give you before I call?"

Melody bit her lip. "Fifteen minutes?"

The hesitation in her voice had him stopping her from opening the door. "If you don't want to do this, say red when you answer the phone and we'll just talk, OK?"

She squeezed his hand. "I won't say red. Talk soon, Ian."

The way his name sounded coming from her made him want to follow her inside, bury himself in her, and find out all the ways he could make her scream his name while he explored the fantasies in her head.

He considered staying in her parking lot while he called her. His house was thirty minutes away with no traffic. Instead, he pulled away and drove to the office, which was only ten minutes away. When he sat at his desk, he tapped her name and hit call.

"Are you always this punctual?"

He chuckled. "I try to be. It's the courteous thing to do. Are you ready for me?"

She didn't say anything, but he could hear her moving around.

"Melody?"

"I'm here. Just getting settled."

"Good girl."

"Oh. I do like that."

The smile grew on his face. "I'll keep that in mind. Tell me about the toy you're going to use."

"It's a Lelo. But I thought I would start with my fingers first."

"Is that how you always do it?"

"It depends. If I'm taking a buzz break, I go straight for the vibrator to get there faster. If I'm taking my time, I like to start with my fingers. It makes the orgasm stronger if I draw it out."

"Two things. One, take your time tonight. And two, buzz break?"

She giggled. "That's what I call it if I'm… satisfying a need in between recording sessions. Some of the stuff I read is pretty spicy, and it gets me all hot and bothered. I have to … relieve the tension if I want to keep recording."

"So, you can write your vibrators off as a business expense."

Her laughter was soothing and arousing at the same time. "I already have quite the collection, but now I'll have to buy more."

"Enough talk, sweet Melody. I'm ready to listen to you play."

"I already am." There was a slight hitch in her breathing as she spoke.

"Naughty girl. I like it. How does it feel?"

"Good, wet. God," she trailed off and her mattress squeaked as she shifted.

After several minutes of labored breathing and small moans, the distinct buzz of the vibrator came through the line.

"Perhaps the next time we do this I'll read you something dirty." He leaned back in his chair and adjusted his pants. He considered masturbating with her but didn't. He would get off reliving the sweet sounds later.

She moaned louder at his dirty suggestion, and he knew she was getting close. "Come for me, Melody. Think about how it might feel when you let me into your bed. Maybe you'll call me next time you need a buzz break, and I can come and help relieve some of your tension."

"Agh, God. Yes."

"Yes, you'll call me, or yes, you're coming?"

She cried out in his ear. "Oh! Mmm. Both. God, Ian that was amazing."

"Good girl. Do you have another one for me? Or are you going to fall asleep dreaming of me?"

"There's no way I don't dream about you." Her voice was heavy, and he smiled.

"Goodnight, sweet Melody. I'll text you in the morning."

When the call disconnected, he sat in his office for a long time, thinking about Melody and their date. And about how he was going to tell her who he was. Damn it, Ian. Why didn't you come out with it from the beginning?

FIVE

Melody looked at her phone and tried to ignore the red notification badge on the *SexyTime* app. She was supposed to be getting ready for a night out with Ian and she hadn't found a way to tell him about her other job. Part of her said it wasn't his business, they were too new. The other part of her—the part that really liked him—said she should give him a heads up before they got too attached to each other. The deal she'd made with herself when she first made the account was that she wouldn't let a relationship be the reason she quit doing it. The work was fun, but she knew a lot of men who used sites like *SexyTime* were hypocrites who would never date a woman who did 'that' kind of work.

She tucked her phone in her purse and finished getting ready. It was their fourth date, and he still hadn't tried to come into her house to sleep with her. When they would finish a date, he would drop her off, give her a gentle kiss, and tell her to call him in fifteen minutes.

On the phone, he would talk dirty and bring her to orgasm over and over until she wanted to pass out. Melody was ready to take things to the next level, but Ian seemed content to take things slow. So tonight, she was pulling out all the stops. She'd put on her sexiest dress with sky-high heels, a sensual smelling perfume, and makeup that she hoped said, "please take me upstairs and take my clothes off".

If all else failed, she would try bluntness, but she didn't do rejection well, so she was hoping he would make the first move.

"What are your plans for the weekend?" Ian maneuvered into a parking space at the restaurant.

She gave him a smile with a flutter of her eyelashes. "Nothing set in stone.

What about you?"

He reached for her hand and brought it to his lips. "I was thinking I could take you some place with me."

"A getaway? We haven't even had sex yet."

Ian winked before he opened his door. "That can change whenever you're ready."

Jesus, I've been ready.

When she opened her door, Ian was there, holding his hand out to her.

"You look stunning tonight," he said close to her ear.

His breath danced across the bare skin of her neck and a shudder raced through her.

"Cold?" He pressed a kiss behind her ear.

"Definitely not." She tried to hold back a sigh.

Ian gave a low chuckle as he lifted his head away from her ear. "Good. I hope you know I'm trying to seduce you tonight, Melody."

She gave him a shaky smile. "It's about damn time."

His head lifted toward the sky, and he let out a laugh. "Someone is impatient, then."

"We've only been dancing around the edges of sex for two weeks, Ian."

He motioned to the car. "We can always skip dinner."

"And waste this dress?" She pulled on his hand and headed toward the entrance.

Inside, wine was waiting for them at their table. Ian seemed to be a favorite at the restaurants they ate in, and she suspected he had at least a little money despite the modest car and average clothing he wore.

"So where did you want to take me?" she asked while he filled their wine glasses.

"There's a place in Colorado that I think you would enjoy. I want to ask you about something else first."

"I am all ears." She was eager to know all the details.

"We've danced around the themes in the books you record, I know you're into it. You know I'm into it. But we've never talked about trying it together."

Melody hoped the dim light of the restaurant hid her blush. "I think I might like that."

"How much experience do you have?"

Melody laughed. "Is this where you tell me you have a secret sex dungeon in your house and you want me to move in with you?"

Ian flashed her a wolfish grin, and the heat in his eyes sent a shiver of excitement up her spine. "Not exactly. I am involved in a couple of kink clubs, though, and I would be interested in exploring with you."

She set the wine down before she spilled it on her dress. "Color me curious." She cleared her throat. "Does that have to do with your weekend getaway idea?"

He nodded and he leaned back in his chair, his eyes boring into her. "One of the clubs I'm part of is in Colorado. There are parties every weekend, but I only get to make it once every couple months. I thought you might like to go as my guest and check it out."

Melody's eyes widened. "Can I think about it?"

Ian smiled. "Of course, sweetheart. I just need to know by Thursday afternoon so I can get you on the guest list."

It was Monday now. That gave her a few days.

"OK. I'll think about it. Maybe you can tell me a little more about the place?"

"I'll answer any questions you have. About there or anything else you want to know."

For the rest of the meal, she peppered him with questions about the club in Colorado, which turned out to be called Club Solitaire. Melody thought it sounded like heaven on earth and she knew she would say yes to a getaway as long as the rest of their night went well. And judging by the way Ian flirted with her all night, she was going to get what she wanted.

By the time dessert arrived, she was ready to drag him to the nearest dark corner to relieve the ache between her thighs. Ian insisted on feeding her the decadent cake and the way he did it was so hot that when they got to the car, she was on the verge of pushing him into the backseat.

At the passenger side door, he pushed her against the window and took her mouth in a powerful kiss. "I think I should walk you to your door tonight," he said when he pulled away.

Her fingers rose and grazed her swollen lips. "You better walk me a lot farther than my door," She wrapped her arms around his neck for another kiss.

His hand came up to cup her cheek, and he gazed at her for a moment. "Would you like to explore something kinky with me tonight, or should we keep it tame?"

She bit her lip. "What do you have in mind?"

He brushed his lips over her forehead. "Nothing too intense. Some orgasm control, a bit of bondage. You'll call me Sir unless you have an aversion to that honorific."

Was this happening? She'd tried to explore kink with a few partners in the past, but when the interest wasn't there or it hadn't worked out, she'd contented herself to fantasize and enjoy it in her dirty books.

"I think I would like that very much, Sir." She tried the title to see how it felt on her lips. She liked it. There was something seductive about the meaning behind it.

The drive was short, and Melody was grateful he'd chosen some place close. In her parking lot, he helped her out of the car and stopped at the trunk, where he pulled out a black duffel bag.

"Bag of tricks?" She was amused he came prepared to spend the night.

He winked. "Something like that. And don't worry, I don't always travel with a bag of sex toys."

"That's disappointing."

He smacked her on the ass and shook his head. "I can always start keeping a bag at your place."

Melody giggled. "You haven't even been inside yet."

"Well then, why are we still down here?"

Inside, she offered him a quick tour and ended in the bedroom.

"Your recording room is impressive. I'd like a closer look later. Right now, I can think of something else I want to see."

Her heart hammered, and she thought it might burst out of her chest, but she flashed what she hoped was a seductive smile. "What's that?"

"You, without this dress on." He stepped closer to her. The dress was short enough that he could graze the hem with his fingertips. She kept her gaze locked with his and lifted her arms above her head. He followed her lead and pulled the fabric up her body until he held it in his hands. It hit the floor with a soft sploosh, and he hummed in appreciation before he reached behind her to unfasten her bra. She hooked her thumbs in the waist of her panties and pushed them over her hips. They fell to her ankles, and she stepped out of them, leaving her in nothing but her heels.

"Fucking hell." His eyes scanned her body. "I just want to bury myself in you. But I promised you something a little more adventurous than that. Where are your vibrators?"

She jerked her head to the nightstand. "Top drawer."

"Lay on the bed on your back with your knees up so your heels touch your thighs."

She got on the bed and crawled to the center of it, where she got into position.

"For future reference, when I give you an order you should say, Yes Sir." He opened the top drawer of her nightstand and pulled out both vibrators.

"Favorite?" He held them both up.

"Black one, Sir." She hoped he didn't notice the tremble in her voice.

He tossed the black toy on the bed, so it landed with a thud next to her head. Then he went to the door where he'd dropped his duffel. The sound of the zipper seemed to roar, breaking the silence, and her pussy clenched. What was he getting?

He held up two sets of leather cuffs when he approached her again. "I'm going to cuff your wrists to your ankles. If it gets too uncomfortable for you, tell me and I'll adjust them or take them off. The point is to instill a sense of helplessness, but I don't want you so uncomfortable that you can't focus on the other sensations."

She swallowed and nodded. "Yes, Sir."

He made quick work of the restraints, binding her like he said, then spread her thighs.

"Such a delicious sight." The strength of his gaze on her felt like it might set her on fire.

He stood where she could see him and stripped off his shirt before he picked up the toy and crawled onto her bed.

She jerked against the cuffs when the vibrator pressed against her clit, and it wasn't long before she was crying out on the brink of an orgasm. The vibrator stopped, and he rested a hand on her thigh. "Are you going to be a good girl and ask to come?" He hovered the vibrator over her pussy.

"Yes, Sir. Please let me come." She raised her hips to touch the toy to her clit.

"Naughty girl, I'll put it back when I'm ready."

She let out a huff and dropped back down on the mattress.

"Not so sure you like this game?" He turned the toy on again.

"Please. I need it," she begged.

"So do I, sweet Melody. Come for me." He increased the speed on the toy, and she came undone.

"Oh, that's lovely," he murmured. "It sounds even better in person."

He tossed the toy onto the mattress beside her and rose to kneel between her thighs. "I want to drag this out, lover, but I'm also dying to feel you."

Melody nodded, eager to have him inside her. She watched as he rolled on a condom she hadn't even seen him grab. "Ready?" He held his thick erection in his hand.

"Please. I'm so ready. You've been teasing me for days."

He flashed her a wicked look and pressed into her soaked entrance. The groan that left his throat gave her a thrill, and she watched with pure lust as his eyes drifted shut and he sank deeper into her. She moaned when he slid out again and thrust her hips up, wanting him buried inside her.

"Fuck me, please," she said when he continued to tease her with long, slow strokes.

Her pleas worked, and he gripped her legs, spreading them as wide as the restraints would allow as he slammed his cock in and set a punishing rhythm.

Melody's cries and Ian's groans filled the room as he fucked her hard and fast. His fingers dug into her skin as he surged on, and thoughts of his fingerprints being left behind had her soaking his cock even further. The ripples of pleasure from the building orgasm careened through her. And when he tensed, she knew they would fall together. She pulled on her restraints as they both came with loud abandon. He called her name, and she whimpered his as the pleasure went off like fireworks through both of them.

Before she realized, he had undone her cuffs and was cradling her in his arms while they both shuddered through the aftershocks.

Six

Ian sat in Melody's living room and opened his laptop. She was in the next room sleeping, something that seemed to elude him, so he slipped out of bed to get some work done. He smiled at Melody's profile picture on his screen. He'd been browsing her social media again before he left work earlier. The profile that was up was her public narrator profile. There was a new post with a promo graphic for the book they were working on now. Not all narrators promoted the books they recorded, but Melody did. He clicked on the comments and felt his blood turn to ice when he saw the top one.

Chelsea O'Donnell: I hear there are some really spicy outtakes from this one.

With a knot in his stomach, he clicked through to his cloud drive and checked the trash. The deleted file was there. He'd forgotten to empty it. He called his assistant.

"Mr. Summerlin, what's wrong?"

"Does Chelsea O'Donnell still have access to my cloud?"

"She does. Marketing put her on *Captured by Carter*, and she said a chapter was missing and that it would be in your cloud."

"Fuck. Can you make sure we cut her access off tonight? I'm worried she might have accessed a file she shouldn't have."

He dialed Chelsea when he was done with his assistant. She answered the phone just a little to cheery.

"What did you do?"

"What do you mean? I'm so glad you called. Want to meet up for drinks?"

"Damn it, Chelsea, I don't have time for your games. Delete the file now and there will be no consequences."

"Aww, did you find another girl to suck your cock and make you feel important? It would be such a shame if that file got sent out as part of the promo package."

"I'll fire you and tell your parents the truth about why."

"You don't want to do that. I'll send the file to everyone I can think of. Her reputation in the business will be shot and she'll never record another book."

"What exactly is your problem with Melody? You don't even know her."

"I met her when she came in for orientation. When the office gossip spread that you were editing the book she was recording, I knew you were into her. You're the CEO. You don't do the grunt work anymore. Unless it gets you something you want. Like a pretty redhead in your bed. Imagine my surprise when I found chapter nineteen in your trash. It was like a present all wrapped up for me."

He laughed. "I dated you out of respect for our family friendship. It's not my problem that you can't get over the fact that you couldn't keep me. I'm hanging up now. If you so much as think about releasing that file, I'll take you to the police."

"You wouldn't dream of it. I'll spill all your dirty little secrets, Ian. The ones you work so hard to keep covered up."

"What secrets?"

"Oh, just your little trips to Colorado."

His laugh held a sinister edge. His trips to Colorado were private, yes, but if they got out, they got out. There were already whispers. He wasn't worried and that meant bad news for Chelsea. He had no problem blowing her world up to get her to stop. Though he had a feeling it wouldn't come to that though. "I mean it, Chelsea. Back the fuck off."

The call ended, and he tossed the phone in disgust.

"Ian, what's wrong?" Melody was standing in the hall, staring at him. Ian motioned for her to join him on the couch. It was time to tell her everything he should have from the beginning.

"Do you know Chelsea O'Donnell?"

"She works for the same studio we do. In the marketing department, I think."

He picked up her hand. "I need to tell you who I am."

Seven

Melody's stomach lurched when Ian told her who he was and showed her the post from Chelsea O'Donnell.

"I can't believe I slept with you. You should go."

"Melody please, just hear me out."

Her limbs trembled as she lifted her hand and pointed to the door. "No. I want out of this contract, and I want you out of my apartment. How can you not see how unethical what you did was?"

Ian lifted his hands in surrender. "I should have told you who I was from the beginning. It never seemed like the right time. I'm sorry."

"You're sorry? Is that all you can say? What do you expect me to do? Especially when it sounds like you have unresolved issues with another woman."

She stalked to the bedroom and grabbed his duffel bag. Back in the living room, she tossed it at him.

Ian backed out of the apartment but stopped in the doorway. "I'm sorry, Melody. You have every right to be upset, but I would appreciate it if you gave me a chance to make this right. I'll assign another editor to finish the book."

"Please, just leave. I can't even think straight. Do I need to be concerned about her leaking this? Does she even have it?"

Ian nodded. "I think she does. The office cloud account traces access points and she opened the trashcan where the file was sitting. It's my fault for not emptying the trash. When I looked at the history, she's been accessing my trash and other files for weeks, probably trolling for something to confront me with. But I'm going to make sure it never gets out. I have a friend in cyber security. He'll help me."

She gave a short laugh. "Great. One more person with access to my most embarrassing moment ever. Just leave."

"Lance isn't like that. I swear. Chelsea is a vindictive person, and she's pissed I ended things with her when we didn't work out. I should have fired her on the spot, but I thought it would look bad. So, I moved her to a new department."

"What are we going to do?"

"You keep asking me to leave and then asking more questions. I want to stay, but if you're kicking me out, I should leave so I can fix this. I need you to trust me. And yes, I realize that's a huge ask right now."

Melody gave a shaky nod. "Just … give me some time and call me later. I'll calm down and can talk rationally about this."

She wanted to ask him to stay. To convince her it was going to be OK. To take her back to bed. But she couldn't concentrate when he was in the room, and she needed to decide what to do.

He stepped all the way out of her apartment and pulled the door shut.

The next evening, there was still no word from Ian, and she was no closer to figuring out what to do about him or the stolen file.

When she got to her computer that morning, she was sure there would be a termination notice or something from the production company. Instead, there was an email from a new producer telling her she was starting on the audio right away and would send her any corrections in the next forty-eight hours.

It disappointed her that Ian hadn't contacted her yet. But at the same time, it was a relief that she wasn't being forced to work with him on the book. She hated herself for thinking they might have been able to develop some kind of relationship.

She didn't have another book on her schedule for a few more days, so she picked up a book and sat in her favorite reading chair to read. But the hero paled in comparison to her short-lived experience with Ian, and she couldn't focus on the story.

She tossed the book aside and woke up her phone and put Ian's name into the search bar. Now that she knew who he was, she could find out more about him. She always worked with people in the production department of Paradise Studios, so she never knew who the owner was. The number of search results took her by surprise. He was a major player in the entertainment industry, even if a lot of his influence was behind the scenes. Why had he hidden this from her? Then again, she had her own secret she'd kept from him.

Curiosity fueled her internet searches, and she ended up on a page for an article about a BDSM club that opened in an old Colorado ski resort. This would be where he wanted to take her. There were whispers on gossip blogs he was a member, along with a handful of other high-profile people.

Her phone rang, and she jumped as it buzzed in her hand. It was a number out of Chicago. Frowning, she swiped to answer and held it to her ear.

"Hello?"

"Is this Melody Warren?"

"It is. Who is this?"

"Miss Warren, my name is Lance Moss. Ian asked me to call you. How are you today?"

Melody's heart rate increased as she looked for the right answer. "I'm not sure. What did Ian tell you?"

"No details, just that a personal file of yours fell into the wrong hands. I wanted to let you know it's being handled."

Melody picked at the fringe of a nearby throw pillow. "What does that mean, exactly? Even if you get the file from her, how do you know there aren't copies?"

"It's a valid concern. But you seem important to Ian, and I'm willing to color outside some lines to make sure that file doesn't see the light of day. As far as I can tell, it hasn't been transferred since it was pulled off Ian's cloud account and I'm great at what I do."

"Thank you, Mr. Moss. I appreciate the call."

"Lance, please. Anything for a friend of Ian's. I hope things work out between you two."

"There's no way for that to happen if he doesn't call me."

She ended the call before Lance could say anything else. There should have been some sense of relief the file was being taken care of, but there was only a sense of sadness that she still hadn't heard from Ian. She picked up the book again and tried to read but it was useless, so she went to lie down. As she was plugging her phone in, it lit up with someone from Paradise Studios.

"And this is where they fire me," she muttered as she accepted the call.

"Melody, hey. It's Samantha. Could you come by the office for a few minutes? It's important."

EIGHT

Melody stepped into the lobby of Paradise Studios, a place she'd been twice, and headed for the reception desk. As she was giving the woman her name, the elevator opened, and two security guards exited with a woman between them.

"You," she said with venom in her voice as they passed Melody. "You're going to regret the day you signed your contract to work here."

The receptionist rolled her eyes and patted Melody's hand. "Don't worry, honey. That bitch won't bother anyone again. She thinks because her daddy is friends with Ian's daddy that gives her a pass to behave like a five-year-old towards anyone she sees as a threat. You can go on up. Mr. Summerlin is waiting for you."

Melody froze with her hand on the visitor badge the receptionist handed her. "Mr. Summerlin? That's who I'm here to see?"

She nodded. "That's right. Just take the elevator to the top floor."

Melody's stomach did somersaults, and she swallowed hard. This wasn't the reunion she'd been expecting.

When she stepped off the elevator on the top floor, her heart jumped. He was waiting for her. His hair was disheveled and his tie hung loose against his rumpled shirt.

"Melody, hi. Thank you for coming."

"So formal."

He dragged a hand through his hair and waved the other one down his body. "Not exactly. I'm sorry for all the silence. I needed to make sure everything was handled before we talked."

He motioned for her to follow him, and she fell into step behind him. When they were in his office with the door shut, he went to his desk.

“I hope you saw Chelsea being escorted out.”

“I’m glad that was Chelsea and not some other woman who hates me.”

He gave her a smile, but there was something sad in his eyes.

“I’m sorry. For everything. Not telling you who I was right away, not being careful enough with the file. Please tell me I haven’t screwed up any chance at all with you.”

She twisted the strap of her purse and stared at him. “I can see that you’re sorry. The file wasn’t your fault, so I can let that go. It’s the fact that you let me walk around for over two weeks thinking you’re a regular guy when you’re some kind of millionaire hotshot playboy.”

He grimaced. “I wouldn’t say playboy.”

“Oh really? Because the number of women you’re pictured with on Google tell a different story.”

“I date a lot. It’s true. But I don’t sleep with all of them. And you’re the only one I want to sleep with now. That’s why I have a proposition for you.”

She lifted one eyebrow and dropped onto the arm of the sofa. “I’m listening.”

“I have two documents here. One lets you out of your current contract with Paradise. The other sets you up with your own studio that we’ll subcontract with. Everything stays the same but we’re not violating any HR guidelines by being together.”

“And if I don’t want to be with you?”

His face fell and Melody’s heart twisted. “If that’s the case, nothing changes. But I’m still willing to set you up with your own studio. I know we haven’t been together long, but for the first time I was able to just enjoy a woman without worrying about what my family thought, what the press would say, or that she was just out for what I could do for her.”

Melody stood and moved closer to him. “Aren’t you worried that’s only because you didn’t tell me who you were?”

Melody picked up the contract and thumbed through it.

“I don’t know if I can sign this.” She tossed the document on the desk.

Ian grimaced but said, “I can take no for an answer.”

Her heart raced knowing what she needed to tell him.

"It's not that I want to say no. There are two reasons I'm not sure if I can sign. First, there's something about me I haven't told you yet and I have no idea how you'll react."

"I have a *SexyTime* account, and I have no intention of getting rid of it. That's where the file I accidentally sent you was supposed to go."

Ian pulled out his phone and handed it to her. "Find yourself and sign me up."

Melody's mouth fell open. "Seriously?"

Ian nodded. "As a heart attack. Sweetheart, we already know you have an exhibitionist streak and so do I. Why do you think I want to take you to Club Solitaire? I would be a damn hypocrite if I had a problem with you putting yourself out there like that. My only request is that if you need a stunt cock you use mine."

Her shoulders sagged and her cheeks heated at the thought of making content with him.

"What was the other reason you don't think you can sign?"

Melody grinned and picked up the contract.

"I can't sign without a revision. I'm going to need some official buzz breaks in here before I can agree to anything."

Nine

Six weeks later

Ian held Melody's hand as they stepped into the tasteful lobby of Club Solitaire. After six weeks of spending almost every night together exploring their fantasies, she had agreed to come with him to the club. At first, Ian hadn't been sure if he liked the content Melody made for the internet, but the first time she let him watch while she made a video, they'd both realized it was going to make their sex life even better. Melody's career was thriving, and Chelsea had moved away. According to her parents, she was traveling across Europe, which was fine by Ian.

Lance Moss leaned against the reception desk, talking with someone behind it, and Ian cleared his throat to get his attention.

"Lance, I'd like you to meet my girl, Melody."

"*The* Melody?" He opened his arms for a hug. "It's nice to meet the woman who has Ian staying home on the weekends."

Ian enjoyed the color creeping into her cheeks. Even with as sexually adventurous as she was, Melody still blushed at innuendo and teasing.

"It's nice to meet you, Lance. Thank you for everything you did for me." Melody accepted his hug.

"I can't say I know what was in that file, but if getting rid of it brought you here, then I'm happy to have done it. Now let's get you checked in and show you around. What convinced you to come check us out?" Lance turned back to the desk.

Melody turned and winked at Ian. "He's been telling me how wonderful it is here, and we've been spending so much time at home. We decided it was time for a new adventure. Time for a little … break."

He smirked at their inside joke and pulled her to him, crushing his lips to hers. While he devoured her mouth, he vowed to give her all the buzz breaks she wanted for the rest of his life.

About The Author

Ivy Nelson writes delicious contemporary romance with kinky alpha heroes and sassy heroines you wish could be your best friend. Club Solitaire is her favorite fictional place to hang out in, and she spends most of her free time spinning tales set there. When she isn't writing, she's probably reading something dirty or drinking wine with her readers on Facebook.

www.ivynelsonbooks.com/newsletter

Encore

Tracie Delaney

Give a woman a
...vibrator ...
And she'll orgasm for life.
PENNY REID

One

Athena

"Close your eyes and count to ten."

Giggling, I shoved at Ryker's hands covering my eyes. "You've blindfolded me. I can't see a thing. What's the point in closing them?"

I estimated an hour, maybe an hour and a half, had passed since Ryker bundled me into the back of a limousine, tied a silk scarf over my eyes, and told me he had a surprise for me.

"I saw you tugging at your blindfold earlier. I don't trust you not to peek."

I gasped theatrically. "Ryker Stone, wash out your mouth with soap. Married for a whole two weeks and already you don't trust me."

"I said I didn't trust you not to peek," he reiterated. "I trust you with everything else. Now shut up, woman, and hold on to me. There's a step here, and I don't want you to fall."

I clutched his forearm. The darkness made me off-balance. Ryker wouldn't let me fall, yet I still clung to him. A hand on my shoulder drew me to a halt. I cocked my ears for clues of where we were. Without my sight, my ears should pick up the slack, yet they clearly hadn't gotten the memo. All I could hear was Ryker's quiet breaths in my ear, and the loud squawk of a pigeon.

"Ready?"

He nibbled my earlobe, making me squirm. I pressed my thighs together to relieve the ache in my core. My beloved husband barely had to touch me to turn me into a mess of wanton desire.

"Always." I sounded breathless, needy, and hungry for his touch.

He tugged on the scarf, and the makeshift blindfold fluttered to my feet. I blinked, the sudden brightness uncomfortable for a few seconds. My vision cleared. Before me, a sleek white yacht sat in her dock. She must have been at least two hundred feet long, possibly more, bobbing in the vibrant blue waters of the Mediterranean Sea. Surrounded by many other superyachts, she was by far the most stunning.

"Happy wedding gift, my darling wife." Ryker wrapped both arms around my shoulders, and rested his chin on top of my head. "I even named her after you."

He pointed, drawing my eye to the elegantly handwritten moniker painted in a beautiful gold leaf. Underneath the word *Thea,* in smaller letters, it read *My Love.* Thea was his nickname for me. No one else called me that.

I spun around, and whatever he saw on my face and in my eyes made his own azure irises glitter with pleasure.

"How … when …?"

"As soon as you agreed to marry me, I made a few phone calls, called in a few favors." He chuckled. "Dropped a few million dollars."

"But … oh God, Ryker. She's *beautiful.*"

"Just like you, Mrs. Stone." He lifted my chin and kissed me.

"So this is why you pushed so hard for us to leave Paris and spend a couple of nights in Nice?"

"Yes. Blindfolding you all the way from Paris to the South of France wouldn't work. The last hour from the hotel was bad enough." He rolled his eyes. "I swear, at one point, I thought I was going to have to drug you just to get you to leave the city."

I pouted. "But I love Paris."

"And I love you." He gestured to the yacht. "How about a tour?"

"Yes!"

I took his hand, and we boarded. A line of people greeted us. The captain stepped forward and introduced himself and the rest of the crew. After the introductions were over, Ryker led me down a set of oak stairs with a handrail in a highly polished chrome.

"First stop. The master bedroom."

I squealed as he hoisted me over his shoulder and slapped my ass. He wasn't gentle about it either.

"That hurt!"

"Don't worry. I'll kiss it all better."

My stomach vaulted. I often wondered whether the intense heat between Ryker and I, one that had built for seven years before we'd finally gotten together, would fade in the coming months and years. I'd voiced as much to him on our wedding night. He'd proved to me—several times over—we were a long way off from that.

He dropped me onto the bed. Satin sheets caressed my bare shoulders and legs where my dress had ridden up. He loomed over me like a predator assessing his prey, his eyes hungry and glistening with desire. I'd seen this look many times, and on every occasion, it made me go weak at the knees, the need to submit overwhelming me to the extent I didn't have a choice.

"Ryker, we can't."

He canted his head. "Why can't we?"

"You said you were giving me a tour."

"And I am. Like I said, this is the first stop."

He unzipped his pants, and my tongue flicked over my bottom lip. His eyes arrowed between my legs.

"Lift up your dress."

I obeyed his instruction, bunching the soft cotton around my waist. I side-eyed the door. Ryker chuckled.

"For a woman who's been around wealth for a long time now, you're still nervous about staff walking in."

I groaned as he laid the truth bare. "All right, asshole. No need to point out the obvious."

His chuckle grew louder. "I've always loved your sassy mouth."

Caging me with his body, he took my mouth in a kiss that sent tingles to my fingers and toes and forced a satisfied noise from my throat. He reared back, tugged off my panties, and pushed himself inside.

"Jesus. Always so good, Thea."

A rumbling noise sounded, and I tightened my hold on Ryker's neck. "What's that?"

"My heart." He grinned, pulling out and thrusting back in with enough force to shift me up the bed several inches. "It's the engines."

"We're moving?"

"Yeah." Another thrust. Another satisfied groan from both of us.

"Where are we headed?"

His jaw flexed. "Thea, questions later, please."

He reared back onto his haunches, taking me with him. He rested his forehead against mine, his fingers dancing up and down my thighs, and my body responded to his touch with a raft of goose bumps.

"Okay, but you know questions are coming."

"Like you, hopefully."

He shifted us both, the new angle allowing him to graze my clit every time he rocked forward. I galloped to the finish line, my eyes falling closed as the orgasm hit me. Dizzy with pleasure, I relaxed into the waves of pleasure, my body undulating, muscles clenching, the drone and pulse of the engines somewhere underneath the hull reminding me of one of Ryker's vibrators that he kept in his drawer of sinful delights at our home in New York.

He collapsed on top of me, his breath hot against my neck, and rolled to the side. His hand sought mine, knitting our fingers together.

"Love you, wife."

"Love you more, husband."

Two

Ryker

I stood, shoved my dick into my pants, and pulled up my zipper. Sprawled on the bed, her hair a sexy, wild tumble of chocolate scattered over pristine white pillows, lay my wife. Eyes heavy with sated desire, her summer dress still bunched around her hips, she smiled up at me. The secretive curve to her lips made me want to bury myself in her all over again.

Plenty of time for that.

Our honeymoon was half over, and we'd spent an inordinate amount of time in bed already. If I'd had my way, we'd never have left the bedroom of our house in Paris. Hell, if we were in the business of granting wishes, I'd keep Athena in bed for always.

Sadly, time passed, and I had responsibilities. To my company, ROGUES, and to the employees who depended on our continued success to pay their mortgages and feed their kids. But mostly, my responsibilities were to my new bride.

God, she was stunning. I could gaze at her all day and never regret a single moment. When I thought back to the seven years I'd denied her, denied *us* and all we were meant to be, I got the urge to smack myself upside the head. All that wasted time when I could have been enjoying her keen intellect, her smoking body, her sense of humor, and canny ability to ground me. To make me feel *alive.*

"Are you going to stand there all day and just gawk at me?"

I leaned over and laid my palms flat to the mattress, either side of Athena's head, capturing her lips in an all-too-brief kiss.

"I could, but I promised you a tour of your boat. And where you're concerned,

Thea, I always keep my promises."

I straightened, reached down, and helped her to stand. She stepped into her panties, then smoothed her dress into place and ran her hands over her hair.

"Do I look like I've just had sex?"

"Yep." I grinned. "Well and truly fucked."

She narrowed her eyes. "There's no need to act so … smug. God, men. You're still back in the caves, aren't you? Beating your chests and bragging about killing boar and nailing your woman."

"Truth." I snagged her around the waist and kissed her hard. "And if you're really lucky, I'll nail you a couple more times before the day is out."

She made a frustrated sound but, accompanied by a quirk to her lips, it lost its impact. She flounced past me, heading back the way we'd come. I smacked her ass as she passed. She threw a grin over her shoulder.

"Hold that thought, lover."

I groaned. Athena owned me. Body, soul, mind. Everything I was, I'd given to her long ago, and I didn't regret it for a hot minute. My main goal in life was to make her happy, and I'd do anything to ensure she was. Slay dragons, fight armies, give up my best friend. Fortunately, I'd dodged a bullet with the latter. Elliot hadn't been thrilled about us at first, mainly because he'd watched me tear through woman after woman while trying to forget his sister, but eventually, he'd come around to the idea. Sort of. He'd pegged me for a player, blind at the time to just how much I'd loved her. But two weeks ago, he'd stood beside me as my best man, and watched as I promised before our friends, family, and God, to put her first. Every time. And I'd meant every single word.

During the entire circuit of the boat, I kept Athena's hand locked inside mine. Touching her soothed me. The earth had shifted beneath my feet ever since I'd made her my wife. A few months earlier, she'd been abducted in broad daylight, and following her release, I'd struggled to suppress the urge to smother her, to keep her with me at all times. Especially with the culprit still roaming the streets of New York. Which wasn't like me at all. I was renowned for my calm and measured demeanor.

Not that Athena would stand for that kind of behavior anyway. She was a free spirit. To clip her wings would be to diminish her, and any man who did that to a woman like Athena deserved to spend the rest of his days with his balls in a vise.

I gave her a complete tour, from port to starboard, bow to stern, and everything in between. We finished up to the rear of the main deck where a plush, cream leather bench provided a perfect spot from which to enjoy the cool spray from the sea and take advantage of the heat from the sun.

Athena rested her forearms on the cherrywood rail that went around the entire boat and stared out at the sparkling blue waters of the Mediterranean.

"I can't believe you did this, for me."

I moved in behind her, wrapping my arms around her waist, and rested my chin on her left shoulder. "I'd do anything for you."

She spun in my arms, curving her hands around the back of my neck. Athena had this habit of playing with my hair at the nape, and every time she did, a surge of pleasure raced through me.

"And I'd do anything for you."

An idea came to mind, and my lips stretched almost involuntarily, the grin wicked and filled with devious intent.

"Anything, you say?"

"Oh God." She raised her eyes to the sky. "What have I just committed to?"

My smile widened, and I tapped the side of my nose. "Wait and see."

"Ryker, would you mind telling me what this is?"

I peered around the door of the bathroom, my face covered in shaving cream. "What's that, my beloved?"

Athena pivoted from the spot in front of my dresser, brandishing a large purple vibrator. "Tell me, husband, when exactly did you purchase this? Because I know it's not from your drawer of tricks back home, nor do I remember seeing it in Paris."

I grinned. Sex toys were my kink. They kept things exciting in the bedroom.

Not that fucking Athena wasn't exciting enough, but there was always room for improvement. And I intended to keep my bride guessing long after most other couples had given up on a rumble between the sheets.

"And what, pray tell, wife, are you doing combing through my personal possessions?"

She gave me that head tilt and arched eyebrow that always kicked my dick into action. There was something schoolmarmish about it, like she was about to bend me over her knee and thoroughly spank me.

See? Kink.

"Nothing is sacred now. I own you. Lock, stock, and cock ring."

She burst into a fit of giggles. I dove back into the bathroom, wiped the cream off my face—I'd shave later—and shot into the bedroom, capturing her around the waist.

"Cock ring is in the next drawer, my sweet." I nuzzled her ear, biting down hard on the lobe. "I had a few things delivered when we docked yesterday. I sneaked them inside while you were sunbathing up on deck. We only have two weeks of our honeymoon left, and I thought I'd crank up the stakes a little."

"Hmm, you did, did you?"

"Yup." I circled my hips and kissed her neck. "And don't even try to hide how excited you are. I can smell it, sense it, feel it." Reluctantly, I let her go. "Hold on to all that sexual frustration, darling. We'll be late for dinner."

I stepped back into the bathroom to finish shaving, smiling at the huff of exasperation that spilled from her kissable, fuckable mouth. God, how the hell had I gotten this lucky? By the time I returned to the bedroom—or rather stateroom considering we were on a boat—I found it empty. Athena had discarded a few dresses which were lying in a heap on top of the bed, and the faint scent of her perfume lingered in the air. I dressed in a black tux, fiddling with—and cursing—the bow tie. But the place we were going to this evening insisted on formal wear. And besides, Athena loved it when I wore a tux. I opened the drawer on my side of the bed and took out the toy for tonight's entertainment. As I slipped it into my pocket, a grin edged across my face. This should be fun.

I moseyed up to the top deck, finding Athena at the bow, leaning on the wooden rail which had the rather fortunate side effect of showing off her peachy ass in the fitted evening gown she'd chosen. I loitered by the steps leading to the lower decks, arms folded, watching my wife as she wistfully gazed out at the twinkling lights of Monaco. We were only here for the evening. Tomorrow, we'd sail for Italy. I'd organized a packed schedule to ensure we saw as much of Europe as possible before the time came when we had to head back to New York. My aim on this entire trip was for us both to make memories that would last a lifetime.

She glanced over her shoulder, a seductive smile on her lips. "What are you doing all the way over there?"

"Looking at you."

Spinning around, she rested her elbows on the rail. "And what do you see?"

I reached her in three strides and pulled her into my arms, I skimmed my nose along the soft skin of her neck and set off dancing around the deck. "The woman who's going to let me use that purple vibrator on her later tonight."

Her giggle made my heart clench. God, I loved her.

"Only if you're very, very good."

"You know how good I am," I murmured in her ear.

A shiver rippled through her, and she virtually melted inside my embrace. "Stop. I'll be a hot mess at dinner at this rate."

"Hot, yes. A mess? Never."

"You know the way to a girl's heart, Ryker Stone."

I flashed a wicked smile. "And her panties." Tugging her bottom lip between my teeth, I slipped my hand south and caressed her butt. "Now let's go eat. I'm starving."

THREE

ATHENA

The restaurant Ryker took me to was decked out in hues of red and bronze with soft, intimate lighting and a vibrant atmosphere. The maître d' seated us at a booth tucked away in the corner. Ryker motioned for me to sit first, then he slid along the bench beside me. A smile pulled at my lips. His signature move reminded me of our trip to Mexico, where he'd proposed. One of the best weekends of my life.

He handed me a leather-bound menu. "What are you thinking?"

"About Mexico." I scanned it. "And your proposal."

His hand traced up my thigh, over the top of my dress, his eyes on me. "We should do it again sometime. Soon."

"Go to Mexico, or have you propose for a second time?"

"Mexico, although I'd happily propose to you every day for the rest of my life."

I closed the menu and set it on the table. "Go on then."

A frown drew his eyebrows low. "Do what?"

"Propose." I grinned.

His slow, sexy smile caused a flood of liquid heat to gather in my stomach.

"If I get on my knees in the middle of this restaurant, there's only one thing I'm doing, and it isn't proposing."

His gaze shifted to the apex of my thighs, and I flushed hot. "Not even you'd go that far."

"Oh, Thea." He shook his head. "Have you learned nothing?"

He made a move to stand.

I snapped a hand around his wrist. "Don't you dare!"

A familiar chuckle rumbled through his chest. He returned to perusing the menu. "Well if I can't eat you, I think I'll choose scallops followed by steak. What about you?"

A warm glow spread through my insides. I was rather enjoying the more relaxed honeymoon version of Ryker. At home in New York, there were a lot of calls on his time, and, as CEO of ROGUES, he took his responsibilities seriously, which often meant a split in his attention. But here, I had him all to myself, and boy, did I plan to savor every single moment of it.

"I was thinking of crab cakes followed by the grouper."

He nodded sagely. "Excellent choices."

I angled him toward me and dropped a quick kiss on his mouth. "God, I love you. No idea why, but I do."

"I know why." He glanced at his groin.

My hand shot up. "Don't say it."

He flashed a smile. "And I love you. Now let's order, so I can snack on you while we wait."

He beckoned to the server and put in our food and drink order. Almost immediately, the server returned with the bottle of wine Ryker had asked for. Ryker dismissed him, assuring him we could serve ourselves. Alone once more, Ryker edged closer to me, his broad shoulders hiding me from view. Slowly, he eased up the hem of my dress.

"Ryker, we're in public," I admonished.

"Then stop me."

The dress brushed my knees, then my thighs. He nibbled on my earlobe, and I only just prevented a groan from spilling out of me. The tables here were well-spaced, and our booth intimately private, but that didn't mean no one would hear me. I had a tendency to be rather vocal when turned on.

"Want to play, sweet wife?" He dropped featherlike kisses along my jaw.

"Play how?" I gasped.

He kissed me rather than answer, his tongue sliding between my lips, dueling with my own. The outside world melted away as I gave myself to my husband. He slipped his hand between my thighs, and I opened for him. A faint buzzing sound penetrated the pleasurable fog in my brain.

I tore away. "Shit!"

Ryker clamped his hand over my mouth, his glittering blue irises full of mischief. He pressed the tip of the vibrator against my clit, through my panties. A violent shudder rolled through me. I pushed his hand away.

"How did you fit that into your pocket?"

"It's only small. A clit vibrator. Too much, given where we are?"

I reached for the wine glass and took a large gulp. "Not now."

"God, you're perfect."

"And you're so damn kinky."

He touched me with it again, and I groaned.

"I'm dying here."

He smiled with wicked intent and pressed the tip harder against me, then began circling it, his mouth covering mine again. I sank into his kiss as a familiar surge began, the muscles in my lower belly rippling. I closed my eyes, too lost in the moment to give two shits about where we were.

And then he stopped.

I snapped my eyes open in time to watch him slip the thin cylindrical vibrator into his pocket.

"What? Why?"

He ran his tongue over his bottom lip. "Should keep you right on the edge for when I get you back to the boat."

I narrowed my eyes, pinning him with a frustrated glare. "That's just cruel."

"You won't be saying that later. Trust me."

He picked up his wine glass and handed mine to me, then clinked. "To us."

I snickered in resigned fashion, then softly sighed. "I'm having the best time."

"Thank Christ for that. I think that rubbish honeymoons spell disaster for marriage."

"I adore this version of you."

"Which version is that?"

"The relaxed one." I put down my wine and made him do the same. I held his hand, playing with the tips of his fingers, and gave him a close-lipped smile. "Promise me something."

"Anything."

"That when we get back to New York, I won't completely lose you to ROGUES."

He cupped me around the neck, the pad of his thumb tracing the length of my jaw. His spectacular blue eyes, the color of the sea at the height of summer, roved over my face, his expression sincere.

"I promise. You're my priority now, Thea. ROGUES is and will always get the best version of me that I'm capable of giving, but it will never come at the expense of your happiness. Of *our* happiness."

I went all soft and gooey inside. This man, he knew just the right things to say at the right time. I couldn't remember a period when I hadn't loved him, but since we'd married, it was as if our feelings had stepped up a level.

The food was spectacular, although I ate faster than I normally would. Lucky for me, I'd barely put my silverware on my clean plate when Ryker called for the check. Still, I couldn't pass up the chance to tease him. "And what if I wanted dessert?"

He raked me with a heated head-to-toe appraisal. "Dessert is on the menu, Thea. You can bank on it. Just a different menu."

The marina was less than five minutes drive from the restaurant. Ryker gave me two orgasms in that time. As we made our way to our stateroom, he couldn't wipe the smug, satisfied grin off his face. I sat on the end of the bed and removed my shoes, groaning as I wiggled my toes. High-heeled shoes looked great, and were necessary with a dress like this, but damn, they weren't the comfiest.

I flopped onto the bed and closed my eyes. At the distinct sound of buzzing, I opened them to find Ryker brandishing the purple vibrator.

"I hope you're not too tired, wife."

I keened and stretched, then ran my hands down my sides and lifted my dress over my hips. "Okay, husband, let's see what you can do with that thing."

Four

Ryker

If I manage not to come in thirty seconds, it'll be a fucking miracle.

I removed Athena's dress, tearing it in the process, but in my defense, she didn't make it easy, lying there giggling as I wrestled with the damn thing. Finally, I got her down to her bra and thong.

"Purple lingerie to match with the vibrator." I grinned. "I'm a fan of parallelism."

I traced the tip of the vibrator around her nipple. It elongated, the point visible through the satin of her bra. I did the same with her other nipple, encouraging it, too, to stand to attention. Already she was writhing, her legs scissoring, and I'd hardly begun.

"Here, hold this." I placed the vibrator in her palm and closed her fingers around it. "Touch your clit with it."

"And what are you planning to do?" She panted the second the tip made contact with the bundle of nerves at the hood of her sex.

I kneeled up and tugged off my tie, unfastening the top two buttons on my shirt while I was there. I snagged her free wrist and wrapped one end of the tie around it. Pushing her legs together to hold the vibrator in place, I captured her other wrist, tying that one, too. With both wrists together, I raised her arms overhead and fastened the tie to the headboard. The position made her tits thrust up and out, her nipples hardening further.

"That's better." I gripped the vibrator. "Now open your legs for me."

She obeyed.

"Wider."

Again, no hesitation. Her eyes tracked my every move, shining with anticipation, her skin flushed, her breath coming in little sips.

"You've never looked more beautiful."

"I'm a hot, sweaty mess, and it's all your fault."

I chuckled. "Like I said. Beautiful."

Shifting the thin patch of material covering her pussy to the side, I ran the point of the vibrator down her slit, all the way to her asshole, then back again, making sure I circled her clit before repeating the entire thing again. Every time she writhed and closed her legs, I stopped. On the third occasion, she growled at me.

"Damn, that's fucking sexy. Do it again."

"Stop torturing me!"

I angled my head to one side. "Am I, though? I thought I was going pretty easy on you."

I increased the speed and pressed it hard to her clit, but before she could come, I withdrew. I'd barely touched her with it, and she was already bordering on climax. I thought the two orgasms I gave her in the car might've taken the edge off. Looked as if I was wrong.

"Ryker." Her breathing came hard and fast. "Please."

Pushing two fingers inside her, I kept up the stop-start torment on her clit. I withdrew, tasting her with my tongue, licking my fingers clean. Her eyes flared. I knew what turned my wife on, and I played up to it. Pleasing her was my favorite hobby.

I parted her folds and nudged the vibrator inside her, then set it on pulse. She gasped. "Jesus Christ."

"Don't move."

I stood to remove my clothes. My dick, impossibly hard, demanded attention, sticking straight out from between my hips. I kneeled between her legs and gripped the base, tugging hard on it. She stared at it, her tongue dampening her lips. *Fuck.* I slowed down, stroking my length. It helped a bit, but my balls tightened anyway. I tugged on the restraint I'd fashioned out of my tie, releasing her hands. She'd need them.

"Lift up your bra. Push your tits together. Play with your nipples. Harder. That's it. Christ."

"Ryker. God."

I swiped my thumb over her swollen clit, barely touching her. It didn't matter. She came. Loudly, gloriously, yanking and pinching her nipples. The vibrator continued to pulse and throb inside her. It was all too much for me to hold on. I came, too, showering her belly and her tits in spurts of cum, my climax unrelenting, never-ending.

Athena pulled out the vibrator, but instead of turning it off, she touched my balls with the tip. I almost shot through the ceiling, especially as my cock still jerked in an effort to empty the remains of my seed.

"Ohhh, payback's a bitch," I said, although I couldn't stop laughing. That was the thing with me and Athena. We laughed a lot, almost as if we were making up for all those years of pain, when laughter was the furthest thing from both our minds.

I fetched a cloth from the bathroom and cleaned her up. She set the vibrator on her nightstand and petted it.

"I'll leave you right here, Purple Pete. I think we'll be playing with you again very soon."

"Purple Pete?"

Curling into me, she flung one of her shapely, downright sexy legs over mine. Her pussy, soaked with her arousal, dampened my hip.

"Well, I mean, I thought of going with Victor Vibe, but that's so cliché." A half shrug. "And I'm … not."

Grinning, I kissed her hair. "I love you, wife."

"Love you more, husband."

"I have a confession to make." I put down my half-finished croissant and wiped my fingertips on a napkin. Athena paused, a fork of scrambled eggs halfway to her mouth, and gave me one of her "what have you done now" looks.

"Dare I ask?"

"I'm volunteering the information."

Her lips lifted on one side. "Give it to me, then."

"Thought I did that last night."

She flashed a glance at the steward who'd come over to refill her coffee cup, a flush creeping over her cheeks. There were many things I adored about my wife, but her coquetry was one of her truly alluring features. I didn't possess the embarrassment gene. Maybe it helped to be male, or perhaps it was just me, but given we were on our honeymoon, I surmised that everyone knew we were having sex, and lots of it. I just didn't see the point in either hiding the fact, or feeling in any way ashamed of it. I'd snared the hottest woman on the eastern seaboard, and I intended to gloat about that at every opportunity.

"Ryker," she whispered, her head angled in rebuke.

A smile of my own pulled at the corners of my mouth, but I waited to speak until we were alone once more.

"With how much noise you make, I think they know we're fucking on the regular."

Her mouth made a perfect 'O' shape, then she clamped her lips together. "Considering you have a confession, you're not endearing me to your cause, mister. Now spill."

I fake shuddered. "Damn, woman, I love it when your dominant side comes out to play."

"Fat chance of that," she groused. "You're dominant enough for the both of us."

Bantering with my wife was one of my favorite pastimes. Bantering about sex took the top spot. Well, next to actually having sex. Not much beat that.

I took a sip of coffee. I wasn't stalling. Not really. But I didn't know how she'd take what I had to say. This was our honeymoon, Athena the center of my world, yet I was about to welcome an interruption. But the chance was just too good to pass up.

"When we dock in Venice tomorrow morning, I have to go ashore for a meeting."

She dropped her napkin on top of her empty plate. "Okay."

I widened my eyes. "That's it? Okay? I thought you'd be pissed that I was interrupting our honeymoon for a work thing."

"I'll have you make it up to me on your return."

I reached across the table for her hand, needing to connect with her physically. Not five minutes went by when I wasn't making some kind of overture.

"It's someone that Sebastian has been trying to entice for a while now, with no luck." Sebastian was one of my partners in ROGUES. He ran our European interests. "Then out of the blue, the guy contacts him and says he's got an opening in his calendar for ten o'clock tomorrow in Venice. I'll be there first thing, I offered to take the meeting."

"Muscled your way in more like," Athena said. "I hope you're not treading on Sebastian's toes."

"He's a big boy. He can handle his ego getting a little roughed up. Besides, it makes sense." I brought her hand to my mouth and sucked on her pinky. "Am I forgiven?"

"Nothing to forgive. ROGUES is an important part of your life. And mine. It's only for a few hours. I think I can entertain myself. It's Venice, after all."

"I'll arrange for security to accompany you."

She sighed, opening her mouth in a ready refusal of a bodyguard, but one look at my face, and she backed down. She knew the drill. After her abduction in New York, she went nowhere alone. Sadly, with enormous wealth came the necessity to protect ourselves, and nothing was more important to me than my wife's safety.

"Fine, but I hope whoever lands the gig likes shoe shopping."

FIVE

ATHENA

I put down my fork and downed the rest of my orange juice. "I can't believe we're going home in two days." I grinned over at Ryker and stroked my chin in perfect villainy. "But I have something very special planned for today."

Ryker arched an eyebrow. "I thought the honeymoon schedule was in my hands."

"And it has been, until now. You already told me that today was a relaxation day, and I've decided it isn't. So, suck it up, Mr. I-love-to-be-in-control-of-everything, because today, you aren't."

"Damn, busted. And I thought I hid my control freakishness so well."

I snorted and got to my feet. "I've laid out the clothes you'll need. They're in the bedroom." I checked my watch. "We leave in thirty minutes."

"You've laid out my clothes?" He frowned. "You never do that."

"Never is a big word." I giggled as I walked away, leaving my apoplectic husband behind me.

He soon followed, his lips twisting in query at the jeans, boots, socks, T-shirt, and hat regimentally set out on the bed. He picked up the hat, turning it over in his hands.

"Why am I getting a bad feeling about this?"

I smirked as I sat on the edge of the bed and slipped my feet into my boots. "Just get dressed."

I jogged back up to the top deck, scanning the sky. White fluffy clouds mingled with pale blue, the temperature a little cooler than of late, perfect for what I had planned. We'd docked last night just north of Bordeaux in the Gironde region of France. A half-hour trip inland would take us to our destination for today's fun activity; horseback riding. I'd ridden some as a child, and I'd been pretty darn good at it, although I hadn't been on a horse in some years. Ryker had never ridden, and I wasn't sure how he'd take to it. Everything my husband did, he excelled at, and I admit that part of the lure was to see how he coped with something new. Knowing him, he'd rock it, leaving me with egg on my face.

We left behind the busy port and traveled into the countryside. Ryker quizzed me the entire journey from the dock to the stables. I told him nothing, but as the driver nosed the car between two brick columns that bridged a black, wrought-iron sign announcing *Arnaud Stud Farm*, my secret was out.

"Riding? We're going horseback riding?"

"Yep."

"Oh fuck."

I nudged him with my elbow. "Can't be good at everything."

My teasing fired up his competitive streak, and he folded his arms. "Wanna bet, sweetheart?"

Michel, the owner of the farm who I'd already spoken to on the phone—fortunately his English was far better than my French—greeted us as we climbed out of the car. Beside him was the cutest dog with a rough tan coat and pointy ears. Michel told us he was called Spike. With those ears, I could see why.

I bent to pet him. "Oh, he's so cute."

"He'll join us on the ride," Michel explained in accented English. "I've tried to make him stay behind, but he follows me anyway, so now I just let him come."

Michel led us over to the stables and introduced us to our horses, explaining that while the saddles weren't what Americans were used to—they were a mixture of American and English saddles, known as Maclellan style—he promised that we'd be fine.

Watching Ryker mount his horse, a gorgeous chestnut named Belle, would, I decided, make the top three of my honeymoon memories. It took him several attempts, which meant I got to see his stunning ass tighten in his jeans over and over again. Eventually, Michel gave him a leg up. Ryker's frown as I easily mounted mine, Estelle, a dappled gray, pleased me no end, and I laughed.

"This is going to be fun."

We set off at a leisurely pace, winding through trails, surrounded by lush greenery and a dramatic mountain backdrop. A hawk rose high into the air, and I tipped back my head, marveling at the vast wingspan and sheer beauty of nature. I called out to Michel, asking him to stop, and snapped a couple of pictures on my phone.

Spike ran on ahead, stopping every now and then to make sure we were following. It wasn't long before Ryker settled into the rhythm of the horse's gait, and he left his stiffness behind, his body moving in time with the horse. On occasion, he twisted in his saddle to shoot me a triumphant grin. But it was when we broke into a trot that I couldn't stop a peal of laughter from bursting out of me. Ryker bumped his ass against the saddle, unable to cope with the change in pace. He cursed.

"My horse is broken," he called out.

I laughed harder. "She will be if you keep bouncing around on her back like that."

I urged my horse on until I was riding beside him. He checked out the way I rocked into the saddle and went with Estelle rather than against her.

"Sit into it," I said.

"Easy for you to say."

"At last." I briefly dropped my reins and clapped. "Something I'm better at than you."

He raked a gaze over me, checked Michel wasn't close enough to hear, then gave me a close-lipped smile. "Keep up the teasing. I'll get my own back, darling wife."

I fake shuddered. "I'm banking on it, darling husband."

About an hour and a half into our ride, Michel stopped outside a rustic café, letting us know it was to give us and the horses a break. As Ryker slid down his horse and landed on the dusty ground, he groaned.

"My ass is killing me."

"Yeah, you might struggle to walk tomorrow, too."

"So will you. Maybe for different reasons."

I burst out laughing. "Challenge accepted."

While we had a bite to eat, Michel picked up Spike, put his cap on top of the dog's head, then plunked him on his horse. He sat there, still and proud while I grabbed my phone to capture the moment. Michel explained that Spike sulked if he didn't get to sit on the horse at least once during each trip.

"God, can we take him home?" I asked Ryker. "He's adorable."

"I think Michel might be rather attached to him."

"Ugh." I stuck out my tongue at him. "Logic sucks."

We set off once again, looping back to the farm via a different route. Ryker began to get the hang of Belle's gait, so when Michel suggested a gentle canter, he was all for it, especially when Michel let him know that canter was easier to master than trot.

All went well for the first ten seconds. Then a rustle in the undergrowth spooked Belle, and she shied to the right, dislodging Ryker. His feet came out of the stirrups, and off he came. We pulled up, and Michel grabbed Belle's reins as she trotted past him. Lucky for Ryker, his fall was cushioned by lots of soft grasses which meant the only real harm done was to his pride.

After satisfying myself he wasn't injured, I burst out laughing. And once I started, I couldn't stop. A dirty smudge snaked up one side of his face, and his ass was covered in dust.

"Very funny." He brushed himself off while my laughter got even louder. I let go of the reins and leaned forward onto Estelle's neck.

"Even Spike's a better rider than you."

He stuck his tongue into his cheek and nodded. "Keep going. I have a long memory. Payback will be mine."

I made a beckoning gesture. "Bring it."

Six

Athena

I swiped mascara over my eyelashes, narrowly avoiding poking myself in the eye with the brush. I blinked, then cursed. How come every time I applied mascara, I always ended up with a big blob of black on the papery skin underneath my eye? Now, I'd have to reapply concealer, foundation, powder. Damn, being a woman was high maintenance. Men, all they had to do was shave their faces, and they bitched enough about that. Imagine if they had to do underarms, legs, and bikini line. Sometimes, I envied men. Their lives were a hell of a lot easier than us women.

Ryker appeared from the bathroom, clean-shaven and dressed, and smelling heavenly. He made a move to kiss me. I warded him off with a raised hand.

"No. I have to redo my makeup, and I'm already running late. No time for your shenanigans."

He pouted, pressing his palm over his heart. "I'm wounded."

"I thought it was your ass that was wounded after your fall earlier today." I canted my head. "Or was that your pride?"

"Ha ha. Like I said, keep it going. The more you tease me, the more you'll beg for mercy when I decide to make my move."

"Really?" I pressed my fingertips to my temples and pretended to concentrate. "My inner psychic says no begging in my immediate future."

"You need a new inner psychic." He traced the tip of his finger over my bra strap. "I approve of your choice of lingerie for the evening, Mrs. Stone. I can't wait to rip it off you later."

"It's La Perla. You are not ripping anything."

"Spoilsport." He fiddled with his tie. "Don't get dressed yet. Christ, this damn tie. I can't get it right."

He stripped it off and moved in front of the full-length mirror to retie it.

"What do you mean, don't get dressed yet?"

He glanced over his shoulder. "You'll see."

Shaking my head, I quickly reapplied my makeup without further mishaps, while Ryker finished tying his tie, then sat on the bed and watched me with hungry eyes. As I got to my feet, he stood, too.

"Just the dress to put on now?"

I nodded. "And shoes."

He crossed to the dresser, opened the third drawer down, and lifted out a black box about three by five inches. My curiosity spiked. I edged closer. He removed something and put it in his pocket, leaving behind two silver balls on a piece of thick string.

I frowned. "Ben Wa balls?" I'd never found them particularly arousing. To me, they just felt like a heavy lump in my vagina. They worked for some women, or so I'd heard, but not for me.

"Not exactly." Ryker took them out of their satin housing and weighed them up in his hand. "Are you game?"

"What does 'not exactly' mean, and what did you slip into your pocket?"

His fierce blue eyes, glittering with desire, bored into me. "Are you game, Thea?"

My sex tightened, and a shiver of anticipation mingled with giddiness raced down my spine.

"I'm game." I spoke in a breathy, almost porn star manner. Or maybe one of those telephone sex lines. Either way, I sounded turned on. "I'm definitely game."

"Good. Bend over the dressing table and open your legs for me."

I did as he asked. He moved my thong to one side, his fingers tickling my flesh. I shuddered. He pushed one finger inside me, then another.

"Damn, always so primed. I'm gutted we don't have time to give Pete another workout."

I giggled. "There's always later."

He palmed my butt, caressing the left cheek. "That's why we're perfect for each other."

He replaced his fingers with the balls. I flinched.

"They're cold."

"Soon warm up. How do they feel?"

"Heavy. Weird."

"But not uncomfortable?"

"No. They'll give my pelvic floor a workout, though."

"Added bonus."

He slipped my dress off the hanger and held it out to me. I slipped it on and lifted my hair for him to zip me up. He captured my hand, his gaze filled with love and heat and desire.

"Ready to go to dinner, Mrs. Stone?"

I nodded. "I am."

We'd visited many restaurants over the last few weeks, but tonight's—set in a medieval castle—beat all the others, hands down. The ancient, thick walls kept the inside cool, while the small windows and clever lighting gave it a cozy feel. Ryker chose a table right in the middle of the restaurant whereas he normally picked a booth or a table tucked away in a corner. I waited for the server to retreat, then frowned.

"This isn't like you."

"No," he replied, an impish tilt to his lips. "It isn't."

My instincts went on high alert. "What are you up to?"

He jerked his chin at the menu. "What are you having? I might go for the oysters."

I narrowed my eyes, but then the server arrived to take our drinks order, and I didn't get chance to question him further.

Turned out I didn't need to.

As he conversed with the server over the wine list, the balls he'd put in me began to vibrate. My eyes widened, and I fidgeted. The vibration increased, and I almost groaned, swallowing the sound at the last minute. Whatever these things were, and how they sat inside my vagina, they were making me hella needy. I squirmed again, shooting a glare at Ryker. He chose to keep his gaze averted, dragging out the conversation about red or white wine. Every few seconds, he turned the dial. Heat spread through my stomach.

Oh God. I'm going to come.

I squeezed my inner muscles, but that only made it worse. He dismissed the server and looked over at me, his eyes glinting.

"Everything all right, Thea?"

I groaned. "This isn't fair."

"On the contrary." He picked up his napkin, flicked it open, and laid it in his lap. "I did warn you payback would be mine."

Another increase in speed. I stiffened and writhed, the urge to get off overwhelming. "Ryker, please."

"Ah, I also seem to remember that I was fairly sure you'd beg for mercy." He made a grand gesture with his hand. "And here we are."

"You are no longer the love of my life," I gritted out.

He chuckled. "I love you, too, Thea. Now, how about those oysters?"

For over an hour, Ryker played with me, increasing and reducing the speed of vibration at will. I'd never teetered so long on the edge of orgasm yet had my release denied. Sweat trickled between my breasts and down the back of my neck, despite the cool air inside the ancient building. When he finally called for the bill, I almost doubled over in relief. I'd never know how I made it back to the boat. I flew downstairs to our stateroom. My dress was off before Ryker caught up to me.

"I don't care what you have to do. Rip the underwear, burn it. Whatever. But for Christ's sake, touch me."

His easy, sexy, self-satisfied smirk went straight to my clit. I jammed my legs together, then crossed one over the other as if I desperately needed to pee and was trying to hold it in.

"I'm serious, Ryker. I'm dying here."

"We are doing this again." He raked me with a heated gaze. "I'd hoped they'd make you hot, but I didn't expect this. Much better than I'd expected."

"Well, good for you." I tugged down my thong and threw it at him. He laughed. Getting on his knees, he applied pressure to the inside of my thighs.

"Open for me."

He buried his nose in the soft curls covering my mound, then swept his tongue over my folds. "Jesus, Thea."

Wrapping a finger around the cord, he gently pulled. The balls popped out, and I orgasmed.

"Fuck!" I didn't swear anywhere near as much as Ryker, but there wasn't a better choice of word than that one for the violent shuddering climax that ripped through me. My body, unable to cling on, succumbed to the precipice Ryker and his remote control had kept me teetering on the edge of all night.

"Better?" he queried.

"Not even a little bit."

He licked his lips when I needed him so badly to lick mine. "Then we'd best do something about that."

Seven

Ryker

"Ready to go home?"

Athena's sad eyes scanned our stateroom, the space emptied of all our personal effects. We'd docked in Southampton on the south coast of England this morning, and my plane was already fueled up and ready to fly us back to New York.

"I suppose. I'm really going to miss this place, though." She tucked her arm around my waist and leaned her head on my shoulder. "What will you do with her?"

"I've already arranged to have her moved to the Bahamas. I've decided to moor her in Nassau. That way, we can get away for the weekend whenever our schedules allow."

She brightened at this news. "I love that idea."

Kissing her temple, I squeezed her shoulder. "Come on, Thea. Let's go home."

The plane soared into the sky, the excellent flying conditions making for a smooth takeoff. Athena stared out the window as we left England behind, and as the plane broke through the fluffy white clouds, she settled back into her seat with a contented sigh. It wasn't long before she dozed off, giving me an opportunity to catch up with work. It was the first time I'd taken a proper vacation since the business I ran with my five best friends had taken off. As ROGUES grew, so did the calls upon my time. But four weeks was a long stretch to be out of the game, and already, I was eager to dive back in.

My inbox overflowed with hundreds of emails, some of which one of the other ROGUES board members had already dealt with, but others still required my input. Sebastian had progressed the deal I'd struck with Giovanni Perucci in

Venice, but there were a couple of things he'd asked for me to look at. I read the draft agreement, made copious notes, and sent it back to him for his review.

Resting back against the leather seat, I glanced over at my sleeping wife, and my heart twisted. Would I ever forgive myself for those lost seven years? All that time wasted when we could have been together. Lucky for me, Athena had never given up on us, and eventually, I'd pulled my head out of my ass and realized a life without her beside me was meaningless.

My email program pinged with a new message from Elliot, Athena's brother and my closest friend. The subject line read "Honeymoon's over, buddy." I chuckled and opened it, soon becoming engrossed in a new business venture he'd proposed. The figures looked good—maybe too good—but the sector excited me. The familiar buzz of conquering something new sent electricity fizzing through my veins. The calling card of an exciting adventure.

"I knew you couldn't resist."

I twisted to face my wife who'd cranked one eye open, a knowing smile on her lips.

"Busted." I grinned. "Am I in trouble?"

"Always." She sat upright, yawned, and stretched. "How long was I out?"

"A few hours." I closed the laptop and held out my arms. "Too long for me not to touch you."

She came to sit on my lap. "Thank you for the best time of my life."

"I sense a wistful tone in there, Mrs. Stone."

She nodded. "I'm sad to leave, because I know that as soon as we get back to New York, a part of you won't be mine any longer."

I opened my mouth to object, but she silenced me with a kiss.

"It's not a complaint. I know the man I married. ROGUES is your life."

"No, *you're* my life. ROGUES is only a part of it. And I meant what I said in Monaco. I will make time for us. I'm aware how single-minded I can get, but things are different now. Our honeymoon was just the start. Making you happy is the only goal I truly care about."

"Well then." She kissed me again. "I'd say you're well on track to achieving it."

We landed at a private airfield in Queens to torrential rain. Immigration boarded the plane to clear us for entry into the United States—one of the many benefits the trappings of wealth brought. I held an umbrella over Athena as we ran down the airplane steps and into our waiting limo. The car glided away, and we arrived at our apartment building forty minutes later. I insisted on carrying Athena during the entire elevator ride up to the penthouse, which brought on a fit of giggles.

"Welcome home, Mrs. Stone," I announced as I strode through the foyer, heading for the main living area. "Let's get you naked."

"Jesus Christ. My ears are bleeding," an all-too familiar voice drawled.

Elliot, surrounded by our friends and family, stood in the center of our living room. Decorations and balloons covered vast swathes of the room, and a huge banner declaring "Welcome home, Mr. & Mrs. Stone" hung across the bank of windows that gave an unrivalled view of Manhattan.

"Oh, fuck." I let Athena slide down my body to land on her feet, an unusual blush stealing over my cheeks as I locked gazes with Karl, Athena's father. Great timing for the embarrassment gene I thought I didn't own to put in an appearance. "Sorry about that."

Karl laughed, holding out his arms for his little girl. "We've missed you so much!"

Cheers erupted, and everyone crowded around, enveloping us in hugs and kisses and demands for us to tell them everything about our four-week European honeymoon.

Just like that, our bubble burst. But replacing it was something even better.

A life I'd never dared to dream of, with the woman I loved beside me.

"Thank you for marrying me, Mr. Stone," Athena whispered in my ear.

"The pleasure, Mrs. Stone, is all mine."

No Fucks Given

by

L. Ann

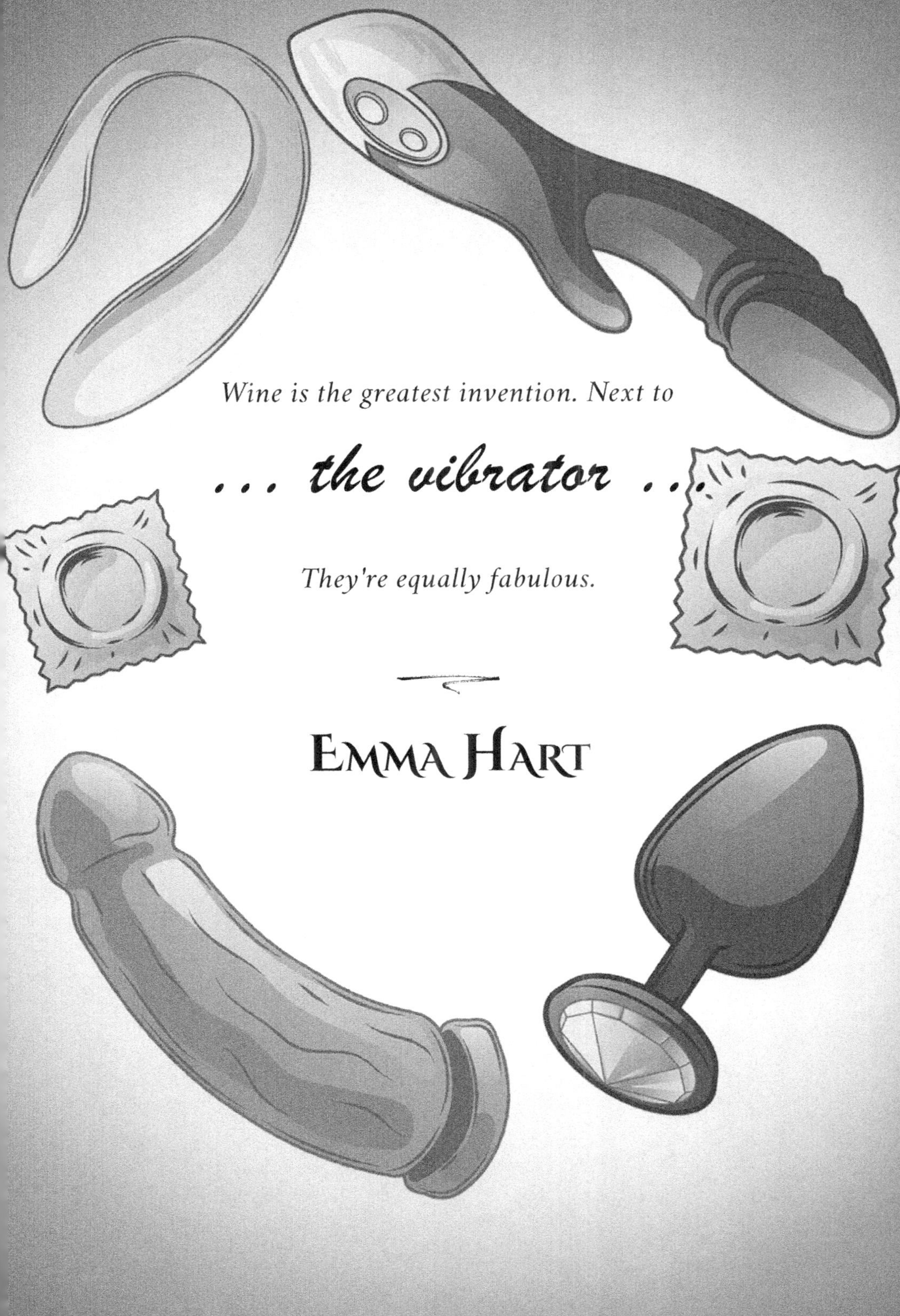
Wine is the greatest invention. Next to
... the vibrator ...
They're equally fabulous.
EMMA HART

One

Rain

The giggling was driving me crazy. I mean the serious 'I'm going to stab you in the face with the nearest sharp object' kind of crazy. I knew what the sound meant. My sister had found someone to flirt with. She'd giggle, pout, rub up against the poor unsuspecting victim, then drag him back to our apartment for a game or two of Plant the Parsnip. By morning, I'd have considered ripping off my ears, numerous times, so I didn't have to listen to her do it again.

I pushed my glass across the bar. "Can I get another?"

The barman hiked an eyebrow. "Already?"

I tapped the rim of the glass. "I'm going to need it. Hit me."

He grabbed the bottle of tequila, tipped it up, and emptied a shot into the glass. I scowled.

"Don't be selfish. Fill that baby up."

His eyes shot up to mine. "I'm cutting you off after this one."

"Yeah, yeah." I gave him an airy wave, waited for him to finish pouring my drink, then snatched it up and knocked it back in one gulp.

He shook his head and moved down the bar, taking the bottle with him.

Spoilsport.

My sister giggled again, high-pitched and fake. I ground my teeth.

"Sororicide is illegal. Although, if that's how she acts all the time, you might get away with a claim of temporary insanity."

The deep, slow drawl came from my left. I twisted on the barstool and came face to face with … a *god*? Eros made flesh. I rubbed my eyes and blinked. Nope, he was still there. Maybe the barman was right, and I *had* passed my limit. *No one* could be that good looking.

"You're staring," Eros pointed out, with a slight curl of his lips.

"I am." I nodded. "I might also be drooling a little. Can I touch you? Just to make sure I'm not hallucinating."

Broad shoulders under white silk shrugged. "You often hallucinate company?"

I jabbed at his bicep with one finger, and my eyes widened. "You're *real* real." My whisper was awed.

"And you're drunk. But that's still no defense against murder."

"I am *not* as think as you drunk I *am*!" I slid from the stool and aimed another jab at his arm.

His lips twitched. "*Riiiight.*" He caught my arm, stopping me from crashing into him. "Shame, really." He rose to his feet, and … just … kept … rising.

"Holy shit. Just *how* tall are you?"

"Taller than you, Tinkerbell. Come on, let's get you into a cab." His fingers curled around my wrist and tugged me through the crowd.

"No. Wait. I'm not going with you. You could be a … a *murder-erer*!" I dug my heels into the floor and resisted his attempts to keep me moving. And by *resisted*, I meant he ignored my pitiful protest and just kept moving. "Seriously, stop! I need to tell my sister I'm leaving."

"I think she already knows."

I blew out a breath. "Oh."

"Yeah … *oh*. C'mon, Tinkerbell."

He jerked his head toward the exit we were heading for, where my sister leaned against the wall, arms folded, one perfectly manicured eyebrow arched as she watched our approach. … Wait, you didn't manicure eyebrows. What the fuck did you do to eyebrows? I searched my tequila-soaked brain for the information and came up with nothing.

"It's called microblading." The god beside me said.

"What? Oh. Wait … how did you know what I was trying to remember?" I peered at him. "Are you *telepathetic?*"

He snorted. "It's telepathic, and no. You were arguing with yourself over it."

"Rain!" My sister's sharp voice reached me seconds before the woman herself did. "Thank you. I'll take it from here."

My eyes swung from my sister to Eros and back again. "I think I'd rather go home with *him*."

My sister gaped at me. "You're not sober enough to make that decision."

The god looming beside me laughed. "I'm not going home; I'm going to a hotel."

"Perfect! Lead the way, Eros!"

"Rain!" My sister, exasperation dripping from her tone, caught my arm. "We're here to network."

I ran my eyes over the guy beside me. "I'm totally planning to network. Look at him. He's a businessman … and a *God*! How much more networking do I need?"

"Rain, you're drunk."

I sniffed. "And you would rather have the apartment to yourself so you can fuck whoever you have lined up without me there to cramp your style. Eros here will look after me." I batted my eyelashes at him, hopefully in a sexy manner. "Won't you?"

He patted the hand I curled around his forearm. "Sure."

Two

Marley

I moved as quietly as I could around my suite, not wanting to wake the girl snoring like a congested walrus in the guestroom. She'd hung on to me like a limpet at the celebrity gala event I'd been forced to attend, and I hadn't liked the idea of leaving her there, in her tequila-drunk state. Knowing how some of the guys who were lurking around behaved, I wouldn't have that on my conscience.

So, when she'd announced she was coming home with me, I didn't argue. She'd tried to kiss me in the elevator on the way up, arms curling up around my neck, those lush curves pressing against my chest. I'd let her; she tasted too good not to. Her hand had dropped to my pants, burrowed its way beneath the belt, curled around my dick and I was so *fucking* tempted to take what she was offering.

But she was drunk, and I wasn't one hundred percent certain she was in control, so I brought her up to my suite, unwrapped her fingers from my protesting cock, and tucked her into bed. I left her there … to sleep *alone*. I didn't do drunk fucks. There was too much risk.

I called down an order for breakfast from room service, asked them to bring it up after thirty minutes, then went for a shower. When I came out fifteen minutes later, a towel wrapped around my waist and rubbing my hair with a second one, it was to silence. I paused in the doorway and glanced around. The main sitting room was empty, which meant my guest was either awake and hiding out in the bedroom or had sneaked out while I was showering. Tossing the towels to one side, I detoured to my bedroom to pull on a pair of black sweats and a t-shirt. I grabbed a bottle of water from the bar in the corner of the sitting room, a couple of painkillers from my 'on tour' supply for morning-after headaches, and tapped on the guest bedroom door.

"Hey, Tinkerbell. You alive in there?"

The door opened a second later, and a hungover red-cheeked blonde-haired nymph was framed in the doorway, wrapped in a sheet.

"Water and painkillers for the tequila after-effects." I held out the bottle and white pills.

"Thanks," she mumbled without looking at me.

"I've ordered breakfast. You have about ten minutes. Take a shower, freshen up. There's clean towels in the bathroom and I'll loan you a t-shirt."

"I'd appreciate that." She took the pills, popped them in her mouth, and then washed them down with the water. "I'm sorry about last night."

"It's fine. I'm often mistaken for the God of Love, forced to fight off a gorgeous drunken woman, who was intent on drilling me in the elevator, and bring her back to my suite with me."

She groaned, her eyes closing in horror. "I did all that, didn't I?"

I laughed. "Don't worry about it. Go take that shower. You'll feel better after it." I stepped away from the door. "Breakfast will be here soon."

"Okay, thanks" She didn't move from the doorway, gnawing on her bottom lip as she looked at me.

"We didn't have sex." I guessed the direction of her thoughts.

The tension left her shoulders and she sagged against the doorframe. "Oh, thank god for that ... I mean ... not that I *wouldn't* have sex with you ... Look at you! Anyone would be crazy not to salivate over that body, but ... I mean ..." Her eyes closed again, her cheeks turning pink with mortification. "Just shoot me now. I'm not crazy, I swear."

I was saved from answering by a tap at the door. A good job, because I was giving serious thought to throwing her over my shoulder and finishing what she started in the elevator. "Go shower," I instructed her and went to greet room service.

The bedroom door was shut and the shower was running by the time I'd tipped the guy and sent him on his way. Ignoring the way my mind whispered about how she would look with hot water sluicing over her body and the way my dick twitched at the image building, I took a second to find a t-shirt and left it on the bed in the guestroom. Back in the main lounge, I poured a much-needed coffee and threw open the doors leading out onto the balcony to let in some air. I was leaning on the railing, looking out over the city when she reappeared.

She moved around behind me, china clinking as she poured her own drink, then she joined me on the balcony, nibbling on a pastry. My lip quirked at the Black Rosary t-shirt, which swamped her form.

"Sooo." She peered at me over the rim of her mug. "Hotel room suggests you don't live here in New York."

"That's correct. Just here for a couple of days."

"Where do you call home?"

"Would you accept Mount Olympus as an answer?"

She moaned, her cheeks firing up again. "I'm *really* sorry about that! I don't usually get drunk. It was just …"

"Working out a way to commit sororicide is stress-inducing. Alcohol and good sex would help with the guilt." I shrugged. "No judgement here. I have a brother. I know how it goes." I turned my head to look at her. "You didn't seem to be enjoying the party last night."

Her sigh was pensive. "I hate them. All the milling around, plastic smiles, pretending to love everyone. And for what? In the hopes someone will take pity and offer you some recognition."

"Music or acting?"

"Music. My label demanded I go and show my face. Be *seen* by the musical elite."

"But you'd rather just be in the studio making music and avoid the bullshit?"

She was nodding along with my words. "My sister loves it. Rubbing shoulders with all the stars, I mean. Me … I'd rather just sing and leave all the business stuff to someone else."

"Can't make connections without being seen."

"No." The word was a sigh. "What about you?"

"Similar reasons. Remind people I exist, see what new talent is around, find out who's fucking who or fucking *over* who."

THREE

RAIN

Was I really standing in Marley Stone's hotel room, wearing clothes that smelled like him, and casually discussing our reasons for being at a celebrity party the night before? This was something my sister would do, not me.

"Not many men would have let me crash in their guestroom," I said when the conversation about the party ran out of steam and silence fell.

"No."

"So why did you?"

"It seemed the least I could do after you tried to climb into my pants." The left side of his mouth tipped up into a faint half-smile when I groaned. "I thought you were amusing," he relented. "Your sister seemed eager to get back to her chosen bed warmer, and I figured it was safer to bring you here than read about your murder charge in the morning. Not when I was on hand to save her life."

"I wouldn't have killed her, not really."

"I wasn't to know that. You seemed pretty intent on planning it."

His tone was so serious, and I questioned whether he genuinely thought I'd been plotting my sister's demise, but then his lips twitched.

"Well, thank you for saving me from prison life. I'm not sure orange is my color."

He turned his body toward me, and I couldn't stop my mouth from dropping open. I'd known he was handsome, but last night I'd been looking through beer-goggles ... well, *tequila* goggles ... and earlier I'd avoided looking directly at him. Frankly, photographs didn't do his raw sex appeal justice. One long finger pressed beneath my jaw and forced my mouth closed.

"Prison Orange might be a bit difficult on the eye, but black suits you." His hand dropped and his fingers brushed against the cotton of the t-shirt I was wearing. "Do you live in New York?"

I blinked at the abrupt change of subject. "Born and bred."

"I'm in town for another two days; then I'm flying back to Los Angeles. Have dinner with me tonight?"

"Dinner? Tonight?"

That half-smile flickered across his lips again. "We can call it networking if you like. We're both in the music business. We can swap horror stories. And then later …" He paused and winked. "We can revisit your attempt to suck those body fluids from my body, if sober-you wants to, that is."

I blinked at him, my eyes dropping to his groin. *Oh shit, look away!* I jerked my eyes back up to his, and his raised eyebrow told me he'd seen where I looked. "I'd be lying if I said I don't want to do that." I placed my coffee mug down on the floor, then straightened and held out my hand. "My name is Rain."

Strong, warm fingers enveloped mine. "Marley." Not that he needed any introduction—sober-me knew *exactly* who he was.

We swapped numbers, he called me a cab and I was back in the apartment I shared with my sister before lunchtime. Piper was waiting for me, blood-red fingernails tapping on the tabletop when I walked in.

"Not dead then, I see."

I tossed the bag containing my dress and purse onto the couch and kicked off my shoes. "Of course not."

"And you know who you went home with, right?"

I rolled my eyes. "Marley Stone. Lead singer of Black Rosary and soon to be co-owner of NFG Records. I'm not stupid, Piper." I flopped onto the couch. "Anyway, we didn't do anything. I woke up in the guestroom, pure and untouched." I tipped my head back and closed my eyes. "He's nothing like the media portrays. He's actually *really* nice."

"Did you know who he was last night? Is that why you flirted with him?"

My eyes snapped open. "What? *No*! I had no idea who he was. That was the tequila talking. I was lucky he turned out to be a gentleman. I thought we were supposed to have each other's backs. You let me leave with him and you knew I wasn't sober."

She sniffed. "You're a big girl, Rain."

"And you'd have gone insane if photographs had been in the papers this morning."

"It wouldn't have done your career any *good*, that's for sure. But Marley Stone is a big name in the music industry. If I'd made a scene, it would have drawn attention to the fact you were with him. And then the shit would have really hit the fan."

"I forgot. Wholesome, small-town girl with the voice of an angel." My tone was self-mocking. "That's the impression I'm supposed to be giving, isn't it?

"Yes! Being seen with the bad boy of rock, no matter how hot he is, won't fit into the *narrative*."

"What does it *matter?* He's a nice guy."

"He isn't the kind of man you take home to meet your parents—and *that*'s what your contract with Remarkable Records demands."

"So, my private life is part of my music contract?" I pushed up from the couch. "I thought we had a lawyer look it over before I signed? Why would I agree to them being able to dictate my life?"

"A lawyer *did* look over it, Rain."

"Well, I need it revised, because I'm going to dinner with Marley tonight." I stomped across the room. "And I'm thinking about sleeping with him, too!"

Four

Marley

"Isn't she the face of Remarkable's teen pop culture?" Karl Daniels, Black Rosary's manager, my friend and my business partner, said when I told him I was taking Rain Silverman out for dinner. "Prince of Rock meets Pop's Princess … I can see the headlines now."

I chuckled. "I've had a promotion. She called me a god last night."

"I don't even want to know what you were doing when *that* happened."

"It was a lot more innocent than it sounds." I peeled off my t-shirt, tossed it to the floor, followed by my sweatpants and underwear, then stretched out naked on the massage bench. The masseur draped a towel across my ass and quietly got to work.

"I'm not sure *you* and *innocent* work together in the same sentence."

"It's just dinner, Karl. Not a declaration of love or marriage. I'm sure Remarkable will be able to deal with that. And if not …" I waved a hand in his direction. "That's why we keep Matt Carmichael on retainer, isn't it?"

"*Your* contract doesn't stop you from dating anyone without the record company's approval."

I lifted my head to search him out, his tone of voice suggesting he knew more than he was saying. He was leaning against the wall, sipping a coffee. "And Rain's does?"

"So, the rumor mill suggests."

"Who the fuck would sign a contract with *that* kind of stipulation?"

"A naive young girl with a terrible lawyer."

I grunted as the masseur dug into a particularly sore part of my shoulder. "How long ago did she sign the contract?"

"A year or eighteen months. Too soon to be able to get out of it easily." Karl's voice was shrewd—he knew where my thoughts had gone without me saying a word. "I don't think a pop princess is what should be our first signing anyway. There's a band in LA whose name is on everyone's lips. I'm going to check them out next week."

"Oh? Do you need me to tag along?"

"Oh, hell no. It's some dive in the Fashion District—Tracie's? Trudy's? Or something like that, anyway. The last thing I need is your face there."

"Fair enough. You'll have to send me a video of them performing."

"I'll do that." He pushed away from the wall. "Right, I'm going. Please try not to get into too much trouble on your ... *date* with the pop princess. NFG Records is too young to go up against Remarkable just yet."

I huffed a laugh. "It's dinner. What could possibly go wrong?"

Jesus fucking Christ.

My final words to Karl came back to haunt me when Rain opened the door and stepped out of her apartment. Her blonde hair had been changed to a dark red—either by a color or a wig, I wasn't sure which—and was in an intricate braid, which fell down to the middle of her back. Her dress was a simple black number, with spaghetti straps, and form-fitting.

"Do I meet with your approval?" Her question was tart when I lifted my eyes to meet hers.

"Good enough to eat." I flicked a finger against her hair. "Disguise?"

She shrugged one slim shoulder. "You know how it is."

"I do." I crooked my arm, offering her my elbow. "Ready to go?"

Her fingers curled over my forearm, and the touch shot right down to my dick. We walked to the elevator bay, where my bodyguard/driver waited.

"I booked a table at Belvedere," I named a high-class restaurant nearby as we walked inside the waiting elevator. "I thought you might want to keep this on the down-low."

"Did we manage to avoid being snapped by paparazzi last night? I did a quick search online earlier and couldn't find anything."

The doors slid open, and we stepped out into the underground parking lot.

"As far as I could tell, there's no evidence of your tequila-loaded murder-plotting ass on the internet anywhere."

FIVE

RAIN

Marley was a lot more fun to spend time with than I expected. There had been so many stories about the lead singer of Black Rosary. Reports about his anger issues, numerous articles about him trashing hotel rooms, brawling with paparazzi in the streets, and loud public arguments with various famous models he dated. I'd half-considered cancelling the date. My sister's insistence I do *just* that, combined with the fact the memory of my hands around his dick was imprinted on my brain, kept me from doing as she said.

My fears about the potential problems he posed seemed unfounded. The entire time we spent in The Belvedere, he was a complete gentleman. He entertained me with stories of what the band got up to on tour and the hard work he'd put in to build up his own record company with his manager and friend, Karl Daniels. He delivered everything in a slow, deep drawl, which kept me leaning forward on my seat and hanging onto every word he uttered.

The passion in his voice when he talked about NFG Records was palpable and it was clear, even to me, there was no way the new record label would be anything *but* successful. A small part of me wished I could get out of my contract and sign with them. A record label run by a musician would be so much more in tune with the artists they signed, but my deal with Remarkable was watertight and the only way out would be my death. And, honestly, I wasn't willing to fake my own death or *actually* die in order to break with them. Anyway, I wasn't the right music genre for NFG—they would be going for rock music: bad boys, loud guitars, aggressive sounds. I was marshmallow and cotton candy—far too sugary sweet for his label.

Dinner was over all too soon, and we lingered over coffee. I didn't want the evening to end and, judging by the way he didn't rush me out of the door, neither did he. When he finally lifted his hand for the check, I swallowed my nerves and opened my mouth, praying he wouldn't hear the tremor in my voice. "Piper is staying with her latest hook-up tonight."

"Oh?" He paused in the process of taking money from his wallet and lifted an eyebrow.

"If you want to come back to my place … for coffee, I mean."

"Coffee," he repeated, and his lip curled into that customary half-smile he was famous for.

My cheeks heated. "Or you could just drop me off if you don't want to."

"Oh, I *definitely* want coffee." He tossed a pile of folded bills onto the table and rose to his feet. "Ready?"

He moved around the table and drew my chair out as I stood. Nothing in his actions, or the way he walked beside me, gave any hint that the dinner had been anything more than potential music associates having a business dinner. Neither of us had touched the other during the meal; there had been no lingering glances or intimate moments. In fact, I'm positive it looked like nothing more than two people having a friendly dinner together and then leaving. We didn't hold hands, and he didn't touch me in any way other than offering his arm when we walked down the steps of the restaurant. He even kept a respectable distance from me. We looked more like strangers than potential lovers. When we got to the car, he opened the door and stood back while I climbed in.

His driver twisted in his seat. "Where to?"

"Sure about this?" Marley asked and, when I nodded, gave the driver my address.

The doors closed, sealing us inside the elevator, which would take us up to my apartment. There were two other people inside. Marley ducked his head and moved to the furthest back corner. I stood opposite him, throwing the other occupants a polite smile. I'd seen them before, not often enough to be friends or know their names, but enough to recognize their faces. Marley folded his arms and propped his back against the wall, his eyes on the numbers as they counted upwards. He didn't look in my direction or acknowledge my presence. The doors slid open on the floor below mine, and one of them stepped out. Marley's eyes flicked toward me, then at the back of the remaining person inside with us. One of his arms dropped; he pulled his cell from his pocket and typed a message. My cell dinged seconds later. I opened my purse and took it out.

MARLEY: I'll get out on floor 15 and come back down.

I gave a slight nod, and his lip curled up. When the doors opened on my floor, I moved past him and the other occupant and stepped out into the corridor. My apartment was only a few yards away from where I stood, and I was inside less than a minute after leaving Marley. I leaned against the door and took in a breath, looking around.

Marley would be here any minute and then … what?

Oh, come on, Rain, I chastised myself. *He's not going to come through the door and immediately strip you naked.*

Truth was, I wasn't even sure he was interested that way. He'd given me no indication he was attracted to me during dinner.

But he agreed to come back for coffee, and everyone knows 'coffee' is code for sex.

I licked my lips. I wasn't a virgin. I'd had sex before … I'd had *good* sex. But not since signing with Remarkable Records. For the past year, I hadn't even had a date. My public appearances had been strictly controlled. I wasn't even sure how I'd managed to go to dinner with Marley without it being overseen by my manager or my sister. But I had, and now he was heading to my apartment.

My heart was hammering against my chest when he tapped on the door. I opened it and stood back to let him in. Fuck, he was tall. Tall, broad, tattooed and handsome. And coming toward me with an almost feral look in his eyes …

My eyes widened when he didn't stop. His hands cupped my face and he kept moving, backing me toward the wall.

"First, we get rid of this." He tugged at the red wig I was wearing. "I don't want to pretend you're someone else." I didn't get a chance to do it myself, his fingers already plucking at the pins securing it in place, and seconds later he cast it aside. My blonde hair tumbled down around my shoulders, and he threaded his fingers through it. "Better."

"I was beginning to question whether you were interested." I gasped when his hand found my breast and squeezed.

"Interested? I had a raging hard-on through the entire meal," he confessed. "Every time you opened your fucking mouth or licked your lips. Jesus fuck, who knew watching someone eat would turn me on."

"Really?"

"Really." His lips brushed across mine, the touch featherlight. "I wanted to be the spoon you licked." He pushed one leg between mine, caught my hand and pulled it down to press against the erection tenting his pants. "This is what you've been doing to me all evening. Knowing I couldn't touch you in the restaurant, in the car, in the fucking elevator was torture. It's all I could think about. Touching you, tasting you."

"Oh …" I breathed the word, surprised at the heat in his voice.

"Yeah," he muttered. "*Oh.*"

Six

Marley

I'd managed to keep it together through dinner—watching those lips as she spoke, the way her tongue swept over them had me imagining how it would feel to have her lick my skin. I tortured myself with thoughts of my dick in her mouth, of burying my face between her legs, but nothing showed on my face or in my voice. Every time she spoke, my dick jumped to attention. It was fucking embarrassing just how much this woman was affecting me. But she didn't notice and seemed oblivious to the way my body was responding to her. And me? Well, I didn't understand it at all, and I didn't care to investigate too deeply. I wanted her. I thought she wanted me. That was all that mattered.

So, when she invited me back to her place, nothing short of a humanity-destroying catastrophe was going to stop me. My plan to kiss her senseless in the elevator was ruined by the presence of two strangers. I was pretty sure they could feel my eyes boring into the backs of their heads the entire time we were cooped up with them, but it didn't make them leave any faster. The fact I was contemplating shoving them out on some random floor told me I needed to take a moment and get my head together. That was why I'd told her I would get out on a different floor. The walk back down to her apartment would give me that much-needed time to get control of myself.

Or so I claimed.

It was a lie.

Because the second she allowed me inside her apartment, I jumped on her like I was starving and she was prime steak. Her skin was like silk beneath my fingers, soft and smooth.

"Will you get into trouble with Remarkable if you're caught with me?" I dragged the thin strap of her dress down her arm.

"Yes." Her own hands were on the buttons of my shirt, popping them open, and dragging it apart so she could smooth her palm over my chest and down to my belt.

"Do you want me to go?"

"I want you to do a lot of things, but leave isn't one of them." She unbuckled my belt and slid it off.

My lips skated over her shoulder, following the path of the strap. "What do you want me to do?" I peeled the dress down further until her breasts were freed from the material. Her nipples were taut, dark pink, and slightly tilted upwards, tempting me.

"Make me fly."

I wrapped an arm around her waist and bent my head so I could run my tongue over her nipples. "You got it, Tinkerbell."

"I better get out of here before your sister comes home."

We were lying in her bed, had been there for hours, and I didn't want to move. Her fingers were tracing over my skin, drawing random patterns, and moving precariously closer to my dick with each sweep of her nails. If she touched me again, I was going to pin her down for round three and I didn't think we had time for that.

"I have to pack to fly back to LA tomorrow." I broke the silence again.

Her fingers stilled. "Do you think we'll see each other again?"

I rolled onto my side, tilted her face up and kissed her hard and deep. "This isn't the end of something—it's the start of it, Rain."

"Remarkable will—"

"Just have to suck it up," I finished for her. "Connections like this don't happen every day. This is special. There's no point in pretending it isn't."

"But—"

"Is that what you want? For me to say goodbye and walk out of your life?"

She caught her lip between small white teeth. "No, that's not what I want."

"Then we'll make this work." I meant every word. There was something here, something worth exploring, something I'd *never* felt with anyone else.

"We'll have to keep it quiet for now. My contract states the record company has control over who I am seen with. They want me to have a specific public personality—seeing the bad boy of rock won't fit with what they want from me."

"Send me a copy of your contract and I'll have someone look at it. I'm sure what they're demanding isn't legal."

"They could still dump me for not being what they want."

I kissed my way down her throat. "I know. I get it, Tinkerbell. Making sure your career is safe is important. I'll be your dirty little secret." I licked her nipple. "It'll be fun. We'll sneak around, meet in shady places, fuck in seedy motels and pretend we don't know each other at public events." My fingers stroked down her body, between her legs, and I pushed one finger inside her. "And while we're circulating and schmoozing at celebrity parties, I'll be imagining the way you moan, the way you fuck my fingers, the way you say my name when you're coming for me." Her hips rose, and I added another finger, thrusting deep, while my thumb found her clit. "But no one else will know, Rain. No one will know how wet your panties get anytime you look at me, or how you're thinking about sucking my dick while you're smiling sweetly at your fans."

She moaned, reaching down to curl her fingers around my dick, and slowly pumped up and down in time with my fingers thrusting in and out of her pussy.

I leaned over her, my tongue teasing her nipple into a stiff peak. "Maybe I'll come to one of your performances and eat your pussy behind the curtain before you go on stage." I nipped and sucked at her soft skin, until she was writhing against me. "I'll stop before you come, and you can perform with hard nipples and wet panties." My other hand spread her open, so I could dip my head and flick my tongue over her clit. "What would your fans say if they could see you now?"

"Marley." She gasped my name, her nails digging into my arm, her body shuddering almost violently with the force of her orgasm.

When her body relaxed back against the mattress, I eased away and rolled to my feet. She gave me a sleepy pout, reaching to pull me back down. I shook my head, pressing a kiss to the corner of her mouth.

"I really have to go."

"But you haven't…" She waved a hand toward the erection I was still sporting.

"You can owe me one."

Truth was, if I didn't get out of here, I wasn't going to leave. That would mean we'd be caught together. The shit would hit the fan, and Karl would have a heart attack. I knew Remarkable Records would *not* appreciate their upcoming star fucking me six ways to Sunday, and they'd go all out to tear down NFG Records before we even got started.

I pulled on my clothes, willing my dick to relinquish its grip on my libido. "Send me your schedule for the next month, and I'll try and figure out a way to be in the same place as you," I told her.

"Do you *have* to go *right* now?"

I chuckled and turned back to her. "Tinkerbell, if I could figure out a way to stay and not destroy both our careers, I'd be back in that bed with you in a heartbeat. But we have to do this carefully, otherwise, it'll explode in our faces."

SEVEN
RAIN

"Are you listening to me?" I jumped, dragged my eyes away from the rain hitting the window and turned to look at my sister.

"Dress to impress. Be ready to leave at nine sharp and not a second later. Wear something sexy, but not slutty. Hair down, not up. Make-up that suggests innocence, not whore." I waved my hand. "Yadda yadda. Same old. I get it, Piper. Pretend I'm not a woman, but still a young girl who's never been kissed. Innocence sells records. Be a positive influence on young girls everywhere."

I'd been listening, kind of. She said the same thing before any public event, so it was a safe bet that all of those things had been in there somewhere. In reality, I was thinking about Marley and the fact I hadn't seen him in almost a month. We spoke most days, we video-chatted almost every night. Heat filled me when I thought about the things we'd done on those video calls.

We still hadn't managed to make our schedules line up so we could meet again, but I held out hope it wouldn't be much longer.

"Rain!" My sister's exasperated tone pulled me out of my daydream again. "What *is* wrong with you?"

"Nothing. I'm just tired. We haven't stopped for weeks. I just want *one night* to myself. To have an early night and curl up in bed with ice cream and a movie. Is that too much to ask?"

"If you want your career to go to the next level, you have to put the work in." Her voice was sharp.

I sighed. "I know. But sometimes I feel like it's no longer *my* career but everyone else's."

My phone dinged.

MARLEY: Sent you something. Wear it tonight.

I frowned at the message. *Huh?*

"What are you scowling at?"

"What? Oh … nothing. Just a marketing text." I shoved my cell into my jacket pocket and stood. "I'm going to take a bath. I think there's a parcel arriving for me. Can you listen for it?"

"What have you bought?"

"I don't remember. I went on an online shopping splurge the other day. Bought some random stuff." *God,* I hoped whatever Marley had sent didn't have his name on it. *That* would be hard to explain. I didn't think he'd do that, though. He had been incredibly careful to always text before calling to make sure no one was around who would ask questions.

I moved toward my bedroom. "Bath, and then I'll figure out what I'm wearing tonight."

A box was on my bed when I exited the bathroom in a mango butter and frangipani scented cloud. I eyed it curiously, closing the door behind me. The box was cream, with no logos or brand printed on it anywhere. Securing the towel around my body, I wedged a finger beneath the edge and prised it open. Black tissue hid the contents and as I unfolded it, a cream envelope fell out.

Picking it up, I peeled it open.

Hey Tink,

Wear everything in this box for me tonight? And trust me!

M

xx

I stared at the note, then down at the box. *Was Marley going to be at the event tonight?* My heartbeat sped up at the thought of finally seeing him again and I pulled the tissue paper out of the box to see what he'd sent me.

The dress I uncovered was beautiful. With my bottom lip caught between my teeth, I carefully unfolded it and held it up. It was long, deep purple, and made from the purest silk. The neckline was high, but the back was cut out in a scoop, which would leave most of my back bare. The side panels were beaded, giving it an almost mermaid tail effect. I lay it on the bed and took out the shoes, strappy, high heels that matched the purple color of the dress. At the bottom of the box was another, smaller box and, opening it, I took out a purple thong and … I blinked … was that a mini vibrator?

There was another note.

Don't forget. Wear *everything.*

I stared at the vibrator. The shape of it was odd, and curiosity got the better of me. I picked it up, discovered a little instruction leaflet beneath it and plucked it out. The images showed me how the vibrator fit snugly into the thong, where it would press over the clit of the woman wearing them, while the curved part would push up inside.

My eyes rounded. Marley wanted me to *wear* that at the event? I couldn't … I *wouldn't* … would I? I tucked it back into the box, covered it with the tissue paper and hid it beneath my bed. The dress and shoes I would absolutely wear. I could get away with that.

But my eyes kept drifting to where I'd hidden the box while I worked on my make-up and hair.

EIGHT

MARLEY

The event was another tedious pat-on-the-back event of suits who knew nothing about music but made millions off the hard work of the musicians they locked into contracts. I had to smile and pretend I didn't hate every single fucking one of them. These people were the reason I'd started my own label with Karl—one that had the best interests of the musicians at heart, not the multi-millionaires who abused their talent to line their own pockets.

I stood near the open bar, a bottle of beer held loosely between my thumb and forefinger as I looked out over the sea of people. My cell was in my other hand, and I flicked through social media—checking hashtags for the band to see what the fans were saying. Karl had left me alone to go and speak with ex-colleagues from the label he left to take a risk with me. He was the networker, the manager, the frontman. I was the bait—the unruly rock star who could entice new bands to join us.

A shadow fell over the screen of my cell and I looked up … and froze, fighting to stop a smile spreading across my face. She was here and wearing the dress I'd sent her.

"Marley." A hand was thrust out, and I pocketed my cell so I could take it. "Maxim Florentino."

I inclined my head. Maxim was one of the top dogs of Remarkable Records and Rain's manager. "Maxim."

"Can I introduce you to Rainbow." His palm landed on the small of Rain's back and she stiffened, then she was stepping forward, her smile warm.

"Nice to meet you."

I placed my beer onto the bar behind me, took her hand and lifted it to my lips. "A pleasure." My free hand dropped to my pocket, where my fingers curled around a small, flat remote control. My thumb swept over the slightly upraised button ... once.

Rain's lips parted, and she gasped, eyes going wide. My lip curled into a half-smile. She'd done as I asked then. "Are you okay?"

"Wh-what? Oh, yes!" The word ended on a breathless yelp when I hiked up the intensity of the vibrator pressing against her clit. "I ... umm ... I need a drink!" She leaned past, grabbed my bottle and drained it.

"Rainbow!" Maxim's voice was sharp.

"Oh, one drink won't hurt her," I said softly. "At least it's not tequila. Right, *Rainbow?*"

She gave me a jerky nod, cheeks flushed. "Right ..." Her voice was faint.

"You're looking a little flushed. Why don't I take you outside for some air?" I pushed away from the bar and offered her my arm.

She glanced at Maxim, who nodded, like I knew he would because I was here as a businessman and not a rock star. Her hand curved over my arm, and we walked through the glass doors thrown open at one end of the ballroom and into the garden beyond.

"I knew that color would look perfect on you." I drew her to the side, away from the view of the people inside. "And you wore my gift as well."

"I wasn't going to."

I checked to ensure no one could see us, then dipped my head to press a kiss to the corner of her mouth.

"But you couldn't resist ..." I pulled the little controller from my pocket and showed it to her. "I thought we could have a little bit of fun. If we can't be together inside, I can still help you get off from across the room."

Her cheeks flushed. "You wouldn't!"

I lifted the controller between us and turned up the setting. She gasped, fingers biting into my wrist. "Marley!"

The way she moaned my name made my dick hard. "Fuck, Rain." I dropped my head against hers. I couldn't kiss her, couldn't touch her the way I wanted to, and it was slowly killing me … so this was my alternative. I could still make her moan for me, make her *come* for me.

I turned up the power on the little vibrator again and she shuddered, her nipples beading beneath the dress. "I'd give anything to be inside you right now," I whispered against her ear. "Feel you wrapped around me, milking my dick while you come."

She panted softly, her breasts pressing into my chest, nails digging into my skin. The sting told me she'd broken through, made me bleed, but I didn't care. I was too busy watching the way her eyes darkened, the way her lips parted. I was listening to her little panting moans as she fell apart for me.

Nine

Rain

My entire body vibrated from the after-effects of the orgasm. If Marley hadn't wrapped an arm around my waist, I was sure I would be a puddle on the floor. But the orgasm, as good as it had been, wasn't enough—would *never* be enough. I needed him inside me, not a toy.

"Rainbow?" Maxim's voice had me pulling out of Marley's arms.

We were both a respectable distance apart when my manager rounded the corner. His eyes went from where I stood to where Marley leaned against a tree trunk, hands shoved deep into his pants pockets. He caught my eye and I saw his lips twitch.

"I'll leave her with you, Maxim." He pushed away from the tree. "A pleasure to meet you, *Rainbow*." He nodded and sauntered away.

Maxim frowned at Marley's retreating form, then turned to face me. "Feeling better?"

"Yes … Ahhh." I bit my lip to stop a gasp when the vibrator between my legs vibrated into life again. *Shit! Shit! Shit!*

"Are you sure? You look a little … frazzled."

"I'm fine." *Oh god*. I was sure Marley had set the vibe to its lowest setting, it was a gentle tremor against my clit, but I was still so sensitive from the recent orgasm that I wasn't sure I could hold it together. "I need to …" I swallowed a moan. "Bathroom."

"I'll show you where it is."

My first step forward was tentative. I wasn't convinced I'd be able to *walk* without coming. Maxim offered me his arm, and I took it, my fingers biting into his wrist.

"Are you certain you're okay, Rain?" he asked when we stopped for the third time.

My vision was blurred, my breath coming in small gasps. Sweat beaded my forehead as I fought against my body's urge to come. I was going to *fucking* kill him. *With* the vibrator currently thrumming against my clit. *Kill him dead.*

"I'm sorry, what?" I was vaguely aware of Maxim speaking.

"You look very flushed. I can call a car to take you home."

My eyes scanned the room, coming to a stop on the broad shoulders of my tormentor where he stood with his back to me, chatting with Karl Daniels, his business partner.

"No ... just ... Where's the bathroom?"

"Through here." He guided me past Marley and Karl, and the intensity of the vibe increased.

"Oh god," I moaned. I wasn't going to make it. I was going to come in front of my manager. I was going to die.

I almost fell through the door of the bathroom, slammed it behind me and leaned against it, panting. My nipples were hard, almost painful. My body was shaking with its need for release and that *fucking* vibrator—

The handle on the door moved and I swore under my breath. The last thing I needed was a witness when I fell apart.

"Open the door, Tink."

I twisted, threw the door open and dragged Marley in by the front of his shirt. My hands were on his belt, dragging it off and shoving his pants down his legs before he'd even locked the door. His back hit the door, and I dropped to my knees. His dick was hard, thick and ready. My tongue swept away the bead of precum, and he groaned above me. I teased him, licking around the head, along the vein that ran beneath his length. I cupped his balls, squeezed gently, rolled them around my fingers, feeling them tighten.

"Fuck, Rain ..." My name was a curse on his lips when I sucked him into my mouth.

I was beyond caring, beyond thinking. The vibrator between my legs driving me to the heights of lust. I wanted to come, *needed* to come, but every time I began to reach the peak, Marley lowered the intensity.

"Stand up." His voice was a raspy demand, and he pulled me off his dick and dragged me to my feet. "Turn around."

I didn't question him, spinning around and planting my hands against the countertop. I watched him in the mirror as he moved up behind me, lifting my dress until my ass was on display. His fingers hooked into the thong, and he slid it down my legs. He dragged a finger through my wetness, and I whimpered at the touch.

"Spread your legs wider," he instructed, pushing two fingers inside me. They slid in easily. I was slick and needy, hungry for his touch and I pushed back against him.

"More." I didn't recognize my own voice, thick with lust and hunger. A third finger joined the first two, filling me, but it still wasn't enough. I needed so much *more.* "Marley ... *please.*"

His lips pressed against the curve of my ass, and then he straightened, pulled his fingers free and I heard the rustle of paper as he ripped open a condom. Finally ... *finally* I felt his dick press against me and slide in. My body accepted him, clamped around him. He thrust deep, sending me forward a step. His fingers moved to my lips, stroked over them, covering my lips with my own arousal. My tongue swept out, and I licked at his fingertips.

His hips slammed against me, his dick branding me from the inside, and I pushed back, demanding more ... *more* ... until his fingers bit into my hips, demanding I hold still. His other hand left my lips, delved back between my legs and found my clit, dancing and strumming over it until I was whimpering, pleading, *begging* to come.

When my orgasm hit, I forgot everything—where I was, *who* I was. All that mattered was this moment, the sensation of Marley deep inside me, his deep groan when he came with me. Lights danced in front of my eyes; my legs trembled, and my heart pounded against my ribs.

Marley's lips pressed kisses along my spine. "I wasn't supposed to be here tonight. I had to wrangle an invitation out of Karl, but I needed to see you. You're making me crazy. You're all I think about. I need you to tell me this is what you want, Rain. If it is, I'll make it work."

I reached back and pressed my hand to his jaw. "More than anything."

His hand circled my waist, helped me upright while he eased out of me. I missed his warmth when he moved away to dispose of the condom. He caught me watching and he smiled, reaching out to stroke a finger down my cheek.

"Freshen up, and then let's do this." He leaned forward and nipped at the lobe of my ear. "Ready to go up against the tide?"

"I think I might fall in love with you, Marley Stone."

"Good. Because I'm already in love with you."

Big Vibe Energy

Lasairiona McMaster

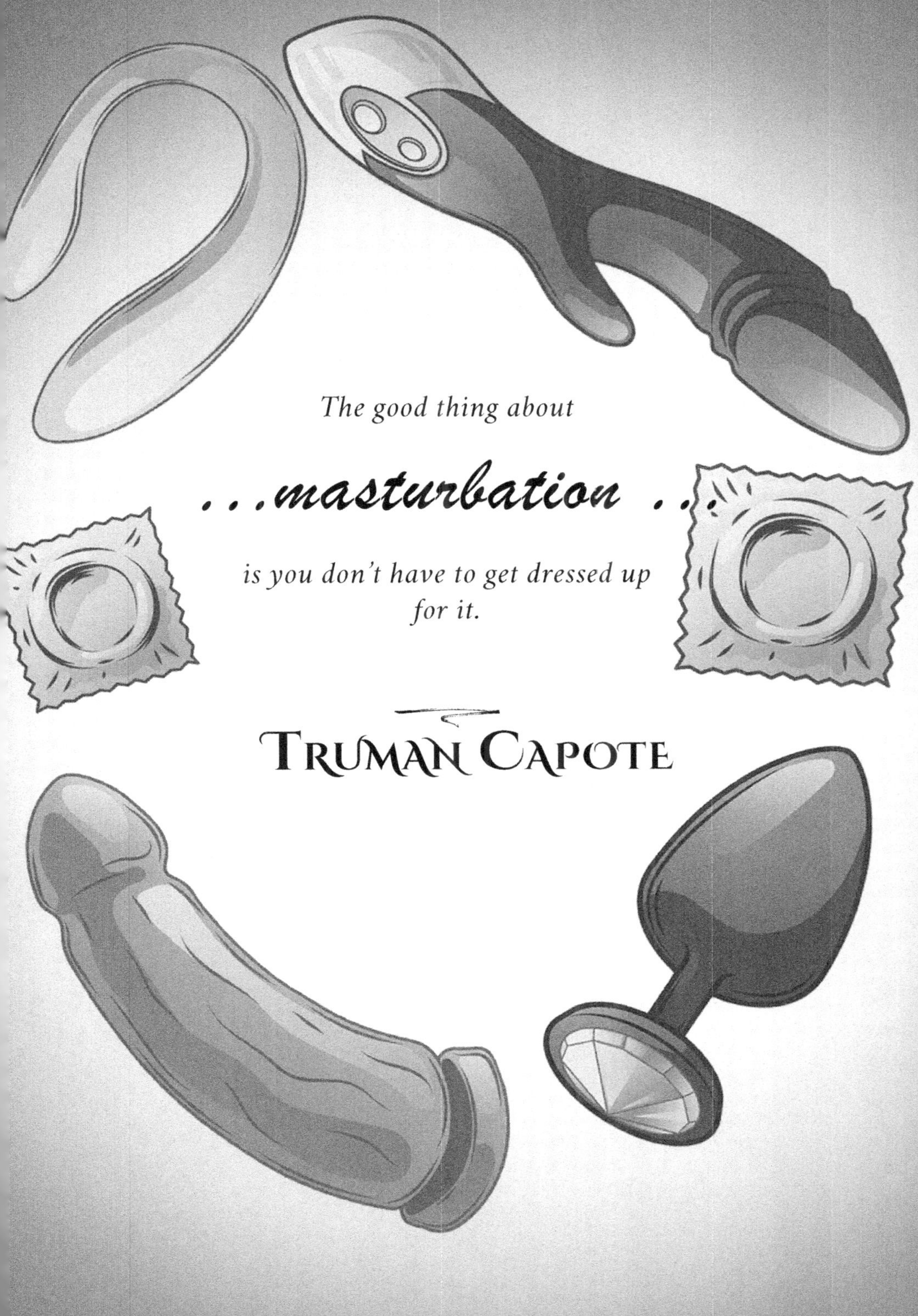
The good thing about
...masturbation ...
is you don't have to get dressed up for it.
Truman Capote

One

Cleo

"Haaaaaaaappy biiirrrrthday, toooo youuuu!'

Cleo groaned as her tone-deaf best friend serenaded her across their small dining table. Molly produced a hot pink paper gift bag from beside her feet and placed it in front of her. In the middle of the pink paper was a bright, white circle with the words 'Good Vibes' printed also in hot pink. "Oh God, you didn't."

"I did. And you're welcome."

"Please tell me there's a gift card in this bag and you didn't … y'know … shop for me."

"I could. It would be a bald faced lie, but if it makes you feel better, I can absolutely say there's a gift card in that bag, Cho-Cho." She twirled a sucker on her tongue, a wide grin splitting her face.

"Thanks … I'll, eh … open it later." Cleo grabbed the bag by the white, twisted string handles and lifted it off the table.

"Nice try. You'll open it now and we can look together. It might be *your* birthday but seeing your face burst into flames with embarrassment at what's in the bag is going to be the gift that keeps on givin' my prudish friend."

"I'm not prudish, I—"

"Yes, yes, I know." Molly waved a dismissive hand. "You like it when he fingers your butthole. So kinky of you, Ms. Vanilla." She winked, jerking her chin at the bag. "Let's see what you make of this lot."

"Lot?" Cleo picked up the bag and gave it a shake. "Oh fuck, how much did you buy?"

"Not much, and nothing too scary. I was going to get you nipple clamps and a spreader bar, but we'll work up to that."

Cleo's eyes flexed wide. "What the hell is a—nope, know what? I'm not going there. Let's start with this." She turned her head away from the gift, dipped her hand into the bag lucky-dip-style, and pulled out the first gift.

"Girl, have you even used that vibrator you bought the day you met Linc?"

Cleo's face was already hot. She shook her head. "Every time I look at it, it judges me. There's public humiliation etched all over that damn box. I know I got the guy, but …" She shrugged. "Isn't it a bit insulting to Lincoln if I use toys while I'm in a relationship?"

Molly rolled her eyes. "It's not at all insulting. You can still have your boy *and* use batteries. Wait. You haven't even unboxed that beauty? Christ, you're a terrible vibrator mother. I'm going to adopt and rehome it."

Cleo giggled, placing a box of sensual hot wax candles on the table. "Don't you have enough toys?"

"You can never have too many toys." She pointed at the box in front of Cleo. "You're gonna wanna patch test that, back of your hand or something. Nowhere … *sensitive.*" She grimaced as though speaking from experience. "Don't ask."

"We'll circle back to that story, Miss Molly." The next box Cleo produced was a set of butt plugs with colored gemstones on the end, followed by a cock ring. She tipped it towards Molly.

"For Linc, obviously."

"Obviously." Cleo dug into the bag to find one last toy. "Satisfyer pro?"

Molly held up two fingers. "Satisfyer pro … two. It's a suction vibratory thing, for your clit. It's *so* fucking good. If I'd given you that before you met Linc you'd never have dated him, or left your room. It's that good."

"Of course you've tried it."

Molly shrugged. "I wouldn't recommend a product to my best friend if I hadn't tried it first. Isn't that like, an unwritten rule or something? I figured we could bring it up at book club, y'know to go with all those smutty books we're reading.

You could start selling them alongside your books when you're a famous author. 'Book boyfriends with a buzz' could be your author tagline. Your logo could be a vibrator on top of a book."

Cleo's mouth dropped open. "Wow. You've clearly put a lot of thought into this."

Nodding, Molly gestured for her to open the box. "I have. I might even design a toy myself. We could go into business." She grunted. "Doctor asked me last week at my pap smear if there was a chance I was pregnant. I snorted and said, 'If I am, I'm giving birth to batteries.' Going through a serious dry patch right now, Cho-Cho. Gotta get back in the game before my vagina shrivels up and dies."

It was Cleo's turn to snort. "So, what? It's been like a week?"

Pretending to be horrified, Molly swiped the box from Cleo's hand. "I'm not letting you deflect from this amazing birthday gift by sex shaming me, Cleo Martinez. And it's been longer than a week. My vajayjay is gearing up for a coup. She's gonna overthrow the shit out of this government. She's whispering sweet nothings about revisiting some exes for some non-BOB time."

Clamping her lips between her teeth, Cleo swallowed down the giggle vibrating its way up her chest.

"It's fine for you, Miss banging Lincoln-fucking-Scott as though it's your Goddamn job. Does his penis provide oxygen directly into your lungs?"

Cleo waved the rose gold toy around before looking at the suction end. "Can we stop talking about Lincoln's penis and get back to this … this …"

"Your new best friend?"

Shaking her head she tucked it back into its packaging and dropped it into the bag.

"Sit with the idea for a while, Cho-Cho. Trust me when I say adding a toy here or there will elevate your sex life with the lovely Linc."

Cleo nodded, already trying to come up with a way to get rid of it. Maybe she'd use it for a giveaway at the Bookaneers book club she'd started as a place to share her love of steamy romance. Plenty of the women in the group were single and would *love* a chance to win a toy that was as good as Molly was insisting. Her friend meant well, but there was nothing amiss with their sex life and she didn't want Linc to think there was. Cleo would figure an inoffensive as possible a way to get rid of it, but she was already one hundred percent sure she wouldn't be using the Satisfyer pro two, or leaving it anywhere it could hurt Linc's feelings about his sexual prowess.

Two

Lincoln

Sweat streamed down Lincoln's spine, pooling in the small of his back. He grunted as he pushed himself forward on heavy limbs.

"Dude, you look like you're on lead legs today. What gives? All that bow-chica-wow-wow with your girl got you all tuckered out?" Russ, Linc's roommate, teammate and best friend, skated past wiggling his hips, tapping the blade of his stick off Linc's ass, and grinning.

"Heavy legs, achy. Not sure what the deal is. Maybe I overdid it with the run before practice this morning."

"Overachievers gotta overachieve." Russ shrugged with one shoulder and smacked Linc's butt again.

Linc grabbed the stick and tugged, hard. Russ's legs wobbled as his weight shifted, and his arms flapped as he fought the pull of gravity to the ice.

"Asshole."

"I know you are but what am I?" Linc tugged again, but Russ was already squatting lower to the ice, his feet spread further apart.

"Fool me once, shame on you. Fool me twice and I get a cold ass. Nice try, Scottie. We doing breakfast after practice?"

"Yeah, and we can talk about what the hell to get my girl for her birthday."

"Isn't it today?"

Linc nodded.

"Didn't you already give her a gift last night because you wouldn't see her until later?"

Linc nodded.

"Then why do you need to get her anything else?"

"I dunno. Something was missing. I mean she loved the special edition copy of Pride and Prejudice, and the book charm for her bracelet, it's just ... feels generic."

Russ chuckled. "You realize you don't need to go one hundred percent all the time, right?"

They rounded the corner of the ice pad, picking up some loose pucks from the boards and shooting them towards the center of the rink. "I know. It's our first birthday together though, I want it to be special. She deserves special."

"And a special edition copy of her favorite book in all the world ... *isn't* special?"

"I guess? It's just not particularly thoughtful, y'know?"

"That's what you get for using all your thoughtful gifts upfront to convince her to date you." Russ elbowed Linc, leaning his weight into it so Linc slid across the ice. "What about getting someone to make her a logo for her book club? Stick it on a mug. That's thoughtful. Sabrina *loves* that freakin' book club." He dragged his glove over his chin. "You might wanna leave it for when she publishes her first book – whenever that is, but that could be years from now. So I vote for it being a now thing"

Linc pulled his helmet off and tucked it under his arm. "That's not a bad idea. I like this new romantic side of you, man. Bre seems to have warmed up your ice cold heart. Good call. I'll talk to Will about it after we're done."

"Talk to Will about what?" Will Morrison, Molly's older brother and team captain for the Snow Pirates, skated beside the two men. "Get your helmet back on, practice isn't over."

Linc saluted his captain with a gloved hand. "Was hoping to talk you into using your computer nerd skills to make a logo for Cleo's book club so I can make a mug for her birthday."

"Her birthday is today."

Russ poorly hid a laugh behind his glove.

"I know that, Einstein. I just wanted to get her an extra present."

"Extra?" Will shook his head. "You don't quit, do you? You realize the more you do for Cleo, the higher the bar is set for the rest of us, right?"

"Still can't convince her to go on a date, eh?" For some reason, Russ always had his finger on the pulse. Team gossip was his specialty. "It's probably that sorry excuse for a lip sweater."

"Fuck you, Stewart." Will reached an un-gloved hand to smooth out his Movember moustache. It was an annual tradition for the team, but that didn't protect them from an annual ribbing that came with attempting to grow in facial hair for the month of November in aid of men's health issues like prostate and testicular cancer. He was still smiling until Finn skated past and his entire demeanor changed, like someone had pulled an emotionless mask over his face.

Finn met Linc's stare and gave a nod, which he returned, but Will froze him out.

"Wanna talk about that?" Linc gestured his stick in the direction of Finn.

"I do not."

"Here for you if that changes." Linc arched an eyebrow at Russ who gave an almost imperceptible shake of his head.

Will nodded. "Thanks. Now, let's do a couple more sets of drills before we call time. Then we can talk about this book club logo of yours."

Fifteen minutes later the whole team lined up on the blue line for one final sprint. As always, Will was driving them into the ground. Salty sweat dripped onto his shirt from the smattering of facial hair Linc was growing for Movember.

The whistle blew. Linc pushed off from the line with a grunt and a groan, willing his legs to move faster. He picked up the pace, but somewhere around center ice when he turned to head back for the last part of the sprint a shooting pain tore through his thigh, settling into his groin. It hit him like a punch to the gut with a battering ram. He crumpled to his knees with a huff of air and a pained wail that sounded as though it came from someone else.

His teammates surrounded him like bugs on honey.

"What happened?" Russ tugged his helmet off and wiped at his sweat-drenched hair with the back of his sleeve.

Helmets came off around the circle. Russ and Finn dropped their helmets, sticks and gloves. Each man hooked an arm under Linc's bicep and heaved him upright, but he couldn't put much weight on his leg.

"Feels like my balls are on fire."

"Groin pull?" Russ turned and draped Linc's arm over his shoulders. Finn copied Russ's movements.

Linc attempted to put his full weight on his leg and yelped. "Think so. I thought I was doing enough strengthening exercises to avoid shit like this."

They took two steps forward and Linc hissed in pain with each step. "Fuck, that hurts."

"Yeah. Let's get you off those skates and home with an ice pack."

"Sorry guys, I'll get it checked out later and report back."

Grim faces, with frowns and sympathetic eyes surrounded him as he limped off the ice. Russell and Finn got him situated on a bench before Russ crouched down to pull off Linc's skates. Finn grabbed Linc's phone from his locker and handed it to him. "Text Cleo. We aren't showering your fucking junk."

Lincoln: Is it okay if I come over? I need your help showering.

Cleo: Intense practice?

Lincoln: Something like that.

Cleo: Ice pack's in the freezer. Want me to get ice for the bath, too?

Lincoln: I couldn't love you more right now, Lizzy. OMW as soon as I get changed.

Cleo: Then I won't tell you there's caldo del res on the stove and mac and cheese in the oven for the next few days of meals.

Lincoln: I think I just came.

Cleo: You … think? We'll have to make sure when you get here. Ride safe, see you soon x

Ride safe. The mere thought of throwing his leg over his bike made his balls cringe.

"Don't sweat. One of us will take your crippled ass home." Finn gave his shoulder a playful nudge from behind. "Call Kenzie. See if you can get in for a checkup."

"Who's Kenzie?" Linc rubbed at the outside of his thigh, even that hurt.

"Mackenzie Cooke, the new physio. She'll have you fighting fit in no time. I'll text you her number."

Russ and Finn helped Linc get his hockey kit off, crammed into his duffle bag, and helped him out to Russ's car. The stabbing pain throbbed in Linc's groin with every step. He was sweating all over again by the time he slumped into the front seat. All he could think on the ride to Cleo's was whether or not he'd managed to do permanent damage, and how the hell he was gonna cope being naked in front of Cleo, but too sore to do anything about it.

THREE

CLEO

Cleo stood agape as Russ helped a limping Lincoln into her apartment.

"Is it okay if I bring some of his things over? Best if he stays in one place for a few days to rest." Russ didn't wait for an answer, or stop at the couch. He helped Lincoln all the way into the bathroom where Cleo had run a cold bath and dumped in a couple of large bags of ice.

She shuddered. No matter how many times Lincoln had told her it helped with aching muscles, she still thought he was bat shit crazy for wanting to steep in ice water for any length of time.

"Get your butt in here, Zelda. I love him, but there's no need for me to undress this man when you're here. I'll go out to the kitchen and call Kenzie, see if she's available to look him over."

Cleo passed Russell on his way out of the bathroom. She smoothed her shirt and steadied herself with a cleansing breath before squaring her shoulders. Whatever had happened to Lincoln, whatever he was facing, they'd face together. When she walked in, he had already pulled his shirt over his head, it lay in a heap at his feet. He was leaning against the bathroom counter. His face was hard set, his lips in a grim line, and pain was etched in his eyes. His jaw twitched and his shoulders were curled forward. It was as though he was using all his energy just to stay upright. A bead of sweat trickled from his hairline down his temple.

"What happened, Lincoln?" She dropped to her knees and tugged his low-riding sweatpants down over his hips, then repeated the process for his boxers. His half-mast dick twitched as she dragged the clothes to the floor before standing and taking his hand.

"I'm not really sure. One minute I was skating, the next I was howling in pain."

She helped him shuffle to the tub and winced in sympathy when he roared as he stepped over the edge of the tub. He sank into the ice water with a long groan. Tension pinched her neck and shoulders as she stood helpless. Lincoln raked his wet hands through his hair and his shoulders softened. Russ was definitely going to have to help her get him out. She should have left Linc's shorts on.

A door opened and slammed shut. "I'll go head Molly off before she comes bursting in to the bathroom. Will you be okay for a sec?"

Linc nodded without opening his eyes. She ran her fingers down his cheek before leaving the room, pulling the door closed with a soft click behind her. She walked into the kitchen where Russell was drinking a soda and a trail of Molly's stuff led from the door to the table where she sat on one chair, and her feet were resting on another.

"Stay out of the bathroom, Linc's … dying a slow and painful death." Cleo made her way to the cabinet next to the cupboard where the glasses lived and pulled out a bag of meds. She only had Tylenol and ibuprofen, but she couldn't bear to watch Lincoln suffer. "I'm going to need your help getting him out, Russ. I didn't think he was quite so bad till he cried out getting into the tub. I'm not even sure we'll manage to get him back out together."

"That's okay. Mackenzie will be over in a while. He can stay there till she gets here."

"He's naked, Russ." Cleo's cheeks flamed hot.

He chuckled. "I know, Cleo. I've seen the boy naked many more times than I can count. It's fine." He took a drink from the can in his hand.

"Russell filled me in, sounds like your boy done got himself a groin pull. Speaking – not quite from experience, but from my wealth of information on the subject of … eh … hockey players – there are varying degrees of injury to the groin. We just gotta hope he didn't tear it up or anything." Molly stretched a hand to give Cleo's arm a reassuring squeeze.

Cleo swallowed. "Tear?" She turned to Russ. "How serious could this be, Russell?"

"Surgery serious." His face was pale, and his usually upbeat demeanour was subdued. "Like Molly says, we just have to hope he didn't fuck it all-the-way up."

An hour, and a change of clothes from getting drenched helping Lincoln out of the tub later, Cleo sat on the sofa, heels tucked up to her butt, facing Lincoln. She, Russell, and Mackenzie the physiotherapist had hoisted Lincoln from the bath. Kenzie and Russ had waited while Cleo and Linc managed to dry him off and get him clothed. Then they had come back into the bathroom to help him out and onto the folding table Mackenzie had brought with her. Kenzie said house calls weren't usually her thing, but she was new and keen to work with the local athletes and had a clear afternoon.

After an examination, more groaning and howling from Lincoln and his outright refusal to go get scanned at the hospital, Kenzie proclaimed on top of treatments with her, he needed rest, ice, compression, and anti-inflammatories. She'd convinced him to rest overnight, and Russ and Cleo would take him in for an X-ray and an MRI the following morning to rule out anything more sinister than a strain.

They'd gotten him down from the table and onto the sofa, Russ had gone back to their dorm to grab a bag of Linc's things and Kenzie had told him straight. Best case it was a grade one strain and would take two to three weeks to heal with physical therapy, massage therapy, heat and stretching and maybe even electrotherapy. She'd said if it was a grade two strain, he'd be out of commission for up to three months. Grade three or four was worst case and would require surgery, but Mackenzie didn't believe it would come to that.

Cleo's heart squeezed as Lincoln deflated in front of her eyes at the words 'months' and 'surgery'. He'd fallen asleep not long after Kenzie had left. Russ had returned, dropped off the bag, helped her get him relocated from the couch to her bed, and told Cleo he'd be back in the morning to help her get him to the hospital. Concern twisted in her stomach. While he didn't want to play pro hockey, the sport still meant the world to him. As she stared at the rhythmic rise and fall of her boyfriend's chest, she wondered how he'd take the news if tomorrow they told him he could never skate again.

FOUR

LINCOLN

Diagnosis was a grade one-verging-on-grade-two groin pull. The treatment plan was rest and patience, neither of which Lincoln was good at. Multiple sessions with Mackenzie would be painful and exhausting, but with any luck, they'd help get him back on his feet without hurting, and eventually back on the ice. He was staying with Cleo and Molly – at least for the first few days post injury. Cleo had insisted. He felt like a burden, and a royal pain in their asses, and super guilty that he'd ruined her birthday with a broken dick. But it was nice to have someone love him enough to want to care for him when he was injured.

Cleo fussing over him had only served to make him love her even more than he already did, and he could certainly get used to her home cooking.

"Need a new ice pack?"

"Please, and another bowl of this beef soup of yours. If there's any left."

Her giggle was like wind tinkling a wind chime. "I'll portion some out for Molly. She will stab you if you eat it all. It's her favorite."

Porcelain clinked, and metal clunked against metal as she worked.

"I really appreciate this, you know. If it gets too much, please say. I don't want to outstay my welcome and get under your feet."

She appeared in front of him, hand outstretched to take his bowl, and in the other, an ice pack wrapped in a kitchen towel. "What you mean is, send you home before we get to the 'I'm never feeding you again' stage of frustration?" She winked.

Nodding, he chuckled. "That's the one. Now I've tasted beef soup, I'm not sure

I can live the rest of my life without it. Is it a family recipe?"

"Yeah, my abuela gave it to my mom, who taught me when I was little. It's a closely guarded secret, though." She tapped the side of her nose. "So you're right to stay on my good side. Though if you call it 'beef soup' in front of my mama, she's gonna smack you."

Stomach full of caldo del res and painkillers, he dozed on the couch with Cleo curled up against him. They were watching an episode of Grey's Anatomy and despite the constant ache in his groin, he was content. Pulling her against him, he kissed her forehead. "I'm glad you're here with me."

"Well, I live here, so there's nowhere else for me to go, really. But I appreciate the sentiment." She shifted her weight and winced. Every time she moved, she waited to see if it had hurt him. Gazing up at him, she kissed the corner of his mouth. He returned the kiss, deepening it, sweeping his tongue against hers. "We need to stop the kissing. I don't want to get carried away and hurt you."

"I think it would hurt in all the best possible ways." He tilted his head towards his groin. "He agrees with me, see?" The outline of his erection was visible in his sweatpants.

"You're killing me." Dropping her forehead to his, she groaned. She dotted light kisses along the curve of his neck and where it met his shoulder. Pulling back, her eyes flitted to his crotch and back to his face. She wet her lips. "Can I? I'll be careful."

He nodded and dropped his head back against the plush couch.

"You need to tell me if it hurts at all, okay?"

"Mhmmm."

Her hand trailed down his chest as she moved across the sofa. She peeled the band of his sweatpants back and scrunched the fabric down, freeing his cock. Her tongue darted out to lap up the bead of glistening precum at his tip. Her warm mouth closed around him and a low groan rumbled deep in his chest. Clasping a hand around his dick, she cast an enquiring stare up at him.

"Fuck, Cleo. You're so damn hot."

Her hazel eyes lit up with mischief and a wicked sparkle, and she grinned, dragging her tongue down his length and back up. Was she sliding her hand down her own pants? Damn, this girl was fire. Cupping his balls in her smooth palm she gave a squeeze as she sucked. The throbbing in his groin increased, dancing along the line of pleasure-pain. Her concerned eyes never leaving his, seemingly searching for signs that he wasn't okay. She rolled her hips against her hand and moaned around his dick in her mouth. Forcing air into his body, he struggled to relax his muscles as pressure built in his groin. "Ow. Fuck. Nope."

Cleo stopped, jerked her hand and head away from his pulsing cock. She reached her palm out, as though contemplating touching him, but retracted her hand. "I'm sorry, I thought it'd be fine if you just lay there and I did the work."

He nodded and hissed through the pain aching in his upper thigh. "Me too. I guess not." He tucked himself back into his pants and shifted his weight with a yelp.

Pressing into the cushion, Cleo pushed herself up and scooted to the end of the couch. "I guess rest means rest for real." A nervous giggle escaped her. Casting her eyes between the TV screen and his face, worry crept into her features. He squeezed her hand, attempting to reassure her he was okay, but the thin line of her lips told him she knew otherwise.

He jumped awake. The TV was off and the couch at his feet was cold, Cleo was nowhere in sight. Light still filtered in through the curtains. It was still daytime and someone had draped a blanket over him while he slept. A faint buzzing caught his attention, followed by a stifled moan and a sigh. Was that Cleo? Was she …? His dick twitched in his sweats. Squashing down a pained 'oof' as he lumbered to his feet, he took a tentative step. His muscles were heavy and stiff, but the pain wasn't as debilitating as it had been the previous day. God bless modern medicine and the miracle hands of Mackenzie Cooke. He inched towards her bedroom. Those panting, hitched breaths made his pulse race.

He froze. Could she see him? He craned his head, but her door was closed save for a sliver of space between the door and the frame. Holding his breath he peered through the gap. Voyeurism wasn't his kink, but his half-naked girlfriend hadn't ever been spread eagle on top of her bed sliding a hot pink vibrator through her slick folds before - at least not when he could see. Guilt flexed in his chest. She'd been worked up before he'd fallen asleep and he hadn't offered to help her finish when he'd stopped in pain. The erection in his pants grew. Her tits were pulled out of her tank top and she was palming one of them with her free hand, rolling her hard nipple between her finger and thumb.

"Oh ... Lincoln. Yes!"

Her eyes were closed, her head rolled back in contented bliss, and her purring noises fueled his desire. He wanted to drop to his knees and eat her like a goddamn ice cream sundae on a scorching hot day, but his leg throbbed.

She moaned again, her breath hitching as she pressed the button to change the setting on her toy. A noise somewhere between a gasp and a shriek slipped out from between her parted lips.

He leaned on the doorframe to take the weight off his leg, and he instinctively reached for his pulsing dick in his pants. He pumped once, twice, but on the third time the muscles around his groin reminded him he was injured and he grunted in frustration.

Cleo bolted upright on the mattress, dropping the toy which buzzed in place on the sheet. "Lincoln?" She yanked her tank top up over her exposed breasts.

He pulled the door open and shuffled inside. Remorse flickered in her eyes as she scrambled to stop the noisy toy. She shoved it into the drawer beside her, hesitating before tossing the bottle of cleaning solution on top of it and slamming the drawer shut with a thump.

"I'm sorry ... I ..." She shook her head and waved a hand. He wasn't sure if she was trying to erase what he'd seen or her gestures were an attempt at explanation. She slid her pajama shorts back on over trembling legs.

Disappointment stirred low in his belly, not because she'd opted for self-service, rather he was broken and hadn't thought about her when their attempt had stalled out earlier. When all else fails, go for the funny.

Her flushed cheeks flared red, and her chest heaved with heavy breaths, she didn't speak when she finally met his eyes.

"So, replaced me already then, eh?"

FIVE

CLEO

"What?" Her hand drifted to cover her gaping mouth. "No … I just … I couldn't help it. I was horny and wound up and you were aslee—"

His face softened, the knot between his brows slackened. He held up a hand. "It's okay, I was kidding. Gotta say though … that was pretty fucking hot, Lizzy. Pretty fucking hot."

He'd called her his nickname for her from back when they'd first met, Lizzy Bennet from Pride and Prejudice, so he couldn't be too upset with her for sneaking away from his sleeping form to masturbate with a sex toy. She was going to kill Molly. Somehow everything was all her fault.

"H-hot?"

"Seeing you there all uninhibited, wet, and needy? Hell yes, it was fucking hot."

Embarrassment radiated from her pores, and while his words said one thing, his eyes said another. He was hurt. She offered a small smile.

"You wanna take it back out and finish?"

Finish? Like … in front of him? Oh fuck no. She was already dying of mortification from the inside out. If she had walked in and found him jerking off instead of coming to her, wouldn't she feel upset? Lacking somehow? Even if she was injured and couldn't … pangs of sadness rippled through her. She shook her head, mute.

He stood a foot from the edge of the bed and stopped moving, he reached a hand out to the bed and dropped his weight onto the mattress, as though he couldn't move his legs another step. He lay flat on his back, she was sitting next to him. "Okay. No toy. Want me to help? I feel kind of guilty. My hands still work though, and my tongue ..."

He wasn't playing fair. She squeezed her thighs together, hoping it was subtle enough that he didn't notice. He did and the corner of his mouth tugged up in a knowing smile. Busted. "Thanks, but it's fine." It wasn't fine, her clit was swollen and throbbing, and she'd been so close to sweet release.

"Why are you lying to me right now, Miss Bennet?"

Why was she lying to him? Embarrassment? Guilt? Fear of judgement? Something uncomfortable stirred in the pit of her stomach and she bristled. "I don't know. But I'm definitely uncomfortable right now. Doctors said you needed to rest, not help your girlfriend orgasm. You know I'm a stickler for the rules. Can we just pretend like this never happened? At least until I unpack and process it a bit? Please?"

The deep frown was back, knotting his brows together in a severe 'v'. He sighed and nodded. "Of course, you know I'd never pressure you into talking about, or doing anything you weren't comfortable with."

"But?"

"But ... I wanna be your safe space where you can talk about anything. No judgement. No shame or embarrassment. I know that takes time. I just hope you know I'm here if you want to talk."

She clamped her lips between her teeth and nodded.

"Wanna finish the episode of Grey's?"

She shook her head. Leaning over him she trailed her fingers across his forehead and bent to kiss him.

"You sure you don't want me to help get you to the finish line?" He ran his hand along her inner thigh. "You can't tell me you're not wet and primed."

Her cheeks heated. "I can't. But I don't want to hurt you."

His fingers inched closer to the still-wet patch of fabric between her legs.

"Want me to stop?"

She shifted onto her knees, shuffled them apart so she wouldn't lose her balance and lowered her hips towards the bed, onto his waiting fingers.

He gave a low whistle of approval. “My dear Miss Bennet, your pussy is simply drenched.” Groaning, he slipped two fingers inside and curled them towards her front wall.

Cleo tugged her tank back down, baring her breasts and teased at her nipples with both hands. She ground herself against his fingers, chasing the orgasm that had been so close only moments prior.

Linc’s face was pallid, prickles of sweat appeared across his forehead, and his jaw was tight. Was he still in pain? Even lying still and only using his arm? Was she pushing him too far? Being too selfish when her boyfriend was suffering? She couldn’t clear her mind enough to relax into his touch.

“You okay?” He tilted his head, his face creased with concern.

“Yeah, guess I lost it? I’m worried about you. Let’s get you up into bed and we’ll worry about screaming orgasms at another time.”

He paused, slipped his fingers out of her, and dragged them over her clit. Hesitating for a beat, he withdrew his hand. “I’m sorry.”

“Don’t be. We just need to be patient and get you better.” She helped him get comfy in bed and changed her shorts. Clenching and unclenching her muscles she willed the pool of heat to cool and the want burning through her veins to dissipate. She climbed into bed next to the man she loved. Snuggling against his side, she wondered how the hell she was going to be able to keep her hands off him. At best, for a few days, at worst, a few weeks, and all she wanted to do was strip him naked and have her way with him.

Six

Lincoln

"Cleo's not home. I think she's at the library. She's not due home until dinner time." Molly held the door half open with one hand, and in the other a taco – somehow still intact and not dripping filling onto the floor. She licked her lips and took another bite, without losing a morsel of food to gravity. She clicked her fingers. "Lincoln? If you want tacos, you're shit outta luck. This is the last one." She gestured the end of her taco at him before shoving it in her mouth.

"I know she's not here. That's why I came by." Linc had moved back to his dorms the previous night, and while movement was easier, it still hurt like hell.

Still chewing, Molly tilted her head, confusion written across her face. "Curious." She spoke around the mouthful of food before swallowing hard and stepping back out of the way. Jerking her head into the room she coaxed him inside. "To what do I owe the pleasure?"

"Almost always dick, right?"

She arched an eyebrow and pursed her lips. "At the moment, almost always my collection of battery operated boyfriends." She shrugged. "You say potato. I say vibrat-o I guess?"

Scrunching up his face, he nodded. "TMI. Serves me right though."

"True statement. What brings you to our humble abode when your good lady isn't around?" She stopped dramatically before she reached the kitchen and spun to face him. "Linc, I'm flattered but I'm not into you. I'm also not that kinda girl, and I didn't think you were that kinda guy."

"What the hell? Christ, you women are watching too many telenovelas!"

Molly laughed. "Drink?"

Shaking his head, he pulled out a chair, wiped a clammy palm on his thigh and eased himself onto the seat.

"No better?"

"Hurts like a bitch. Miracle woman Kenzie is helping, but damn if it doesn't burn like the fires of hell when she's done working me over."

Molly rolled her eyes. "That innuendo is too easy, I'm just letting it go – but please note it's hard not to make a joke right now." She plonked onto the chair facing Linc and took a sip of her drink. "It's gonna take time Linc. The secret to healing is, you just gotta be ..." Glancing over each shoulder, she dropped her voice to a hushed whisper. "Patient." She held up her palms. "I know. You jocks loooove to be told to hurry up and wait." Leaning back in her chair she rocked it on its back legs. "Wanna tell me what you're doing here? Don't get me wrong, I like you and all, but one-on-one time with Lincoln-fucking-Scott wasn't on my to do list today. Oh! Are you here for a juicy exclusive? Do I need my notebook?"

Lincoln blinked, then blinked again. "Are you on Speed?"

"I've had four cups of coffee."

"It's only noon."

She shrugged. "It's a multi-cup kinda day."

"Fuck. I'm glad you've moved onto water."

"Oh, honey, no." She shook her water bottle and the ice clinked against the metal. "This is cold brew."

He chuckled, shaking his head, and shifted his position on the chair. "I, eh ..."

"Linc? You got real serious in a heartbeat. What gives? Do you need surgery?" Concern flared in her eyes, sparking warmth in his chest. She might be the little sister of his teammate, and the best friend of his girlfriend, but she cared about the players and she was becoming his friend in her own right, weird as it was.

"No, but I do need your help."

"I'm listening."

He swallowed. He sighed. And he looked everywhere but at her eyes. "Cleo said you got her some ... stuff, for her birthday. I'd like to know what you got her. She seems to be ... I dunno, shy about the whole toy thing. Well, sex in general really, and I want to help her feel more comfortable."

"And you're not a toy fan?"

Shaking his head he rubbed at a spot on the table. "I've never ... I mean, I don't really need them." He shrugged and slipped his hand behind his neck, rubbing the muscles slowly, willing the tension to leave.

"Are you embarrassed? Linc, this is adorable." She leaned forward and pinched his cheek. "Everyone 'needs' toys. Wait ... lemme go grab the bag and some beer, sexy toy school is in session."

"Oh God." Raking his hand over his head he covered his face with his palm. "No. This isn't what I signed up for, Molly."

She ignored him, striding towards Cleo's room. When she returned she had a broad grin on her face. "Well, well, well, Cho-Cho you sly dog."

"What?"

Molly didn't have a bag in her hand, but she had a collection of unboxed adult toys clutched to her chest. She put them on the table before grabbing two beers, popping them open, and handing one to Linc. "It's five o'clock somewhere, Lincoln. Don't judge me. Day drink with me."

Picking up the rose gold toy by the handle he examined it. The white tip at the opposite end to the one he was holding had a small hole. "How does this even work?" He waved it at Molly.

"First things first – Cleo has opened all of these. Not sure if she's used them or just stared at them in terrified wonder, but I'mma go right ahead and clean them, just in case." She spritzed cleaning solution over the toys in front of her and wiped them down with a cloth. "That, my dear uneducated friend, is the Satisfyer pro ... two." She tipped her beer bottle towards him before taking a long drink. "That white hole, goes over her clit. You gotta get placement juuuuust so, turn it on and Bam!" She slammed her open palm on the table. "Sucks her very essence out her clitoris, and gives her the best orgasm of her life."

Lincoln's face scrunched up in disbelief without his instruction. He placed his finger into the hole and pressed the button, a soft sucking tickled his fingertip. Testing the rest of the settings he was surprised to find his finger wasn't bruising by the time he turned it off.

"See? Great suction, yeah? That's what she said." She snorted behind her hand before taking another drink of her beer. "This is a butt plug – it does exactly what you think it does. These are wax candles. This is *the* origin story. *The* hot pink vibrator that landed on your foot that fateful day, and this … Well, this is a cock ring."

She spoke so matter-of-factly that Lincoln couldn't help but wonder if she was the exception to the rule, or if most women spoke so frankly about sex toys. His mind was whirring. "Wax? For ambiance?"

Her laugh was like a braying donkey. "Shit. Lincoln." She clutched her ribs. "How can you have the God of BDSM on your team and *not* know this stuff?"

"You learned all of this from Austin? Fuck, your brother will lose his shit."

She brayed again. "No, dummy. I learned this stuff from my l-o-v-e-r-s. But I thought Austin was the team sex guru?"

He shrugged. "I've always been happy enough with my healthy, pleasurable, no-need-for-toys sex life. I never really thought about them, to be honest. I mean, I see guys chatting with Austin, and I've seen his …"

Molly's eyebrows shot up her head. "Say it, Linc. Say *it*. You've seen his schlong haven't you?"

"I've seen every Pirate's dick, yes."

Molly clapped. "Are the rumors true?"

"Bro code, Mol. I can neither confirm nor deny whether Austin has a pierced cock."

She squealed. "I knew it. If he wasn't … well … Austin, I'd wanna climb him like a goddamn tree."

Linc winced. "Ew. Just, no. Back to the wax." He picked up the box, turning it over in his hand. "You just, pour it on each other?"

"Looks like she's already tried one, hopefully on her hand or somewhere. I didn't read the instructions my first time, and, well, let's just say I'm pretty sure there's still a scar on my nipple."

He groaned. Holding up one hand as a stop sign, he covered his face with the other. "Jesus, Molly."

"I can't help it, Linc. I've never seen you mortified before and it's charming. I wanna see just how red your face can go."

"You know I'll never ask you for help again, right?"

"Lies. My lesson is fun, educational, and relaxed. I only poke fun at those I care about." She reached over and poked his bicep. "Besides, you'll do anything for our Cho-Cho – even if it means enduring my teasing."

"This is embarrassing."

"That's what society wants you to think, my friend." She slugged another mouthful of beer while Lincoln peeled at the label on his. "And you're here to try to help Cleo be less embarrassed, right? That means you gotta give less shits. If you're embarrassed, and she's embarrassed, ain't nobody gonna have a good time. Relax. It's just the two of you. You've seen every square inch of each other naked." She nailed him with a smirk and a knowing stare. "You love each other and whenever you're together in the bedroom it's a safe space. Sometimes sex is about the queefs and shiggles. That's what real love is, Lincoln. It's not the fancy dinners and the walks on the beach. It's working through the tough times and still being able to look each other in the eye, even when your vagina makes farty noises."

"Shiggles?"

"Shits and giggles."

"Of course." He sipped on his beer, letting her words filter through his anxious mind. "Hey, when did you get so smart about this kinda thing?"

She shrugged, but something was behind the small, clearly fake smile she was offering him was an answer.

"Wanna talk about it?"

"No thanks." Sipping on her beer, she leaned back. "I'm good. You got any other questions?"

He picked up the cock ring. Rolling it around in his hand he glanced at his crotch.

"I'm pretty sure it'll fit. I went with a larger size." Draining the last of her beer, she plopped the bottle onto the table with a clink. "Look, not that you asked, but we both know I give my unsolicited opinion regardless. You're going to be out of commission for at least a bit longer, right? You have options, they're just not great. Wait a few days and hope to be able to *perform* with your hand – or face – without your body crapping out on you from exhaustion. Wait a few weeks until you can get pelvic again. Or, and for the sake of all your friends and family, I'm hoping you choose option 'C' here, try the toys. I'm not sure 'death by sexual frustration' is an officially recordable cause of death, but I don't need either of you exploding. And you're gonna be pissed off enough at not being able to play. Going out on a limb here, but you're probably gonna wanna feel like you can still do *something*."

Swallowing his mouthful of beer with a cough he shook his head. "Can you stop being so sensible? It's freaking me the fuck out."

She smiled and stole his beer. "Go get the girl, Linc. And while I don't require a play by play, post-game analysis of your bedroom antics, I *do* encourage you to try. It's fun. Trust me."

SEVEN

CLEO

As soon as she closed the door to her apartment behind her, something felt out of place. Had it not been for the subtle scent of cucumber on the air, and the low, dulcet tones of music emanating from her room she'd have been creeped out. Dumping her backpack next to the couch, she kicked off her shoes and stripped off her many layers, draping her clothes over the arm of the sofa. She felt ridiculous creeping towards her own bedroom door, but if Lincoln was already asleep she didn't want to wake him.

He'd left the door half-open, the room was dim, lit only by a slew of candles, and soft music played from his laptop, open on the floor. He was shirtless, on his back, and his hands were tucked behind his head. Eyes closed, his chest rose and fell with long, even breaths. "You coming in? Or are you just gonna stand there staring? Pervert." He peeked at her through a barely open eye.

"How'd you know?"

"I always know when you're staring at me. I feel it right in here." He touched the skin over his heart. A dreamy sigh escaped her. "Well, that, and I heard the front door close. I expected you a while ago though. Books hold you hostage in the library again?"

Nodding, she unbuttoned her jeans and dropped them to the floor before stepping out of them and kicking them out of her way. "Researching a project." She unhooked her bra and slid it out from under her tank.

Lincoln, both eyes open, regarded her as though she was the world's greatest magician. "I still don't get how you make such light work of those things." He pulled back the comforter and patted the bed beside him.

She climbed onto the bed next to him, gliding over his chest with her open palm as he pulled the blanket back over the two of them and rolled, with a grunt, onto his side to face her.

"I missed you." His murmur against her neck as he kissed her sensitive skin, made her giggle.

"I missed you too." Her heart thumped in her chest. His fingers left a trail of fire and want over her skin. Skimming her collar bone, the swell of her breast, he caught the fabric of her shirt and tugged. He palmed her breast, rolled her nipple between his finger and thumb, and blew across the sensitive bud. A delicious shiver passed through her body, and she arched her back to meet his touch. "We … fuck, Lincoln." Her breathy voice was swallowed by his mouth closing over hers. "We … don't … have to," she gasped between kisses.

As though answering her, his erection pressed against her thigh. "Do you want me to stop?" His hand paused, hovering over the apex of her thighs. The air was thick with heat and desire.

Spreading her legs for him, she shook her head. It wasn't his fingers that glided across her clit, it was something else, something cold, something hard. Every muscle in her body froze.

Lincoln shook his head against her neck, never slowing his butterfly kisses, dotting them over every inch of skin he could reach. "If it doesn't work, we'll figure something else out. Just enjoy it."

Giving herself over to him, she sucked in a breath, and nodded her consent. When he pressed the button, the small vibrations coursed through her entire body. She was soaking wet and needy. It had only been days, but she'd already adjusted to having her fill of Lincoln Scott whenever she felt like it. Not being able to be intimate with him had driven her closer to losing her mind than she cared to admit.

He pressed something and the vibrations intensified.

"Won't … take … long."

He smiled against her skin. "Good. Don't fight it. Come for me, Lizzy."

Another press on the handle by Linc, and stronger, louder buzzing ensued. Her breath hitched. She closed her eyes, rolling her head back. White sparks danced at the edges of the darkness behind her eyes and her entire body tensed. Her hips jerked and bucked of their own will. Air caught in her chest before bursting from her in an ear splitting scream, and what seemed like a gush of liquid escaped between her legs.

Curling her nails into his shoulders, he pressed again and the vibration increased once again. "Linc … I can't. Too … much." Her whole body trembled, her muscles and limbs no longer responding to commands from her brain. She was almost completely sure the bed under her ass was soaking. Did she still even have feet? She couldn't get an answer from her toes. Wave after wave of bliss coursed through the very fabric of her being. Was she dying? If she was, this was the way to go. Lincoln's tongue was exploring her chest. His free hand had made its way behind her neck, snaking over her shoulder, and was squeezing her nipple and the blissful buzzing between her thighs was driving her relentlessly towards the edge of the cliff. Her second orgasm hit her before she realized what was happening, cresting over her like the tide on the shore. If she was screaming, only dogs could hear her. Somewhere a few miles away, Lincoln was growling against her skin, and if she didn't know better she'd have said she wet the bed.

After what could have been ten minutes, or a week, her twitching muscles pulled her back from the land of what-the-fuck-just-happened.

"Back in the land of the living?" He brushed his lips along her clavicle.

"I'mma go with nope."

"I have no idea what you were trying to say, but let's give it a couple more minutes before you try talking again, 'kay?"

"Everything's broken."

"Seemed to all work fine to me, Cleo." He trailed kisses along her jaw. "Ready for round two?"

Holding up three fingers she shook her head. "Don't you dare. I'm not even sure I have feet anymore."

"You do, and they're still adorable feet. So …" He waved her vibrator between them. "Does this mean Molly isn't re-homing your vibrator?"

She nodded. "I feel like we could give it a good home just here. As long as you don't feel emasculated by the hot pink bringer of orgasms and wet sheets."

He chuckled. "I don't feel emasculated at all, but my new goal is to make you come like that without the toy. Challenge accepted."

EIGHT

LINCOLN

FOUR WEEKS LATER

A sting flickered across Lincoln's palm from the smack he'd skimmed across Cleo's ass. She was on all fours in front of him, her fingers strumming her clit like a musician on the strings of a guitar. Her face was buried in the quilt and her ass was in the air. He had been given a clean bill of health and the first thing he'd done was bury himself, balls-deep, in his beautiful girlfriend.

Fingers gripping her hips, he rammed his dick hard, grunting with every movement.

"Yes! Lincoln! Don't … stop!" Her words were panted pleas between thrusts and slaps of sweaty skin colliding.

"No intention of it, Lizzy. I have a few weeks of pent up frustration to take care of."

Her walls tightened around his cock. Groaning, he clenched her hips.

"We've done things …"

"You think any of that comes close to being inside you? Shit, Cleo. There's no competition." The familiar pressure grew in his balls. He picked up the small bottle of lube and one of the toys he'd kept out of sight behind his foot and dropped a blob between her ass cheeks.

She giggled. "Linc, you've been putting your finger in there for a while, I think it's safe to say you don't need lube."

Closing the bottle top with a click, he tossed it next to them on the bed, slowing his thrusts to lazy strokes for a moment. He brushed the tip of the metal plug against her tight hole, relishing the shudder that traveled through her body.

"Is that one of my plugs?"

"It is. Want me to stop?"

"No! I'm ready."

It slid into her with a satisfying pop, the gemstone glistening in the sunlight. It was met with a low hum from Cleo. "Feel okay?"

"Mmmhmm." She pressed herself back against him, as though encouraging him to pick up the pace again.

"So impatient."

Reaching behind his leg he lifted the wand and pressed it between them, against her clit.

"W-what is that?"

"Just 'cause I'm fully healed, doesn't mean we don't have space in the bedroom for some mechanical assistance. You game?"

"Absolutely. Now would you stop threatening me with a good time and fuck me already?"

Acknowledgements

I know, I know, this is an anthology and people don't usually write acknowledgments in the back of these things but hey, we're already breaking the stigma of sex toys, so why not push the expectations of the back matter as well?

Firstly, if you bought this book, read it on KU, or shared it on social media – thank you. I truly mean it. I thank my readers in every book I write, but this time ... this is different. With Amazon and Facebook not letting us advertise a book with a hot pink vibrator on the cover, we had to rely on word of mouth advertising – this book wouldn't be what it is if it wasn't for you. A million thank yous.

The group of steamy authors who convinced me to put this set together. What can I say? What started out as a joke in our Facebook group for another anthology resulted in one of my favorite book releases of 2021. For the enablers who convinced me to buy the cover, and follow through to publishing – thanks. I didn't know it at the time, but this project helped me grow and I needed it.

The authors who wrote the stories, thank you for taking a chance on this anthology, thank you for helping to break the stigma and for coming along on this crazy fun ride. Thank you for not falling apart when my red pen tore up your stories, and thank you for putting them back together again. This has been a lot of fun, I think we've all learned a lot and maybe once I've recovered we can do it again some time.

Our beta readers, Sarah Budd, Savannah Medina, Corinne Basmaison, and Jessica Potts, thank you all so very much for your time, feedback and obsession with these stories and this book. Your continuing support means the world to me.

And finally, Lee Ann (L. Ann), my partner in crime, author bestie, and the person who hears my crazy ideas and goes 'Let's do it' without hesitation. One day the world will be ours, and when we look back we'll say our origin story started with a vibrator and a busted can of biscuits. Thank you for encouraging me to be better and to never settle for ordinary when I can be extra.

Made in the USA
Las Vegas, NV
16 March 2022